Th

Heart

Of War

To Julie,
Thank you for your
friendship & support !
Fondly,
Juliann Dorell

Juliann Dorell

Cover by Marilyn Droz

Dedication

To Tristan, Sienna, Fallon, Addison, and Harlow…
I love being a 'grand.' You make me so proud.
May you always approach the future without
forgetting the past.

Acknowledgements

To Marilyn Droz for sharing her great, great,
great, grandfather –

Corporal Edwin N. Josselyn

Corporal Josselyn of Zanesville, Ohio, was nineteen
years old when
he and his friends volunteered for the "three month
war that would
save the union." His Civil War journal and letters
home are priceless.
Reading about his journey both during the
war and after
gives one an incredible sense of being there.
My deepest thanks to Marilyn and her mother,
Cleo Ellis,
for sharing Edwin Josselyn's precious memorabilia.
There is no substitute for the real thing!
And…..
Pat Seiler, Lynnie Clark, Janet Slick – what
wonderful,
supportive friends, readers, and muses you are!

Marilyn Droz – your talent and cover art is
amazing!

…and to Marnie, with love.

Table of Contents

The Cold Heart of War

Come, you men in the fields – lay down your plows.
Come, you men of the forest – lay down your axes.
Come, you men in the factories – lay down your tools.
Our precious Union is in peril!
The color blue will be your garb,
a gun your constant friend.
The cannon's roar will greet you now,
each day a bitter end.
The days of war shall take their toll,
through numbers and bad weather,
The miles you march will age your soul,
and naught will make it better.
Cities, towns and villages burn,
and families all will suffer,
While battlefields run deep with blood
from brother killing brother,
The war that now divides our nation will
rage and take its toll,
Take care, dear soldier, guard yourself,
ere your heartturns bitter cold.

Juliann Dorell

PROLOGUE
December 1858 - Fairfax, Ohio

Beatrice Bradley was a proud, intelligent, and well-educated woman. She wasn't given to vapors and other emotional nonsense like some women allowed themselves to suffer. She and her sister Kathryn comported themselves with dignity at all times like their mother had taught them. If there was a problem – emotional or otherwise, she simply discussed it with Kathryn and she handled it. Period. The one and only subject never discussed, was Beatrice's periodic melancholy. This she did not share with anyone, even her loving and devoted sister. Beatrice would simply seek alone time where she could reminisce in private and deal with her emotional pain. It was the only time she allowed herself to shed her tears and have regrets of a time past. It was the only time she indulged in weakness. For to Beatrice, that is what it was….simply weakness.

In her daydreams she returned to a special time in her life and remembered the young man who had loved her and made her feel so wonderful. But he left her. Not because he wanted to - but because *they* had killed him. The sheriff said it was an accident, but Beatrice was no fool. The Rev. Ben Pattison was a very competent driver who loved his horses and could control them. No --- no runaway team had killed him; cracked his skull, broken his ribs….a gang of scurrilous, violent men in her town had done that. And she would never forgive them. She thought she knew which ones had killed him –

she had her suspicions – and she would pay them back. Not by hurting them physically, she didn't have the power to do that. But she had other ways to hurt them and make them suffer for what they had done. She would take something from these men that made them money and excited their evil needs. Saving as many runaway slaves as she could would be one thing and then taking away their means of living would be another.

Her sister Kathryn's wedding was soon. She had to take part and celebrate with her family. She would be miserable, but would never let on. She was happy for Kathryn and wanted to be with her. It was only proper to put on a gracious face for the public. Her mourning was now private. There was no jealousy of Kathryn. Beatrice loved her sister and Kathryn returned that love and loyalty. She had even wanted to postpone her wedding day, but Beatrice had refused to let her do that. Even her parents had agreed. But it had been over a year. Life had to move on. Somehow she would make everyone know that she was fine and completely recovered from her loss.

Beatrice sat in her rocking chair alone in her spacious room. She let her gaze take in the soothing colors of peach, blue and yellow of her comforter and wallpaper; the lovely peach roses she had placed on the mantel. She closed her eyes and let her mind drift back. It felt good to see herself on that day when she first saw him. She had loved the dress she wore that day -- still had it in her hope chest. No more hope – just memories.
Ahhhhh….there he is….she could see him now…..

Chapter 1

The Revival

The traveling preacher, the Reverend Ben Pattison, came to Fairfax, Ohio, in the spring as the talk of war began. He was given permission to pitch his tents in the big field owned by the Bradley family. This was very exciting news for the town and the surrounding area. Most folks loved a good "gettin' together" and a revival meeting was the source of much celebration. It would mean picnics and meetings, camp fires and singing. The children would all be excited because they knew they could attend almost all of the events as well. Folks would come from miles around and pitch tents and set up cook fires to share with other families. The nearby Ohio River would serve as both a place to bathe, a place for recreation, as well as drinking water. Yes, there was reason for all the excitement. The Rev. Pattison would be here for three weeks of preachin', prayin' and singin'. It was a grand time for the folks of Fairfax and the surrounding towns. Hundreds of people would attend and most would stay for the whole three weeks!

At the end of the first week, when he started talking about the issue of slavery, a group of southern sympathizers told him to clear out and not come back. That kind of talk could hurt their businesses. Most all of their whisky, cotton and other goods came from the south where the slaves did all the work. The Rev. Pattison tried to soothe their unrest, but it was clear that while a lot of the people were listening – there was a rowdy group of men who were becoming more hostile by the hour. Rev. Pattison was pretty sure that alcohol was fueling their tempers. He knew this was an area with a large anti-north population, but he was surprised at their vehemence.

The Bradley sisters, Beatrice and Kathryn, had attended all of his revival meetings. They listened to his preaching about the sin of making people slaves – the fact that they were not savages but human beings. Beatrice Bradley had decided she was in love with the preacher. She had been to all of his smaller lectures and bible studies and was mesmerized by his voice and delivery of his message. She always sat in the front row, even when her sister or parents didn't come with her. He watched for her and always smiled right at her. He was a young man, tall and so strong. His longish black hair was below his collar and shined in the lantern light of the tent. Sometimes she thought he had a halo over his head. He had eyes the color of the blue bonnets that grew in mama's garden. When he sang hymns he would look at her and smile and her heart almost stopped beating. She would talk to him while he ate lunch, and sometimes when he ate dinner, because she brought him the food from her house. Her parents gave their cook permission to feed the Rev. Pattison. And, Bea made it her duty to bring the food out to him for each meal. Her parents had no idea of her attachment to the Rev. Pattison.

The Reverend slept in a wagon next to the main tent where the people gathered for the large meetings so he could stay long into the night with people who wanted to be saved. Everyone was looking forward to being baptized in the river at the end of the week. Even their town minister, Pastor Franklin, was going to be a part of that ceremony. He attended some of the revival meetings and used the pulpit for bible readings and lectures. He never
preached about slavery though. Before Rev. Pattison, no one had talked against slavery or that it was a sin.

One night, Beatrice and Kathryn stayed after an evening meeting and asked the reverend what they could do about slavery and he told them to meet him after all the people had gone home. The girls sneaked out of their house at midnight and met him by his wagon. They walked deeper into the trees at the end of the field and he told them about how they could help hide the escaped slaves. It was dangerous work, he warned them. They needed to think long and hard about what could happen to them if they were caught helping escaping slaves. The Fugitive Slave Act of 1850 made it a crime for anyone, citizens or officials, to help slaves escape, which included a $1,000 fine and imprisonment. The reverend spoke of a way people were helping the slaves go along a "Railroad to the Promised Land."

Beatrice and Kathryn were amazed to think that they could actually save people from this horrible abuse but didn't think that their parents would ever consider allowing them to do anything for the cause. Young women of good breeding would never consider involving themselves in anything that could be considered improper or dangerous. But the idea had taken root in Beatrice's mind. No one would ever suspect the most proper sisters of any kind of ill behavior. After all, they were held in high esteem by the people of their town. Beatrice and Kathryn exchanged looks and it was a given that they would think very hard about helping this noble cause. Rev. Pattison made them swear on a bible. With shaky hands, the sisters made their vow to help in secrecy, never revealing any people or places they knew of in the organization of the Underground Railroad. Once they had taken the oath, he told them about the people who were already involved in the Underground Railroad and how they would work together if they chose to do so.

The sisters had much to think about. Beatrice wanted to do something to help the poor slaves and be a part of something the Rev. Pattison believed in enough to risk his own life. But Kathryn was engaged to be married to Weston Floyd Granger. She wanted to help and would have to figure out a way to do it. But right now she had a future husband to consider. Weston and she hadn't discussed topics like slavery and politics. She would be a proper wife and mother for his children. She knew he would not approve of her wanting to possibly risk her life to help the escaped slaves. Any involvement on her part would have to wait until after she knew more about her future husband's feelings and what part she could play to help Beatrice. His parents had never owned any slaves. And, she would be living in his parents' large estate ten miles away. She couldn't sneak behind his back, but she did want to help this cause and her sister.

Beatrice's heart was full of pride for the handsome preacher and the life he lived. She had made up her mind to spend time alone with the reverend. She had to know that his eye contact with her was as special as she hoped it was. When he touched her hands as she gave him plates of food, those brief touches were electric to her. His gazes deep into her eyes couldn't be just her imagination – or could it? She even wondered if she might go with him when he moved on to another town. She blushed at the thought. Maybe he didn't feel as strongly about her as she did about him. Beatrice needed to know. She couldn't believe that she was thinking about leaving her beautiful home and her precious sister, Kathryn. But this feeling she had for Rev. Pattison was starting to consume her every thought. She had to be brave and talk to him about it. The time when he would leave was fast approaching. She had to know.

The next evening when Beatrice brought dinner to Rev. Pattison, she stood in front of him and waited for his eyes to look up at her. He was concentrating on his bible notes and had reached for some food with his fork when he paused and looked at her feet, then slowly raised his eyes to her face. The sudden flash of electric blue eyes was startling and Beatrice almost turned and fled.

"Was there something you wanted, Miss Beatrice?" Rev. Pattison laid his fork down and leaned back in his chair.

Beatrice squeezed her hands together and took a shaky breath. "I wanted to talk to you, Rev. Pattison."

"Yes….about?" he questioned with a smile.

"Uh, hem," Beatrice cleared her throat, "I was wondering-----oh my, this is so difficult." She looked down and tried to summon more courage.

Rev. Pattison's smile was growing larger as Beatrice became more flustered. She looked up directly into his eyes. His smile made her feel like he was challenging her. She stood taller and dropped her hands in fists by her sides, "I was wondering if you feel a certain attraction to me."

Beatrice's chin went up and she proudly stood waiting for his reply.

"Well, yes, I do think that there is some sort of spark between us whenever we are together." He smiled at Beatrice, "Yes, I do feel it. But I wasn't going to do anything about it, Miss Beatrice. You're a lady, living in a fine house, and I'm a traveling man of the gospel. Not much to call my own except my bible, the tents and wagon. Your parents must want you to do better for your future than to be attracted to someone like me," he said quietly.

Beatrice relaxed her hands and put them on the back of a chair across from the reverend. "I don't really care what my parents want for me. I'm 24 years old, and I am confident that I know my own mind. I have felt attracted to you since first we met. If you feel the same then we can keep company and get to know one another better. If you are in agreement." Beatrice replied primly. She held her breath and waited for him to turn her down.

Slowly, Rev. Pattison stood and carefully put his napkin beside his plate. He swallowed and cleared his throat, using the time to prepare his answer. He knew that what he was about to say would change his life. "I have traveled the last ten years preaching in towns and cities all over these United States. I have met many young ladies, but none have attracted me as much as you. You stood out in the crowd that first night I preached. I watched you, hoping you would come back the next night so I could know if I would feel that same attraction again." He waited.

"And did you?" Beatrice asked in a hushed voice.

"Indeed I did. And when you offered to bring me food, I was glad that I could see you more often. That night you met me after midnight to talk about helping runaway slaves, I saw your hair sparkle in the starlight and I wanted to reach out and touch it. I was tempted to take your hand, but I thought I'd frighten you."

He walked around the table as he talked and stopped next to Beatrice so that she had to look up to see his face. "My name is Ben. You need to think very carefully before you make any decisions about spending more time with me. I have enemies now. Some of those men who were vocal during my sermons could become violent and run me out of town. It wouldn't be the first time I was asked to leave a gathering." He chuckled. "Our country is on the brink of breaking apart if our leaders can't bring themselves to agree about the sin of slavery. There could be a war. By spending more time with me, you could be in danger. And, if you went against your parents, if they don't approve of me, they could cast you out and forbid you to return to your home. Have you thought about that?" He softly touched her cheek with the back of his hand.

Beatrice leaned into his hand and closed her eyes. "I don't care. I want to be with you, Ben. Will you come to my house and talk to my father about us spending time together?" She looked up and he smiled down at her and took her hand. "If you're sure you want this. I will only be here for one more week unless I extend my stay. Let's see what your father says first, shall we?" he inquired as he stroked her cheek.

Mr. Bradley approved of the Rev. Ben Pattison. He had spent some time with him discussing the gospels that he preached and found the reverend to be intelligent and a man of good character. Her mother, sweet and innocent, thought he was thrilling and handsome. Her opinion would never have been in opposition of her husband's. She was a loving mother and obedient wife. One stipulation Beatrice's father made was that the Reverend had to stay in one place. Mr. Bradley would build a church for him if he had to, but his daughter was not going to go traipsing all over the country in a wagon and live in a tent. NO SIRREE! Before any talk of courting began, Rev. Pattison had to make a choice – his daughter his way, or the road.

Ben Pattison loved preaching. He had chosen to take the gospel on the road reaching many more people than he ever could in a single church. But lately, he had been thinking about settling down. He knew there were big changes about to take place in the country. More and more, the towns in the south he passed through were showing signs of unrest with the government. Talk of ending slavery by the vocal abolitionists in the north was causing anger among the southern plantation owners. A way of life that depended on slavery was a cause for talk of seceding from the Union. His attraction to Beatrice was powerful. She was a good woman; perfect for a town preacher with her good manners and intelligence. He enjoyed talking to her and knew her opinions about slavery matched his. And, her desire to aid escaped slaves would make her a good helpmate with his goals, too.

Having his own church built anywhere he wanted by a wealthy father-in-law was a pretty powerful incentive, also. He had dreamed of his own congregation, but most large churches had ministers placed by religious organizations. Without Mr. Bradley's help, he could only hope to have a small, poor church in some little town with a small population. Rev. Pattison was eager to serve the people, but his ego and aspirations would make it easy to accept Mr. Bradley's generosity. All large cities and towns had more than one church. He knew that he had the ability to lure people to his church, no matter what city he chose to settle in. He gladly agreed to end his travels and begin courting Miss Beatrice Bradley. He would give one final grand evening of preaching. A little fire and brimstone about the

evils of slavery would be his final night.
Tomorrow he would save souls by baptizing them
in the Ohio River.

Chapter 2

The Baptism

It was a picture perfect day for baptizing the large gathering along the banks of the river. The blue sky and white puffy clouds made Rev. Pattison think of heaven. He could imagine that a heavenly chorus of angels would soon be joining the voices of the folks who were already singing their joy and praises to the Lord. Those being baptized had removed their shoes and stockings and were wading into the river, arms raised, their voices singing, "Shall we gather at the river, where bright angel feet have trod…." Rev. Pattison, also barefoot, and wearing a white robe-like garment holding his bible, followed his flock into the water. The voices grew quiet as he raised one arm toward heaven and intoned, "And he showed me a pure river of water of life, clear as crystal, proceeding from the throne of God and of the Lamb."

One by one the men, women and children came forward to be held and lowered backwards into the cool water. Handing his bible to the elderly Rev. Franklin, who waded into the water behind him, Rev. Pattison carefully held and blessed each soul as he lowered them into the water. Soon the river was full of happy faces smiling with delight, believing they were saved and would join their Lord in heaven when the time came for their passing from this world. The Rev. Pattison gave a last blessing and turned to lead his flock out of the river. The singing began again, "Yes we'll gather at the river, the beautiful, beautiful river. Gather with the saints at the river that flows by the throne of God."

It was the culmination of his time in Fairfax. His success was complete as he had been given donations of food, as well as money for his coffers. These would all be used for his new church, for Mr. Bradley, true to his word, had promised him a church and congregation for marrying his daughter. Rev. Pattison's real prize though, was Beatrice, for she was everything he had searched for in a wife and partner: she was intelligent, loving, believed in God and would be a good mother for their children, of which he wanted many.

Yes, life was good and he was grateful for stopping in Fairfax, Ohio. Tonight would be his last sermon in the big tent. He would give the people one last talk about the current issues of slavery and possible war, and the consequences that could occur. His work helping escaped slaves would not be affected by his marrying Beatrice. He knew she would help him save those poor, unfortunate folks. He would be proud to have her at his side. They would not announce their engagement until things were settled about his new church and where it would be. He had agreed with Mr. Bradley to let him make the announcement when the time was right. Rev. Pattison would remain on the Bradley property until then and they would be properly chaperoned.

That evening, it was very dark, the stars obscured by clouds. The wind was pulling the tent walls back and forth making the poles groan with the strain of holding them down. Rev. Pattison knew he would have to talk as loud as possible to be heard over the impending storm. He would take great care in securing the kerosene lanterns inside the tent. Their flame could quickly ignite the tent into a deadly conflagration. He had extinguished all the outside lanterns he could, including the ones around his own wagon. He didn't want to worry about anything except delivering his sermon and saying goodbye to all the attendees. Rev. Pattison was looking forward to enjoying the rest of the evening with Beatrice. They had so much to discuss.

The men who had filed into the back of the tent were rowdy during his sermon. Several people had turned to quietly chastise them for their rudeness, only to be met with stern glares and whispered epithets threatening them to mind their own business. One group of people moved to get away from them, remarking among themselves that they could smell hard liquor on the men's breath.

Rev. Pattison, using his loudest and sternest voice, extolled the virtues of treating all men as equals; that slavery was wrong and the work of the devil. It was against God's principles to enslave men, women, and children, and to sell them, breaking apart families for profit. He ignored the fact that his audience was becoming more and more uncomfortable with his sermon. He believed in his words and knew the people would be uneasy about them but shouldn't feel threatened by them. He was preaching against a way of life that had gone on for many years. But what he was proposing was a threat to their business and economy. Never a rich community, Fairfax traded with the South and didn't want any change. The few slaves who had been caught and returned from the area were not discussed, not even in their churches. Rev. Pattison was stirring up trouble.

Beatrice and Kathryn were sitting with their parents in the front row and could feel the crowd stirring restlessly during Rev. Pattison's sermon. The rumble of voices way in the back rows was growing louder and people were edgy and wriggling in their seats. Beatrice wished he would finish soon. He needed to change his topic to something more than his current harangue. Mrs. Bradley was clutching her hanky so tight that the lace around the edge had come loose. Just as Beatrice was about to stand to attract the reverend's eye, he bowed his head and closed his sermon with one last prayer. She heaved a sigh of relief.

"And the Lord said, if my people, who are called by my name, will humble themselves and pray and seek my face and turn away from their wicked ways then I will hear from heaven and forgive their sins and heal their land," he spoke with a deep and resonant voice, "Amen. Our last hymn will be 'Sing Praise to God Who Reigns Above.' Please rise and raise your voices to the Lord and give thanks to Him."

It seemed as if everyone was relieved to be done this night. The storm was gaining strength and would make it a difficult night for those who were staying in tents. Cook fires would be out of the question till morning. The hymn soon ended and all the people filed out, many shaking Rev. Pattison's hand, but most scooting out the other side entrance wanting to get away from him and the men in the back row who didn't seem to be in a hurry to leave.

Mr. Bradley approached Rev. Pattison with Beatrice close behind him.

"You might have gone a little lighter on the slave issue, Reverend. Folks around these parts need the South and the slaves to deliver crops to them. The talk of war is making people uneasy as it is, and you got a little stern with them," he spoke as he did when lecturing his daughters on their behavior.

The Rev. Pattison frowned and placed his hand on Mr. Bradley's shoulder, "It's a difficult topic, I know, but one that must be spoken about.

The treatment of slaves is harsh and it's wrong to own another human being, no matter his color. If not a preacher reminding the people of God's word, then who, Mr. Bradley?" He glanced up and looked at the men in the back of the tent. "I am not afraid to do God's work. I spoke the truth and you all know it," he stated loudly facing them.

"All the same, you'd better stay close to our home tonight. Those men have been drinking and were making some pretty serious threats while you were preaching. The sooner we get you and Beatrice settled in a new area a little farther north, the better for you both."

"I intend to spend a very nice evening with you and your family, Mr. Bradley, but first I told the Donahues that I would help them move their family home. Tom Donahue is loading his tent, children and things in my wagon right now and I will take them down the road and return before long. I appreciate your hospitality and won't miss a minute more than I have to." Rev. Pattison smiled warmly at his new 'almost family.'

Mr. Bradley turned and took his wife's arm. "Let's go and prepare a little something for us all to eat and give these tempers a chance to settle down. Beatrice, are you coming?" He turned and started to walk away, "Please join us at the house as soon as you can, Reverend." Mr. Bradley hesitated and waited for his daughter to join him.

"I'll be right there, Papa." Beatrice took hold

of Ben's hand and pulled him outside where they could have a moment alone. He was so close to her so that they were touching from shoulder to knee. She could see every line on his face. His features were so strong: his chiseled nose and cheek bones were prominent. She loved his dark eyes. They showed all the emotion he felt and wasn't ashamed to voice. Closing her eyes, she locked his face in her memory. She trembled with love for this good man. He thrilled her down to her toes and she felt the gentle power of his strong hands and arms as he put them around her and held her tightly against him.

"Ben, please come to the house now. Let Tom Donahue take your wagon and we can go and get it tomorrow after the storm. I'm worried about those men," she implored, her hand cupping his cheek.

Ben couldn't move away from Beatrice. He kissed her long and deep. All her longing and his mingled into a wondrous kiss that lasted until they both had to take breaths. Ben stepped back and forced himself to let her go. It wouldn't be right for anyone to see them like this.

He smiled down at Beatrice, "They're just trying to frighten everyone with their mean stares and words. I'll be alright. I'll be back soon, then I need to see that the lanterns are all turned out and my horses are settled for the night. This storm is going to rage on for a while. There are lots of folks around and these men know it. Don't

18

you worry now, Bea." He gently kissed her lips and squeezed her hands. Then he pushed her toward the house. "I'll be with you soon, my love."

Beatrice was reluctant to leave him. She didn't like the grim expressions she had seen on the men's faces. She didn't trust any of them, especially one of them. He was a troublemaker who lived down the road named, Hank Colby. He made her skin crawl with the way he looked at her and Kathryn. Reluctantly, she turned and hurried to catch up with her parents.

That was the last time Beatrice was with the Rev. Ben Pattison. His body was found early the next morning by the side of the road in a ditch. His wagon was turned over, his body crushed underneath. The team of horses he loved were standing nearby, their harnesses dangling --- torn loose from the wagon. Several men who had attended the gospel meetings wrapped his body in a sheet, and brought him back to the Bradley's house.

Beatrice hadn't slept all night and was in the kitchen drinking a cup of tea when the noise of horses brought her running to the front door. Her face was filled with relief as she threw open the door and raced out onto the porch. She couldn't wait to throw herself into Ben's arms and hold him.

The faces greeting her were filled with sorrow. Beatrice saw the men taking a long wrapped bundle down from the back of a horse. She was still looking for Ben and couldn't understand why he wasn't with these men. Then, she knew. The long bundle was her Ben. She didn't feel the arms of her father holding her, couldn't hear the voices telling them what happened. She heard screaming, then everything started to spin around her and the morning turned black.

Beatrice awoke late that evening in her bed. The house was quiet, even the crickets were silent. She turned her head and saw her sister, Kathryn, sitting in a chair next to her, sound asleep. Her throat was sore. She remembered hearing someone screaming. Had she screamed? Closing her eyes she still saw the body wrapped in the white sheet. Ben was lost to her now. She knew as sure as she knew her own name that he had been killed. Beatrice believed she knew who had done it. The men who had been standing in the back of the tent during Ben's sermon, talking and plotting. Of course, it would never be proven. Her analytical mind was rapidly considering the possibilities. No, the storm would be blamed. Hatred and loathing filled her mind with thoughts of revenge. She wanted them all punished.

Never more would she treat those men with anything but disgust. They had killed her kind and gentle man who preached that all men were created equal under the eyes of God. Well, these men would never be treated as her equal, nor would she treat their families with kindness or good manners ever again! Her father was a rich and successful man who had many businesses the people of the town needed every day: the lumber mills and factory that made carriages, wagons, harnesses and bridles, the fields of corn, wheat, vegetables, and the large mercantile store in Fairfax were all owned by her father. These men and their families depended on credit for their existence. Mr. Bradley was also half- owner of the town bank where anyone wanting a loan had to pass his approval. Beatrice was her father's right hand. She would influence her father and prevent him from giving any of those men or their families, who she believed had hurt Ben, any more credit, services, or loans in the future to help them....*ever again*!

She could taste the bitterness of hate on her tongue. From this day forward, her life would never be the same. She would take something else from that cruel bunch, something that made them money and gave them a sick excitement for their evil needs. They used the Fugitive Slave Act as an excuse to go hunting for runaway slaves. She would save as many of them as she possibly could and serve the Lord and Ben's memory. Somehow, in secret, she would do whatever she could to help them. Her parents wouldn't be involved. She needed to think and plan. Kathryn would help her, and she knew there were others who would help, too. This would be her life's mission. Not a husband, or children, or a happy home. She would dedicate her life to this new cause.

Beatrice rose from her bed, and woke her sister. She would start planning today. NO! She had to prepare a funeral for her dear Ben. He had told her he had no family. It would be up to Beatrice to see that he was buried with all the respect he deserved. She would delay her plans. It was a comfort to know that she had something to keep her sane. Losing Ben had destroyed her heart, but not her inner strength. She needed a purpose. She had a mission now. That was all she had. Her life would be lonely, but full of purpose.

Chapter 3

The Wedding

Kathryn Louise Bradley's winter wedding was the talk for miles around. Everyone knew that she and her childhood sweetheart from nearby Colton Springs would eventually marry. Both families had money so it was a given their wedding would be one to impress the town folk… and it was. The Saturday in November chosen for their wedding day had received a light dusting of snow making the countryside beautiful and bright with snow crystals shining in the sun. Deep red rose bouquets were everywhere in the church mixed with white roses and deep green foliage, all grown in the Bradley greenhouses. Wide red and white satin ribbon tied in elaborate bows and roses were attached to each pew on the aisle of the Baptist church the Bradleys attended.

Kathryn's sister, Beatrice was the eldest daughter and should have married first, but it wasn't to be. She lost the one man that could have been her husband. Before the Rev. Pattison had come along, none of the many suitors who approached Mr. Bradley for permission to court her were approved by the fussy Miss Beatrice. Then, she met the Reverend and she told her parents he was the one. But tragedy struck and now, to her parents' great disappointment, Beatrice was destined to be a spinster. The town thought she had become hard-hearted and callous by the way she treated some folks.

Both sisters were beauties, everyone agreed. They were cultured, educated, intelligent and lovely. Their first attraction to eligible suitors was that they were daughters of a very rich and prominent family. To their credit, the Bradley sisters were also charming and down to earth. They volunteered where needed, sang in the church choir, and were present at the Ladies Society meetings where they contributed time quilting, sewing, knitting and sharing Cook's recipes for fundraising to help needy families, the library, and an orphanage in Cincinnati.

Knowing that he would never have sons to take over his businesses – and there were many - Mr. Bradley trained his daughters to understand business and finances. Kathryn was good with figures for the accounting and books, but Beatrice was exceptional at managing men and organizing the workers' schedules and maintaining supplies. The Bradleys were a very close family and widely respected. This wedding was the largest event in the history of Fairfax, Ohio.

The wedding party was ready, the guests were all seated, and the overflow of late arrivals were crowded in the vestibule and around the edges of the pews. Mr. and Mrs. Bradley took one last look at their beautiful daughter in the full-length mirror.

"You're absolutely the most beautiful bride

Kathryn," she said tearfully. Pulling an expensive hankie from her satin reticule, she dabbed at her eyes. Mrs. Bradley arranged Kathryn's long veil for the hundredth time and looked sadly into the mirror. "I can't believe you'll be living so far away from me now," she choked.

"Mama, it's only ten miles from here. We'll see each other for Sunday dinners each month and all the holidays. And…." She turned to her father and touched his rose boutonniere, "you'll see me whenever you come to visit me. You know you're always welcome. But I am sorry that I can't work for you anymore, Papa. I hope Mr. Carver will be competent with the books and accounting." Kathryn hugged her father then took his arm. "I'm ready, Mama. It's time."

She turned around, looking for Beatrice. "Oh, Bea!" Kathryn cried out reaching for her, "I am going to miss you so!" She rushed over to her sister and they hugged tightly. They exchanged looks knowing the deep regret in Kathryn's eyes told Beatrice that she knew today would be difficult for her.

"Don't you dare cry now, Katy! Weston will worry you're having regrets about marrying him." Beatrice pulled herself up, squeezed her sister's hand, and took a deep breath. She would force herself to enjoy this day for her dear, beloved sister.

"No he won't. He knows I'm plum crazy about him!" Kathryn hugged her sister once more and laughed.

Mr. Bradley knew he had to break this up and get the wedding underway. "Okay my beauties. It's time to make that long walk down the aisle. I'm the envy of everyone who sees my three beauties. I'm looking forward to everyone getting a good gander at the three of you on this fine day." He sighed. "It is a bit sad to think that this is the last time we will be together like this." He wanted to say more. He wanted to tell Beatrice he understood her pain. But he didn't want to allow her sadness to take over the moment. This day belonged to Kathryn. He would watch out for Beatrice all day just to make sure his beloved daughter wouldn't suffer too much without her knowing her parents loved her and were always there for her.

Beatrice took over. "Okay, Bradley family. Out, out, out!" She walked over and opened the door motioning for everyone to leave. Once in the vestibule, Beatrice nodded her head and the signal was given for the organ to begin playing the wedding march. The six bridesmaids dressed in long-sleeved red velvet gowns were going to make people gasp when they entered the church. On their heads were wreaths of red and white roses, baby's breath and small bows of narrow red and white ribbon which also trailed down their backs. The groomsmen all wore tuxedos with tails, white vests, ties and red roses in their lapels. In the crook of their right arms they each held top hats with narrow red ribbon hat bands.

Beatrice's gown was also red velvet, but because she was the maid of honor, her dress had a more dramatic drape of material in the front and a longer train. Head held high she waited for everyone to file down the aisle. She turned and watched as their father gently pulled the wispy veil of silk down over her sister's beautiful face. Beatrice smiled and exchanged a last look, then blew her sister a kiss. Precisely when the time was right, Beatrice nudged her groomsmen and they started down the aisle.

As she knew they would, a gasp went up when the congregation saw her sister and stood to watch Mr. Bradley and Kathryn. Even the new minister, Reverend Hawthorn, his eyes widened when he saw Kathryn approaching him. Her dress was the dream of any young woman who wanted to be a bride. Designed in Paris, made in New York City, Kathryn's wedding gown was something no one had ever seen in Fairfax. Yards and yards of silk, and white velvet gracefully draped the bride's lovely figure. The pearls and rhinestones on the veil, bodice and sleeves captured the candlelight and sparkled as she walked. Kathryn's long train and veil streamed behind her and she seemed to effortlessly glide as she walked next to her proud father. At the end of the wedding when the groom placed his ring on Kathryn's finger, more gasps were heard when the diamonds glimmered brightly. The happy couple turned and Rev. Hawthorne loudly said, "May I introduce Mr. and Mrs. Weston Floyd Granger."

Beatrice had never seen her sister happier or more beautiful! For just a brief moment she allowed the pain to surface and to imagine it was she standing there with the love of her life. But it was not to be. There would be no one who made her heart skip a beat as Ben had done. There was no one she wanted to spend every day and night with. Perhaps there never would be.

The elaborate wedding reception was held in the church basement which had been transformed into a dreamland of silk swags, candles, roses and ribbons. Against the wall, long tables covered with rich white brocade were laden with trays of beautifully prepared roasts of beef, turkey, and pork. The many side dishes were in crystal bowls placed on intricate white and red doilies. Standing nearby in neat black suits and dresses with white gloves were servants ready to serve each person who attended the wedding reception. Being served and eating such expensive food was a first for most of the people flowing down the stairs. They were stopped at the bottom and prevented from rushing to the seats. Mrs. Bradley had taken the time to place seating cards with elegant calligraphy names for all who had been invited to attend. There were tables further in the back for the people who came at the last minute without invitations. Everyone was welcome!

At the end of the reception, Kathryn and Weston went around the entire basement greeting all the attendees. All the cards and presents would be waiting for them at the Bradley house when they returned from their honeymoon to New York City. Beatrice approached her sister and whispered in her ear that their carriage was waiting for them. They would be taken to the railroad station to enter their private car which would take them all the way to New York City in style. The story of this day: the dresses, meal, and private train car would be discussed for months. Beatrice smiled at her sister and hugged her tightly against her breast. She felt like she was losing another big part of her life.

"Have a wonderful time. I'll want to hear all about your time together in New York City," she whispered.

Kathryn blushed, "Well, surely not everything Bea!" she gushed.

Kathryn laughed loudly, "Certainly not!" Kathryn was pulled away by the crowd and well-wishers. Her father and mother waited by the carriage. Beatrice watched them struggle with tears as they hugged and wished Kathryn goodbye. Weston stood patiently holding the carriage door open. Mr. Bradley shook his hand and Mrs. Bradley hugged him and then wept into her hanky as Weston and Mr. Bradley pushed Kathryn's wedding gown and veil into the carriage. Kathryn turned once she was seated and hollered, "Yoo hoo," to the crowd, then threw her bouquet out the carriage door. Beatrice held back. She didn't want any part of trying to catch the beautiful roses and have everyone look at her. It was a stupid superstition thinking that you would be next to marry if you caught the bride's bouquet. She was beyond thinking of a wedding happening.....*ever*!

Beatrice looked around for another buggy to take her back home. She needed to escape. Big John, her parents' main butler and trusted employee, saw her and stepped up. "Ready to go home now, Miz Bea?" he asked kindly. Beatrice nodded her head. Suddenly she was exhausted. The house would be lonely and quiet without her sister. From now on she would attend all their functions and meetings without Kathryn. Oh, well. She would adjust. That's what competent ladies did.

The big black man took her arm and gently helped her into the buggy, then drove her home. Big John had a deep and abiding affection for this young woman and her family. Years ago, her father had brought him and several other men and women from a plantation in Kentucky. The owner who was bankrupt and dying gave them manumission which freed them all. Mr. Bradley gave each one a job either in his home, mill, wagon works, or fields. They were treated as equal employees by most all of Mr. Bradley's other employees. They even had small cottages near where they worked in the mill and fields. They were grateful and loyal people. Several now had wives and children. Mr. Bradley had purchased them and freed them, too. Big John's job was to run the large estate home. He did just that with joy and competence. The entire household couldn't run without him.

The happily married couple returned after three weeks of a very joyful honeymoon. Their first stop was an overnight at the Bradley house to open their wedding gifts. Kathryn's bedroom had been prepared for the couple by Beatrice. She was excited to be with her sister again and to hear about their trip. Kathryn and Weston had many stories about attending the opera, plays and museums -- and they had brought back presents for everyone, even the servants. It felt like Christmas had come early as each person was given their gift and opened it.

Soon, it was time for Kathryn to leave for her new home. Once again, sad goodbyes were said and hugs were given as if they were the last. Weston was eager to reach his home as he had a sore throat and wanted to relax in the comfort of his own bedroom with his new wife. Beatrice wished he had spoken up earlier as she would have gone to Mary Leland's cabin for something to relieve his throat pain. Mary and her mother were women known as "healers." They could do almost everything a doctor could to take care of sick people – even birth babies! When she mentioned it to Kathryn, she just waved her hand and said it was just a little sore throat and he'd be okay in a day or two.

Once home, Weston returned to work in his family's factory. The large building was drafty and he developed a cough. Kathryn tried to get him to stay home, but he insisted that because he had taken so much time off for the wedding that he shouldn't miss any work. Now concerned that the cough was turning into something more serious, Kathryn told Weston that she would write to her sister for potions, and other medicines from Mary Leland, the healer who would help his affliction. Weston was appalled! He didn't believe in 'healers' and wouldn't be using any grass and twigs for any reason.

Within a week, Weston's cough was much worse and he had a high fever. By that week's end he was bedridden and Kathryn was truly alarmed! She sent a note by messenger to her sister and begged for help and medicine.

As healers, Mary, and her mother Grannie Rose, cared for people who were sick or injured, mothers who were about to give birth, all came to them for help or sent for them in the middle of the day or night. Together, they set bones, cured fevers and birthed babies. In payment they received milk, butter, eggs, chickens or chopped wood and sometimes small amounts of cash. Once in a while, a grateful patient or relative would fix their old roof or fence. And then sometimes they only received a tearful thanks. Most always people gave what they could when they could.

Within two days, Mary Leland, Beatrice, and her mother arrived at the Granger estate and rushed to Weston's bedside.

"Why didn't Weston see your local doctor?" Mary was alarmed at Weston's high fever and difficulty breathing.

"We don't have one right now. Colton Creek's only doctor is away treating his wife's mother. Weston wouldn't let me contact you earlier. He doesn't believe in people who are healers." Kathryn was wringing her hands with worry. "Can you help him, Mary?" she cried.

Mary looked at Weston. "I can try, Kathryn. But he's very ill," she said as she started unpacking her large baskets.

After three long days and nights, Weston died from pneumonia. After the funeral, a devastated Kathryn packed her belongings into several trunks and left her husband's estate. His family begged her to stay, but she couldn't face each day without Weston and without her family close by to help her. She chose to be with them and return to her old bedroom. She would never love again. She would never have children or a separate home of her own. No other man could ever take the place of Weston.

Beatrice was very sympathetic. Even though she was the strong one who didn't tolerate weakness, she understood her sister's love for her husband and complete despair. Eventually, she knew her sister would recover from her mourning and rejoin the world just as she had done. Beatrice would tolerate nothing less!

Mr. and Mrs. Bradley were both filled with frustration and deep sadness for their beloved daughters. They had lost a son-in-law, their daughter a husband, before they had a chance to establish a married life. Beatrice had been denied even her church wedding by her tragic loss. And, the fact that there was no doctor in their town to take care of the more serious health issues was a problem. Not everyone believed in the healing powers of Mary Leland and Grannie Rose. Weston's death was a direct indication of the need for a medical doctor. They agreed that as leaders of their town of Fairfax, Ohio, it was necessary for them to seek out a doctor who would be willing to move his practice to Fairfax. They would contact the medical board in Cincinnati and schedule a trip there immediately.

It would be a matter of only six months that tragedy would strike their beloved town again. A blackness was descending that would forever change Fairfax, Ohio.

Chapter 4

The Epidemic

Even though it was sometimes a long trek, Mary Leland, her son Tom, and mother Grannie Rose, made house calls rather than having seriously sick folks travel to their home. Their family was poor but they didn't go cold or hungry. Mary's son, Tom, could read and write and do sums. He was becoming more and more helpful to his mother and was growing into a fine young man. Mary Leland had used the bible to teach Tom how to read and used match sticks for addition and subtraction.

Tom had wished he could go to school but it was too far to town without a horse or mule and he was busy helping Ma and Grannie Rose most days anyhow and they needed their only horse, Ole Ned. His pa died a long time ago, when Tom was only five years old. Ma told him he had been a good man and had loved his only child very much. Their farm grew crops then. There were fields of corn and smaller plots of land with seasonal vegetables; enough to feed their family and some they took to town and sold at the mercantile. His pa had been a successful farmer.

Mary had a feeling that the coming months would be increasingly uncertain for people because of the talk of war. Their friend, Samuel

Washington, a former slave who worked at Bender's Tavern, was constantly hearing angry talk about southern states leaving the union. A group of rowdy drinkers who were regular customers, were even talking about getting back at people in their town who sympathized about freeing slaves and telling the southern states what they could and couldn't do. Mary was always nervous when traveling because she didn't trust the men Samuel told them about. Her hope was that because she and Grannie Rose were healers and had treated their families, even some of the men themselves, they would leave her family alone.

This cold morning, a young lad awoke Mary by banging on her door with a metal cup she kept on the porch for drinking water from the well. She cautiously opened the door a crack and peeked around to see a panicked young boy.

"Miz Mary! You gotta come on to my house right quick! Ma's ailin and so's my baby brother and little sister. Pa says they's got the fever real bad. Can you come on with me now, pleez," the young boy pleaded.

"Who are your folks? I don't recognize you." Mary pulled her robe closer around her body and opened her door.

"I'm Caleb Dooley's son, Miz Mary. You remember me. You fixed my arm up real good when I fell in the barbed wire fence last year, remember?" The young boy smiled showing his missing front teeth.

"Well, my goodness! How you've grown. What's your name son? You want to wait and go back to yur house with me and Grannie Rose, or do you want to hurry on back and tell yur pa we're comin'?" Mary was packing her medicine bag while she spoke to the boy. She remembered how brave he had been when she had to clean his wounds from the barbed wire. He was a real nice boy.

"I'm Patrick, Miz Mary, and I'd a soon as be with you. Pa says I can't go in the house no more till everybody's okay agin." He dragged his shirtsleeve across his nose and sniffed. Mary watched him and hoped he wasn't coming down with the same fever his family had or if he was trying to keep from crying. She approached the boy and gently placed her hand on his forehead checking for a fever. Finding none, she breathed a sigh of relief.

"Wait here, I'll get changed and get Grannie Rose and Tom to go with us."

The young boy nodded and leaned against the cabin door. Mary quickly changed and woke up Grannie Rose and Tom telling them about the sick family they had to visit. Tom dressed and hurried outside to hook up their horse to the wagon. He tossed a feed bag into the back of the wagon filled with food for the horse and blankets for his ma and Grannie Rose. He couldn't depend on the family for feed for their horse, they were poor and might not have enough for their own stock. He tossed in some baskets of herbs they might need, a couple of jugs of water, and a large kettle to boil it in and ran back into the house. Grannie Rose was moving slowly so he took her arm and helped her out the door and into the wagon. Mary came out with the boy carrying her large bag and some more blankets.

"We're goin' to the Dooley's farm Tom. Seems the family's ailin' with fever." Mary hoped it was something she could easily nurse these folks through. They were nice folk.

Tom made sure Grannie Rose was settled next to him. His ma was in the back with the boy and the supplies. Tom slapped the reins and the horse took off at a trot. He wished he had been given time to eat some breakfast. His fast-growing body always made him feel like an empty bucket waiting to be filled up. He hoped maybe he could help his ma and grannie then hurry home to some oatmeal and bread with honey he collected. The young boy, Patrick, stood up behind Tom and held onto his shoulder, giving him directions and urging him to hurry.

They soon reached the farm and saw Patrick's father pacing on the porch his breath coming out like fog. When he spotted them, he rushed forward with relief painted on his face.

"Thank the good Lord you're here Miz Mary! My family's ailin bad. I didn't know what to do 'cep call on y'all!" He helped Grannie Rose down and then started helping Tom unload the wagon. Mary and Grannie Rose went into the cabin to take a look at the sick ones inside. Tom knew to start a fire outside to get the large kettle boiling water. His ma and grannie would use it for all matter of things while they tended to their healing.

"Just pile all the supplies on the porch by the door. We'll need that big fire for this kettle and as much water in it as you can keep hot." Tom knew it would be good to keep Mr. Dooley busy while his wife and children were being examined. "Patrick, you can put the feed bag on my horse while I unhook the wagon. Lead him over to your fence over yonder and hook him up by the water trough. You keep an eye on 'em and in a little while take the bag off and let him drink. That way I can help my ma and not worry about anything else, okay?"

Patrick puffed his chest out, "I'm right pleased to help ya Tom. I can take good care of yur horse." The little boy stretched up and unhooked the lead from the wagon and led the horse over to the fence and tied it with a good knot. "Looks like he's a might thirsty, Tom. I'll hook up the feed bag after he gets some water."

Tom smiled, "You're in charge, Patrick. Thank you kindly."

Meanwhile, Mary and Grannie Rose were examining Mrs. Dooley holding a crying baby. A little girl lay asleep in a bed nearby. All three were shivering and the two that were awake had bright fevered eyes.

Mrs. Dooley groaned, "I'm feelin' so bad I can't rightly soothe this baby, Miz Mary. Can you help me?"

Mary picked up the baby and handed him to Grannie Rose who immediately sat down in a rocking chair next to the fireplace. She opened up the blanket surrounding the baby's body and pulled away the night gown he was wearing checking for any sores or a rash. The baby's temperature was high and needed to be brought down. Grannie Rose removed the gown and blanket and laid the baby across her knees on its stomach so she could inspect his back.

"Tom! Need you inside to help us." Tom trotted up the porch and went to grannie's side. "This high fever has to be brought down. I need you to fill up a washbasin with cool water so I can start on this little one."

The screaming baby was too ill to do much other than cry as Grannie Rose removed his nightgown and soggy diaper. "Look ahere now, Mary. We got us a rash goin' in this little one's neck. You see anything on Mrs. Dooley yet? I'll check out this other little one. She looks like she's burnin' up."

Grannie wrapped the baby back up in the blanket and laid him down on the bed, then turned to the little girl asleep on the bed. "Oh my Mary! She is burnin' up! Tom," grannie hollered,

"We'd better get their bath tub and fill it up too."
Pulling back the covers from the little girl, she
saw that her rash went from her cheeks down her
body as she lifted her night gown. The girl
moaned and opened her eyes. "She's got a runny
nose and a rash." Grannie Rose looked at Mary,
"I think we're dealing with measles." Grannie
sighed.

"Doesn't look good. We're gonna be here all
day and night for these folks, Mary. Better check
on Mr. Dooley and little Patrick."

Mrs. Dooley was crying. Mary held her hand
and tried to soothe her, "Now Mrs. Dooley, we're
gonna do everything we can to make you all feel
better. Grannie Rose and I think you all have
come down with the measles. Do you know
anyone who has been sick with fever and a rash?"

"Fever and a rash? My husband and I went
over to the Mercer's farm for a potluck last week
and one of her little girls had a cold and was not
feeling real good, but played with my Melanie all
afternoon. I ain't seen em since so I don't know
as any of the others are ailin." She grabbed
Mary's hand, "We're gonna be okay, right, Miz
Mary? Please say we're gonna be alright." Mary
patted her hand.

"Grannie Rose and I will stay with you and get
you through this, Mrs. Dooley. You just
concentrate on getting well again." Mary got up
and went to the door. Tom was carrying the wash
basin filled with water back to the cabin.

"Tom, after you fill the bath tub up, I want you to take the horse and ride over to the Bradley's and tell Mr. Bradley that I'm afraid there's gonna be a lotta sickness with measles real soon and to alert all his men at the mercantile, bank, mill and wagon works. Then go on over to Bender's Tavern. You tell them about the Dooleys having measles and that anyone who's been in contact with them in the last week may come down with them, too. Folks need to stay away from each other as much as they can. Tell Mr. Bender to put a note on his door and warn people about being sick. If anyone needs us we will be here at the Dooley farm for a couple of days. If a lot of people have been together with the Dooleys or the Mercers, this thing's gonna go through our town like a barn on fire!"

Mary opened her satchel and started pulling out herbs and laying them on the kitchen counter along with her stone and pestle to grind them up. The willow bark would be ground, then boiled and made into a tea to be drunk for fever. The eucalyptus leaves had already been prepared by boiling the leaves then mixing them with oil. Mary had several jars in the wagon which she would use to make poultices for chest congestion. She took the kettle and filled it with water from the kitchen pump, lit a burner and put it on to boil as she talked to Tom. All her remedies would be used today. She only hoped she had enough to treat the many she was afraid would come down with measles in the next few days. Mary had only treated folks for measles one time before when Tom was a little boy. She and Grannie Rose had been summoned to a town a few miles across the Ohio River. Luckily, she had had measles when she was a little girl so she didn't have to worry about getting them again. Tom had come down with a mild case then so he would be fine to help with the sick ones. At the time, they had worked round the clock for over a week and had lost many people, young and old to pneumonia which was a complication of the measles. It seemed like the people who had died had been older folks and babies. She looked over at the baby, still crying and said a prayer for him.

"When you get back, Tom, I'm gonna teach you some more healin' cause if I'm right, we'll be splittin' up to cover all the ailin' folk who'll be needin' us." Mary pulled her hair back and tied it with a ribbon from her pocket. "Hurry up now, and send in Mr. Dooley and Patrick. Might as well check them out, too."

Mr. Dooley came in with Patrick and stood twisting his hat by the door. "Tom said you wanted to see us, Miz Mary. Are you gonna be able to help my family?"

Poor man, Mary thought. "Mr. Dooley, have you ever had measles? Because that's what I think your wife and children have."

She approached Mr. Dooley and felt his forehead for fever. He nodded his head, "Yes ma'am, I have had the spots when I was a little feller like Patrick. I don't know 'bout my wife. Not much reason to talk about that kind of stuff." He looked down at Patrick. "Don't believe this one's ever been with it or not."

Mary felt Patrick's forehead. He didn't feel too warm, but he did have a runny nose, which concerned Mary since that would be one of the first signs he was coming down with the measles. Only the next day or two would show if he was going to be ill.

"Mr. Dooley, I know you have work to do on your farm. Just go on about your business, and Grannie Rose and I will take care of your family. We'll also see to the meals while we're here. Hopefully, in a few days, your wife will be feeling much better and can finish taking care of your daughter and the baby. You might be needed then to help her. She's gonna feel a little worn down for a while." Mary smiled and led him to the door.

"What about Patrick, Miz Mary. Should I have him helpin' me out or keep him here in the cabin?" Mr. Dooley placed his hand on Patrick's shoulder.

Mary smiled down at the boy, "What do you think, Patrick? Do you feel up to helpin' your pa?"

Patrick looked up at his pa then at Mary, "I feel okay, Pa. There's nothing I can do here and I sure am tired of listening to the baby cry."

Mr. Dooley patted Patrick's shoulder and smiled, "You're my right-hand man. I can use your help out there. But you start ailin' 'n I want to know it right fast. All right, son?" Patrick nodded.

Obviously, Mr. Dooley was a loving father. He took Patrick's hand and went out the door. Mary could hear them talking as they went. She wouldn't worry about the boy. Maybe he wouldn't be sick.

Tom jogged back to his cabin and saddled up his horse for the ride to Bender's Tavern. He was hoping that Colby and his gang would not be there. They were unpleasant men when they were sober, but mean and nasty when they drank. His friend Samuel Washington worked there and told him and his ma that lately they were talking about punishing folks who were talking abolition and they thought were helping the escaped slaves. But he needed to warn the people. His mother's concern was serious. This sickness could already be spreading through their town!

The tavern was a dark, wooden cave of a building. On the weekends, a piano player made good music but the tavern was filled with boisterous voices now. As he feared, Colby's gang was in the back laughing and drinking. Tom saw Mr. Bender behind the bar with Samuel standing next to him. They were deep in conversation and didn't see him until he stood before them.

Mr. Bender looked up in surprise, "Well, Tom, what are you doing in here? Can't say I've ever seen you in the tavern." Tom smiled at him and Samuel who also looked surprised.

"My Ma sent me, Mr. Bender. There's a sickness that could be goin' 'round and Ma's real worried about the town folks. She said to tell you to make an announcement and post a notice so people can read it." Tom took a breath, "Her and Grannie Rose are out at the Dooley's farm. Miz Dooley, her little girl, and baby are real sick with measles."

"Your ma isn't one to panic folks, Tom. Measles is something we should be worried about. I will tell all the folks and post a big note on my door. You also need to stop by Rev. Hawthorn's and the mercantile and train depot, too. How 'bout I make the signs and you and Samuel can cover more places thata way?"

"Thanks kindly, Mr. Bender. Can I wait for you and Samuel in the back? I don't like being 'round Colby's bunch." Before Tom could move, Hank Colby saw him talking at the bar and lurched over to him.

"Howdy, young Tom!" He slapped Tom on the back. Tom winced and started to step away from Colby but he grabbed his arm, "Hey, where you goin', boy?" His rotten teeth and odorous breath turned Tom's stomach. He frowned and pulled his arm back while trying to move away. "Whoa, whoa, boy. Now I'm talkin' to you. You respek yur elders now boy, ya hear?" Colby lurched against Tom, pinning him against the bar.

"You are nothing I respect, Colby. Step back away from me. I have important business here with Mr. Bender." Tom pushed Colby and he stumbled. Before Tom could resume talking to Mr. Bender, several of his gang rapidly approached looking angrily at Tom.

"Whatcha doin' pushin' Hank around, boy?" He strutted up to Tom and hitched his pants up over his big belly and belched. "We don't take kindly to bein' pushed around. Especially by a young snap like you, eh fellers?" Colby's friends nodded their heads and grunted their agreement while crowding closer to Tom.

"Okay now you men. Tom's here to warn us about a sickness that might be goin' through our town. His Ma's out at the Dooley's farm and there could be others that have it. It's measles, men. People can die from this and we need to have folks know about it and stay away from each other for a while." Mr. Bender looked at each man and saw that what he said was slowly filtering into their inebriated brains.

"Whoa now Bender. You ain't shuttin' down the tavern now, are ya?" the big man shouted.

"Walt, don't you have a missus and little ones down at your farm?" Bender looked at him, "You mean to tell me you're not a little worried about them?" He stared the man down.

Walt shifted his feet and cleared his throat,

"My missus can take care of my kids just fine. I ain't a'tall worried 'bout 'em."

"Well, that's fine then, Walt. But you do know that if they haven't had measles before, they're all liable to get it, and you, too."

The men started to look a little worried. One man was even white-faced. "I remember a time back when I lived in Hampton. The measles went through the people there and a lot of folks and babies died including my older brother! I think I'm goin' on to my home and hope my wife and kids ain't gonna get sick. I already had the spots, but I'm not sure 'bout my wife." He hurried out of the tavern and some of the other men looked like they wanted to run, too.

"I'm putting up a sign I want y'all to read, folks," Mr. Bender said loudly. The loud voices in the tavern died down and all the people turned to look at Mr. Bender. "We've got measles at the Dooley farm. If any of you have been around the Dooleys or their kids, you need to be watchin' now for fevers, runny noses or rashes on your bodies. If you have had measles, you can't get em again, but if not – you can get real, real sick. I'm gonna post a sign on my door and probably close down the tavern for a while. Report any sickness to Mary Leland or Tom. She can help you if you need any doctorin' so make sure you get some help." He looked over the bar at people who now were murmuring among themselves. "This can get real bad for us. Go on home now, and take care of your families."

By week's end, Mary Leland had her hands full trying to find enough hours to treat the sick. She was worried about Grannie Rose who wasn't feeling well but tried to fool Mary that she was doing fine. She thanked every day that she had Tom to help out. He was taking on more and more healing responsibility. Mary was so proud of how competent Tom was becoming.

The normally bustling town of Fairfax slowly ground to a halt over the next two weeks as more and more people became ill. When folks started dying, the town council made a special place in the cemetery to store the bodies until they could be properly buried. Fear now raged in the town and people were afraid to go anywhere they could be around folks who might be sick. The knowledge that the "spots" as people called the disease, could be passed from one person to another was just plain scary. The bank closed, the tavern, and most of the other town businesses closed as well. There was no school and the mercantile took orders for delivery only. The town newspaper, The Fairfax Bulletin, published information about what symptoms to look for and for folks to take their loved ones to either the church or the school as the number of sick people increased by the day. There were no church services while the epidemic raged.

The Bradley family did all they could to help the town folk by furnishing cots made in their

Wagon Works and Mill, and sending as much bedding as they could to the church and school. Beatrice and Kathryn donated jars of fruit and vegetables, and bags of flour so that the people who could not work and had no money would not starve. Mr. and Mrs. Bradley packed their bags and left on the train for Cincinnati to hire a doctor for their town. They couldn't expect Mary Leland and Grannie Rose to save their town when serious medical issues affected so many. It was time to do what was right for the people.

A heavy curtain of sadness hung over the town. Rev. Hawthorn and his wife moved all the church pews to the walls and the room became a hospital ward. The school nearby did the same, moving desks and making pallets on the floor. Instead of traveling from farm to farm, Mary, Grannie Rose, and Tom had only to drive to town with their wagon of herbs and potions. Gradually, over the next several weeks, there were fewer demands to treat the sick folks. The school and the church sick beds dwindled down to just a few people in each place.

Mary had sent Grannie Rose home earlier in the day with Samuel who made sure she had a kettle on for tea. Grannie Rose had been visibly slowing down the last few days and complained of being very tired. The long hours treating and traveling had taken their toll on her. Mary was not going to let her leave the cabin for the next week now that she and Tom could handle the few patients who were left at the school and church.

Mary and Tom returned home late one night to a dark cabin. At least one lantern was usually lit by Grannie Rose before she took a nap or went to bed. Tom pulled the wagon close to the front porch so that they could easily empty all the baskets from the back. After helping Mary, Tom released the horse and put him in their small corral with food and water.

Mary entered the dark cabin and struck a match to light the lantern by the front door. As she turned to place the lantern on the table, she saw Grannie Rose asleep in her rocker by the hearth. Only a small flame remained in the fireplace casting a shadow across Grannie Rose's body. Even before she took a step, Mary knew what she would find when she reached out and took Grannie Rose's hand. A shudder went through Mary and she cried out, "Ma!" Mary knelt next to Grannie Rose. "Ma," she cried clutching her body to her chest.

Tom came through the door and immediately ran to his ma. He knelt down next to her and took Grannie Rose's other hand.

"She's gone, Tom," she sobbed. "I knew she was tired lately, but I let her keep coming with me and workin' when I knew she was *tired*!" Mary leaned forward and hugged Grannie Rose. Tom released Grannie Rose's hand and stood up, tears running down his cheeks.

"We'll need to prepare her ma. It's late now,

so we'll take her in the morning to the church, I guess. Rev. Hawthorn can hold a service for us and Grannie Rose, even if it's only for you and me."

Mary lifted her face and looked at Tom. "Thank you Tom. I won't expect many folks to stand with us and bury Grannie Rose," she said sadly. "Probably just the reverend, the Bradley sisters, and a couple of others. You better go on over and let Beatrice and Kathryn know." Mary smoothed her hand over Grannie Rose's head. "But first, let's say a prayer and lay her down in her bedroom with her bible." Mary's tears were clogging her throat. "You say the prayer, Tom. I can't."

Tom had loved Grannie Rose so much. She had patiently taught him so many things about finding and picking out herbs that were so good for treating people's ailments. Grannie had made a game out of tramping through the forest and finding lichen, mushrooms and other healing plants and leaves, then hanging and drying them. The first time Tom had tried to grind up the potion Grannie Rose had put together, he made a mess all over the table. He felt bad to waste any of the precious herbs, but Grannie Rose just laughed and showed Tom how to hold the pestle and carefully grind the herbs together.

She was always like that. Nothing ever made her lose her temper except meanness in folks. Now this patient, loving, wonderful woman was gone. His ma would really be lonely now without her counsel and love. Ma was truly alone now. He was her only family left.

Tom picked up ma's bible and started to read, "So do not fear: for I am with you, do not be dismayed, for I am your God, I will strengthen you, and help you, I will uphold you with my righteous right hand. Amen."

Mary and Tom were shocked when they saw all the folks waiting in the churchyard for them to bury Grannie Rose. Rev. Hawthorn stood tall and impressive in the special white robe he wore for funerals and weddings. Mary smiled and greeted all the folks. Grannie Rose would be so proud to see them gathered here for her.

"We are gathered here today to honor Rose Milton. A woman who lived all of her fifty-six years here in Fairfax. Grannie Rose, as she was known, took care of most of you at one time or another. She had a deep well of love and caring. No complaint was ever ignored. I look around and see a few of you who have Rose to thank for being the one who helped bring you into the world. She will be missed by all of us. We must celebrate the life of this wonderful woman. Her life here has ended, but she is not truly gone for she will live on in the hearts of those who knew her and surely we will meet again in Heaven."

Rev. Hawthorn looked over the crowd and nodded to Samuel in the back of the crowd. He put his harmonica to his lips and slowly played,

There is a Balm in Gilead. Mary knew the words as she learned them from escaped slaves she had treated and hid in her root cellar. She softly sang the words to herself as Samuel played: "There is a balm in Gilead, to make the wounded whole." It was a beautiful addition to the brief ceremony and Mary would thank Samuel for his thoughtfulness later.

Usually, after a funeral there would be a luncheon for the mourners, but because of the recent epidemic, everyone would just say goodbye and return to their homes. Mary and Tom would stay with Grannie Rose's coffin as the gravesite was filled in with dirt. They had flowers and herbs to plant that would mark Grannie Rose's grave. She wouldn't rest here alone for next to her were the graves of her husband and Mary's husband. She was in good company. It was a warm summer day so the planting and watering of the flowers couldn't be delayed. Grannie Rose would forever sleep beneath one of her favorite red roses growing next to the heavy wood crosses of her loved ones.

Mary and Tom stood alone at the grave of Grannie Rose. A last prayer was said, then it was time to leave but Mary was reluctant. Tom looked up and saw that Beatrice, Kathryn, Big John, and Samuel were waiting for them by the church.

Big John approached and removed his hat, "Miz Mary, Miz Beatrice is havin' you and Tom over for a little supper now, if'n you please?"

Mary smiled at Big John, "Why that would be very nice, Big John. I really wasn't ready to go home and face Grannie Rose's empty rocking chair right now." Mary turned to Tom, "You made sure enough water covered the roses, didn't you, Tom?" When Mary turned to look back at Grannie Rose's grave the tears began to fall again.

"Yes, Ma, I'll come back every coupla days to get 'em through the hot days, you can be sure." Tom took his Ma's arm and turned her toward the waiting buggy and their friends. "We need to go now. There's nothing more for us to do here."

Tom kept his hand on Mary's arm to guide her through the cemetery. He wished he had enough money for one of the fancy markers they passed. But they were simple folk. He would visit here more often now. Tom said a quick prayer for his grandparents and father and added that he didn't want his ma taken away from him for a long, long time.

Unfortunately, Mary and Tom didn't have any time for mourning, for that night a message was sent from another 'depot' that Tom needed to guide three escaped slaves to his cabin for they were sick and not able to travel to the next depot on their journey to freedom. He would hide them in the root cellar that he and Samuel had dug when he was just ten years old.

The Lelands' cabin had two root cellars: one

inside the small barn close to the house, which was a secret place used for the escaped slaves. The other was next to the barn but built into a small hill between the barn and the house. A wood door opened to an 8x10 interior with shelves on both sides and in the back from floor to ceiling. This cellar was always filled with potatoes, canned goods, and other kitchen staples. There was an emergency tunnel which connected the two root cellars only to be used in case of an escape from the barn cellar. A narrow tunnel in the side facing the barn was hidden by two wooden bins full of corn husks. The tunnel went under the barn to the other root cellar. That secret door in the far back was covered by dirt over a large flat rock. It was Samuel who had built the hidden root cellar in the old barn with Tom's help. He told Ma and Grannie Rose about the escaped slaves and "them havin' trouble gettin' to the Promised Land" which was really Canada. He also told them about how they were sold to plantations - sometimes beaten and even had to wear chains. Right away Ma said that she would help.

That's when their cabin became a stop along the Underground Railroad for the sick and injured. If the runaway slaves were healthy, Tom was a conductor who made sure they made it to the next stop or 'station,' twelve miles away. It used to be an easy trek for Tom. But lately, bounty hunters and other men hunted the slaves down and got a reward for their efforts. Mary was always scared when Tom was gone. Luckily, Tom knew the countryside like the back of his hand. Even darkness couldn't keep him from traversing the fields and valleys in the dead of night. But it took longer now that he had to hide their trail as they traveled.

Chapter 5

The Rescue

Tessa finished lunch alone and sat gazing out the window watching the hummingbirds flit among the flowers in her aunts' garden. She knew she would be happy here. Cousins Beatrice and Kathryn treated her like a grownup and she loved her new bedroom --- all pink and white and frilly. All during her train journey from Philadelphia to Fairfax, she looked forward to her new life here. Her stepmother had tried to be friends with her, had even given her pearl earrings and a matching necklace, but Tessa just couldn't accept her. She was sleeping with Tessa's father in his bedroom for heaven's sake --- replacing her mother! Tessa couldn't bring herself to think about what they did there without feeling a little ill. It wasn't proper to think about that behavior. Now there were little ones! Her father hadn't wasted any time replacing her with twin daughters, Tessa thought crossly. Although they were sweet little angels, Tessa just couldn't bring herself to love them and wanted no part in their lives. Her father had a new family now. They had invaded her home. It was time for Tessa to get her own life.

After all, she was sixteen years old. Many of her friends were already engaged to be married!

She didn't want to be engaged or married to any of the silly boys who had attended cotillion classes with her. They giggled as they stood over her and requested her hand for the next dance. NO! She would live with her cousins here in Fairfax for the next year and then move to Columbus and attend the Litchfield Academy for Young Women. She was already registered for attendance. Her future was set for the next three years at least.

Her father had looked sad when she told him she had written to her cousins and they had invited her to live with them and that she was leaving. She had written to them and told them she had her father's permission to stay with them until she attended school. Her cousins had even sent money for her train ticket without consulting her father. She had purchased her ticket and left a tearful stepmother who told her she hadn't meant to drive her away, and her father who blew his nose several times before giving her an awkward hug good bye. It was funny, really, that she hadn't felt more than a little regret to be leaving. Tessa missed her mother who had only died three years ago. She had never been very close to her father. He was always so busy working that she was accustomed to the house without him -- except Saturday afternoons and Sundays. Now with her stepmother, he was always underfoot.

The day was fresh spring and blue sky lovely. Tessa looked out over the garden and saw the white blossoms of the apple orchard in the distance. How beautiful! She knew they had a sweet fragrance and she thought they would look lovely in a vase by her bedside. She quickly cleared her place and rinsed her dishes. The cook would wash them if she left them in the sink so she hurried outside eager to walk amongst the beautiful apple trees on this lovely day.

Hank Colby held the flour sack and string tightly in his hand as he sneaked through the apple orchard. He had a hankerin' for chicken dinner and knew the Bradleys had a chicken coop full of ripe fat hens that would taste mighty good when his wife cooked 'em up. He regularly took stock of them and borrowed a few now and then. He chuckled. The Bradleys were uppity folk and thought they was better'n him. It wasn't as if they couldn't spare a hen or two. He even brought his boy Willie to help him round up eggs from time to time. His skinny ole chickens din't put out their kind of eggs. Yep, he'd have hisself a good meal this day,

Suddenly, he saw a blue dress up ahead. He didn't recognize the young gal wearing it. Hadn't seen her before. What a beauty! Hank hid behind the large bushes that lined the edge of the apple orchard and watched the gal sniffin' the apple blossoms and hummin' to herself as she walked. Hank was mesmerized. He couldn't take his eyes off her. Boy! What he wouldn't give to have a woman that purty! His woman was skinny and whiney. Always beggin' him for this and that. Lately, she din't want him in their bed – din't that beat all? Even told him there'd be no more little ones. Well, he'd bide his time and get his way soon enough with a coupla good whacks. Right now all he could think about was that gal. She was a real looker. His gang at the tavern would sure wish they could see this! He took out the bottle from his hip pocket and took another swig. He'd been drinking since early that morning after he had a talkin' to from his wife. Women always thinkin' they'd git their way. Wouldn't his friends like to share a piece of this here gal?

Hank rubbed his hand over his mouth. An idea was forming as he looked around to see if anyone else was walking in the apple orchard. He listened real careful. Nope, not a soul. He checked to see if his mule was still tethered on the other side of the bushes. She was, eatin' grass and not paying any mind to anything else. Hank looked at the gal to see where she was at now.

He was thinkin' as soon as she turned her back, he could sneak up on her and put the flour sack over her head. She couldn't see anything then – 'specially him, he thought. He might have to whack her a little so she wouldn't fight him too much. The gal din't look too big…..he could tie her hands with the string. Slowly, Hank crept around the bushes to the next clump. So far….so good. A 'nother cuppala bushes and he'd be close 'nuf to grab her, he thought excitedly. Her next step picking apple blossoms had her back completely turned away from Hank. That's all the time he needed and he pounced.

Tessa started to scream and Hank covered her mouth with his dirt-encrusted hand. "Don't fight me gal," he growled. "I don't wanna have to hurt ya, just stand still." Hank forced the flour sack over Tessa's beautiful blonde hair, pulling some strands out as he did. She tried to scream again and Hank punched her in the back a couple of times.

"Uff!" Tessa felt like her legs would fail her with the pain in her side. She tried to kick out at the man behind her, and staggered back.

"I tol' ya not to fight me, dang it!" Hank punched her again and Tessa started to fall. Hank lost his balance and Tessa fell on the ground in the dirt. Hank had the flour sack on her now, covering her face. He held her head and thunked it twice on a rock. She lay still then and he used the time to secure her hands together in front with the thick string. Hank was disappointed he hadn't had a chance to look at her close up.

Quickly, he looked around. No one around yet, as far as he could see. Good thing that ole blackie, Big John, who worked for the Bradleys, wasn't around. He couldn't fight him off very well. The girl was still quiet on the ground. Hank bent over and hoisted Tessa up and tried to get her over his shoulder. He couldn't get her up high enough so he decided to drag her over to his mule.

Hank looked down and paused for a brief moment when he saw blood on the rock he had hit her head on. His stomach rolled. He couldn't have killed her with that little whack, could he? Hank put her on the ground and got down on his knees to feel her chest to see if she was still breathing. Yup, she's still breathin' he thought with relief. He felt her again, not for her breathing but because she had felt real nice. With a sly grin he looked around. He didn't have enough time to have her here. He could still get caught. Even his friend the sheriff couldn't help him if he got caught havin' his way with this gal. 'Specially not one who was at the Bradley house. No sir. He best get her out of here as far as he could go. Then figure out what he was gonna do with her after.

He ran over to his mule and pulled the reins, urging the mule closer to the girl. The mule pulled back and refused to walk around the bushes. Hank yanked hard on the reins and growled, "Get up you bucket o' bones!" He pulled again, nothing. Hank reached down in his pocket and found a small dried up apple he had saved for a snack. He put it near the mule's nose and quickly pulled it away. The mule's ears perked up and it stepped forward. Gradually, step by step it walked closer to the girl's body. Finally it was close enough and Hank put the apple back in his pocket.

He put the reins down on the ground and put his foot over them to keep the mule in place. He pulled at the girl's arm and lifted her up against him and the mule. With a huge effort he got her over the mule's back and climbed on behind her. With one last look around, Hank steered the mule away from the apple orchard and kept going. Hank took a deep breath, brought out the bottle of whiskey from his back pocket and took a big swig. Wiping his mouth with the back of his hand he spilled some whiskey on the girl's back.

"Dang it! Cain't waste my hooch thata way!" Carefully, Hank pushed the cork back in the top of the bottle and put it back in his pocket. Looking around he decided he'd take a long circle around the Bradleys' property and stay where he knew there were no houses. He had a place in mind to take the gal and wanted to get there as soon as he could. Hank took the bottle out again and this time, dropped the cork. He would drink it as he was ridin' he thought. Celebratin' his lucky find! Whooee! He was gonna have some fun this day all right. Wisht the fellers could see this gal. Hank started to whistle Dixie then thought he'd better quiet up or else someone might hear him. He took another swig and smiled.

Tom had been gone all day and was tired and eager to get home to his bed. Even his horse, Ole Ned, was walking slowly. He'd been gone from home since early morning. If he wasn't careful, Tom would fall asleep and fall to the ground. At least he wouldn't lose Ole Ned. He'd just hold up and eat while he waited for Tom to regain his seat in the saddle. The slaves he and Ma had taken care of in their root cellar were now at the next depot on their way north. It was a good feeling that they were safe to this point. He hoped they would make it all the way to the Promised Land.

He heard a scream—then nothing—or was that the wind? He started running. When he reached a dense group of trees, he saw a very dirty, disheveled man struggling to hold something down. In the little bit of light from the bright moon, Tom recognized the man - his name was Hank Colby. He lived down the road from Tom's house. Tom knew Colby was a very mean man who beat his wife and children and mistreated the animals on his farm. Tom's mother told him never to go near his house for any reason. He knew that his mother disliked him because she never referred to him as "Mr. Colby" just Colby and that meant that she had no respect for him.

As he got closer he saw that Colby was leaning over a girl. Tom knew it was a girl because he could see long hair mixed with leaves and mud. She was moaning now, he was holding her down. Tom saw him pulling her dress up. He was pinching her now and poking at her, putting his fingers where he shouldn't be touching her.

Tom knew he was going to do bad things to

her. His ma told him, "Tom, you never touch a girl with mean hands," and "A man never puts himself inside a woman's body unless he's married." Hank Colby was married to someone else. Who this girl was, he didn't know. Even though he was only sixteen years old, Tom knew that what Colby was trying to do was wrong. He also knew that he had to stop him from hurting her somehow. Looking around he found a short, thick branch.

Colby hadn't heard him yet because he was too busy pawing at the girl. Silently, Tom approached them. Suddenly the girl started fighting Colby and he made a fist and hit her....hard. She fell back and stopped moving. Swiftly, Tom moved closer and swung the branch as hard as he could and struck Colby in the head. Without turning around, he fell forward on top of the girl and was still.

Tom nudged him with his foot. He didn't move so Tom leaned over and grabbed him by the arm and pulled him off the girl. She wasn't moving either. She was really dirty, as if she had been dragged through the mud. There was blood mixed with the leaves and dirt on her head. She might be dead. Tom felt rage starting to grow deep down in his gut. The kind of rage his ma said he wasn't supposed to let out. She was just a young girl without enough strength to save herself from this piece of trash and that was just wrong.

Gently, Tom felt for the pulse on her neck. He

could barely feel anything so he knelt down and placed his head on her chest and listened for a heartbeat. Her heart was beating but her breathing was very shallow. Tom knew that he had to get her back to his house where his ma could clean her up and see to her wounds. He didn't care if the man was hurt. He could lie here and freeze to death for all he cared. Unfortunately, it wasn't really cold enough for that. Colby wouldn't be getting up any time soon—-on top of being clobbered on the head, he smelled like rot-gut whiskey and throw-up.

A malnourished old mule was standing nearby, his reins hanging down. Tom was tempted to use it to take the girl home with him. But the poor creature belonged to Colby and if the mule was discovered at Tom's house, the sheriff could get involved and that wouldn't be good for his ma, and this poor girl, if she survived. The fact that one day his pa went out to hunt and was found two days later in the forest near where he had just found the young girl made it plain that a person couldn't be too careful. Tom's dad had been covered with leaves, his head bashed in and his pocket watch – his one and only treasure, and his rifle were missing. The townspeople who found him reported it to the sheriff, but he did very little to find out who murdered his pa. His pa was buried next to his grandpa and Grannie Rose in the church cemetery in town.

The fewer people nosing around to see what

his family did on a daily basis, the better, especially what they did at night helping the runaway slaves. Helping the runaway slaves who were on the underground railway could get his family in big trouble. Kentucky and Virginia, just across the border, were both slave states. Since their town of Fairfax, Ohio was not far from the border of these two states, there were many folks who didn't like people who helped the slaves escape from plantations. They were sympathetic to the slave owners and the Fugitive Slave Act. They would even help catch the slaves and give them to the hunters who came looking for them. Tom knew they received a bounty for each one they returned. Anyone who helped the slaves went to jail. He had seen a couple of the bounty hunters on their horses with guns on their hips and whips laid across the horns of their saddles. They even had special dogs, folks called 'bloodhounds' that track slaves through the dense forest. It was dangerous work helping the escaped slaves, but Tom and his ma knew they were doing the right thing. Even the sheriff and the town judge cooperated with the bounty hunters. They both knew it could be dangerous to go against a group of southern sympathizers especially since it was against the law to help the slaves. Tom didn't like or trust the sheriff. He didn't know the judge, but he wasn't sure if he was good people or not. He wasn't about to hope that they would help him or any of the folks involved in the 'railroad.'

The little town of Fairfax, didn't have a doctor. The old doctor had died five years ago and hadn't been replaced. Samuel, a freed slave and friend of Tom's family, worked at the local tavern and listened to folks talking: the town was supposed to get a new doctor, but no one knew exactly when. Samuel was always listening to the townsfolk and travelers when they talked, and reported back to Tom's ma about what he heard. He could give warning to be careful when tempers of the town folk were stirring about tales of escaped slaves. The Lelands' and several neighbors were his friends, and he wanted to protect them by letting them know what was being talked about in town even if it was only rumors. Fairfax was a mixed town of folks; some were southern sympathizers called Copperheads, and others favored the north and the abolition of slavery.

Lately, rumors were a part of every conversation from the hardware store to the tavern about the fact that soon the nation could go to war. There was talk that some of the southern states were going to leave the union. Tom didn't know how he felt about that. He just knew that he would do what he could for the escaped slaves and the people who helped them. And right now that meant he had to help this poor girl. Whatever she had been doing out here alone he didn't care. He got her away from Colby. He stared down at her mud-smeared head considering what would be best to do. He could go and get a horse from home, but that could take too long. She could be discovered by someone looking for slaves or Colby could wake up and take her away. Tom was not going to let that happen.

Nope, he would carry her home. He was strong and tall for his age, almost the size of a grown man, but he might have to stop and rest a couple of times since he was about three miles from home. Glad that it was dark, Tom would stay in the shadows of the trees as much as possible. Someone could come along the road any time and see them. Tom didn't want to answer any questions about this girl and why he was out on the road so late at night.

The trek home was longer than Tom had thought. Since he had to avoid the road, it took longer to go around the dense bushes and large rocks in the fields he had to cross in the limited light. He rested twice, but didn't want to take any more time because the girl was softly moaning and her head was still bleeding. As he struggled along, he was grateful that the cool evening breeze wasn't a hot, humid night. Tom didn't want to stop and bandage her up if he could help it. She would need a lot of cleaning up first and he couldn't do that without fresh water.

Thankfully, he finally saw a light up ahead. He knew it was his home because his ma kept a lantern burning in their window until he arrived home safely whenever he was out at night. She would be waiting for him in her old rocker next to the fireplace. Ma always kept watch when he went out at night. Tom was a 'conductor' – he helped slaves who had escaped from plantations in the nearby states of Kentucky and Virginia. His job was to escort the slaves on the Underground Railroad from one 'depot' or safe house, to the next in his area. Tom would give his "passengers" to another conductor, that is, if they were well enough to keep traveling. More often than not, they were starved, wounded or sick and needed a few days' rest. Some gave birth to children they hoped would never experience the life of a slave. Some even died but were grateful to die as a free person and not as a slave. Eventually, their final destination was somewhere in Canada, "the promised land." When the runaway slaves arrived at a "depot" where they would spend the night or two, a message was sent along to the next depot that folks were coming so they could have their hideaway ready.

Tonight, Tom had helped three people to a nearby "depot" which was actually a root cellar on the Beasley farm. He was lucky because none of them had needed anything more than food. Normally, potatoes, canned goods, fruit, and seasonal vegetables were stored in root cellars. This root cellar was hidden inside the Beasleys' barn and had cots and blankets for three or four people. The temperature was bearable in the cold of the winter, and the hot, humid summer, which was good because there was no source of heat in the underground cellars. Mr. and Mrs. Beasley were the "station masters" because they hid people -- runaway slaves - - in their root cellar, until another conductor came and took them to the next station. This wasn't the only "station" nearby. There were probably a half dozen within thirty miles of Tom's home. The largest one was at the Bradley sisters' estate. Kathryn and Beatrice Bradley could hide more folks there because they had large wagons with false bottoms on them that could accommodate six to eight escaped slaves. Since the wagons had regular routes where they delivered cotton and other produce, those wagons could travel all the way to Columbus where the escaped slaves could then get in other transportation that would take them on to Canada. In "the promised land" they would be free to live like regular folks did without fear of arrest or punishment from escaping their masters in the south. The farther north they got, the easier it was to transport them without fear of sheriffs or trackers or farmers who would turn them in for bounty money. In Canada there was no Fugitive Slave Law.

Ma would help this poor girl. She knew how to do almost as much as a regular doctor; like stop a fever, set broken bones, birth babies and even pull teeth. Tom had helped with all that except birthing babies. He wasn't ready to help do that….probably never.

Tom would not undress this girl and check her body for wounds or broken bones. His ma could do that and give her a bath. Tom knew how to mix herbs and make poultices for the sick. He had been taught since he was a little boy and helped gather herbs in the woods. He could even go into the forest alone because he knew which plants, herbs, tree leaves and bark to pick. He and ma wound them together with string so they could hang under the porch roof to dry. They always had a good supply to use. Tom would take some down and use a big stone to grind them up. His ma would tell him which ones she needed. He would mix them together and grind them into powder. Then, the powder would be made into a tea or a poultice. They always kept jars of herb water so they could easily have it available for emergency poultices and drinks for the sick and ailing. When they needed bandages his ma used sheets donated by the Bradley sisters. Ma was careful to tear the strips to just the right size. They couldn't afford to buy new sheets at the mercantile. If too much material was purchased, the storekeeper might wonder why they needed so much even though his ma treated most of the folks around Fairfax. They couldn't be too careful. Ma didn't want anyone to notice what they were doing. Nosy people could be dangerous.

Tom was completely exhausted when he finally reached the house. As he struggled up the steps, his ma pulled the door open. Without saying a word she helped him bring the girl into the house and pulled back the blankets on the bed in the back room where they gently laid her down.

"Who is she, Tom?" his ma asked as she started pulling back her dirty, blood-matted hair.

"I don't know. I found old man Colby beating her and trying to, uh, you know, have his way with her. She was trying to fight him but he hit her and knocked her out. I don't know what other wounds she has besides her head wound. I didn't check, just hurried to get her home to you. She's awful dirty."

Tom put his hand on her arm, "I hit old man Colby....real hard, Ma. I knocked him out and left him there. He could be hurt bad, but I don't care." Tom looked guilty, "He can rot for all I care."

Tom didn't watch as his ma undressed the girl. "I'll fetch some water for you in the big basin. I'll put more water on to boil....will that be enough for now?

"I'm going to need more water, so fill up the kettle and all the big pots and put them on to boil. Use the outside fire pits to get them all done right away. Then get some bandages as well as the herb basket on the porch. I think her ribs are pretty bruised, but I don't think they're broken."

She gently examined her, "But she may have a broken arm. And her lip and cheek are both cut where he must have hit her."

She turned the girl's head and tsked, "And the back of her head has a cut, too. Looks like I need to put a couple of stitches in her head wound. Bring a sharp knife so that I can cut off her clothes. They're so torn and dirty I won't even try to save anything she's wearing. You can take her shoes off and put them over by the fire. We'll clean them tomorrow after the mud dries."

When Tom handed his ma the scissors he grimaced and turned away as she started cutting and pulling away the mud-soaked dress, petticoat and bloomers. Tom's ma was softly touching the girl's arms, chest, and stomach. Then moving down to her legs looking for more wounds and broken bones. Mary tried to turn her, "You'll have to help me turn her over."

"Oh, Ma!" Tom felt his cheeks burn. "I don't want to look at her naked, Ma!"

"Then just keep your eyes shut 'til I can cover her up. I can't move her by myself without hurting her. You have to help me if we're going to save her. The head wound's gonna be a real worry, probably concussed. She's chilled to the bone, too. If she gets pneumonia she's a goner for sure. The sooner we clean 'n stitch her up and put on the medicine, the better her chances. It's gonna take a lot of water to get her clean."

Tom's ma worked steadily as she talked.

"Just to be sure, you mix up one of the poultices for her chest. Not much more I can do for the poor thing."

Carefully, she pulled the girl's hair away from her face. She gasped, "Dear God!" Mary recognized her! "This is the Bradleys' cousin, Tessa! She's only sixteen years old! What in the world was she doing out at night? She's just here visiting her aunts. Where'd you find her, Tom?"

"I found her about two-three miles from here. I didn't see anyone else besides her and Colby. She couldn't ah been conductin' and I never heard nary a message 'bout travelers tonight. Should I go back an' see if anyone's hidin' out in the forest? I don't know how bad I hurt Colby when I whacked him over the head. I could pretend to be out huntin' if you want an' 'accidentally' find him out there."

Tom didn't really want to go back out, but he didn't want any poor souls left without a chance of getting to safety. He might have to take Colby home, too, but he wouldn't help heal him.

"No, after we take care of her, I'll send you over to the Bradleys' house. You'll have to tell the sisters what happened. Ask them if she helped someone conducting tonight. Somehow she got caught by Colby. If she was with someone and they did have passengers, where are they now? On second thought, you better hightail it over to the Bradleys' house soon's you get the water to boilin' and let em know we have Tessa and she might be here a few days. They'll need to make up a story to cover her being gone and then figure out a story for her wounds. No need to get folks a waggin' their tongues about such a nice young lady. Colby won't want to reveal that he took her so we're probably okay there."

Suddenly, Tom's ma looked panicky, "Tom! Did he see you?" She grabbed his arm and shook him. "Did he see you?" she pleaded.

"No ma'am. I don't think he even knew I was comin' up behind him. He was too busy tryin' to hurt the girl. I found a thick tree branch an' hit him over the head with it before he could turn 'round."

Tom was wracking his brain. Could Colby have been pretending to be unconscious when he was looking over the girl? No, Tom thought, with the drink and the hit on his head he was probably still lying on the ground where he fell. But what if there were passengers out there? There were too many folks around who would turn them in for the bounty.

"Should I go back an' look for the passengers? What should I do, Ma?" Tom asked.

"For now let's just worry about this poor girl. The Bradley sisters will let you know if they need your help. Any poor folks left out there will have to stay put for now unless the Bradley's people can help them."

Mary Leland worked swiftly trying to clean the mud and grime off poor Tessa's head. The head wound needed treating first. She'd work from top to bottom and as fast as she could to get her clean. Tom would have to fill the bath tub and help her put the young girl in a fresh tub of water to get her really and truly clean when he returned. Ma knew he would be embarrassed, but it couldn't be helped. If he was to learn how to care for folks in need he would have to get over his embarrassment. If they didn't get a new doctor, Tom would be the only one to help her. But times were dangerous now, what with their town and surrounding countryside occupied by Copperheads who didn't want a war between the north and south, but they hated abolitionists so they turned folk in who helped slaves and the men in town who wanted to get rid of all the do-gooders helping the runaway slaves. If any of them thought she and Tom were helping escaped slaves, there would be hell to pay.

Without a town doctor she and Tom were the next best thing to help people in need, even if there were people who would do them harm. They couldn't let the townsfolk know how many other people they were helping. It was getting more and more difficult to keep the two sides separate.

"Help me get her in the tub, then hurry over to the Bradleys' and come right back in case I need you. She's too heavy for me to be liftin by myself."

Tom dragged in a large bath tub and filled it

up with steaming water. He added some ground lavender and inhaled the musky scent. It would help soothe the young girl while his ma soaked the mud and grime off her. Hopefully, she would wake up soon and be okay. Tom had great respect for Miss Bea and Miss Kathryn. They were his ma's friends and did a lot of nice things for people. He tried not to look at the girl, Tessa, but it was hard not to. As his ma cut away her clothing, Tom could see that she had beautiful milky white skin, the prettiest thing he'd ever seen. He quickly turned away.

"Okay, Tom, I have her covered with a towel. Help me lift her into the tub."

"I can put her in the tub, ma. Just get on the other end by her feet and help me place her proper in there." Tom looked down at the young girl and gently put his arms around her and lifted. She moaned and tried to pull away from him, but he held on and soothed her with his voice. "It's gonna be okay. Ma and me won't let anything bad happen to you I promise."

Tessa moaned once more, then went limp. It made it easier for Tom to put her in the tub. He felt bad because she probably thought she was still fighting Colby and not safe with him and ma.

"Boy! The Bradley sisters are gonna be mad as wet hens when they find out what that mean ol' cur did to their cousin. Ain't they ma?" Tom frowned when Tessa cried out as the warm water covered her scrapes and bruises. She started thrashing and Tom held her arms. Suddenly, Tessa opened her eyes and looked panicked!

"Tessa, my name is Mary, and this here's my son Tom. He's the one who rescued you. We're gonna help you, honey. This is a nice warm bath to clean all the mud off you. We're not gonna hurt you, just clean you up. We're healers, Tessa and friends of Miss Bea and Kathryn. Do you understand?" Mary smoothed her hair back and cupped her cheek, looking into Tessa's eyes.

Tessa, relaxed a little and started sobbing. Mary tried again, "Tessa, can you understand what I'm saying?"

She nodded her head, but sobbed louder, leaning her forehead on the edge of the tub. "hhh--hurts!" she cried.

"I know you prob'ly got a fierce headache. After I wash your hair, I need to take a couple of stitches in the back of your head. These scrapes and bruises prob'ly hurt, too, but you're gonna feel much better when you're clean and in a nice warm bed. Just hang on a little longer, okay?" Mary motioned Tom away. "Tom's gonna go to your cousins and let them know you're here and okay."

Mary stood up, "Don't lollygag, Tom. I'm gonna need to put her in another tub cuz this one's gonna be too dirty to get her real clean. So hurry up now."

Mary was thinking about a story for Tessa's injuries while she worked on her. The Bradley sisters would have to figure it out. If they had a decent sheriff, Colby would go to jail. But he was a friend of the sheriff and there would be an investigation. It would be embarrassing for Tessa. She was too tired and worried about this poor child. She'd let the Bradley sisters decide what they wanted to do.

Quickly, she finished washing Tessa's head wound and prepared to stitch it closed without removing her from the tub. After several stitches the flow of blood slowed to a small trickle. At least it seemed like she had only a mild concussion because she had finally opened her eyes and wasn't throwing up. A brain injury wasn't something that Mary knew how to fix. She offered up a little prayer to the Almighty. He would have to help out a little if Tessa was going to be all right.

Chapter 6

A Story for Tessa

Tom arrived out of breath at the Bradley sisters' home. He banged on the door and it was answered by Big John. "Evenin' Tom. What's got you out of breath and in such a hurry?" he chuckled. Big John was a free slave who Mr. Bradley bought from his owner when the sisters were little girls. He was the first free slave in the whole state of Ohio, Tom thought. He loved Miss Bea and Miss Kathryn like his own daughters of which he had six.

"I need to see Miss Bea right away, Big John. There's trouble. Would you get her, please?"

"You sit down in there," he pointed to a chair in the parlor, "and I'll get her fo ya."

Big John looked concerned, but hurried away to get Miss Beatrice. Minutes later, Miss Bea rushed into the parlor where Tom was waiting. She looked really upset. Miss Kathryn was on her heels, "Tom, we can't find our cousin, Tessa. She's only been here a week and…"

Tom stood up, "That's why I'm here, Miss Bea. She's at our place and ma's takin' care of her. She's hurt…."

"Ohhhh!" the women cried. "Thank God she's safe! Where did you find her? She went for a walk after lunch in the apple orchard, and disappeared. We've been all over the property trying to find her!"

"Let's get on back to my place and I'll tell you all about it on the way. Ma may need me and I was supposed to hurry up back to her."

"Big John, can you please have the buggy brought around? Call off the men and tell them she's visiting with Mary Leland, forgot the time and didn't think to tell us she had gone there on a walk. Don't tell anyone yet about her being injured. I want to see her first and bring her home."

Big John patted Miss Bea's shoulder, "Don't you worry none, Miss Bea. I'll have the buggy here in no time." He hurried out onto the front porch and went to the stable out back at a run. A little while later, Tom heard the buggy approach with Big John driving.

"Here you go, ma'am. I needs to drive that horse for yuh, so you get there fast and safe to bring young Tessa home soon's you can." Big John hooked the reins around the brake and helped Miss Bea and Miss Kathryn into the buggy.

Before Tom had a chance to settle in, Big John slapped the reins and the horse took off at a run toward Tom's cabin. On the way, Tom told the sisters about how he had found Tessa.

"That hunk of Satan! I'd like to horsewhip that guttersnipe Colby! He'll rue the day he laid a hand on our sweet Tessa! I hope he lays dead out there where you found him, Tom. Don't lay a finger to help him if he shows up at your house for help, either!" she fumed and grabbed a hold of her seat as they went round a corner fast. The buggy swerved and Miss Bea hollered, "Get up Midnight! We don't have time to waste!"

They quickly covered the mile to the Leland's' house. When they arrived, Miss Bea jumped down as soon as the horse screeched to a halt and was up the steps and in the house before Tom got down and helped Miss Kathryn. Big John tied the reins to a post and followed Tom up to the door.

Tom turned to Big John, "We'd better let the ladies be alone in there. Ma had her in a tub trying to get her clean when I left. She's awful dirty and hurt. I clobbered Colby over the head. He's prob'ly still out there. I don't care if I did kill him. He was treatin' her awful bad, Big John."

Big John put his big hand on Tom's arm, "Don't you be worrin' now, Tom. He's a right bad man and deserves a whippin' for what he done. I ain't gonna feel t'all sorry fur em if'n he does die. Dat mangy sheriff sure wudn't do a thang."

Big John sat down on the porch step and Tom sat on the porch rocker. They could hear soft voices inside the cabin. "It might be a while until ma is finished healin' Miss Tessa." Tom sighed and rubbed his stomach. He was hungry.

"I could sure nuf eat a meal right now. How 'bout you Big John?" Tom rubbed his growling stomach.

Big John laughed, "Oh you knows me Tom, ah can eat what's laid down in fronta me long's it ain't movin' on muh plate. But I don' see a thang for eatin' 'roun here none. Whyn't you tell yur ma we gonna take a quick swing by Miz Bea's kitchen and see if we can rustle up some goods ta eat while theys patchin up Miz Tessa?" Big John got up and climbed into the buggy. "Ya'll tell em we'll be right back."

Tom knocked on the cabin door and waited. He stepped back when the door opened as he didn't want to see inside in case the young girl wasn't decent. Miss Kathryn peeked out, "Yes, Tom? You can't come in yet, we're still, ah, attending to Tessa." Her cheeks were pink as if she was very embarrassed. She was a very proper lady and was probably shocked to see her cousin naked.

"Since y'all are goin' to be busy for a while yet, me and Big John are going back to your house and pick up some foodstuffs for us and y'all if you want. I haven't eatin' since early today an Big John says there's leftover dinner I could share if it's ok with you and ma." Tom's stomach let out with a loud grumble and he stepped back, "Scuze me mam," and he ducked his head.

Miss Kathryn smiled, "I'm sure you're most

85

welcome to get something to eat, Tom. My sister and I are so grateful for what you've done by saving our dear cousin, Tessa, that you are welcome to anything in our kitchen. A growing young man like yourself needs a great deal of sustenance for strength and vitality. You go on now and help yourself. Just make sure you come on back in about an hour. I'll tell your mama what you're up to and I'm sure it will be fine."

She looked out at Big John, "You drive safe now and be back in an hour. Be sure and help yourself, too, since I know you want to." Kathryn smiled at Big John and closed the door.

The men drove back to the Bradley house at a slower pace than earlier. "What else was goin' on when you found Miss Tessa, Tom?"

Tom's hands fisted on his legs, "I hit him over the head with a tree branch and I'm not sure if I killed him or not." He looked at Big John, "Don't care either," he said fiercely.

"How far 'way was dat agin?" Big John looked thoughtful. "Mayhap I could send a feller round there and take a look. Fact is he might be out huntin' and cum 'cross that skunk by accident. Never can tell." Big John smiled at Tom. He turned toward the road, "Yep mayhap we'll get lucky an' find a dead skunk or at least one we can leave to die in peace."

Big John slapped the reins, "Giddy up there Midnight, we gotta hurry up now." Big John drove the buggy to the barn and called a couple of the men over. Tom could see him talking quietly and the men grinning back at him. No one liked Colby, especially the black men and women. He was a mean man who liked to taunt and bedevil people. He could make big trouble with his friends against anyone he took a dislike to. It was obvious these men would delight in seeing an injured or dead Colby.

"Come on Tom, these fellers have some huntin' to do." Big John led Tom to the back door of the Bradleys' kitchen. "Let's see what the kitchen's got to offer us."

Tom had his fill of the Bradley cook's larder: meat and vegetable pasties and apple pie, as well as some baked potatoes filled with cheese and sausage filled Tom's plate. He was going to ask if he could take some home for his ma.

"This is sure good eatin' Big John." Tom said with a mouthful. "My Ma's a good cook, but she don't hold a candle to Floreen. I'd never tell ma, though," he smiled and stuffed some baked potato into his full mouth and smiled.

Big John smiled back and stuffed his mouth as well. "The Bradleys' don't do nothin' half way, that's fo shure." He wiped his big hands on a towel and handed it to Tom. "We best git on back to yur ma, Tom. See if theys needin our help any."

"Yeah, my stomach's full now and I'm ready to fall asleep if I don't get movin," he chuckled.

Tom and Big John were both quiet on the way back to Tom's house. "I might've killed someone tonight. It doesn't seem real. I feel bad, but not as much as I think I should, Big John." Tom looked up at the big man driving the buggy, "You spose I oughta be askin' God to forgive me?" He looked at his hands in his lap. "Even though he was a sorry excuse for a man, should I be askin' for His forgiveness anyway?"

Big John looked at Tom then out at the road ahead, "Well, Tom. Seems like you got two things to be thinkin' 'bout. One, that mean varmint was hurtin' a precious young lady and you stopped it from happnin' and saved her. And, two, you might have got rid of a bad man you din't plan to kill at all!" Big John looked at Tom. "Way I see it, that man deserves a lot worse than bein' hit over the head and dyin' in a muddy field. All the time's he up to no good 'specially at night time. So it seems to me that ifn you ax the good Lord to understand what you did and why, well, bein' the good Lord that he is --- he's gonna understand. You know, it's 'bout like this here war y'alls talkin 'bout. Fightin' man to man, brother to brother's bad. But it ain't the fightin' man's fault when he's sent out to fight and kill. Y'alls defendin' the folks like me and mine, ya know what I'm talkin' 'bout, Tom?"

"Yeah, I guess I do, Big John." Tom fidgeted around in his seat, "I just came up on seein' a bad thing happenin' and did what I thought I had to do. If it ends with a bad man dyin', well then so be it. But I will talk to the Lord and explain. If only to be able to sleep at night."

Big John patted Tom's knee, "You do just that, Tom, ain't nobody gonna believe you killed that man on purpose. Besides, mayhap nobody's gonna find that varmint."

Tom put his head down, thinking about what Big John said.

"You know Tom, I dun reckon I know how many years I am. Each year jus' goes into the nex' and I feel like a lucky man. Mas Bradley bought me and my crew years ago and we all got free papers, but none wanted to leave him and his family. Now, I takes care of the whole household and I love them folks as if'n they's mine. The others -- they work in his fields or the mill or wagon works. It's all good. We got food, a good place to live and some's got a wife and chil'rens. Ain't nothin' better than not havin' to worry about food and a home. We feel nigh on to as safe as can be here. 'Cept for Colby and his no good comp'ny, we all been treated like folk. Seems like you gotta keep yur eyes on what's mos' important in yur life and jus' keep on a goin' thata way like the Lord's leadin' ya. Then the res' most likely'll take care of itself."

Big John smiled. "Here we are, Tom, you go on in and tell folks we're back and see what they all need. I'll just wait outside for yuh."

Tom took the wrapped up food and went up to the cabin door and knocked. The door opened and Miss Kathryn stepped back to let Tom inside. Tom wiped his feet and ducked his head, afraid he might see something he shouldn't. "It's alright, Tom. Tessa is asleep now in your Grannie's old room. She's going to stay here a few days until she's a little better." Kathryn smiled and reached out for Tom's hand. "We can't thank you enough, Tom. You saved our darling girl," she sniffed and reached inside her cuff for a hanky.

Not sure of what he should do, he shifted his feet and looked down, "I just did what was needed, Miss Kathryn. Didn't even know who she was 'til I got her to ma." Tom looked for his ma hoping she was nearby.

"Here's your dear boy now, Mary," she cried. "Tom, we can't thank you enough for saving Tessa." Beatrice grabbed Tom's hand. "She is the sweetest child and did not deserve that piece of Satan's garbage to do to her what he did. I shudder to think what would have taken place if you had not happened on them when you did!"

Tom stood still looking down and turning red. Luckily, his ma joined them and placed her arm around Tom's waist. "Thank you, Bea. Tom's just glad he was in the area and could save her." Mary stepped in front of Tom and pulled Beatrice away toward the fireplace, motioning for Kathryn to join them.

"Now why don't we have some herbal tea and relax for a few moments. Tessa's gonna sleep most of the night and Tom and I will take turns sitting with her. You ladies should go home after we decide what story we'll tell everyone about Tessa's injuries. Mary seated the ladies in Grannie's old rocker and a padded chair in front of the fire. Tom busied himself making the tea from a pot that always held hot water inside the fireplace. A small ball of wrapped herbs was placed in the tea pot and set aside to steep. Mary pulled a stool over near the ladies and sighed as she sat down.

"It seems to me like we all need to get our stories straight. I didn't tell you earlier but Tom hit Colby over the head with a stiff branch and knocked him unconscious. Tom thinks there is a chance that he could be dead." Both Kathryn and Beatrice loudly inhaled. Kathryn's hankie was pressed to her mouth and Beatrice clenched her lips together. They exchanged looks and then looked at Mary.

"We will say whatever is necessary to protect Tom and Tessa." Beatrice sat tall and looked from Tom to Mary. "Several people from the Wagon Works were out looking for her. We can say she went for a walk, fell down and Tom found her and took her to your cabin. No mention of Colby is necessary. That drunken oaf could have just hurt himself for all anyone knows."

Tom placed a tray with the teapot and

cups next to his mother. "Ah, Miss Bea, I told Big John about my clobbering Colby and thinkin' I might've killed him. So he sent a couple of men from your place out to go huntin' and see if they can find Colby. If he's bad hurt or dead, they're just gonna leave him be but at least we'll know one way or another."

Tom stood waiting.

Beatrice looked thoughtful, "It seems we should just go ahead with our story and not concern ourselves with Colby. He won't be able to tell anyone what he was doing anyway." She looked at Mary and Kathryn. Both women nodded their heads in agreement. "Once Tessa's awake we'll let her know what we've decided and she can relax and not worry about wagging tongues. Her hair is thick and will hide the cut on the back of her head, not that anyone but our staff will see her. The front wound isn't as bad, but we will say it caused a concussion. She won't go out in public or have visitors for a while anyway." Beatrice poured the tea and gave Mary and Kathryn their cups while she was thinking. "The one problem we have is where Tom found her. The men combed this whole area and never found her. What would she be doing so far from home? We have to think up a reason." Beatrice stood up and paced while drinking her tea.

"She was a good two-three miles away, Miss Bea," Tom said. "Too far for a young lady to be walkin'."

"Yes, Tom, you're right." Beatrice paced back and forth.

Kathryn looked at Tom, "But what if she was closer to home? Tom, you know this area well. Is there a place she could have fallen down and the men wouldn't have seen her?"

Tom put his head down and thought. Was there an old well or place that would work for their story? He'd grown up playing in every possible corner of this whole area, surely he could think of one place no one knew about. Then it came to him. There was a little hill and rocky area with tree roots that stuck out. He had fallen many times climbing there to hide out when he was a kid. It was a good place for someone to climb to see the valley and town. If Tessa had caught her foot and fallen, she could have been under the large rocks and would not have been seen in the dusk.

"Well, I think I know of a place." Tom looked at Miss Bea and proceeded to tell her about his old hideout. "But, do you think folks are gonna wonder what she was doin' there?"

"You're right, Tom." Beatrice thought a moment. "Are there any flowers there or anything she could have been attracted by?"

Kathryn spoke up, "Why couldn't she just be looking for a good view of the area? I mean she's new here, maybe she just wanted to look around?"

"That's it then." Beatrice said with steel

in her voice. "She went exploring and fell." She looked at Tom, "And you, Tom, were out looking for a lost….." she implored Tom.

"I was lookin' for our cow to bring her home to milk an thought I'd look 'round the valley an' I found Tessa under one of them big rocks." Tom smiled and looked at his ma, then Beatrice and Kathryn. They all smiled at each other.

Chapter 7

Healing and Young Hearts

Tessa slowly came awake the next morning. She had a terrible headache and the room spun around when she tried to raise her head. She started to panic until she remembered that she was safe. Some lady had cleaned her up and cousins Beatrice and Kathryn had been with her. She heard voices in the next room as she carefully looked around her room. It was a small bedroom with only a bed and a small chest with a tiny mirror above it. She felt the blanket covering her and picked it up. The quilt was old and worn and had been made of soft flour sacks stitched together. A combination of tiny flowers and faded colors on a backing of striped ticking covered her. It smelled like lilacs and gave her some comfort when she held the blanket up to her nose and inhaled. She wasn't wearing her night dress but a plain chemise. Tessa didn't want to move. She hurt all over: her chest, back, legs, and her head. There was a big scratch on her right arm and her left elbow was just covered by rough, raw skin and some sort of salve. Her mouth was parched and her throat felt like she'd swallowed fire.

Mary went to check on Tessa and found her looking around, "Good morning, Tessa. Are you ready for a nice cup of tea and some bread with jam?" She smiled at the young girl but inside she cringed. Poor Tessa! Her face was a mass of bruises and scrapes. Mary knew her body was pretty bruised and scraped up as well. Today would be unpleasant for her, but Mary would keep her as comfortable as possible. "You just rest right there, and I'll fix it up for you right away."

Tom came in as Mary was fixing Tessa's tray. "Tessa's awake Tom. She's doin' pretty well and is goin' to have a little tea and bread. Hopefully, she won't have any trouble keeping it down." Mary took the tray into Tessa's room and paused. She was so pale and beat up it hurt Mary's heart. She didn't want to put the tray on her lap because Tessa would have to sit up and that might not work right now. "Do you want to try to sit up or should I just feed you?"

Tessa turned her head to look at Mary and winced. "I don't think I can sit up, would you mind feeding me, ma'am?"

"I'm Mary, Tessa. I'm so pleased to see you doin' so well. Beatrice and Kathryn are gonna be so relieved, too. I'm gonna send my son Tom over and let them know right now." Mary took a cloth and placed it over Tessa's chest and pulled a stool over next to the bed. She sat down and put the tray on her lap. The tea was still hot so when she dipped the spoon in the tea cup she gently blew on the liquid before placing it on Tessa's tongue. "My son Tom's the one who found you and brought you home to me. He's about your age and a real nice boy. You can meet him later."

Tessa jerked back, "Oooh, it's a little too hot on my lip! Perhaps I should just have some cool water." Her eyes teared up and Mary felt bad.

"I'll just dip a little piece of bread and see how that goes. I'll add more cool water to your cup of tea and a little sugar. That should taste good, too." Mary smiled encouragement and placed a piece of soggy bread in her mouth. "Soon's yur ready, Big John's gonna take you back home. Won't that be nice now? You'll be back in your own room with your family 'n healin' up just fine."

Later in the morning, Mary had to leave to visit a nearby farm with sick ones who needed to be treated. She left Tom to give Tessa lunch while she was gone.

Tom carefully opened the bedroom door. Tessa was awake, but when she heard Tom enter the room her eyes widened and she clutched the blanket, trembling with fear.

"Afternoon, Miss Tessa. My name's Tom. Uh, I'm the one that found you, um, with, um….well I mean I brought you home to my home for ma to help you and, uh….." Tom felt so awkward. He didn't want to tell her what he saw when he found her. He was stuck for words. "I, uh gotta lunch here for ya. Ma says I might need to help you out if you can't feed yurself yet." Tom felt Tessa's fear. "I won't do anything to scare ya but if I don't get you to eat somethin' she's gonna be mighty disappointed in me. I'll leave it if you want or I can keep you comp'ny or help you…. if you'd like?" Gently Tom put the tray down on the small table and waited for Tessa to speak.

Tessa watched the tall boy. She thought she remembered his voice. If he was the one who saved her she should thank him. It was embarrassing being here in her night clothes but she felt herself relaxing. He had nice big brown eyes with long lashes and he looked very kind. "I would like a little help to sit up. I seem to hurt a lot when I try by myself, and my wrist is stiff under this bandage."

Tom carefully helped Tessa sit up. His large hands covered her shoulders and long blonde hair. He liked the feel of the thickness under his hands. The color reminded him of a field of wheat and he thought it was beautiful. He looked at her face as she looked up at him. Her eyes were the bluest he had ever seen! Even with her injured face she was a pretty girl. Looking at her made Tom feel like he had bubbles in his stomach.

Tessa smiled at Tom, "I need to thank you for saving me. I don't know how you got me away from that man then brought me to your mother, but I will forever be in your debt."

Tom was speechless! He even liked the sound of her voice! "Well….I, um, it's okay, um…you needed savin' and I was there is all." Tom backed away. "You okay now? I mean, can you eat by yourself? Ma said I should help you eat if you want me to." Tom backed up some more.

"If you put the tray on my lap. I think I can feed myself. Thank you though, Tom. I'm much obliged."

Tom picked up the tray and gently placed it on Tessa's lap. He held it steady for her. "Can you hold it okay while you eat?" Tessa placed her hand over Tom's which was holding the side of the tray. Tom froze.

"It's not too heavy, but maybe if you took the glass of milk off while I eat the broth, then I won't accidently spill it if the tray moves."

Tom took the glass and placed it on the table. "If you want, I can stay here while you eat an' give you the glass of milk."

"I think I wouldn't mind your company. My face feels terrible. I must look a sight." she said and shyly dipped her face. Tessa took the cloth napkin and placed it on her chest. "What were you doing out at night when you found me?"

Tom hesitated, "I was out lookin' for a lost cow." He swallowed and hoped that Tessa wouldn't ask any more questions. He didn't want to be the one to tell her about what he saw.

"I guess I've had enough broth. You can

hand me the glass of milk now, Tom."

Tom removed the tray and gave Tessa the glass. She took a big swallow, "Oh, this tastes so good!" She smiled at Tom and he felt his cheeks flame.

"Well, uh, I'll take this tray an' leave you be to finish yur milk." Tom started backing away and his foot caught on the rug by the bed. He caught himself and stuttered, "Uh, I'll come back a little later an' uh, check up on ya." His face was really flaming now.

Tessa's smile was bigger, "Careful Tom, you almost fell. I'm sure your mother doesn't want another patient." She chuckled as he closed the door.

Tom didn't like her teasing. He didn't normally trip and stutter when he talked. She had him all aflutter doggone it!

The next day when Big John saw Tessa, his hands fisted and he had to hold himself still. He wanted to find Colby and kill him with his bare hands! To do something so cruel to such a beautiful young girl was just wrong. He was a "hunk of Satan" like Miz Bea said. Carefully, he picked her up and walked outside to the waiting carriage. A large blanket on the seat was wrapped around her. Beatrice sat next to Tessa with her arms supporting her for the ride home.

Tessa was dizzy and sick to her stomach. She hoped she wouldn't lose the bread and tea Mary had carefully fed her. She let her hair hide her face because she could feel her face was swollen and ugly. Earlier she had touched places that felt like deep scratches on her cheek. The back of her head felt like hammers pounding and she ached all over. She hoped no one would see her like this for a long time. Last night she had awakened so frightened she'd been afraid to go back to sleep. A terrible nightmare was so real she waited for the man to grab her again. She could smell his rotten breath as if he was still holding her down. She would never be the same again. She could never walk in the apple orchard or the garden alone. Even the thought of going into town and shopping was scary. Whatever was she going to do?

Later that afternoon, Mary was preparing to make calls on some folks who needed her poultices and salves. As she loaded her wagon, Sheriff Vinton and two dangerous-looking men with dogs turned into her driveway and approached her. Immediately, Mary was alarmed. These men were bounty hunters and just last night, Tom had taken three runaway slaves from their root cellar to the next depot.

"Mornin' Miz Mary, Tom." The sheriff leaned on his saddle horn with one hand and placed his other hand on the pistol on his belt. "You seen any runaway slaves 'round yur house lately?" While the sheriff had been talking the two dogs ran around the yard sniffing and whining.

"Morning, Sheriff. Tom and I have been pretty busy what with so many folks bein' sick and all. And, of course, I just buried my mother." Mary glared at the men.

"What 'bout you, Tom? Seen any black folk runnin' 'round here?" Tom stood on the porch and watched the two men with the sheriff climb off their horses. They were dressed in dirty black shirts and vests. Their boots were old and caked with mud, and they had gun belts, rifles and a coiled whip on their saddle horns. A chill went up Tom's back as he watched them approach the porch where he was standing. He stood still as they approached, unsure of what to do. They kept walking and shoved him aside as they passed.

Mary screamed, "Stop! What do you think you're doing?" She started to run to Tom but the sheriff moved his horse in front of her and wouldn't let her pass. "You have no right to go in to my cabin without my permission. How dare you let those men go in there?" Mary was furious but very frightened. She was scared they could hurt Tom and the sheriff would do nothing to help him.

"Well you see now, Miz Mary, these here bloodhounds got the scent of some runaways and it led us right up to yur property. So these here bounty hunters are thinkin' they'd be in yur cabin. I don't have to tell you that it's agin the law to help them runaways, now do I?" The sheriff smiled and it turned Mary's stomach.

Mary glanced out to the yard to see what the dogs were doing and found them running around in circles. She wanted to smile but held herself back. It wouldn't do to let on that the scattered eucalyptus leaves that covered most of her yard, the entrance to the barn, root cellar and the porch confused the scent of the dogs. She had mixed in some alum with the eucalyptus leaves and sprinkled it in front of the different entrances so that any bloodhounds sniffing around would have a numb nose making it impossible for them to track the runaway slaves.

Mary heard breaking glass and dodged the sheriff's horse and ran into the house. Tom was right behind her as they saw the two bounty hunters knock jars of herbs onto the floor. "Stop! Those jars filled with herbs I use to take care of people. Get away from them!" One of the men picked up a jar and looked at Mary as he dropped it on the floor. Tom started to walk toward the man and Mary grabbed his arm and pulled him against her. "There is no one here except my son and me. Get out!"

The men shoved Mary and Tom aside and laughed as they walked back outside. The sheriff was still sitting on his horse waiting for them, a nasty smirk on his face. "The dogs ain't gotta smell. I guess she's tellin' the truth. Might's well get on now." The sheriff looked at Mary, "You make sure you turn in any runaways now, Miz Mary. I don't wanna have to put you and

Tom in jail and burn yur place down. It'd be a real shame when we need yur healin' powers from time to time."

He turned his horse around as the two men mounted their horses. They all rode over to the barn. One of the men dismounted again and opened the door to the root cellar and looked inside. The men exchanged some words but Mary couldn't hear what they were saying. She had her arm around Tom and stood and waited for the dogs and men to leave her property. It wasn't until they had started down the road that she finally took a deep breath.

"Well, I guess my leaves and alum did the trick. Those dogs were so confused they didn't know what they were smelling and won't for several hours. I'm so mad at the sheriff for lettin' those men in our cabin, and them breaking my herbs jars, that I think I'm gonna make the sheriff sicker next time he comes to me for his stomach ache." Mary bristled with anger.

Tom had been silent until now. He pulled away from his ma and stormed back into the house. Taking the broom, he started sweeping up the broken glass and herbs. He knew they couldn't be used now because they could have glass pieces mixed in and they could hurt a person if they were used. "I couldn't do a thing to stop those men. I just had to stand there." Tom swept the glass and herbs into a pile and took a piece of cloth and picked up as much as he could. His shoulders were hunched over as he walked to a waste bin and opened the cloth so that the debris could fall into the bin. "If pa had been here they wouldn't have done this. They wouldn't' have come in our cabin!"

"You're wrong, Tom. Your pa wouldn't have been able to stop them, either. The sheriff has the law on his side and he knows it." Mary looked sadly at her son, "Do you want to come along with me? I'll make a stop at the Bradleys'. I want to tell them about the sheriff's visit. You can talk to Big John and let him know about the bounty hunters and their dogs. We're gonna have to be real careful for a while until we know they've moved on. We might want to have Samuel do some checking and make sure it's safe to conduct if we get a message." Mary finished loading her wagon and Tom hooked up Ole Ned to the wagon.

"Yeah, I'll go with you, ma. Just let me close up the cabin. You think they'll come back while we're gone?"

Mary thought for a moment, "They might. We can't stop them, but I might have one of Big John's workers keep watch from the trees and let me know if they do anything while we're gone." Mary got up on the wagon and moved to the side. "You drive, Tom."

Tom climbed up on the seat next to his ma and shook the reins. Ole Ned picked up his head and started down the drive. He was a good old horse, but he was getting on in age. He'd have to think about some kind of trade for a new horse. He'd talk to Big John while his ma was talking to the Bradley sisters. It wouldn't hurt to get another horse before Ole Ned gave out. That way he could use him to ride places when his ma was out with the wagon.

Over the next two weeks, Tom sat with Tessa to keep her company as she recovered from her ordeal with Colby. They had become friends and Tessa looked forward to Tom's visits. He was relaxed in her company now and read to her from his Ma's bible. Tom wanted to take her outside but Tessa was afraid. After talking to her and insisting that it was time to go about her normal day she panicked. To comfort her fear and give her courage he read Psalm 46: *"God is our refuge and strength, always ready to help in times of trouble. So we will not fear, even if earthquakes come and the mountains crumble into the sea. Let the oceans roar and foam. Let the mountain tremble as the waters surge."*

Tessa smiled at Tom and he returned her smile, "I don't know what an earthquake is exactly, but I know it has to be sumpthin' real bad if the bible said people feared it." Tom looked at Tessa's face and it made his stomach tingle. She seemed to really like the Psalms when he read them so he decided to read them each time he visited. Tom believed reading them would help her get better. Even though she could read the bible by herself, it became something she looked forward to and missed him on the days he didn't visit.

Chapter 8

The Journey to Cincinnati

Mr. and Mrs. Bradley arrived in Cincinnati and checked into the beautiful Baldwin Hotel. They had an appointment the next morning with the state medical board to consider several resumes of doctors who would be willing to set up their medical practice in Fairfax. That evening they had a delicious and elegant dinner in the hotel dining room. Their spirits were high and they both agreed that it was good to be away from the pallor of sickness in Fairfax. They took an evening stroll and Mr. Bradley held his wife's hand on his arm with pride. Mr. Bradley was thoughtful as they walked. He was a wealthy and a powerful man. -- life was good. He was going to enjoy their time together here in this beautiful city. Tomorrow they would choose a new doctor for their town and return home.

Mr. Bradley was rewarded with five resumes of very qualified doctors. But one stood out: that of a thirty year old doctor from Boston. He was currently in Cincinnati and was able to join the Bradleys for luncheon. They knew by the end of their meal that Dr. Bradford Phillips was the doctor for Fairfax. He was a handsome, qualified young man and when Mr. Bradley shook his hand

and offered him the job, Dr. Phillips was thrilled to accept.

Two days later, Samuel Washington came rushing in to Mary Leland's cabin all excited, "Tom, Miz Mary! Mr. and Mrs. Bradley hired a new doctor in Cincinnati! Mayor Brodt told Mr. Bender that the town council got a telegram tellin' them he's on his way now! Ain't that the best news?" His dark face clouded with concern, "What will happen to you and young Tom now, Miz Mary? Cain't rightly see how you won't still be needed here, too. But I hope he don't have a problem with y'all."

Tom was excited too. "Well don't that beat all? Hope he's a good one, huh Ma? Don't you worry about us, Samuel, this is good news. After the last few weeks I will sure welcome a new doctor, 'specially if he knows some new medical ideas to help the sick. There's plenty folks for us to help. And, if the new doctor approves of our healin', we'll get along just fine."

Mary looked up from working on her dried herbs, "I think we'll do just fine still helping those folks in far-reaching places." Mary looked thoughtful, "He might even be a doctor who cares about all kinds of folks," she pondered.

Samuel knew she meant "all kinds of folks" was the escaped slaves she helped. He watched Mary mixing the herbs and preparing them for grinding with a smooth rock. She ground them without even looking at them as she talked; a familiar task she had performed hundreds of times.

"You could be right, Miz Mary, but he could be some stuck-up Copperhead who's agin the war, too. The town council had letters from Mr. Bradley 'n they musta liked what they read cuz they hired him right then and there!" Samuel rubbed the back of his neck, "Sure hopin' they're all right 'bout him. Don't need no more mean folks around these parts."

"Well we'll just have to wait and see Samuel. After these past weeks I just hope he's a good doctor who will know how to take care of our town folk. And, I hope he's not an old man who can't get around when he's needed out in the countryside. Lastly, I pray he's not gonna be against Tom and me caring the old fashioned way with my herbs and potions." Mary thumped her pestle down on the table to make her point.

The Bradleys had enjoyed a wonderful evening of dinner and dancing in the hotel's ballroom. Mrs. Bradley had worn a new gown and her husband had told her several times how beautiful she looked. They had to wait for two elevators full of people to exit before they could take it to the 15th floor where their suite was located. It felt like a second honeymoon and Mrs. Bradley had told her husband shyly that he was as handsome now as he had been then.

"I declare I feel like a bride this night. I thank you, dear, for such a wonderful time. It's not often that we make a trip like this and I have enjoyed every bit of it," she exclaimed.

"Yes dear, I noticed you blushing a few times. It's still very becoming." Mr. Bradley smiled down at his wife. "Our daughters will enjoy all the fripperies you bought today, I'm sure." He smiled, "I suppose there'll be some more purchases before we leave tomorrow, hmm?"

"Well, I did see some lovely gloves for the girls and myself. I might take another look at them in the morning. I will be all packed and ready to go so I can take some time to make a last purchase, surely," she smiled coquettishly at her husband.

"My dear, I wouldn't have it any other way." Mr. Bradley leaned down and placed a kiss on his wife's mouth.

"Oh my sakes alive! We're in public! What will people think?" Mrs. Bradley's cheeks were bright pink as she stepped into the elevator.

Mr. Bradley kissed her again, "That I'm a very lucky man." He winked at her as they arrived at their floor. Thankfully, they were alone as they walked down the corridor to their suite.

The sound of running feet in the corridor and muffled voices awoke Mr. Bradley. Quickly, he donned his night shirt that he had removed and tossed on the floor. He stepped into his slippers and robe, glancing at his wife. She was still sleeping, her white, creamy shoulders and back above the covers. He smiled down at her. She was still the love of his life. He closed the bedroom door and hurried to their suite's outer door and opened it to see smoke billowing thickly as people hurried down the corridor.

"Fire!" A man screamed as he ran, pushing people out of his way. "Fire on the floor below us!"

Mr. Bradley closed the door and hurried back to his wife. "Leona! Leona," he hollered as he removed his robe and night shirt. "Get up, Leona! There's fire and we have to leave now!"

Mrs. Bradley threw back the covers and grabbed for her dress from the previous evening. "There's no time for that! Put your night dress, robe, and slippers on! Hurry, Leona! Hurry!"

Mr. Bradley had his shirt and pants on and was putting on his shoes when they heard an explosion. Without tying his shoes he ran to the window. It was tightly latched so he took a chair and broke out the window. Looking down his, face fell with disappointment. There was no outcropping wide enough that they could exit this way to safety nor were there iron stairs. Their only hope was to try to escape down the corridor like the people had done when he looked out. Grabbing his wife's hand he pulled her to the door.

"If the smoke is thick, put your robe over your mouth and try not to breath in the smoke."

"What will you use?" Mrs. Bradley looked

around and saw her shawl. Quickly she grabbed it and gave it to her husband. "Here, this should work for you."

The Bradleys held tight to each other and stepped out into the corridor. Immediately they were shoved back by the crowd who were panicked and shoving each other trying to get to the other end of the hallway.

"The stairway should be at both ends of the corridor, I think." Mr. Bradley hollered to his wife. "We can't consider taking the elevator. I just hope we can get down the stairway without this crowd running over us." He pulled his wife to the wall in front of him and started pushing and edging their way down the corridor.

Another explosion with the sound of breaking glass had several people stopping and screaming in terror. Mr. Bradley took advantage of the brief lull and pushed Mrs. Bradley to the stairwell door. The opening was full of people trying to walk down the stairs, pushing and shoving. They joined them, and again, Mr. Bradley went to the far wall of the stairwell pulling Mrs. Bradley behind him and holding onto her arm. Mrs. Bradley grabbed hold of his shirt and held on. He began shoving people aside and moving down the stairs as fast as he could. Up ahead he saw more smoke billowing in from one of the doors. He looked up and saw that it was the twelfth floor. They still had a long way to go to reach the ground floor. Mr. Bradley pulled his wife and pushed harder against the people in front of him. He gained another floor when he noticed the smoke was getting much thicker.

Over his shoulder he hollered at his wife, "Keep your robe over your mouth, Leona! The smoke is getting thicker down here as we go."

"I fear we won't make it to safety, Stephen!" Mrs. Bradley choked and started coughing.

"We will, my love, we will. Try not to breathe in too deeply." Mr. Bradley started coughing as well.

Up ahead there was a turn in the stairwell and Mr. Bradley used the wider opening to forge ahead of more people. As they turned the corner, he saw that flames were coming out of the top of the door to the tenth floor. Now, visibility was almost nothing but black smoke. "Crouch down, Leona! We must try to keep this smoke out of our lungs!"

Mr. Bradley put his arms around his wife and pulled her down lower from the smoke. Together, they pushed ahead of more people who were coughing and choking in the heavy smoke. "Surely one of these floors will be without fire," he hollered while trying to stay low and push people out of their way.

Mrs. Bradley stumbled and almost fell out of his arms. "Leona! Keep your robe over your mouth!" He could hardly see her now.

Suddenly, they could go no further. There

was too many people now backed up and stalled in the stairwell. Many were down on the ground blocking the stairs. Mr. Bradley could feel bodies around his legs and he couldn't push them away. Crouching down he tried to move them, but lost hold of his wife's arm. "Leona!" He couldn't feel her. "Leona!" He started choking and fell to his knees.

Later, the Cincinnati Firemen opened the hotel's stairwell and when they reached the third floor, after clearing away the debris, they found stacks of people lying on top of one another. The ceiling had collapsed and prevented people from reaching the ground floor. The smoke was so heavy that they had all died from lack of oxygen. Most of the people, although covered in gray ashes and smoke, looked like they were sleeping.

The Reverend Peter Hawthorn and his wife Penelope assumed the duties of the largest church in Fairfax with gusto. They had made fast friends with Mr. and Mrs. Bradley and received the news of their deaths with great sorrow. The entire town was in mourning with black ribbons hanging on every store in town. The town council had had an emergency meeting to elect a new member to replace Mr. Bradley and make plans to honor their exalted former member. Mr. and Mrs. Bradley had been the most prominent couple in Fairfax by owning and controlling most businesses and the town bank. Their loss would seriously impact the town and there was much discussion about what would now become of their town.

The town folk were worried. Groups of people gathered to discuss their concerns thinking all their jobs were at risk. 'Who's gonna run all the businesses if Mr. Bradley's not here anymore?' was the main topic. It was decided that a town meeting for all to attend should be called as soon as possible. That night a large crowd gathered in the council's office. The rabblerousers with Hank Colby among them were talking about taking over the Mill and Wagon Works. Angry voices could be heard as a carriage arrived and screeched to a halt outside the office. Several men on horseback arrived behind the carriage. It was soon apparent the men were from the mill. Miss Beatrice and Miss Kathryn got down from the carriage and were soon surrounded by the men from the mill. Dressed all in black with black veils, the women made a powerful sight.

Not waiting for the men, Beatrice pulled open the door of the council office and stormed into the room toward the men seated around the council table. The crowd automatically parted for her as she walked. You could hear a pin drop after all the yelling suddenly ceased. After reaching the table, Beatrice turned to face the crowd. The mill men, with Wilson Meyers in the middle, stood guard at the back of the room, rifles held across their chests.

Beatrice with head held high addressed the crowd. "My sister and I are in mourning for our parents. But it was brought to my attention that there was a town meeting where my family's businesses were being discussed." She hesitated and scanned the faces of the people, "I am appalled to think that after all these years you all could disrespect my parents like this!" Beatrice stood tall with her hands held in fists at her sides.

"The Mill and Wagon Works, the orchards, the Fairfax Mercantile, the bank and other concerns will continue to operate without fail!" She glared at the people, "My sister and I have worked with our father and know about the accounts and supplies, and other responsibilities -- for the past five years! We know the complete workings of all – I repeat *all* of *our* businesses! We will close down the businesses and fields for the funeral, the information will be posted in the church and in the newspaper. You may all attend. As of right now, all business will resume," Beatrice paused and scanned the room, "at eight o'clock in the morning as usual. If you value your jobs you will close this meeting, go home, and stop discussing this nonsense about taking over or interfering with our businesses in any way."

Big John, who had stayed in the background, came forward and took Beatrice' arm and escorted her and Kathryn out to the carriage. Before they reached the doors, Hank Colby's rabble didn't move to let them pass. Beatrice made eye contact with the man in front of her who was one of the leaders of the gang, "Titus Gelbey, step aside." Before Beatrice could take a step, Mr. Wilson Meyers and his men shoved the gang aside and made a path for her, Kathryn and Big John.

"Yur ah uppity woman, Miz Beatrice," he drawled. "Y'all wanna be careful now you don't have no powerful pa to protect y'all."

Mr. Meyers stepped in front of Gelbey, "And you might want to think about what might happen to you for threatening Miss Beatrice and Miss Kathryn." The mill men pushed the gang further back with some forceful shoving that made them stumble.

The Rev. Hawthorn was waiting by the carriage and took Beatrice' hand, "My wife and I will call on you and Miss Kathryn tomorrow morning."

The mill men mounted their horses and followed the carriage back to the Bradleys' house. The meeting was adjourned and the people all dispersed. Hank Colby's gang went in search of whiskey and more talk about what they wanted to do to the mill. It seemed that more and more the town was split into two factions: one influenced by the north, the other, the south which created short tempers and dangerous attitudes.

At the Bradley house, two large wreaths with black ribbons adorned the large front double doors. Beatrice and Kathryn moved silently through the house, dressed in black bombazine clutching their hankies continually wet with tears. They had received a telegram with the dreadful news about their parents' death from the Cincinatti Police Department. Kathryn had fainted when Beatrice read the telegram out loud. Even Big John swayed and had to sit down. The Mill and Wagon Works had shut down when the men received the news and it was left to Beatrice to stay strong and begin preparation for their bodies to arrive on the train and to make arrangements for their funeral.

The Reverend Hawthorn arrived the next morning and was waiting in the parlor. Beatrice had ordered tea and was ushering Kathryn into the room. This would be a painful time for the sisters. The last thing she ever imagined was her parents' passing. Certainly never by this kind of death. The next step would be for her and Kathryn to take over their parents' businesses. They had been groomed to be a part of the businesses, but never to be the managers issuing orders. Beatrice refused to think too much about that now. She had a funeral to plan. The last one she planned, she had her parents to support her. Now, she knew that it was up to her alone with some support from Kathryn. She walked into the parlor and greeted the Reverend and his wife.

"Thank you for coming, Rev. Hawthorn and Mrs. Hawthorn." Beatrice motioned for them to be seated. Silently, Kathryn entered the room, whispered a greeting, and sat down in a chair. Beatrice smiled sadly at her sister and turned to the Hawthorns, "I appreciate your visit so timely for us. I have made some notes for you. We know what our parents would expect including their favorite bible readings and hymns. Would you assign a place near the rose garden for them in the church's cemetery for us? We would like to have room for a bench, special rose bushes we will plant, and perhaps have it near a tree?"

"I am truly sorry for what happened last evening. Penelope and I took the initiative before we came to see you, Miss Bradley. We believe that we found the most appropriate place for your parents' final resting place and by chance it does have what you require. I also took the time to speak to Mr. Dow about the headstone. He has a plan for a grand monument and will contact you at your convenience. He will have a design for your approval by tomorrow. If you and your sister agree, we can hold their funeral ten days from today. I understand their bodies will arrive by the end of the week. If they have been prepared for burial, I shall hold them in the church for viewing. Otherwise, I will alert the Higgins Mortuary to prepare them for you and then have them brought to the church."

"That will be fine, Reverend. Thank you." Beatrice handed him several sheets of stationary, "This is what we would have you incorporate into

your service for our parents. We will prepare a dinner for the congregation for after the funeral. Kathryn and I would appreciate it if you would post the information about the wake, funeral and dinner on the church message wall. I will have it posted in the Fairfax newspaper as well."
Beatrice stood up, "If that is all for now, I hope you will excuse us. We have much to do with regard to our father's businesses and employees."

"We understand. You have our sincerest sympathy for your loss Miss Beatrice and Miss Kathryn. You and your sister are much too young to have suffered so much loss. We will pray for you." Mrs. Hawthorn hugged both ladies and patted Kathryn's back as she held her. "They will be truly missed. If I can help you in any way, please do not hesitate to ask."

Beatrice closed the door and leaned back against it. "We have much to do, Katy. You and I need to sit down now and make decisions about how we will share the responsibilities." She stood up and straightened her cuffs. Striding down the hall she called to Kathryn to follow along. Kathryn smiled at Beatrice's back. It was just like her to dive in and take over. Nothing ever stopped her sister for long, even the loss of her love, Rev. Pattison, only slowed her down for a few hours. She then planned his entire funeral. Beatrice was a formidable force when she had a purpose. Not even Colby's rabble could scare or deter her determination.

When Kathryn reached her father's study, Beatrice was seated behind his desk with a pen in her hand and papers ready for them to discuss. "We will take each company in order of the amount of work to be done. I think the Mill and Wagon Works should be first, the Fairfax Mercantile next, the bank, fields and rental properties last. Is that satisfactory, Katy?" Beatrice laid out the papers into different stacks and looked up at her sister.

"Bea, I don't really care how you do it, just tell me what you want me to do. I am perfectly happy keeping my job with the accounts. You're much better at ordering the workers and overseeing their labors. I will give you any support you need, I could even add ordering all the supplies, but please don't make me have to be in charge of anything. I'll leave that to you," Kathryn pleaded.

"Now Katy, you are perfectly capable of handling any of these areas and you know it."

"Well maybe that is the case, but I don't want to and I don't enjoy being in charge like you do, sister dear." Kathryn sat back in her chair across from Beatrice and finally let herself relax. "I leave our future in your capable hands, dear one. Leave me to the books. I would rather deal with inanimate numbers and ledgers in a quiet room."

"Well, if that's the way you feel I shall endeavor to sort out what I must accomplish and move forward. I shall begin this very evening if you don't mind. Please tell cook we can dine early. That way I can work afterward and make a good start." Beatrice looked up and smiled with tears in her eyes at Kathryn. "We shall make it through this latest tragedy, dear one. We will not falter. I am of the persuasion that with this talk of war, we will soon have need of more wagons. I will have much to discuss with Mr. Meyers. Please keep me apprised of our cash flow and any outstanding bills. I will depend on your expertise with figures. Perhaps we should have regular meetings with Mr. Meyers so that we shall know everything that is occurring. What do you say?"

"Yes, Bea, I think that would be just fine. How would each Thursday afternoon at tea time? I will bring a report for you to peruse and you can give me an accounting of the businesses. You can have Mr. Meyers bring his books as well."

This was a good beginning Beatrice thought. She was grateful that her father had engaged them to be informed about his businesses and investments. But she knew she had a lot to do to really take over the reins. Another great hurdle would be for all her father's employees to accept her as the new head of management – the ultimate decision maker. Hopefully, Mr. Meyers would help her make the transition as easy as possible at the Mill and Wagon Works. Perhaps that would help for the others to follow suit. If not, Beatrice was prepared to make it known that she was not to be trifled with.

Chapter 9

The Funeral

"The bitterest tears shed over graves are for words left
unsaid and deeds left undone."
Harriet Beecher Stowe

Mr. and Mrs. Bradley's caskets were
delivered to the church in Fairfax. The wake was
held and it was the day of their funeral. The week
had been a quiet one with only Hank Colby's
gang still angry and trying to stir up trouble while
drinking at Bender's Tavern. Beatrice and
Kathryn arrived at the church precisely one hour
before the funeral. The Reverend Hawthorn
stood on the church steps waiting to greet them.

Rev. Hawthorn warmly greeted both sisters.
Big John had followed them up the steps and
removed his hat and took Rev. Hawthorn's
outstretched hand. "Thank you, Big John, for
bringing your people to the wake last night to pay
their respects."

"I was right glad to be able to attend like all
the folks, Reverend." Big John turned and spoke
to Beatrice. "Miss Bea, I'll be right at the back of
the church with all your house folk waiting to
drive you to the cemetery."

"Thank you Big John. Please thank everyone
for their prayers."

Beatrice and Kathryn entered the church. It

was the last time they would be with their parents. Penelope Hawthorn was near the altar lighting candles. Two ornate mahogany caskets sat side by side near the altar stairs. Tall candelabra sat on each side with eight candles on each. The caskets had already been sealed.

Penelope greeted the sisters and smiled as they walked forward. "Would you like some company for prayer? Either I can stay with you or both Rev. Hawthorn and I will."

"You're both very kind, but my sister and I would like to be alone." Beatrice smiled at the reverend and his wife.

The sisters joined hands and prayed silently for their mother and father. A heavy black cloak of sadness covered them as they huddled together. They had been a close and loving family. The next weeks and months would be difficult. Beatrice knew she and Kathryn would have to be very strong.

The women stood and placed their hands on the caskets of their parents. Tears ran unchecked down their faces as they said another prayer, "Fear not, for I am with you; be not dismayed for I am your God; I will strengthen you, I will help you, I will uphold you with my righteous right hand."

Both sisters had been holding black bonnets with black netting attached. They placed the bonnets on their heads and the black netting fell around their faces and shoulders like a shroud.

"We must be strong now, Katy," she whispered as she hugged her sister. "Mama and Papa would expect us to carry on."

The church was filled to capacity and people overflowed into the vestibule and stairs. It seemed the whole town and people from surrounding towns were in attendance to pay their respects to the Bradley family. Rev. Hawthorn addressed the gathering with a thundering voice so that he could be heard in the vestibule. He spoke about his friendship and admiration for Mr. and Mrs. Bradley and their accomplishments. He urged the people to support Beatrice and Kathryn during their mourning period and whatever decisions they made regarding the businesses. He impressed on the people the importance of the Bradleys to the success of Fairfax. He ended his sermon with a prayer for peace and understanding for the nation.

Beatrice was impressed with Rev. Hawthorn's sermon. She was pleased that he had gained so much respect for her parents, especially for her father, in the brief time since he assumed leadership of their church. At the end of the service, the people stood and sang "Rock of Ages."

Tom and Mary Leland sat behind Beatrice and Kathryn. Mary had her arm around Tessa Bradley, supporting her. Tessa's thick blonde hair fell over her face like a golden curtain. She was sobbing into a handkerchief. Mr. Bradley was her father's brother and had always treated her like one of his daughters. Her stepmother was ill so her family was unable to attend the funeral. Tessa had hoped to be a part of the Bradley family until she left for school. Now both her aunt and uncle were gone.

Reverend Hawthorn announced that Beatrice and Kathryn would host a dinner for everyone. He raised his arms high in the air and intoned a last message from the bible, another of Mr. Bradley's favorites from Philippians: *"Fear not, for I am with you; be not dismayed, for I am your God; I will strengthen you, I will help you, I will uphold you with my righteous right hand..."* Twelve men picked up the two coffins and carried them down the aisle to the outside. Mr. Casey, the undertaker, wearing a formal suit and top hat, stood respectfully between two glass-topped hearses. Great white plumes adorned the headpieces of eight horses' bridles. Black material was draped along the bottom of the windows and were held in place by silver ropes tied in elaborate knots.

The caskets were loaded into the hearses and the doors closed with a loud click. Beatrice stood and waited while Kathryn sobbed into her hanky. Kathryn wanted to rip open the door and throw herself on her mother's casket. Leona Bradley had been a source of constant love and support for her and Beatrice through all of their trials of sorrow. Kathryn feared the future without her parents. She was not strong like Beatrice. Her mother always knew what to do and what to say when Kathryn was tongue-tied and fearful. Who would be her rock now? She held her breath and shuddered. Beatrice felt it and gently placed her arm around Kathryn and held her, "Kathryn, you can be strong," she whispered.

The journey to the cemetery was only a short distance from the church. The crowd followed the hearses on foot and stood silently as the caskets were taken out and moved to the two prepared gravesites. Beatrice shuddered when she gazed down at the two deep holes which would house her beloved parents forevermore. For a moment she almost lost her rigid control. Next to her, Kathryn began to weep and that brought new resolve to Beatrice. She would not allow herself to sob and grieve in front of the town folk. Holding tightly to Kathryn's arm she gently shook her. The sisters made eye contact through their black netting. Kathryn stood up straighter and with a hiccupping breath regained her control. Rev. Hawthorn stood at the head of the gravesite and folded his hands over his bible, "Dear Lord, we ask you to receive Leona and Stephen Bradley into your precious arms. They were the Christian pillars of this church and community and they will be sorely missed by all. *There will be no more sorrows or crying or pain for their old world and its evils are gone forever more. May they rest in peace.*" Rev. Hawthorn raised his arms up to the sky, "The lord said, *I am the resurrection and the life. Those who believe in me, even though they die like everyone else, will live again. They are given eternal life for believing in me and will never perish.* Amen."

Big John had taken charge the day before and ordered the cook to prepare food for the community who attended the Bradley funeral. He and men from the mill brought three wagon loads of food and serving dishes to the church. The Bradley house staff took care of setting up and serving the meal. Beatrice and Kathryn greeted the folks and spoke to each one until the dinner ended. When they returned to their home, they were too exhausted to do anything but retire to their beds. Kathryn had been very withdrawn all during the day. Beatrice had let her be, but tomorrow she would have a talk with her sister. They had to be united and strong to show anyone who had doubts that they could do what needed to be done to keep the town businesses productive and successful.

Chapter 10

A Doctor for Fairfax

Dr. Bradford Phillips arrived in Fairfax, Ohio, driving a large wagon full of medical supplies and furniture including eight chairs which hung – four on each side - on his wagon. Behind him was a smaller wagon being driven by a tall black woman wearing a large, wide-brimmed beige bonnet. Peeking out from under her seat were two little black faces.

The small caravan stopped in front of a large building with a sign that read Town Council. Dr. Phillips climbed down stretching his long legs and back. He was tired and needed a shower and a decent bed for the night. Looking around he saw that he had drawn a small crowd of curious folks. Looking back at the other wagon, "Well, we're finally here, Gussie."

Smiling, Dr. Phillips removed his hat, wiping the sweat off his brow and smacked the hat on his pant leg making a small cloud of dust. Looking around at the people he decided to address them, "Afternoon folks, I'm Dr. Bradford Phillips, your new doctor." Immediately, he was surrounded by handshakes and exclamations of greetings.

He walked back to the second wagon and took the woman's hand, "This lady here," as he helped her down, "is my assistant, Mrs. Augusta

Brown, and her two daughters, Lottie and Lissie."
The children disappeared from the front of the
wagon and he could hear them giggling.

Faces were poking out of doorways of the
many stores that lined the street, and pressed up
against windows, looking out at the new arrival
with great curiosity. The doctor was tall with
broad shoulders. The shirt he was wearing was
dusty and dirty. His sleeves were rolled up to his
elbows showing dirty arms and hands as well.
He had pushed himself and his horses to arrive as
soon as possible for this new job because he was
anxious to set up his medical practice in Fairfax.

Phillips was truly sorry that Mr. and Mrs.
Bradley were not here to welcome him. He had
taken a real liking to the couple. Mr. Bradley
would probably have become a friend had he
returned to Fairfax with his wife. Their tragic end
was incredibly sad.

Dr. Bradford Phillips came from a wealthy
family in Boston. Against his father's wishes he
left Boston and finished his medical studies in
New York after his fiancée ended their
engagement. After five years treating wealthy
self-absorbed socialites, he was an embittered
man looking for a way to make his life matter.
Newspapers telling tales of escaped slaves being
hunted down and returned to cruel plantation
owners made him want to be involved in helping
these unfortunate people. He heard about an
organization called the Underground Railroad

being used to get them to freedom. When Augusta Brown came to his home looking for work, he hired her. She gladly took his job of housekeeper because he had no problem with her having two little children who would live with her in his home.

When Mr. Bradley and his wife went to New York looking for a doctor for their town, Dr. Phillips jumped at the chance to move to Ohio and make a new start in his life as well as find a way to help out the people who needed him. His new housekeeper wanted to go with him as well. Fairfax was a much smaller town compared to Boston and New York, but he liked what he heard about the town and looked forward to his new life and medical practice.

One man pushed forward through the people and took Dr. Phillips arm, pulling him away from the crowd. The Mayor, Arnold Brodt hollered, "Welcome! Glad to see you've arrived."

Dr. Phillips removed the man's hand and stopped walking. "Mayor Brodt, I'm glad to finally be here in Fairfax. Mr. and Mrs. Bradley told me to report to you for the keys to my home and office. I'm very sorry that they were killed in the hotel fire. They were mighty fine people."

"Yes, they were the backbone of this community and will be greatly missed. Their daughters have assumed all of their business responsibilities. In fact, when I saw you pull up I sent a messenger to the Bradley home. Miss

Beatrice and Miss Kathryn will want to greet you as well. You'll find that they are very important since most of the businesses in Fairfax are owned by them now." Mayor Brodt leaned closer, "You might want to get on the good side of the ladies. They wield a lot of influence when you need something," he wagged his eyebrows and winked.

Dr. Phillips frowned. It was apparently no different in small towns or big cities. There was always someone who had to be impressed if they were important. He sighed and resigned himself to making "nice" to the young ladies. It wouldn't do to get on their wrong side too soon. After he was settled in and treating patients it would be different. This town needed a doctor – needed him. He wouldn't put up with any nonsense from any one when people's health and welfare were at stake.

Augusta and her daughters still stood by the wagon. They had not been welcomed like the doctor. A few ladies had smiled and nodded at her, but had not engaged her in conversation.

A carriage was rapidly moving toward them driven by a large black man who was smartly dressed. Dr. Phillips could see two frilly hats blowing in the wind: one pink, the other yellow - the sisters Bradley he assumed. He was disheveled, dirty, tired and short-tempered. Not a good combination to meet two young influential women but he would try to be his most civil mannered.

The carriage stopped and the driver quickly got down, opened the door and helped the two ladies disembark. Mayor Brodt rushed over to greet them, "Good day Miss Beatrice, Miss Kathryn. Good news! Fairfax now has a doctor!" He smiled and waved his arm toward Dr. Phillips, "May I introduce Dr. Bradford Phillips?" He waved his arm back toward the ladies, "And Dr. Phillips, may I introduce Miss Beatrice Bradley and her sister, Mrs. Kathryn Granger?"

Phillips nodded his head to the ladies, "I am pleased to meet you. May I offer my sincere sympathy at the loss of your parents? I found them to be extremely good people and I enjoyed their company in Cincinnati. It is such a terrible loss for you and for this community." Turning back toward the wagon he motioned for Augusta and her daughters to come forward.

"This is Mrs. Augusta Brown and her daughters, Lottie and Lissie."

Beatrice came forward and offered her hand, "I am pleased to make your acquaintance, Dr. Phillips and Mrs. Brown. Indeed, my parents are a tragic loss for us all. But I am so grateful that they were able to secure your employment before their deaths." Dr. Phillips liked what he saw when he looked into Miss Beatrice's eyes. She was obviously intelligent, and there was no simpering or nonsense as with many of the ladies he had known in Boston and New York.

He turned to the other sister as Kathryn

extended her hand, "I hope you will be happy here in Fairfax, Dr. Phillips and Mrs. Brown. We will be pleased to extend our hospitality for dinner this evening as I am sure you are not prepared with foodstuffs as yet." Looking at the woman, she smiled, "And of course Mrs. Brown and the children are included."

"Thank you, ma'am, but we have been on the road several days and are in great need of a bath, food, sleep, and laundry facilities. I hope you will extend your invitation to another day. The little ones need tending too as well. We hope you will excuse me, I would not be good company for you." Dr. Phillips smiled at first Kathryn, then Beatrice.

"We certainly understand, Dr. Phillips. I will send a dinner to your residence and make sure you have all the necessities for your kitchen and bath. I have taken the opportunity and placed a cook for your convenience as part of your contract. I am sure you have much greater need of settling into your practice and do not need the additional worry of unpacking and making your office ready as well as your home." Beatrice turned to Big John, "This is Big John Cooper. He will be bringing your supplies and staff within the next hour." She turned to Dr. Phillips, "He is an indispensable member of our family."

Dr. Phillips offered his hand to Big John. "Pleased to make your acquaintance, Big John." He found his own large hand enveloped by the much larger hand of Big John.

"I'm much obliged to meet you suh." Big John smiled at Dr. Phillips. "Mr. an' Mrs. Bradley were wonderful folk who's missed ever' single day." Big John turned toward Augusta, taking her hand, "I'm right pleased to meet yuh, ma'am." His smiled widened as he held her hand.

Augusta returned his smile but quickly looked down. "I'm glad to meet you." She stepped back and didn't return his look.

Big John stood staring at Augusta. With a warm smile he kneeled down to say hello to the little girls. "My, ain't you two de purtiest little ones ah've seen in a long time?" The little girls tried to hide behind their mother's skirt while giggling.

Augusta turned and looked over her shoulder and said softly, "Come on out now. This nice man just paid you a nice compliment. Come on now, what you say to that?" The little girls shyly came forward but looked down and kept quiet. Augusta looked up at Big John, "I thank you for your kind words. Their names are Lottie and Lissie."

Mayor Brodt pushed forward. "Ladies, you may return to your home. I will take Dr. Phillips to his new home and office for you. Thank you for coming so quickly to welcome him." He turned away, dismissing the sisters.

Beatrice was having none of his behavior. "Dr. Phillips, I will stop by your office tomorrow morning. What time is most convenient? We have some things to discuss and I have the final contract for your signature."

Dr. Phillips was impressed, "You may come by any time after 8 o'clock, ma'am. I will be in shirt sleeves, but will stop my work at your arrival." Replacing his hat on his head he nodded to both sisters and turned to Mayor Brodt, "Mayor, I would appreciate being shown to my home/office now. There is a lot that needs to be done before we can retire for the evening."

Big John approached, "Dr. Phillips, I'll return real quick an' make sure you got heated water fur all's yore bathes, supplies fur cook and help fur unloaden' and puttin' away yur things." He turned and helped Beatrice and Kathryn into the carriage, closed the door and tipped his hat and nodded at Mayor Brodt, Dr. Phillips and a smile at Augusta Brown. "Afternoon."

Dr. Phillips watched the carriage drive away. Mayor Br,odt walked up to him watching them as well, "Quite a pair of ladies, wouldn't you say Doctor?"

"Indeed. Quite a lovely pair. Miss Beatrice is very assured and intelligent. Her father spoke highly of both his daughters. I see why now." He turned to the mayor, "I'm ready to go. I will follow you if you'd like or you can give me the keys and address and that will suffice." He was more than ready to end his journey.

Mayor Brodt, nodded at the people gathered

to watch the new arrival, got into a small buggy that he turned toward the end of the street. Dr. Phillips ignored the crowd, helped Augusta and her little ones back in their wagon, got back on his wagon and made a wide turn around on the street to follow the mayor. He looked straight ahead and didn't acknowledge the faces in the store windows as he passed by. Fatigue was pulling on him like a heavy, wet blanket. A bath had sounded good, but now he wanted only a meal and a soft bed. He would refuse the mayor if he insisted on a tour of his office and new home. Phillips didn't want to lose his temper so soon. He had little time or patience for self-important people and Mayor Brodt struck him as that sort of person. He would be more in the mood for tours and information tomorrow. It hadn't escaped his notice that the mayor had ignored Augusta and her little daughters.

Big John arrived at the Bradley home and prepared the wagons with boxes and bags to take to Dr. Phillips. He had already placed them together in the barn earlier in the week when he found out that the doctor was coming so it made it easy to load up quickly for his return to town. He was glad the cook, Desdemona, was already at the house waiting for Dr. Phillips. Miss Beatrice had placed her there just the day before so that she could clean and make the house and office ready for the doctor.

Two black mill workers who had volunteered

to help Big John unload climbed aboard the
wagon and settled back asking Big John about the
doctor. "Well, he's a might tired and dirty from
his travels here. He don't seem like the kind of
man to take folks' guff. I hope he's gonna be a
good doctor for all us folks but only time's gonna
tell that. We just gotta hope that Mr. Bradley
made a good pick when he chose him." Big John
shook the reins and the team picked up speed.
"He got a mighty fine woman, Miz Brown, with
him. She gotta coupla lil ones, too. I think it's a
good sign of what kinda man he might be. He
made quick travel to git here. Seems like he's
wantin' to be our doctor." He thought a
moment, "But I hope Miz Mary will still be
mixin' up her potions. A lotta our folks just ain't
gonna want to trust a new doc." Big John smiled,
"Miz Bea sure seemed to take a likin' to im
though," he chuckled, "Yep, she sho did. Git up
Deacon, gitty up, Bishop. Gotta git these here
things to our new doc." Big John hoped he'd see
Augusta again.

When Mayor Brodt stopped at the new house
and office he got down from his buggy and waved
for Dr. Phillips to stop. "If you go down to the
end of the block and turn down behind the
houses, I will meet you at the back of the house.
There's a small barn for you to keep your horses
and wagons. It's a nice piece of property owned
by the Bradleys'. I think you'll be right pleased."

Dr. Phillips slowed down his wagon and

nodded his head at the mayor's instructions. Following the road around, he was pleased with the quality of the houses, large lots and the land around them. Five houses down, he saw the mayor standing in the middle of the road. On the right side he saw a small corral and barn where he turned in and stopped. The horses snorted and stomped their feet, eager to get water and feed. Dr. Phillips patted their necks as he took the harness and pulled them around to back into the barn.

"If you come on up to the house, I'll give you the grand tour," the mayor smiled, "you can let Big John and his fellas take care of your things."

"I thank you for your help, Mayor Brodt, but I have some pretty important supplies in this wagon that I would prefer to take care of myself. I'll let Big John take me through the house after he arrives and we unload." Dr. Phillips removed his hat and held out his hand to shake the mayor's hand. "I look forward to living in Fairfax. Thank you for your welcome and guidance here."

The mayor frowned but handed him the keys, "Well, you'll find a lot of good folks here in Fairfax. We're proud of our community and you'll meet a lot of them with all the welcome dinners the ladies have planned for you. I have to tell you, Dr. Phillips, a good-looking single doctor like you is going to attract the ladies, that's for sure," he guffawed. "I can't wait to watch them swarm you like bees to a new hive." The mayor laughed and softly punched Phillip's shoulder.

Dr. Phillips held his temper. Just what I need, he thought, a bunch of silly females making my life miserable. Well, he'd nip that right in the bud from the very first meeting.

As Mayor Brodt stepped up into his buggy, a very large wagon pulled by two immense horses turned down the street. Dr. Phillips saw the black man he had met with the Bradley sisters driving the wagon and two other black men riding with him. He was relieved to see they were all big men and would make short work of unloading and carrying into his office all the contents of his wagon. He touched the brim of his hat as the mayor drove off. Community events would be important for him to attend, but he needed a few days before he would be ready to assume his new life in Fairfax.

Big John pulled the horses to a stop. "Here we come, Doc Phillips, jus' like I said. We'll have you unloaded right fast now." Big John lashed the reins around the long break handle, "This here's Elijah and Louis. We all work for the Bradleys; me at the big house and the boys in the mill." Elijah and Louis touched the brims of their hats and sat waiting for Big John to tell them what to do. Big John reached into the bed of the wagon and pulled out a large wooden basket covered with a red and white cloth. "This here's your dinner for tonight. Whyn't you and Miz

Brown and the youngins go on into the house and tuck yursef into this meal whilst we take care ah yur things?" Big John walked up to Dr. Phillips and pulled back the cover on the basket, "Why you just take a sniff of this here meal and you won't waste another breath on worryin' 'bout unpackin'." He smiled and held out his arm gesturing toward the house. "You can meet yur cook Desdemona, whilst we bring yur belongins and she'll setchu up wif this good eaten."

Dr. Phillips looked at the two men in the wagon and then at Big John, "Well I guess you can unload this wagon, but I have some delicate medical supplies amongst my belongings in my wagon so I insist that I be with you when we unload those things." He looked sternly at Big John with a look that intimidated most people.

Big John smiled, "Sho nuf Doc. I'll come gitchu when we finish dis wagon." He chuckled softly as he walked away. Yessuh, he thought, sparks were gonna fly between him and folks here in town when Doc wanted his way and he was gonna enjoy seein it happen, yes-suh-ree.

Big John was still chuckling when he walked back to the wagon, "Come on now fellers. We gonna unload and put alla these here supplies in Doc's house. Won't take but a blink a time."

Elijah leaned close to Big John, "We saw that new woman. Whooee! She's a real looker she is!" Big John gave him a sour look. "Whatcha think about the new Doc, Big John? You think

143

he'll be a doc for us, too?"

"Well, I think we'll just have to wait 'n see what happens when one a us gits to ailin' and needs the doc." Big John reached into the wagon and lifted out a large bag, "If not him, I'm good with Miz Mary for my ailin'. Hurry up now, my dinner's awaitin' up at the big house."

Dr. Phillips watched the men drive away. "Well, Gussie. Let's see what our new home and office looks like." He ushered her and the little girls in front of him and entered the back door of the house. A young woman was waiting in the kitchen smiling at them.

"Welcome y'all. I'm Desdemona. Miz Beatrice said to tell you I'll be yore new cook. I can houseclean fur ya too." She was not as tall as Augusta, but she was rounder. Her smile was genuine and Dr. Phillips liked her on sight.

"I'm glad to be here and welcome your help. This is Augusta Brown, Lottie and Lissie, Desdemona. She is my medical assistant but will help you with the household. I'm hoping you can be friends as well as employees." Dr. Phillips inhaled and sighed. "I think we are about to enjoy a good lunch, Gussie." He rubbed his hands and looked down, "But first I need to wash about a hundred miles of dirt off of my hands."

"Yessuh, Doc. Me and the girls will wash up and join you shortly. Desdemona, if you'll show Doc his room we'll just use the kitchen this time."

Desdemona took Doc through the kitchen,

"This here's the back way upstairs for ya, Doc, if you don't mind me using yur Gussie's name fur ya."

"Not at all, Desdemona. We'll be working together in the same house. I don't stand on stuffy rules of society. I'd appreciate your befriending Gussie and her daughters. You can show her around town, you know, shopping and such. If you attend church, I'm sure they will want to go along with you if you don't mind."

"I'm real pleased to do just that Doc," she giggled. "I think we all will do just fine together." Desdemona motioned with her arm and Doc walked down the hallway in front of her. "This here room is yur bed and bath. This floor's got three other rooms. Then the downstairs is yur office and the front room is big with a nice fireplace for folks to make em cozy while they wait on ya. We can look at that later. Big John placed all the boxes in there and the office." She paused, "Is Gussie and her girls staying up here?" She looked worried, "Cause the town busybodies sure will have a mouthful of words 'bout that doncha know it! But for tonight one of these rooms will be jus fine for Gussie and them lil ones. We can worry bout dat another day," she frowned.

"Oh! Well, I didn't think about that. Where do you live?" Doc stopped and leaned against the bedroom door.

"I've got me the room offa the kitchen. It's

got 'nough room for me, but not much else for a woman and chil'ren." Desdemona smiled, "But ya know what? There's a small carriage house attached to the barn. Ain't been used in a long time, but it just might be good for Gussie. Her youngins can play in the backyard where I kin keep an eye on im." She smiled, "Yessur, me and her kin git that place fixed up no time atall."

Doc smiled, "Desdemona, I think you're going to be a treasure. If your food is half as good as it smells and you're this helpful --- why, I think you're about the best way to start my new life here in Fairfax." He smiled at her as he closed the door.

Desdemona had a big smile on her face as she returned to the kitchen. She was humming a tune as she started placing the food on the table. She told Gussie about the carriage house and they were talking excitedly when Dr. Phillips returned to the kitchen. They stopped talking and waited for him to be seated.

"Will you say the prayer, Doc, or you want me to?" Gusssie put napkins on her girls' laps as she spoke then sat down.

"I'll say it if you don't mind." He sat down at the head of the table. "Desdemona, if you haven't eaten we sure would enjoy your company. Matter of fact I would like all of us to partake meals together from now on unless there is an emergency and I'm away. We'll have to talk about working together as well, but not until tomorrow. I'm thinking we'll retire early tonight." Dr. Phillips cleared his throat, then bowed his head, "Lord, we are gathered together in our new home here in Fairfax, Ohio. We are grateful to you for seeing that our journey here was safe. We ask that you bless this food, and all who are seated here. Amen."

"Well Gussie, what do you think about Desdemona's idea about the carriage house? You think you want to give it a try? Otherwise I will look into renting something else close by." Phillips took a bite of the food on his plate, "My, my, my! Desdemona – it's been a few weeks since I sat down to a meal. Gussie did a good job on the journey, but I must tell you this is a wonderful meal. I look forward to your culinary excellence in the future."

Desdemona, sat down at the end of the table and smiled with pride. "Don't know much 'bout dat. I learned to cook when I was 'bout as big as these youngins standin at my ma's side. 'Nothin better'n havin' the range full of bubblin' pots and the oven full of pies."

"We're gonna get on just fine, Desdemona, just fine all right." Gussie smiled at each of the faces at the table.

After the meal was over, Gussie helped Desdemona clean up. Dr. Phillips wandered around his new house. He was pleased. It was plenty large enough for him and his practice. When he entered the rooms he would use for his patients he was pleased with the shelves and glass cabinets that were clean and shining, waiting for him and Gussie to put away all his supplies and medications. Mr. Bradley hadn't said enough about this home when he described it to him in Cincinnati. As tired as he was he still felt a tingle of excitement. This was the place. He would be the best doctor Fairfax ever had.

The next day, the new doctor's office was abuzz with activity. After a good night's sleep and a full breakfast, Gussie and Dr. Phillips were emptying boxes in the surgery and patient examination room. The little girls were playing with their rag dolls on the back lawn under a tree. It was a surprise when Desdemona announced Miss Beatrice had arrived. He couldn't believe the time had passed so quickly. This would be a test to see how he was received by Miss Bradley without his coat or tie and his sleeves rolled up to his elbows.

Dr. Phillips thought about his appearance but before he could lower his sleeves, Miss Bradley stood before him. "Good morning, Dr. Phillips," she said with a smile.

"Good morning to you, Miss Bradley."

Just then Gussie came in and with another box to unpack. "Oh! Good mornin' Miz Bradley! Mighty fine house and office you have here for Doc. We'll have this place together in no time atall." Gussie paused, "Doc, whyn't you take Miz Bradley in the front room and I'll fetch you some coffee."

"Good morning, Mrs. Brown. I'm glad you like this home. It's always been a favorite of mine. My father purchased it after our last doctor passed away. He allowed me and my sister, Kathryn to choose new wallpaper and drapes. We also chose the paint for all the rooms." Beatrice smiled as she looked around.

"You should just call me Gussie like the Doc here does. No sense using that Mrs. Brown name. I'm just plain ole Gussie to all my friends."

"Well, I'll be pleased to call you Gussie then," she smiled and reached out to take Gussie's hand in friendship.

"I think me and the Doc are gonna be real pleased with Fairfax. Thank you ma'am.

"Then I think you should call me Beatrice like all my friends do. Please let me know if there is anything you and your daughters need or anything that will be needed for the doctor's office, Gussie."

Gussie beamed, "I'll do that. Yes I will. Right now Desdemona and me will get the office settled, then I hope you don't mind but, I would like to clean out the carriage house next to the barn for a place close by for me and my girls. Desdemona said she thought it would be a fine place for us. We didn't think to ask you first."

"I have no objection. In fact, I think it's perfect! There might even be some furniture stored in there if I remember right. Use anything that is good and throw out anything you don't like or need. The church has storage in the basement where we can put any furniture you don't want. I should have cleaned out the carriage house long ago. I think this arrangement will work just fine."

Beatrice turned to Doc, "Dr. Phillips, shall we go into your front room and finish our business?"

"By all means, please proceed." Doc exchanged a grin with Gussie. "Would you kindly ask Desdemona to bring some tea for us, Gussie?"

"Yes sir, I sure will."

When Doc turned the corner into the front room, Beatrice was already sitting in a chair, gloves removed, holding a sheaf of papers.

"I have your contract, Dr. Phillips. If everything is satisfactory you may sign right here." Beatrice turned the paper around. "In addition, I know there are probably other important needs you have that I advise you about. You can settle in first, then contact me or if you know of anything now, please let me know. I'm sure you will need a couple of days yet to finish organizing your office." Beatrice looked up waiting for Doc to respond.

"I have found everything very satisfactory. Fairfax appears to be just what I was looking for. I thank you for placing Desdemona here with us. She and Gussie have already formed a friendship and will work together very well. I prefer to let

Gussie handle my household and office affairs and organization.   I will endeavor to be the type of physician who is available for the folks of Fairfax whether in my office or at their homes if needed." Doc signed the contract and handed it back to Beatrice.

Beatrice put the papers inside a folder then looked at Doc. Gussie appeared before she could say anything. Leaning forward she asked, "Shall I pour?"

Doc looked at Gussie and she quietly disappeared. "Of course."

"Do you take cream and sugar?" Beatrice paused with the small pitcher poised.

"No thank you. I prefer my tea black, thank you."

After handing Doc his cup and saucer and preparing her own cup, Beatrice still hadn't said anything. Doc thought he would wait her out. Obviously there was something else she wanted to say.

Finally, Beatrice looked at Doc, "We have been without a doctor in Fairfax for quite some time." Doc waited for her to continue.

"Even when we had a doctor, families in the outlying farms were sometimes unable or did not have the economic ability to use the doctor's services." Beatrice looked away as if she was trying to decide something.

Beatrice turned and looked at Doc with a very serious expression, "When those families were ill or injured they would seek out a different sort of medicine. And," Beatrice cleared her throat, "when we had a measles epidemic, we were grateful to have Mary Leland, her mother Grannie Rose, and her son Tom who are healers. In my opinion they saved this town. When more than half the people of Fairfax came down with measles, Mary and her family went from house to house as well as to the school, and church, which they set up as temporary hospitals to treat and stay with people who were dangerously ill. We lost only three people: two older folks and one child. Mary Leland's mother, Grannie Rose died after working many long hours during this time."

Beatrice leaned forward and looked at Doc. "I know that most physicians frown on people like Mary Leland, but she was more successful with healing ailments and birthing babies than our former doctor. I hope you can find it in your heart to allow them to continue helping folks and not feel as though they are encroaching on your medical practice." Beatrice looked at Doc expectantly, waiting for an argument.

Doc watched Beatrice as she talked, thinking how attractive she is. He liked the tenor of her voice filled with emotion for the people she was defending. He also liked that about her; that she would defend someone who was doing something that might be socially acceptable in most cities. He wanted to meet and talk to Mary Leland.

Doc smiled, "Miss Beatrice, I am aware of

people who do healing with potions, salves and ointments. That is a longtime way of helping people and much of what they do is very effective. I will be delighted to meet Mary Leland and her son. I am sure we can agree on the fact that all of our citizens deserve to be helped in time of illness – whatever ailment they have."

Beatrice sighed. She had expected to do battle with the new doctor. "I am pleased to hear you say that, Dr. Phillips. Mary and Tom are friends of my sister Kathryn and me. They live near my home about a mile away. If you would like I can accompany you some morning or afternoon and introduce you."

"I would be very pleased to have you accompany me, Miss Beatrice." Doc set his cup and saucer on the tray, "That is, in a few days. I want to settle in and organize my office first. I would imagine that I might be needed by someone anytime now that the word is out that I have arrived."

"Yes, yes of course." Beatrice returned her cup and saucer to the tray and stood up. "I will go now and allow you to return to your office. If there is anything I can help you with I hope that you will feel free to contact me. My offer for you to dine with us is an open invitation. You have but to send a message and you will be welcome."

Beatrice walked toward the door and turned, "There is one other subject that I believe you should be aware of," Beatrice hesitated. "I do not know your position regarding all the talk of the south seceding from the union, but here we are quite divided.

There is a rather unsavory group of men who are quite vocal and possibly violent about defending the south and the issue of slavery. Bounty hunters come through Fairfax quite often. As you know, defending or helping escaped slaves is against the law." Beatrice sighed, "I employ a large group of black men and women who are freemen. They and their families live near the Bradley Mill and Wagon Works. We have had night riders who burn the property of those they feel are union sympathizers. I do not condone this behavior. The sheriff of Fairfax has a different point of view and is more inclined to support this radical faction." Another sigh, "I am not asking for you to voice your opinion on this issue, but I did want you to know about the temperament of some of our citizens."

Doc had followed Beatrice to the door and now stood with his arms folded as he listened to her. "I am a doctor first, Miss Beatrice. I treat the sick and injured no matter their faith or color. I came here to Fairfax to help people. I do want the union to stay together but I cannot support the desire to have slaves or to hunt them down like animals when they strive for a better life."

He opened the door for Beatrice, "We will talk again, Miss Beatrice. I thank you for this information. I shall inform Gussie that she must be careful when she's going to shop or to church." Doc offered Beatrice his arm and they descended the stairs to the sidewalk where her horse and buggy awaited.

Doc helped Beatrice up onto the buggy's seat, "Good afternoon. I look forward to dining with you and your sister. Please extend to her my felicitations." He smiled as he watched her drive away. She is quite a woman, he thought. He really did look forward to being with her again.

In the afternoon, Gussie was cleaning out the carriage house when a wagon pulled up outside. Big John got down and proceeded to unload lumber, a large coil of rope and boxes. He looked up as Gussie walked toward him, "Good afternoon Miz Brown. I brought a few things to help you settle in to yur new house."

"Why that's real nice of you….um," Gussie stammered. She wasn't sure she should call him Big John because she didn't know him and it was too informal a name when they didn't know each other.

"I wish you'd call me Big John, ma'am. Mah last name's Cooper, but no one's ever called me anything but Big John. Seein's how we'll be friends an all I think it's all right. And if I have your permission, I'd like to call you Miz Augusta, if it pleases you."

Gussie felt her cheeks redden. "I think that would be all right, Big John, everyone's always called me Gussie." she said softly and smiled.

"Well now, that'll be Miz Gussie for me then." He put his hand on the wagon, "I got a load of things fo ya. I thought I'd take this here wood and make a nice swing on that big tree over yonder by the Doc's house fo them purty girls ah yores. Nothing like swinging for a good time. Then Miz Bea and Miz Kathryn thought you could use some extra blankets and linens and such. So they asked that I fetch em with this load of wood fo ya. You just show me where I can put em, and I'll put em there befo I start work on the swing."

Gussie was a tall woman but Big John Cooper made her feel like she was a foot smaller. His big hands easily picked up two large boxes stacked on top of each other and he started walking to the house with ease.

"I haven't done much today except empty out the house and start cleaning the rooms. So I think it's best if you just put the boxes on the floor in the main room."

Big John followed Gussie into the house and put the boxes down and removed his hat, "My, my, my you have done a mountain of cleanin in here. I only looked through the windows a cupla times but I know there was a world of cobwebs and stacks of junk coverin' the place. You done all this work yoself? I woulda gladly come over and helped you." Big John walked into the other next room that was not as large but had a

156

fireplace. This here will be yore bedroom? Where will the little ones sleep?" He walked around and checking out the fireplace and the windows."

"My girls will sleep on a trundle bed I found. It'll fit just fine with the bed I'll be sleepin on."

"Seems okay." Big John walked over to the fireplace and looked inside. "I think I'll come back with a cupla fellas and clean out this fireplace and wash the windows fur ya. Cain't havin you do too much work when you got Doc's stuff to put up, too." He smiled at Gussie. "You'll be needen a large stack ah wood for both houses and I will take care of that, too."

"I don't want you to go out of your way. I can take care of the cleaning just fine. I'm so grateful with just this that you've brought me."

Big John was pleased that he had made Gussie happy. "Yur a right fine woman, Miz Gussie. I'm a pleased as can be to help you out. I'd like to have you come to church with Desdemona this Sunday if you please. That is if yore used to attenden services?"

"I did have a church I attended back in Cincinnati." Gussie thought for a moment, "Do you have enough black folks for your own church, or do you attend the church here in town?"

"Yes ma'am we got ourselves a nice church right down the road past the Mill. You gonna be pleased as punch to meet up wif some real nice black folk. We's all freemen and most of us work for the Bradleys in some way or nuther. I'm proud to tell ya that I'm preacher there and I'd be right pleased to see ya Sunday morn."

Big John chuckled, "We do a lot of singin' and shoutin' to the Lord and then we have meal together. Desdemona can tell you what to bring witcha. I think yur little ones'll have a good time, too."

"Then you will see me Sunday morning for sure. I thank you again." Gussie walked out with Big John following her. "I'll let you get on with the swing. Doc may be needing me, so I will bid you goodbye."

Big John watched Gussie as she walked across the road and up the small hill to Doc's house thinking that he liked everything about her. He was looking forward to seeing her again and knew he would think of more reasons to visit her. He would write a good sermon to impress her for this Sunday.   Smiling as he unloaded the wood Big John felt younger and full of energy. Yessuh, he thought, his life just got a bushel of happiness all right. Big John sang softly one of his favorite hymns, *The Lord, by Moses to Pharoah said, Oh, let my people go. If not I'll smite your first-born dead. Oh, let my people go,"* as he worked.

"What's that yore singin' mister?" the little girl asked.

Big John turned around. Gussie's two little girls were standing together holding hands watching him work.

"Why ahm singin' a church song, an y'all be hearin' it agin come this Sunday mornin when you attend church with yur mama an' Desdemona." Big John crouched down almost level with the little girls.

"My name's Big John, what's yurs?" he smiled. They giggled and just smiled at him.

"Well, I guess I'll have to guess then. Hmmm, you must be Miss and you'll be Missie, right?"

The little girls almost collapsed giggling and laughing.

"It's too bad I don't have yur names right as I got here in my pocket a right fine candy that I was fixin' to share wif y'all." Big John stood up and started to turn around.

"I'm Lissie and this here's my sister, Lottie."

Big John chuckled and put his hand in his pocket and brought out two pieces of candy and held them out to the girls. They both stood still with their hands behind their backs.

"Well go on now. There's one for each of ya."

The girls looked at each other, "Mama might get mad at us," Lissie whispered to Lottie.

"We cain't take em Mister Big John. Not without our mama sayin' we kin."

"Yore mama's right down there? Why'nt you run and ask her? I'll be here workin' on a surprise for y'all."

The girls turned to run then quickly turned back, "A surprise!" they squealed.

"Shore nuf. Go on now, for dis candy gets into my mouth."

"Mama, mama," they screamed as they ran. "Mister Big John gots candy for us, can we have it, please?" They crashed into Gussie almost knocking her down.

"Girls, girls, now what this about?"

"We can have a piece of candy from Mister Big John if you say it's ok with you. Puhleeze!" Lissie begged.

Gussie looked up the hill at Big John who had his back to them. "I guess it would be alright, but you set yourselves down before you put the pieces in your mouth, you hear? I won't tolerate any chokin' on candy or it'll be a long time afore you can have another."

"Yes'em mama. We hear you." They were running back up the hill as they answered Gussie. Suddenly, they stopped half way, "And, Mister Big John' makin up a surprise, too!" Lissie hollered. They turned and continued to run to Big John.

Big John turned around and smiled at Gussie as the girls stopped in front of him. "Here ya go. Now you mind yur mama and set down over there. Don't be steppin round me while I'm workin' so's you don't get a knock on yore heads from this here swing I'm buildin'."

"A swing!" the girls shouted together.

"You're makin' us our very own swing?"

"Yup. Gonna have a good time on this I can tell you." Big John started humming.

Lottie and Lissie sat down on the grass and carefully held the candy to their lips and smiled at each other as their tongues licked the sweet peppermint. Gussie watched and felt a happiness she hadn't felt in a long time. This is a good town for my girls, she thought. A good new life here in Fairfax for me and for Doc, yessiree!

Chapter 11

The Road to the Promised Land

Beatrice and Kathryn entered the Bradley Mercantile Store as Big John held the door for them. "Jus' let me know when y'all are ready to leave and I will git yur packages and load up the buggy, Miz Bea and Miz Kathryn." Beatrice smiled at Big John, nodded her head and proceeded Kathryn into the store where she was met by two ladies who stopped in front of her.

"Oh, Beatrice! Have you met the new doctor? Wait til you see him, land's sake!"

Beatrice couldn't escape Dolly Thornton's hand as she grabbed her arm. "The new doctor has arrived and he's oh so handsome!" she gushed. She leaned forward and whispered loudly in Beatrice' ear, "Quite handsome, in fact, I almost swooned when I saw him."

Beatrice pulled back and frowned at the woman. "Dolly Thornton, the man is our new doctor and you're a married woman."

Dolly turned her nose up and clutched her reticule with both hands, "Of course I'm married but I can still recognize a handsome man when I see one." She pushed aside the woman she had been talking to and squeezed past Beatrice and Kathryn in a huff. "Good day Beatrice," she said primly and stalked over to the closest counter. "I swear Janeen, Beatrice Bradley can be so rude!

As I was saying, we'll have to invite the new doctor to a welcome party. Can you just imagine what the mothers of our single ladies will think when they get a look at Dr. Phillips? Besides, with all this loathsome talk of war we need a party to enjoy something better than all that nonsense." Dolly put her hand on her heart and closed her eyes, "It's just thrilling to have such a handsome professional in our town. Simply thrilling."

Kathryn heard Dolly talking and leaned close to Beatrice, "Should you warn Dr. Phillips about Dolly Thornton? The poor man is about to be inundated with the biggest gossip in the county. If he attends her party he will be surrounded by every available marriageable woman for miles and miles," Kathryn chuckled.

"I think Dr. Phillips can take care of himself, Kathryn. I've been told that he can hold his own with the men of the town. He's been stopping at Bender's Tavern and has made friends with Wilson Meyers and the men from the mill. Mr. Meyers told me he has become a welcome addition to their discussions about politics. Even Mr. Sutton has him sit and talk almost every afternoon and they discuss the telegrams of news and what should be printed in the next edition of the newspaper. As the owner and editor of the Fairfax Courier, that's quite a compliment." Beatrice sounded impressed. "Mr. Meyers said that Dr. Phillips is definitely on the side of the union. He doesn't even seem to be intimidated by Hank Colby and his gang of ruffians."

"Well, if Mr. Meyers and Mr. Sutton like him, then that puts him in favor with me." Kathryn giggled, "You do have to admit, Bea. Dr. Phillips is quite a handsome man."

Beatrice smiled, "I don't have to admit any such thing." Beatrice thought Dr. Phillips was definitely a handsome man. But she wasn't interested in him. She had already been in love. She still bore the pain of her loss.

Later as Big John helped put packages in the back of the buggy, he told Beatrice that he overheard Dolly Thornton talking to some ladies outside the Mercantile Store. "She was tellin' them all about how she was havin' a party to introduce Doc to the town and how handsome and refined she thought he wuz." Big John shook his head, "I think you should warn im, Miz Beatrice, he's 'bout to be overrun by them women. Yeah suh, he don't know it yet, but Miz Thornton's gonna roughrod im into a tussle of women filled with ideas a movin' into his new house. You mark my words, they'll be loads of food bein' dropped off. Miz Gussie and Desdemona's gonna have their hands full keepin' em outta the parlor." Big John shook his head, "Poor Doc. Heh, heh, heh."

"I'm afraid you're right Big John. Dolly Thornton's a force to be reckoned with for sure."

A few days later, Dr. Phillips was ready to

lock his doors and escape. True to Big John's prediction the kitchen counters were filled with plates of cookies, cakes, bread and jars of everything from fruit to jams, jellies and meat. Poor Desdemona swore this morning that she was barring the door to any more gifts and especially to the intrusion of over-scented pushy females. In addition, he had been invited to a special soiree in his honor so that all the town folk he hadn't already met could greet him and welcome him to Fairfax. Even the mayor, Mr. Brodt, stopped by to make sure he attended. He had half a mind to ignore the invitation. His only hope to avoid attending was if he had an emergency. He would much rather attend a dinner at the Bradley home. He truly enjoyed the time he spent with Misses Beatrice and Kathryn. Perhaps he could attend the soiree with them as his protectors. Miss Beatrice held a lot of power in town. She had the respect of Wilson Meyers and Homer Sutton and that said a lot.

Doc went out the back door and smiled to see Lottie and Lissie swinging together on the swing Big John had made for them. Desdemona had told him that every week she and Gussie attended the church where Big John was the pastor. She also told him that she thought Big John was sweet on Gussie. Doc approved. He thought very highly of Big John. He was an intelligent, thoughtful man. Gussie couldn't do better if she decided to remarry. The way he doted on her little girls was very special. They surrounded him every time he stopped by and they now took turns giving him hugs when he arrived to visit and drop off wood for the fireplaces.

But right now, he had no new patients waiting so he decided to visit Bender's Tavern. He enjoyed his talks with the men who frequented the tavern. The owner and his wife, Jacob and Stella, were good people and always friendly. It was a good place to hear the news about the area and local and national politics. Doc had made friends there and he enjoyed having a beer and relaxing among the men. The Benders were good people. They had a black man, Samuel Washington, who worked for them and they treated him with respect. The unruly group that met in the back of the tavern were not allowed to mistreat Samuel. Jacob and Stella even told the sheriff that people were to act civilized while drinking in their tavern. Doc wasn't sure he liked Sheriff Vinton. Tempers seemed to be too high lately with arguments about north versus south. Too many times he saw the sheriff in the back drinking and whispering among the men who were a motley lot and didn't get on well with Wilson Meyers and the men from the mill.

Doc thought highly of Wilson Meyers and Homer Sutton, and counted them as trusted friends. Both men were already enjoying a beer together when Doc arrived.

"Hey Doc," Wilson greeted him. "How'd

you sneak out of your office so early and escape all those females who've been visiting you?" He looked at Homer and laughed.

"Very funny, Wilson. You and Homer should stop by and pick up some cake or cookies. I've also got a supply of canned goods I could share with you, too." The men all laughed.

Samuel stopped by their table and placed a large tankard of beer in front of Doc. "Good to see you, Doc. You're a bit early today."

Homer and Wilson laughed. "He's escaping all them females who've trying been to impress him with their kitchen skills." The men laughed and Samuel joined them.

"Yeah, Doc. Seems like yore the talk of the town. Big John said there's big doin's at Miz Dolly Thornton's home to welcome you in style and give all the mothers a chance to meet their daughters." Samuel chuckled as he gathered the empty glasses and wiped the table."

"I'll have you men know that I came here for peace and quiet and a little conversation. I can deal with the ladies of Fairfax, don't you worry." He shook his head and took a long drink of his beer.

The men settled into their drinks and talked about the latest news. Quietly, they had spoken about the escaped slaves who frequented the area from time to time. Wilson and Homer had exchanged looks when Doc asked them what happened to the slaves when they were in the area. When neither man was quick to answer, Doc leaned forward and very quietly asked, "Have either of you men heard about something called the Underground Railroad?"

Both Wilson's and Homer's faces paled and they sat back. It was apparent they knew something. "I swear to you I am only asking because as a doctor I feel it is my duty to help any man or woman in need. I don't want to get anyone in trouble. I know about the penalty for helping. Just know gentlemen, I am a friend, not a foe," Doc sat back, "and with that I will take my leave."

After he left Wilson Meyers said thoughtfully, "Well what do you think? He's been here a few weeks now and I really like the man. Whenever we have discussions he is right with us in our opinions. I think I'll discuss putting him in our group if Miss Beatrice approves. Do you agree?"

Homer Sutton thought a moment, "I agree. Doc's a good man. I think we might trust him to help when needed, but Miss Beatrice should be advised. It couldn't hurt to get her opinion." Homer looked around, "Mary Leland could use the help with some of the more difficult injuries before they're transported in the wagons."

Wilson Meyers nodded his head in agreement, "We'll start by letting him know about Mary and not Miss Beatrice and transportation in the Bradley wagons."

After Doc left the tavern, he decided to take the opportunity to visit Mary Leland instead of returning to his office. They had met in town and she had invited him out to her home. She said that he could take some of her prepared ointments to use if he wanted. It was a good time to go, he might be able to use her skills.

Doc turned his buggy down the back alley to his home and office and stopped. Desdemona saw him through the kitchen window and came to the back door.

"Desdemona, please tell Gussie that I will be at Mary Leland's if she needs me. I will return before dinner." Doc shook the reins and his buggy shot forward. It was a nice day for a drive into the country. As he left town behind, he slowed the horse from a quick trot to walk so he could enjoy the late spring bloom of wild flowers along the road. The yellow mustard blossoms and purple lilac bushes buzzing with bees. Fairfax was a beautiful valley that was enhanced by the flow of the Ohio River. The fields were rich with dark brown soil that was currently filled as far as the eye could see with rows of corn.

Just as the road turned in a wide bend, his eye caught movement in the cornfield. Since the corn was only knee high, Doc could see something large was moving low to the ground. If it was an animal that had been injured he would see if he could help it without being injured himself. Doc stopped the buggy and got down slowly and approached the corn field. As he got closer he was shocked to see that it was a black man crawling to get away from the road.

"Stop! I can help you if you're injured." Doc looked back over his shoulder to the road to see if anyone was coming. "I am alone, no one else is coming. I can help you. I'm a doctor."

The man turned over and tried to sit up, but fell back. "Cain't get caught. Gotta hide. Dogs be comin' fur me."

"I understand your fear. I'm going to help you into my buggy and take you where I can see to your injury. Do you understand that I'm a friend?" Doc leaned down. The man groaned and tried to evade Doc's hands.

"Cain't go back. Gonna be free! Got to keep a goin' if I can." The man's shirt was torn and hanging in strips. Blood was seeping down one shoulder.

"I will help you get to freedom if you will let me help you up and into my buggy. I'm not going to turn you in. You have my solemn promise." Doc bent over and pulled the man up. He put his arms around him and as he stood up the man started to fall back down. Doc pulled him over his shoulder and walked back to the buggy.

His horse nervously pulled at the reins when Doc approached. "It's all right boy, just going to put a little more weight in the buggy. That's it, thaaat's it." Doc took hold of the reins and pulled back gently. The horse stilled and Doc placed the man on the floor of the buggy where he wouldn't be as likely to be seen from a distance. Doc took a blanket he always kept in the buggy and tucked it around the man. He was going to have to take a chance and see if Mary Leland would help him. For some reason he felt the kind, soft-spoken woman would help him. Mary and her son Tom seemed like the kind of folks who would help anyone who was ill or injured. He'd have to trust his instincts about people.

Doc picked up the reins and snapped them. The horse took off and soon was galloping down the road. It was only another mile or so to Mary Leland's home. Doc hoped the men hunting for this man were not too close by. Hopefully, he could hide him and take care of his wounds without anyone knowing he had helped him. He was about to trust his life and the life of this poor escaped slave to someone he barely knew. Only God could guide him now.

Mary was mixing herbs and tying them together to hang under her porch eaves to dry when she heard a buggy turn into her yard. Tom was leaning against the open front door playing his harmonica. They stopped and watched Doc Phillips quickly gallop up to the porch and pull his horse to a stop. There was a large mound on the floor next to him. He jumped down and pulled the blanket down revealing the injured black man.

"Can you help me young Tom?" Doc looked around while Tom hurried over to help him. "I'm going to trust that I have come to the right place," he said as he pulled the man up on the porch and into the cabin.

"Why, what have you brought us, Dr. Phillips?" Mary asked trying to sound innocent. If her instincts were right, he had an escaped slave in his arms. She followed them inside while Doc and Tom laid the man down on the floor. Tom backed up and watched in surprise as Doc revealed an obviously injured and feverish black man.

Doc looked up at Mary then Tom. "I swear by all that is holy, Miss Mary, I came to Fairfax, Ohio, to help people. This man is obviously an escaped slave. I want to help him. I am hoping that you will help me. I know you could be in trouble with the law, but I pray that you will help me and show me where I can hide this man after I treat his wounds and fever."

Doc leaned over the man and started removing his torn shirt. "I have heard there are people who help escaped slaves. Perhaps you know of them and could let them know that I need their help. You would need to keep my secret and I swear I would never reveal your help or the help of anyone else." The man groaned then went silent. Doc bent over and listened to his chest. "He's alive, but has fainted." He sat up and looked at Mary and Tom. "Well, can you help me? If not will you allow me to leave without telling the sheriff?"

Mary and Tom smiled at Doc. "You've come to the right place, Dr. Phillips," Mary said with relief, "Tom and I are part of the Underground Railroad. We have a special place to put this poor man while we do everything we can to make him well and put him on the road to safety. They call it the 'road to the Promised Land' you know."

Tom squatted down next to the man and looked at Doc. "We need to put him in our cellar, Doc. He'll be safe there. I'll take some alum powder and eucalyptus and pour it in yore buggy. That'll keep the dogs away from the scent if he's got bounty hunters after im."

Doc heaved a sigh of relief. It was going to be okay. He could relax and concentrate on treating this man's wounds and fever. He smiled at Mary, then Tom, "I heard about people like you – people who are helping the slaves to escape from the southern plantations. This Underground Railroad -- I want to help, I swear I do."

Doc gently lifted the man, "I'm hoping to convince you that I'm not a spy and I won't for any reason divulge the names of the people you work with or any facts I learn about how you are helping the slaves escape. Mary, I will treat this man for fever and infection if you will keep him here for me. Do you believe me?" Doc waited for Mary to reply.

"Alright, Dr. Phillips, I will believe you. You've already left yourself open to a fine and jail just bringing this man here. Get your medicine bag if you have it in the buggy, then you and Tom can bring him into the cellar." Mary grabbed her basket of herbs and some jars of ointment then hurried outside. Tom was leading Doc to the small barn. They hurried, afraid any moment they would hear the baying of dogs and the pounding of horses' hooves. "Tom, you get this man inside where he will be safe. I'll leave my things here while I go back and put a mixture around Dr. Phillips buggy and the floor of the cabin. You can help the doctor. Hurry now!"

Tom opened the door to the hidden cellar. Only a little light showed them the interior. "I'll light the lantern, Doc after we put him on a pallet."

The man awoke, groaned and started to struggle, "It's okay now," Doc said softly. "We're going to help you. Just relax and let us get you settled. My name's Dr. Phillips and this is Tom. His mother is Mary. They're part of the Underground Railroad. Do you know what that is?" Doc was removing the man's shirt as he talked.

"Yessuh, I do know 'bout dat, but I ain't had the luck to meet up wif no one who was of a mind to git me help. I got caught up by a bounty man and hiz dawg and he tried to whup me and I had a good fight and got away through ah bunch of trees and a big river. I fell under the water and got into a tree that was floatin down then the tree got caught up and stopped movin' so I crawled up into the cornfield. I saw the road and knew I was goner there so I tried to get into the cornfield to hide -- and, well, here you found me, and ah thank you most kindly, suh." The man started moaning and lost consciousness again.

"Let's get this fellow out of these bloody clothes. After I get them off, I think you'd better burn them." Doc and Tom carefully turned the man over. Tom sucked in his breath when he saw the damage someone had done to his back.

"I just don't get it, Doc. How come people can mistreat another man like this? Can't hardly believe in the Bible and bring on this much misery." Tom lifted away what was left of the man's shirt carefully trying not to touch all the blood.

"I know, Tom. In my years of being a doctor, this is a first for me. I've never seen what a whip can do to the body's skin. It's not something we should have to see. I'm sorry you have to be here helping me. But I know this man's going to be mighty thankful as am I." Doc looked up at Tom and his smile was more of a grimace. Tom exchanged a look with him and just nodded his head.

Tom hesitated to tell the doctor that he had seen the damage done to a few of the men and women he and his ma had helped. Maybe someday if he knew him better he could trust him and tell just how much he had seem and done for the escaped slaves. He watched Dr. Phillips as he worked. Tenderly he swabbed the open wounds even though the man wasn't aware that he was being treated.

"The important thing here now as you probably know is that infection can set in and that's where a person can get into real trouble. I can already tell he has a fever. If we can get this all nice and clean and put some ointment on opened skin, we have a chance to get him through the fever. Otherwise, if those cut open places start to fester, we'll have a real fight on our hands to save him." Doc looked up at Tom, "But any way you look at it, this man's not going anywhere for at least week or more. Can you and you mother keep him here that long and care for him? I'll try to stop by, but I can't be too obvious. People might start to wonder why I'm visiting here so often." Doc kept cleaning the man's back until all the dirt had been cleaned away.

"I need to fetch my bag in my buggy. Can you keep these cuts clean while I'm gone? I want to stop the bleeding and oozing if I can." Doc paused and watched Tom. He smiled as he walked out of the cellar into the barn.

Mary was just finishing up with placing the herbs to fool the blood hounds in Doc's buggy and on the floor of the house. "You must have a lot of experience with those herbs if you know they'll be effective."

"Yes, Dr. Phillips. Unfortunately, I've had to do this before. Sheriff Vinton has visited here a few times. The last time he had bounty hunters with him an' they did some damage to my jars that hold my potions. I made it difficult for the bloodhounds to know where they were going." She chuckled. "How is the man doing? He looked like he had a fever. I have some fever medicine all made up if you'd like?" Mary looked uncertain. "I mean, I would understand if you wanted to use your own medicine. I won't take offense if you object to using mine."

"On the contrary, Mrs. Leland. I would be glad to use your potion. If you don't mind my asking – what is the formula that you used to make it?"

Mary guided Doc into the house and showed him the jars and bottles of her medicines. A mortar and pestle still was full of ground powder. She picked up a small bottle and handed it to Doc. "My mother taught me how to make all these potions, ointments and poultices. I've taught Tom now as well. I use ground up willow bark for both pain and fevers."

"After we get our guest settled, will you tell me about all these jars and ointments, and the hanging herbs?" Doc was amazed at the large collection this woman had that she had grown and hunted for in the forest and meadows and then made into medicine.

"I'm surprised, Dr. Phillips, that you have such an open mind about all these things." Mary motioned with her hand. "Our last doctor told everyone who would listen that I was a fake and a swindler. Selling my potions and such was bad for people." Mary chuckled, "It didn't keep most people away though. 'Specially when I ended up helping someone the good doctor had failed to help."

"You're a truly good woman, Mrs. Leland. I heard about how you saved the town during the measles epidemic. I'm just sorry you lost your mother."

"Thank you, Dr. Phillips. Yes, Grannie Rose was a treasure and is very missed by all who knew her. She was a wonderful mother and grandmother to Tom. He's lost both his father and Grannie Rose in such a short time." Mary walked next to Dr. Phillips carrying a basket of herbs and ointment. "Most everyone calls me Mary, Dr. Phillips. But if you would rather not it's okay."

"I would like that very much, Mary, but then you must call me Doc."

"All right. Doc it is." Mary was pleased. This was a good man. If he was half as good a doctor, the town of Fairfax was very lucky. He wasn't the kind of doctor who would look down on her and Tom. She was now sure that everything would be all right.

Mary returned with Doc to the cellar with

medicine to help the man. Doc was pleased to see that Tom had done a very good job cleaning his back. Mary was surprised when Doc used her ointment before he wrapped his back with strips of cloth.

The man awoke as Doc finished wrapped his upper body. "Ah've gotta thank y'all. I wuz hurtin' pretty bad befo." He looked around, "Could I bother y'all for a drink of water? I cain't 'member when I had any, 'cept jus the river an' it was full of mud."

Tom lifted the man's head so he could take a drink from a gourd filled with cold well water. "We'll bring in some food for you if you feel up to havin' some? You'll be very safe in here but we don't have any windows an' we have to close up the door but I can leave a little space open. If you hear any kind of noise, you gotta close it up fast an' be as quiet as you can no matter what you hear outside. Here's another way out if you really get found out. This here opening takes you through a tunnel – it's not long, but it'll take you to the root cellar next door. You'll see a place you can push open and get in there. You understand?" The man nodded head. "I'll leave some candles and matches for ya, umm,…what should we call you?"

The man smiled and took Tom's hand. "Ahm called Zeke, suh. When I git to the Promised Land ahm gonna choose my last name. Ain't right that ah never did have one 'cept fo mah massa's and he was a orn'rey man to be sure, and it ain't likely ah wud evah want his name."

Tom shook Zeke's hand, "Well you can call me Tom. And I'm glad to make your acquaintance." Tom looked up at Mary and Doc, "And this is my mother Mary and Doc."

"Ahm very glad to meet y'all. Ain't never had nobody to be nice ta me and treat me good like y'all. Ah ain't got no way to repay yur kindness 'cept to thank y'all."

"Zeke, you don't need to worry yourself over paying. Just by being safe and getting you to the Promised Land is all the payment we need. Now you just rest yourself and we'll be back later to check on you." Mary and Doc started to go outside when she turned back, "Can you read, Zeke?"

"No'um. It's agin the law fur us slaves to be book learned. I guess that's anothah thang ahm gonna git mahsef whin I git der." He smiled and looked so happy, Mary's eyes felt teary.

"Well, I wish I had something for you to do in here. I guess you'll just have to rest yourself and get well." Mary smiled and leaned to feel Zeke's forehead. She looked at Doc, "I think we'd better work on that fever he's got. Should I give him some willow bark or would you rather give him something else?"

Doc was thoughtful and watched Zeke for a moment. "Let's see how he does with the willow bark. I'll come back tomorrow morning unless you send Tom to get me sooner. I think you've done a good job. Let's get the willow bark in him with lots of water then cover him up and let him sleep for a while. You can keep an eye on him tonight." Doc walked toward the door and looked around. "This is quite a clever room you have here. Did your husband build it?"

Tom stood up next to his ma and placed his arm around her shoulder, "No, my pa had died before that. It was me and Samuel who dug all this out. We worked for days hauling the dirt out and putting out in the orchard. We had to make sure no one saw all the fresh dirt so's they wouldn't wonder where it was comin' from." He chuckled, I thought we'd never dig down far enough. Then we had to make sure you can't tell there's a doorway here." Tom looked around, "Yep, I'm purty proud of what we did. Can't tell you how many times we've used this room."

The three walked out together. Tom made sure the small door was partially opened, but that the bags and tools that were used to camouflage the door were close by in case it had to be hidden.

"While I'm here, Mary, I sure would like for you to tell me about your medicines that you use."

"Why I'd be pleased to show you and tell you about them." Mary walked ahead of Doc and Tom. "My mother, Grannie Rose, taught me everything about potions, poultices and how to make ointments for just about every ailment there is." Doc walked up to the porch and Mary pointed above their heads. "This is where I hang the herbs and such after Tom and I gather them. Once they are dry we use the mortar and pestle and grind them into powder. We only have a couple of Eucalyptus trees around here. I steam the leaves and use them for colds and I boil them down and make an oil that I use on people's chest for congestion and fever."

Doc walked into the house and over to the area where Mary had baskets and bottles neatly lined up. "And what do all of these containers hold?"

"These baskets are filled with herbs which I chop up then soak in water for a day before I mix them together and make ointments with them." Mary held a basket up to Doc's nose, "I also dry them out like these in this basket. Then I put them in some hot water and after a little while they become a poultice. I put them on injuries and cover it with a bandage." Mary watched Doc walk along the shelf and sniff into each basket.

"Mmmm. I can smell mint in this one." Doc picked up a leaf and crushed it between his fingers and held it under his nose.

"Yes. That's mint and this," Mary held it up to Doc's nose, "is chamomille. I make tea out of these. They help with upset tummies and indigestion."

"I have no idea what you do with these." Doc picked up what looked like a root of some large bush or small tree. "Is this a root of some kind of plant? What would you do with these things?"

Mary took a jar down from the shelf. It was filled with an oily substance. She opened the jar, took Doc's hand and smeared some on the top, rubbing it in. "These are roots and bark from trees. Tom cuts them away and I dry them out then boil them for a long, long time. Then, I take olive oil or oil from almonds and mix them together. It makes a powerful mix that I can make into salves for healing any kind of wound."

"Well I'll be." Doc looked at Mary and Tom, "This is nothing short of amazing Mary. Tom, can you make all of these things as well?"

"Yes sir, I can. My Grannie Rose had me grinding up these herbs when I just a youngin'. She'd take me out to the fields and talk to me the whole time she was pickin', tellin' me this and that about all these things here." Tom picked a large jar that held a sticky yellow goo. "This here is about the best honey you ever tasted. I know where all the best bee hives are and I know when to open em up and take the honey away. We use it for eatin' as well as healin'." Tom opened the jar and held it out to Doc. Doc stuck his finger in the jar and pulled out a finger dripping with honey.

"Mmmm,mmm,mm! You're right, Tom. This is about the best I ever had." Doc smiled. "Now just what is it you put honey on?"

"Why I use it like my other healing salves and ointments. It's real good for wounds and really good for burns. Especially those that get swelled up and red."

"You don't say." Doc was so amazed by this woman and the knowledge she had just shared with him. He was thinking that he just might use some of Mary's medicines along with the ones he was accustomed to using.

"This has been a really nice day, Mary. I can't tell you how glad I am to have met you and Tom, and have you share all this with me. I would like to able to visit you whenever I'm out this way."

"You're very welcome any time, Doc. We'll enjoy your company any time." Mary handed Doc a large jar of honey. "You take this to Desdemona. She'll make good use of it for you I'm sure." Mary smiled and walked Doc out to his buggy. Tom followed along, "I'll take a regular look at Zeke. He might need me during the night if his fever gets going. I know what to do, but you might want to stop by tomorrow if you've a chance. Just to…..you know…take a look."

Tom liked Doc and hoped they would see him often.

"Not a problem, Tom. I'll be here sometime in the afternoon. Thanks again, and you both stop by when you're in town."

Chapter 12

'Doc' Tom

Doc's visits with Mary and Tom began a regular routine. Zeke healed up enough within a week's time that he was able to leave and move on the next leg of his journey. Doc wondered how he knew where to go, so one afternoon, he and Tom were sharing lemonade on the porch and Tom told him how the Underground Railroad worked. Doc was so amazed especially when Tom mentioned the Bradley sisters being a part of the organization. Doc didn't ask many questions but he thought he now knew why Homer and Wilson had looked guilty when he had asked them where the escaped slaves went.

Tom would stop by Doc's when he was in town. Soon it was apparent to Doc that Tom came into town just to see him. He would walk into Doc's office and study all the instruments carefully. Doc even gave him a few textbooks he had from medical school. Tom had read them and then asked if he could have more. Some afternoons, if Doc wasn't busy, he and Tom would sit in the kitchen drinking milk and eating Desdemona's cookies and talk about the books and questions Tom had about treatment of illnesses and surgery.

One day Doc put Lissie and Lottie up on his examination table and taught Tom how to use the funny looking tool that you put in your ears and on a person's chest. Doc laughed and laughed when Tom's eyes almost bugged out when he heard their heart beat. "Gawww-ly Doc!! This is about the most amazing thing I ever heard! I've listened to a person's heart beat before, but never this loud! I can't wait to tell Ma about this. What's it called?"

Doc handed Lissie and Lottie each a candy from his pocket and they giggled and ran out of the room. "It's called a stethoscope. It is pretty amazing isn't it?" Doc put the ear pieces back in Tom's ears. "Now listen real close. You can hear the rhythm of the heartbeat going thump, thump. That's the sound of the blood rushing through the chambers of the heart." Doc walked over to his book shelves and took down a large book. After thumbing through several pages, he came to some pictures. "See here? That's a picture of the heart. And see here? That's a picture of the chambers of the heart. These here are called valves."

Tom was fascinated. "Can I sometime come here and read these big books and see all the pictures?"

"Of course. Any time you want. I can explain anything you don't understand. But watch out. There are pictures of what men and women look like without clothes. That may be a bit of a surprise." Doc watched Tom's face. Tom turned a few more pages then slapped the book closed.

"I don't know anything about girl parts," he whispered.

Doc couldn't help himself, he laughed out loud. "Even to me the human body is still pretty amazing, Tom. God did a glorious thing when he made us."

"I'll say. And what's this thing here?" Tom held up a long-handled device with curved arms on the end, sort of like scissors without the blades.

Doc rubbed the back of his neck. "Well, those are called forceps. They are used for child birth."

Tom's face got red and he quickly put the forceps down. "I don't know anything about that. But my ma has birthed a lot of babies over the years." He looked down, "I don't hardly know what I'd do if my ma wasn't around for that. I just make sure she's got lots of boiling water and towels, then I disappear outside with the men while they wait. Sure is a lot of screamin' and moanin' going on. That I do know." Tom quickly moved on to another glass-enclosed cupboard.

Doc just smiled and waited for Tom to ask another question. "I haven't done any stitchin' up of folks yet. Ma's done that a lot, too." Tom opened a leather pouch and looked at all the needles inside. "Some of these are almost round. The ones Ma has are just straight."

Doc picked up a needle, "Yes, the reason they are curved is so that they go through the two pieces of skin easier for the one doing the stitching." Doc moved his hand as though he was actually stitching some skin. "I'll bet your ma uses string, right?"

"Yeah, she does. What do you use?"

Doc handed Tom a spool of string, but it didn't look like the string his ma used. "What's this made out of?"

"That's cat gut. Used to be made from sheep intestines, but this works better. When I have to take stitches inside someone, it melts away after a time."

"Well I'll be swaggered. That's pretty amazing." Tom pulled out the string. "So this stuff melts, huh?"

"Yes. But when I stitch on the outside of the body, I wait a week and remove the stitches. That way there is less of a scar."

"I gotcha. I've taken out stitches that ma's done before. I can see how the longer there're in they might pull the skin down. It don't bother me none to remove em."

"Have you thought about going to school to be a doctor, Tom? How old are you?"

"I'm almost eighteen. How old do you have to be to go?" Tom didn't believe he could ever consider going to medical school. His ma could never afford to send him.

"You're about the right age. How much

schooling have you had?" Doc leaned back against the examination table and crossed his arms.

"Well, my ma and Grannie Rose taught me to read with the Bible. I learned my figures by all sorts of ways. I'm pretty good at learning. I like to read. We don't have many books, but my pa had a book of some plays by Shakespeare. I like those and I've read that book several times." Tom straightened some jars on the shelf, "I don't know if I could ever go to a big school like medical school. That's way beyond a fella like me. I'll just be a healer like my ma." He looked over at Doc. "But ya know? I could maybe help you out from time to time." Doc chuckled, "You bet you can. Anytime you want, I'd be glad to have you. Tom, you and your mother are what they called in medical school a homeopathic type doctor and I am an allopathic type doctor." Tom smiled and shuffled his feet, embarrassed by Doc calling him a doctor.

"Oh, Doc. What are you sayin'? I'm not a real doctor. You had all that school and I just learned herbs and potions and such from Grannie Rose and my ma."

"Tom, you and your mother, Mary, are two of the best doctors I know. By homeopathic I mean that you use herbs and powders to make your patients well. But you can set broken arms and legs, birth babies, and pull teeth just like real doctors do --- maybe even better than some."

Doc smiled and laid his arm on Tom's shoulder, "As an allopathic doctor, I treat my patients with patent medicine and surgery when needed. But I think I have the best of both worlds now because of you. From now on I'm going to include all the herbs and powders you use as well as all the medicines I use to treat my patients. That's going to make me an even better doctor." He smiled at Tom and swatted his shoulder before walking away. Tom smiled, would wonders never cease! He was almost like a doctor, by golly. If he could only be as good as Doc. That would be his goal.

All during the summer, Tom came in to Doc's office to help him. Summer months were slower for sickness, but accidents were plentiful so that Tom learned a lot more about stitching people up and putting splints on broken arms and legs. Tom was very competent and not at all bothered by blood or broken bones. He was steadily reading Doc's medical books and asking questions about what he read, constantly challenging Doc's knowledge. They formed a friendship that gave Doc great pleasure and pride in the young Tom.

Doc was also becoming a regular at the Bradley house for Saturday night dinner. Big John always greeted him on the front porch where they would be seated for a quiet chat about the 'travelers' and information that was passed along as they were transported to another depot. Beatrice and Kathryn would join them and then talk would turn to the possibility of war and the effect it would have on the people of Fairfax and the town.

Doc enjoyed talking to Beatrice. He valued her opinions and sense of humor. She was an attractive woman; her chestnut brown hair always pulled back and wound in a figure eight with just a small curl by her ears, and her figure perfectly covered by soft colored dresses that showed only a little of the top of her full breasts. Beatrice always wore a gold locket around her neck and sometimes small pearl earrings. Her sister, Kathryn, was also very attractive, but more quiet and shy. She dressed like Beatrice but never wore any jewelry except a gold band on her left hand. Doc knew that she had once been married and was a widow. Kathryn wore her light brown hair braided in a coronet on top of her head.

The Bradley sisters were as regal as princesses, but were kind and gentle, not affected by their obvious wealth and education. They were the owners of several successful businesses in Fairfax, with many employees, yet they treated everyone as an equal. It was clear to Doc that Beatrice was the one who made most of the decisions. She was an impressive woman and Doc enjoyed being included in their home. Amazingly these two women were a major part of Ohio's Underground Railroad, risking their own freedom and wealth to participate in rescuing perhaps hundreds of escaped slaves.

Big John joined their conversation saying he was worried about what would happen to his people, meaning the slaves who were still in the southern states on plantations if war was declared. When he preached on Sundays in his church attended by the black people, most of them employees of the Bradleys', they still had loved ones in the south and they worried about what would happen to them. There was so much they didn't know, with so much speculation and gossip, that emotions and tempers were high.

Big John sighed, "I wish'd I cud hep em all, I do. If we do have a war, I hope there will be sumthin' fur me ta do. I feel as if the Lord is pushin' me somewhares – I jus' don' know where that is." He looked at Doc with a pleading expression on his kindly face.

"Well, Big John, none of us is sure what the next year is going to bring. If we do have a war, many say it won't last long. It seems to me you are already helping folks what with your church and the Railroad." Doc patted Big John's shoulder, "Only time will tell us what our role will be. For now, we keep helping your people on the road to the Promised Land."

Chapter 13

The Night Riders

The Fairfax newspaper put out a special edition and posted the front page on the main office window about a fellow named John Brown and a group of his followers who raided an arsenal in a place called Harper's Ferry. They had had a big stand-off and battle with soldiers and town folk. They eventually lost and Brown was hanged, but they had stirred up folks and tried to get all the slaves to revolt. When a patron at Bender's Tavern made the announcement about how they had tried to rile folks up, Hank Colby's group mounted their horses and rode through town whooping, hollering and shooting their guns.

The fall night air was cool as Tom rode through the trees toward the place where he would meet up with a conductor and take three escaped slaves on to his cabin. Ma had prepared their root cellar to hide the folks he would be bringing back home. The note had been brief as it always was, with no signature. "3 riders. Round tree rock by midnight." Tom pushed his hat way down on his head, tucked his coat collar tighter around his neck, and lowered his head against the breeze as he rode. Always listening to the night sounds as he rode, he thought he heard thunder in the black night.

Samuel Washington, a black man who worked at Bender's Tavern, was sound asleep in his cabin behind the tavern when he was awakened by the pounding of horses' hooves as they flew down the road. He jumped out of bed to peer through his window curtain. It was just past midnight. A group of men he saw on horses made his skin crawl. Especially when he saw they were wearing bandannas over their faces and holding lit torches as they rode.

Samuel ran outside after they passed and saw Jacob and Stella Bender standing outside their house in their nightclothes huddled together, fear on their faces. "They're up to no good, Samuel," Jacob hollered. "Might be a good idea if one of us followed them to find out where they're going."

"I'll go, Mr. Bender. I can ride fast without a saddle. No reason to bother the sheriff. He'd only call me names and go back to sleep anyway. But at least I can get to the Bradleys' house for a bucket brigade to save as much as possible if it's not too far." Samuel ran back inside, quickly dressed and raced outside to get Mr. Bender's horse. Bender had already put a bridle on the horse and was standing ready to boost Samuel up on the horse's back.

"I'll head on over to see if I can help, too. You stay outta them fellas way now, hear? You're too valuable an employee to lose." Bender patted Samuel's leg.

"You mean slave, doncha Mr. Bender?" He laughed as he kicked his heel into the horse's side and galloped away. Because of the Fugitive Slave Act, it was a secret only a few knew that Samuel was a freeman.

The Bender's Tavern, was known as "bend yer arm" by some of the townspeople because folks came there to drink from large tankards, share information and gossip. The town newspaper owner had a permanent table there where he spent his days listening and making notes. Secretly, the Benders were abolitionists and they pretended to own Samuel for his own safety, but he was really a freed slave, a freeman. He wore his freedom papers in a secret pouch inside his belt. Jacob's brother had owned Samuel and through manumission: when an owner died he could give freedom papers to free all the slaves on his plantation, he told all the freed slaves to go north as far as they could. He told Samuel to go to his brother's tavern for safety. Samuel had heard about the Underground Railroad and followed it to Fairfax, Ohio, and the Benders. They agreed to take him in to work there and help them. The Benders treated Samuel like a son. Because of the Fugitive Slave Act, they pretended that they had purchased him from Jacob's brother. They had fake papers stating that fact if they ever had to prove ownership. Conductors alerted Samuel and the Benders to every group who came through the underground route near Fairfax.

Samuel helped the Underground Railroad by passing on information that he heard from customers in the tavern. Bender's Tavern had a secret room they used to hide escaped slaves when an emergency arose and they couldn't make it to the next destination. They were good people, the Benders. Another reason for Samuel wanting to know who was escaping was that he was waiting and searching for someone. He'd been in love with a woman who lived on a neighboring plantation. They vowed to marry, but when Samuel was freed he found she had been sold and sent away to another plantation. Their last time together, she vowed with tears streaming down her cheeks, to escape and find him in Ohio. Samuel prayed each night for that day to happen. He prayed that Suedaleen could be one of the escaped slaves he knew were somewhere in the night right now. A slither of fear went through him as he thought of those dangerous men he was following who hoped to find the escaped slaves trying to get to the next depot. He prayed that someday he would find her and men like these would not.

Samuel Washington tried to be invisible as much as possible in the Tavern so people would hardly notice him. His last name he had chosen in honor of a man who had been a brave soldier and father to the country. Samuel was a very quiet man; always moving softly. Keeping his face void of expression, he listened to all the Tavern patrons' conversations and reported to the Benders and the Bradley sisters or to Big John, his close friend. Jacob Bender and Samuel hunted each week and often used that time to move slaves on the Underground Railroad.

Samuel carried the 100-pound wooden kegs over his shoulder as easily as another man would carry a 25-pound sack of flour. Gently, he placed them in the wooden cradles behind the bar. He was a good man with a keen intelligence. He could read, and do sums as a result of his previous owner's gratitude for Samuel's loyalty and service.

It was against the law to teach slaves how to read and write. He was grateful for his good luck in having been owned by a good man and then given his freedom. He was better-educated than most of the people who came in to the tavern. His only wish was that he could share this good life with his love, Suedaleen. Even if he had married Suedie, her status would not have guaranteed that she could stay with him. Samuel was bound that someday he would find her and they would marry. They would "jump the broom" together. He saved almost every penny he earned at Bender's Tavern. Someday he would leave and go looking for Suedie. With the talk of war, that journey might be sooner than he knew.

The group of mean-spirited men who were

regulars in the tavern stayed in back drinking and bragging about how the south was going to rise up and take over the union, ignored Samuel's presence unless they loudly demanded he serve them. It was not unusual for one of them to deliberately trip Samuel when his hands were full of steins overflowing with beer. They would laugh and call him 'dumb niggah.' The men treated him like a pet dog most of the time. Once in a while one of them would trip and kick Samuel when he was on the ground. When Jacob or Stella would chastise the men about their behavior and wild talk, they threatened to burn down the tavern and the Benders' home which was behind the tavern. Several times, the sheriff was in the Tavern and never intervened to help Jacob and Samuel. He was afraid of the gang of men and had joined their ranks. Samuel didn't want to call attention to himself. He did his job of bringing in the kegs of beer, cleaning the floor and tables, and waiting on customers when Jacob and Stella were too busy. It was the price he had to pay while waiting for word of Suedie so they could start their life together.

The Fugitive Slave Act, also known as the "Bloodhound Law," because of the dogs used to hunt down escaped slaves, meant that officials who did not arrest runaway slaves could be fined $1,000. Law officers had to arrest anyone aiding escaped slaves in any way; food or shelter. People accused would receive six months in jail and the $1,000 fine. Anyone who captured slaves received a bonus or work promotion. In addition to this, slaves no longer had a right to a trial and were locked up, chained, and returned to their owners. Most all people were afraid of the law and those who enforced it. Hank Colby's gang got more agitated with the talk of war. Tavern arguments included Copperheads: people who argued that there should be no drafting of men to go and fight. They saw blacks as inferior people and thought the union should stay together and just let slavery take place in the south. Men who were Copperheads ran for office and were elected in Illinois, Indiana, and Southern Ohio.

The Fugitive Slave Act allowed the Copperheads what they viewed as hunting rights. Collecting the bounty given when slaves were caught gave them money and a feeling of power. They started night rides: hunting and scaring the people they thought were abolitionists and would help escaped slaves. They torched and burned down farms, fields, barns, and homes of the people who argued or disagreed with them but only in the dead of night wearing masks. Most people figured out who the men were but could do nothing to make them stop.

Tom heard the thunder coming closer now and knew it was men on horses. He quickly looked around for a place to hide and moved further into the trees. He was still too close to the road but thought the dark night would hide him.

Soon he saw light and saw the masked men riding hard towards him carrying torches lit and ready to burn someone's fields, barns or houses. Tom waited several minutes until he started the horse up again. Luckily, where he was going was to the right and the riders had stayed left going down the road. There had to be a way to stop what he knew they were going to do from happening, but Tom couldn't follow them. There was more important business he had to attend to.

The employees and their families who worked at the Bradley Mill and Wagon Works lived in a series of cottages built by Mr. Bradley for them. The cottages were within walking distance from the Bradley Mill and Wagon Works along the Ohio River. They were attractive small abodes with two and three bedrooms, furnished kitchens, and room for vegetable gardens in the back. The rent for the cottages was reasonable and were for the workers who had a wife and family. A boarding house at the edge of town took care of the single men. The black families and workers lived further down the road, but their homes were the same as the cottages for the white workers. The three single black men lived together in one of the cottages.

Beatrice had received notice from Samuel that he had overheard gang members talking about their next night ride. They talked about setting more fires and the mill was mentioned because the Bradleys employed black workers instead of them. One of Colby's gang had an argument with the manager of the Mill and Wagon Works, Wilson Meyers. He had fired the man for being lazy and insolent when told to work.

Because of Samuel's warning, Beatrice and Wilson set up a warning system with night guards after the mill closed. Three mill workers were assigned each night to patrol the grounds without being seen. A siren that was activated by turning a large handle on a device would put out a shrill wail that could be heard for miles. Wilson Meyers had designed a large cylinder made of a stout barrel. Attached to the cylinder was a hand pump that sprayed water to put out fires in the lumber which was stored in stacks around the perimeter of the mill works and in the summer months became dry as tinder. The cylinder was mounted inside a specially built wagon so that it could be moved by the large draft horses when needed. The barrel held rainwater and could be filled from the nearby river in case of fire since the mill was surrounded by piles of lumber and could easily be destroyed by fire. A fire hose with a large nozzle was attached so that water could be sprayed on buildings or piles of lumber to stop fires.

When Colby's gang made plans to set another fire, their target was the Bradleys' Mill. Samuel told Miz Beatrice that he heard them talking in the tavern and figured out their mill would be the next target.

The siren could be heard in the cottages of the mill workers alerting them to some type of danger. Big John heard the siren blaring and woke the household up. All hands in the house would be needed if there was a fire at the mill. Quickly he organized the staff to be ready to board the large buckboard and go to the mill. A bucket brigade would be made up of mostly the women to ferry buckets filled with water from the river when needed to help refill the water wagon.

Beatrice told Big John to have a wagon loaded with coffee and sandwiches for the workers who would be at the mill for whatever emergency the siren was warning them about. When they arrived at the mill, the fire was almost completely out. The mill workers had arrived in time and together had put the fire out before hardly anything more than one stack of wood had been damaged.

While working together to put out the fire, they heard a scream and saw a man running with flames on his arm. From the shadows of the stacked wood, another two men ran toward the burning man. The mill workers let them run away. They had no desire to go after them.

When Big John, Beatrice, and Kathryn arrived they were pleased to see that none of the mill workers had been injured and the mill had been saved. Before they started to clean up the damage, a cheer went up and the smiling, smoke-faced men patted each other on the back and laughed. They were proud of the job they had done together. Beatrice and Kathryn joined in and thanked the men. A monetary reward would be given to all the men for saving the Mill and Wagon Works. Hereafter, the new security measures would be in place each night.

The day after the fire at the mill, a scruffy young boy knocked on Mary Leland's door, hat in hand. "Miz Mary, my ma tol' me ta fetch ya. My pa's got a rite sore burn on his arm and needs yur healin' potions fur it. He's hollerin' sumpthin fierce! Can ya come quick, Miz Mary?"

Mary wanted to take pity on this poor scraggly little boy, but she immediately had a suspicion about a man having a burned arm, especially if it was one of Hank Colby's. If this boy was related to someone who tried to burn down the mill there was no way she'd help. She would alert Beatrice, Wilson Meyers, and the sheriff first. Mary was not sure that the sheriff would do anything about Colby and his gang if they had set this fire, but she had to tell him anyway. "Which youngin' are you?" Mary frowned down on the boy.

"Name's Willie Colby, Miz Mary." The boy nervously strangled his dirty hat and swatted his leg with it. He was impatient to be gone with Miz Mary and her medicine for pa.

"I heard the siren at the mill go off last night," she looked down at Willie. "Tom went over and helped fight a big fire." Mary leaned closer to Willie's face, "Is that where your pa got burned, Willie?"

The boy kept swatting his leg and wouldn't look up at Mary. "Cain't say," he choked out. "Please, Miz Mary, Ma's frettin' sumpthin' awful and Pa's gonna thrash me sumpthin fierce if'n I don't come home with a potion," he whined. Finally he looked up at Mary, pleading.

Mary gritted her teeth and looked away. She didn't want this poor boy to be punished, but Lord help her --- she just couldn't help Hank Colby. "You go on back to your ma, Willie. Tell her I'll be comin' round soon and take a look at your pa. You just tell them I was out of the right potion and I'm makin' some up and I'll be there shortly," Mary said and she guided Willie out the door. Mary shook her head. Colby deserved to suffer, but his poor family didn't. Her first stop would be at the Bradley house. Beatrice could notify Wilson Meyers. After saving the mill he would be very interested to hear about a burned arm on that no-good Hank Colby.

Mary was right. The sheriff said that wasn't enough proof. Nobody had seen Colby at the fire so there wasn't any reason to bring him in. Besides, he was badly burned and was suffering. Beatrice and Wilson Meyers just shook their heads. The only way Colby would be punished was if someone had witnessed him and his gang or if he confessed, which would never happen.

Mary took a small jar of burn ointment to the Colby farm and told his wife that she would not look at his burn and there would be no more ointment for him. Mrs. Colby nodded her head without looking at Mary. She was a poor skinny, bedraggled woman married to a worthless mean man. Mary returned to her home feeling sad for Colby's family. Their whole farm was a rundown mess. She knew the children probably often went hungry. Someday, she prayed, may God punish Colby for all his evil deeds.

Later that day, Mary told Beatrice and Kathryn about Colby after she talked to Sheriff Vinton who dismissed her accusation that Colby had been burned in the Mill fire. The sheriff told her to mind her own business. Colby probably hurt himself working at home. Mary practically choked, "Have you seen the Colby place, Sheriff Vinton? It's a pig sty. Hank Colby hasn't done a lick of work as long as he's lived there."

"As I've told you Miz Mary, you mind your own business. When I have time I'll go out and talk to Colby. He might just have fallen into a candle burnin' after he got home from Bender's Tavern."

Mary shook her head and walked away. She knew her suspicions would go nowhere with the sheriff.

Chapter 14

Colby's Demise

About a week later in the early evening, Tom was walking through the apple orchard. He had worked long hours picking the apples. Some men from the Bradley farm had come over and helped him. They kept several bushels for their work and the rest Tom would take to the Mercantile Store, except for two bushels which would be put down in the cellar. Ma could make a real good apple pie, and Tom enjoyed sitting on the porch eating the juicy fruit at the end of the day. Tomorrow should be the last day of picking since there were only a few trees left to pick.

Tom heard a commotion and stopped to see what the noise was. Hank Colby was in his apple orchard! There was no way Colby was going to trespass here. Swiftly, Tom walked toward the pair. He would order them to get off his property.

Colby had his arm around a little boy who struggled to keep Colby from falling down. The man was hobbling more than walking. As Tom got closer to them he saw that Colby's face was red and blotchy. He held a dirty hanky and swiped his face with it. His left arm was wrapped in a dirty, bloody bandage which he held against his chest.

"Good! You can hep me git to yur house.

I gotta have yur ma take care ah me right quick."

"That's not gonna happen, Colby. You get off my property this minute. Ma gave your wife ointment for your burned arm. That's more than you deserve since you probably got those burns by trying to burn down the Bradley Mill. Now get. off. my. land!" Tom turned away and Colby lurched forward and grabbed his arm. His hand was blazing hot. Tom could see that he was burning up with fever.

"Now you looka here! Yur jist a no-'count northern lover who don't know 'bout respectin' hiz elders. Ahm a tellin' yu to gimme yur arm so's I kin git to yur ma! Now hep me out. This here youngin' ain't no hep atall. He's 'bout as worthless as y'all." Colby knocked the little boy down with the back of his hand. The boy scooted out of the way.

Tom wrenched his arm away and Colby staggered, almost falling down. "I will not help you and my ma's not gonna give you anything more. You got yourself in this fix. Go ask your gang to help you out."

"Why you worthless piece of shit, boy! You ain't no better'n yur pa! He was a north lover, too. He wuz ahways puttin hisself up like he wuz sumpthin. Oh yeah! He got hiz comeuppance that's fo shure. Haw, haw! Yu betcha he did! Why he just stood and stared at me when I shot im."

Tom gasped! "What the hell are you

saying? You shot my pa?" He was shocked! No one knew what had happened to him. He was found days later when he didn't return from hunting.

Colby's mouth hung open and his eyes were wide. He looked scared.

A blast of fire hit Tom's brain! This dirty, lazy excuse for a man had killed his pa! Without thinking Tom flew at Colby using his head he hit him square in the gut, knocking him to the ground. The air whooshed out of Colby's lungs. Tom's hands were fists and he started hitting Colby's face, pounding and pounding on him until he could scarcely breathe. His hands found Colby's neck and he squeezed and squeezed until small hands pulled at his arms.

"Mister Tom! Mister Tom! Yur gonna kill im! Ya gotta stop Mister Tom!"

Tom rocked back on his feet, almost sitting on Colby whose face was now covered in blood. The only sound he heard was his own harsh breaths and the little boy sniffing next to him.

"Is he dead?"

Tom just sat staring at Colby.

The little boy got up and started to run back the way they had come, then stopped and slowly walked back.

"Mister Tom?" The boy slowly walked to Tom and Colby.

Colby still wasn't moving. Tom stood up

still gasping for breath.

With a sneer the boy said, "I hope he is dead. He ain't never treated me an my fam'ly like we wuz his kin. He likes to hit us and he laughs if we cry. He beats my ma sumthin fierce. Sumtimes she cain't even walk. One time he hit her so hard her jaw all swelled up an' she cud hardly eat. So if'n he is dead, I'll hep you bury the ol jackass."

Tom squatted down next to Colby and shook his shoulder. Nothing. No movement or moan. Tom started to sweat. He thought he once had killed Colby when he struck him with a large tree branch. But he hadn't. Not then. Dear God! What had he done now?

The young boy reached out and poked Colby's face. When he didn't respond, the boy squatted down next to Tom. "I think we should bury im and not tell a soul." He looked up into Tom face. "I kin hep ya. No one's gonna miss this ol fool. Even his gang duz'n cum 'round no more since he got this burn. I cud jus tell'im he went to town an' never cum back. My ma ain't gonna miss im that's fur sure, it is."

Tom was starting to feel strange. The anger that took over his mind and body was draining away. He reached his hand out and held it on Colby's neck to feel for his pulse. There was nothing that he could feel. He dragged his hand down to Colby's chest and pressed down to feel his heart beating. Nothing. Tom laid his head on Colby's chest and listened, shushing the boy to be quiet. Again – nothing. This time he had killed Hank Colby.

The boy reached into Colby's pocket and pulled out some coins and put them in his own pocket. He got up and went around to the other side and reached into that pocket and pulled out a pocket watch.

Swiftly Tom reached out and captured the boy's hand. "What have you got?" Tom let go of the boy and took the watch out of his hand. He held the watch to his chest and looked up at the sky, tears in his eyes. "It's my pa's watch. It's my pa's." Gently he held out the watch to see it better. "He must have taken it when he killed him."

"Well, looks like yuh got it back now. Ain't gonna do him no good. Belongs tuh you anyhow." The boy placed his hand on Tom's shoulder. "Don't feel bad, Mister Tom. He was a bad man. I think there's a heap of bad things he's done to folks. You got my word I ain't gonna tell nobody nuthin. We can spit an make a 'pack' by shakin' hands. Thata way ah gotta swear to y'all and y'all tuh me that we ain't never gonna tell on no a'count what we did here."

Tom cradled the watch against his chest. With his other hand he spit on it first then took the boy's hand and shook it. "I don't know. I feel like I should tell someone but I'm not sure I want to. I think I'll go over to the Bradleys and

talk to Big John. He'll tell me what I should do.
I can't tell my ma just yet." Tom got up and
started walking then stopped and turned back.
"Want to come along?"

The boy looked at his pa then at Tom. "I
think ah'll jus wait fur y'all. Ya gonna cum right
back, ain'tcha? It's gonna git dark soon an' I don
wanna be out here alone wif him."

"I promise. You wait here and I'll be
back as soon as I can with Big John." Tom
started walking fast then broke into a run. He was
out of breath when he reached the Bradley's
house. Tom ran around the back to the kitchen
and rapped on the door. The cook, Floreen,
answered, "Why Tom! Are you okay? You look
a fright! Come on in and sit down right now.
Y'all need sum water?"

"No, Floreen, I need to speak to Big John.
Is he here?" Tom leaned back on the doorframe
and tried to catch his breath.

"Why a course he is. Ah'll git im right
quick."

Floreen started to leave the kitchen and
Tom stopped her, "I just need to talk to Big John.
I don't want to disturb Miss Bea or Miss Kathryn.
It should only take a minute if you please."

Floreen looked puzzled, "Ok, Tom. Ah'll
be right back."

In a few minutes Big John pushed through
the kitchen door. He was only wearing an
undershirt and his arms were damp like he had

been washing up. "What's wrong, Tom? Floreen said you busted in here like a flock of devils wuz on yur tail."

"Big John, I need your help right away if you can." Tom looked at Floreen then at Big John.

"Ok. I kin cum wif you right now if'n you need me Tom. Is yur mama all right?"

"Yeah, ma's just fine. This is something else. I just need you, Big John. Right now." Tom started out the back door and Floreen stopped them, "You fellas gonna be all right? You want I should go with y'all?"

"No, Floreen. We'll be ok. I just need Big John to help me with something. He'll be right back."

Big John walked out with Tom and as they got to the bottom of the outside stairs he took Tom's arm and turned him around. "What's this about, Tom? Somethin's not right here. Tell me now what it tiz."

"I need you to trust me, Big John. There's something I need to show you." Tom pulled Big John and started walking. "We need to hurry. It's getting dark and we have to hurry."

"Ok, Tom. Let's go see what's gotcha so riled up."

When Tom and Big John reached the apple orchard it didn't take long and Tom could see the little boy standing near where he had left Hank Colby. As they got closer Big John suddenly started trotting and stopped next to Colby's body.

"Has he moved or tried to breathe while I've been gone?" Tom asked the boy.

"Nope. He ain't moved or breathed a'tall. I think he's daid for shure, Mister Tom."

"Dear God almighty," Big John whispered. Colby's dead?"

"I think so, Big John. I did it, too. I told him to git offa my property and he got mad and started talkin' 'bout what he thought of me and that I was jus' like my pa and that he had killed my pa. I just don't know what happened. I just flew at im and the next I know this boy was pullin' at my arms and my hands were around Colby's neck and.....what do you think I should do, Big John?"

Big John kneeled down next to Colby and leaned close to see if he was breathing. "Yur right, boy. Colby's a dead man, that's fo sho." Big John looked up at the boy, "Ain't you hiz boy?"

The boy looked at Colby then at Big John, "Tha's right. He's my pa. But he's a real stinker. Ya ask me, it's good he's dead. Ain't never done a right thing in his life. Me and Mister Tom made a 'pack'. We spit and shook on it. We ain't never tellin' no one 'bout this. My ma an' me an' my sister an' brother ain't gonna miss him no how."

Big John put his hand on the boy's shoulder. "I know he was a bad man, boy, but he was still yur pa. We need to say a few words over him and see that he's buried. I won't say nothin' 'bout dis. When we done here we walk away like nothin' ever happen. Right? Tom?"

Tom looked at Big John, "I guess so. I did a terrible thing. You sure I shouldn't turn myself in to the sheriff?"

"Oh hell no!" Big John stood up and grabbed Tom's shoulders and shook him. "You done took care of somethin' that should have been done a long time ago. He killed yur Pa! Ain't nobody I know's gonna care dat dis….." Big John hesitated and looked at the boy, "…Colby is dead."

"Okay then. We might as well bury him somewhere." Tom looked at Big John, "Where's the best place to do it?"

"You ain't gonna do nothin. Ahm gonna git some ah duh boys and we's gonna take care ah Hank Colby." Big John looked down on the boy, "You go on home now. Ya gotta ack like ya don know nothin. When yur pa don't come home you ack surprised. Never! Never say nothin to nobody, ya hear?"

The boy smiled at Big John and Tom, "Ahm gonna try not to have a party. This secret is one ahm never gonna tell. My ma's gonna be happy he's gone. Ahm gonna git a job and take care of her an' my famlee. We can do a lot of stuff we ain't never got to do before. Y'all don' worry 'bout me. Ahm a right happy feller now."

214

The boy started walking toward home and turned, "Does this mean we be friends now?"

For the first time in several long minutes Tom smiled, "Yes, we're friends." The boy started walking again. "Hey! What's yur name, boy?"

"It's Willie. Willie Colby, the head of the Colby famlee," he said proudly and kept walking.

"Well, ah'll be." Big John watched the boy disappear into the darkness of the orchard. "That's quite a boy. Ah don think he'll be a problem a'tall." He looked at Tom, "Ok, Tom. Y'all head fur home. Me and the boys'll take care of dis here piece ah garbage. You just put it out of yore mind right now."

Tom reached into his pocket and took out his pa's pocket watch and held it out to Big John. "The boy, Willie, took this out of his pa's pocket. It's my pa's, Big John. It just proves he took it when he killed im. My pa was proud of this here watch. It was his prized possession and he wouldn't have given it to a man like Hank Colby. The only way he got it was when my pa lay dead on the ground."

Big John held the watch and looked it over, then handed it back to Tom. "Yur right, Tom. Ain't no way Colby got a good thing like this without taking it. He always did hate yur pa. He was always hollerin' at im cuz yur pa tole im to stop beatin' that poor old horse ah hiz. Then when his pigs got out, yur pa tole im to fix the

215

fence up. Colby just always wuz sayin' how yur pa was uppity and needed to be brought down a peg. Well," Big John pushed Colby's foot with his foot, "Looks like he bin brought down a peg or two hisself. An' there's nobody to blame but hisself." Big John looked at Tom, "I dun forgot. I wuz gonna say some words over him but the boy's gone now." Big John thought a moment, "On second thought, I ain't gonna waste any words on this piece of Satan's trash. He don deserve nothin noways. He ain't goin' to heaven, an' where he's goin' ain't no words gonna hep him anyhow. Go on now, Tom. Go home an' let yursef just let this go. You say yur prayers tonight an' ask the Lawd to understan' an' forgive ya. He's gonna do just that you mark mah words. Now go on now....git home to yur ma. Someday soon, you choose the right time to tell her what happen here. She's gonna understand, too, an' hug you to her heart. She'll be proud to think you made things right for yur pa. You'll see. Miz Mary's a brave woman. She be by yur side. Now git." Big John turned Tom toward home. "Everythin's all right now."

Big John walked back to the Bradley house and around the back to the cottages where the house workers lived. He knocked on a door and it was answered by a tall black man. "Ah'll be needin' yore help Johnson. Kin you pick up Nathan and Jubal and come with me real quick? We got a 'portant job to do and we gotta keep real quiet."

Johnson closed his door and started walking with Big John. "Ah've gotta git some tools so you go on an' git the other boys and meet me at the end of the drive road. Ah'll tell y'all 'bout it soon's we meet up." Big John kept walking and got three shovels out of the barn.

The men met up and walked in the shadows to the Lelands' apple orchard. When they arrived at Colby's body the men all sucked in their breath and looked at Big John. "Didcha kill'im, Big John?"

"No, I din' kill 'im, but he's daid all right. We gonna dig a hole and bury 'im then we gonna go on back home an' not say a thing to no one. We don't know nothin' 'bout Colby being missin' an' we don' know nothin' 'bout nothin'. Y'all know dis here' 'bout de worst trash der evah wuz an' ain't nothin' bad 'bout im bein' daid. So, let's git to work. I think dat over der looks good 'nuf for a big hole. Ain't no one gonna plant anotha tree der so dey ain't nevah gonna find his body." Big John looked around, "If'n any you hears a peep – we all freeze up an' don move or talk til we know what's up. Y'all know we be in a heap a trouble if'n anybody ketch us burin' a body, even if it's ol Colby."

The men made quick work of digging a deep hole. Big John picked Colby up and tossed him into the grave. Then the men heaped the dirt back in the hole over the body. When they were done, Big John took a branch and dragged it several times all around the grave, then picked up leaves and rocks and threw them on the area where the hole was covered up.

"Thata 'bout duz it, boys. Johnson, it look all right? Cain't have no one lookin' an' seein' this hole we dug." The men paused and looked around then nodded at Big John.

"That's it. We go on home now. An all y'all 'member ---- y'all don know nuthin'," Big John made eye contact with each man.

Johnson stepped forward, "Big John, you don' have nothin' to worry yursef 'bout. Not one ah us has a good word 'bout dat man. Many a blackie been mistreated by him an' his gang." Johnson spit on the ground. "Good riddance." Each man in turn spit on the ground then started walking back to the Bradley estate.

When Tom returned to his home, his ma had left his dinner on the back of the stove keeping it warm. He didn't have an appetite, in fact, he felt sick and just wanted to curl up in his bed. But wasn't prepared to tell his ma what had happened out in the apple orchard. She was in Grannie Rose's rocker in front of the fireplace gently rocking while sewing small bags she was making from flour sacks to store the herbs she crushed. She looked up with a big smile on her face, "You're late tonight. Are the apples all picked?"

Tom tried to avoid looking at his ma. He

didn't want her to see how upset he was. "No. They should all be picked tomorrow. Just gotta a few trees left. The men took most of the bushels away. I saved one and will keep the other tomorrow." Tom stood in front of the stove and stared at the plate full of food waiting for him.

"What is it, Tom? You're more than just tired. I haven't seen your face look like that since you came home carrying Tessa."

Mary stopped rocking and put the bags down on the floor. She paused, then got up and walked over to Tom. "I know you so well, son. Did something happen today? It's not like you to just stare at my beef stew. Especially when I know it's your favorite." Mary reached out and ruffled Tom's hair, pushing it off his forehead. "I know you're getting to be a full-grown man, and you're gonna have private thoughts, but I don't like to see you so sad. A mother's always ready to listen no matter what her child has to tell her." Mary let her hand fall to Tom's arm and she waited.

"I wasn't gonna tell you tonight. I was gonna wait for a time and then tell ya." Tom sighed, I think you'd best set down in Grannie's rocker. I'm gonna git the bible, then I'll tell ya what happened."

Mary felt like her heart was being squeezed. Tom was never this serious except when he had come home and told her how he had hit Hank Colby over the head and might have

219

killed him. Something really bad had happened. She hoped they could fix whatever it was. Mary sat down in the rocking chair and said a quick prayer asking the Lord to be with her and Tom and give her guidance.

Tom picked up the bible from the mantle and removed the doily that was wrapped around it. He patted the loved book and held it to his chest. It gave him a sense of comfort holding Grannie Rose's bible. It was so old and it was a precious part of Tom's life. His pa had read from it in the evening while Tom sat by the fire, and ma and Grannie Rose had read to him when he was a boy and didn't feel well. Tom gave the bible to Mary and sat down on the hearth, facing the fire.

"I did somethin' out of anger today that I can't take back. You might not want to forgive me for what I'm gonna tell ya, and if anybody finds out what I did I could be in some real bad trouble."

Mary clutched the bible to her heart. "Why Tom, nothing in this whole world could ever make me turn away from you. You are my son and I'll love you to my grave and after." Mary waited for Tom to speak.

He was quiet for a while, watching the flames flicker and change from orange to yellow to gold. "I killed Hank Colby for sure this time."

Mary gasped and cried out, "Oh Tom!" She leaned her head back against the rocking chair and tears ran down her cheeks. "I don't know how this happened, but I am so sorry you had to see him again after knowing what a bad man he is."

"Yeah, he was about the baddest man I know. But he won't be around anymore to hurt anyone again. 'Specially his own family." Tom picked up a small bag and played with the string that pulled it closed. In a soft voice Tom told his ma the story of how he came to kill Colby. When he finished he sat quietly, letting his ma take in what he had done.

Finally, Mary took a hankie from her pocket and wiped her face with one hand while she held the bible with her other hand. She took a deep breath, "Where is he now? We need to bury him in a place no one will find."

Tom looked up at her with surprise. "It's all done. I went to Big John and brought him back to Colby's body. He told me to go home, Willie, too. He said he and some men would take care of burying Colby and no one will ever know. Even Willie's glad his pa's dead. I'm glad he's dead too, but I have a bad feeling about myself that anger took over my whole body and drove me to kill him." He looked up at Mary, "Does this make me a bad man, too, Ma?" Tom's eyes filled with tears. "I don't even remember much after he told me he shot Pa. Not 'til Willie was grabbin' my arms telling me to stop."

Mary got down on the floor next to Tom

and pulled him against her. She wrapped her arms around him and Tom reached up to help hold the bible.

"You will never, ever think you are a bad man. Hank Colby was the worst possible man he could be. Everything 'bout him was evil. Your anger was because he murdered a truly good man. Your pa was everything Hank Colby could never be and he hated him for it. When Pa tried to help him, or get him to fix up his fences or told him to take better care and stop beating his animals, Colby hated him even more. But I never thought he could have killed him. I know to kill is wrong, but so help me Tom I'm glad he's dead. Big John's right. Do you think we can trust little Willie? I know you and he agreed not to tell, but he's only a little boy."

Tom nodded his head, "Willie said he's the head of his family now. He was glad his pa wouldn't be 'round to beat any of them anymore. I think he's older than his years. He won't say anything. Big John asked him, too. I think he'll be all right about it."

Mary held Tom tightly and leaned her face against his head, "We can't tell anyone – 'specially not the sheriff. If any of Colby's friends found out, they would come for you. He's not worth a hair on your head. I won't allow anyone to hurt you. We will pray to the Lord tonight and never speak of this again. Never."

Tom and Mary bowed their heads and

together they held the bible, "Lord, we have sinned this day. We ask that you forgive us and understand why we have committed such a terrible sin. We pray for You to help us live with this tragedy. Please be with us Lord. Help us to live good lives each day and be the kind of people you can welcome into the kingdom of heaven. We ask this in Your name's sake. Amen."

Both Tom and Mary had tears in their eyes. Tom held his mother and whispered, "I love you ma. You are the best person on this earth. I swear I will never sin against the Lord again, so help me." Tom kissed his mother's cheek and went on to bed. He lay under the blankets and shivered. He was cold all the way to his soul.

Mary stayed in Grannie Rose's rocking chair until the fire was just a few embers. She had prayed to her mother for her wisdom and to her husband for peace. She felt guilty because she was so proud of her son – and so desperately sad because he had been forced to take a life from this world.

It was almost dawn when Mary got up and went to her bed. Tom mustn't see her fret. This new day would be just that: a fresh start to their lives.

Colby's son, Willie, needed a job to help his family. Since Willie was used to hanging around Bender's Tavern to take his drunk father home, Jacob Bender took pity on the boy when he came looking for a job. Bender gave him a job sweeping and cleaning up the tavern with a young black boy whose father worked at the mill. Willie liked the boy and stepped in to defend him when he was knocked down by one his father's gang.

"Leave Lester alone!" Willie bent down and helped the smaller boy stand up.

"Whatchu thinkin' boy? This here's jus' a no-good blackie. You best step aside an' mind yur own bizness."

Willie grabbed the man's arm as he tried to shove him aside. "My pa said jus' like you all blacks were no-goods, but seems tah me that as hard workin' as this boy here is, an' his pa at the mill, they cain't be called no-goods now, kin they? Just how hard did y'all an' my pa work 'cept tuh saddle up yur mules an' horses an' ride 'round causin' troubles fur the folks?"

"Why you young pup! I'll fix you for makin' lies like that!" As the man raised his arm to strike Willie, a loud click was heard behind them. The man stopped and turned to look, his eyes grew wide.

Standing behind the bar Jacob Bender aimed his shotgun at the man. "Get out of my tavern, Gus Stratton, and don't ever darken my door again. And if you think to cause any harm to us or these boys, you'd better think again. Things er gonna change 'round these parts real soon. You might's well just keep on ridin' right out of this county. You ain't gotta job here 'bout an' no home to speak of, so I suggest you just keep on ridin' ya hear?"

"You might be high an' mighty now, Bender – but the South is gonna kick the north's ass an' then you'll be beggin' for us southern boys to keep this here tavern. Just you wait!" Gus hit the tavern doors hard and stormed out cussing under his breath.

"Thank ye kindly, Mr. Bender." Willie saluted Bender and went back to work sweeping. When he passed Lester who was cleaning tables he punched him on the shoulder and laughed, "Ain't we a pair, Lester! We got us a good job, ain't we?"

Lester smiled back and shook his head at his pal. While he worked he thought about the war and what would happen ifn the south won. He wud prob'ly have tuh sneak out wif his fam'ly an' head as far north as they could for safety. But if'n the north won, he might jist have a good future here in Fairfax. He'd know purty soon what wif de war only gonna last a few months. He'd save all the money Mr. Bender paid him jist in case. Never could tell 'bout nothin'. Lester smiled at Samuel who smiled and nodded his head. Mr. Bender was shurnuf a good man to give out jobs the way he did to people a lot of others wudn't give a mind to. He'd make him glad he gave Lester a job. Before he saved too much he decided he'd stop by the Mercantile Store on his way home an' buy a candy to suck on. Ain't ever day he had cause to celebrate. Might's well do it now in case the town was overrun with Johnnie Rebs.

Chapter 15

War Declared

"It is well that war is so terrible, or we would grow too fond of it."
General Robert E. Lee

In March, 1861, President Abraham Lincoln was inaugurated.   The southern states had started to secede from the Union and ordered the Union troops to evacuate Fort Sumter, near Charleston, South Carolina. Lincoln sent a message to the governor of South Carolina that his troops should not leave the fort, and that the Confederates should abandon the harbor. The Confederates refused and reinforced the harbor making it impossible to send food and supplies to the small group of Union troops occupying the fort. Starting April 12, Confederate cannons fired on the fort for two days and forced the outnumbered soldiers to surrender while a crowd of townspeople watched. Outraged, President Lincoln ordered 75,000 volunteers to put down the rebellion. As a result, four more southern states seceded and joined the Confederacy --- thus, the Civil War began.

The news about the fight in South Carolina circulated quickly among the people of Fairfax. The newspaper was filled with stories from people who had witnessed the battle. When the paper mentioned the 'war' and that it was soon to be declared, the article said that men should enlist in the army to save the union. In Bender's Tavern a verbal fight broke out between men talking about enlisting in the Union Army and others wanting to enlist in the Confederate Army. Sheriff Vinton threatened to run out of town anyone who enlisted in or sympathized with the Union Army and a cheer went up from Hank Colby's old gang. Colby was still mysteriously missing.

Doc was sitting in the tavern having a drink with Wilson Meyers and some of the men from the mill when he heard the sheriff make his threat. Wilson watched the tightness of Doc's face as he turned to look at him and the other men with him, and knew he was very angry. "I've had about enough of the sheriff and his gang," he said quietly to Wilson.

Doc stood up and faced the sheriff, "You need to decide if you're going to be a fair and honest sheriff or continue to be a lying double-talking member of this gang, Sheriff."

The tavern was so quiet you could hear a pin drop. Sheriff Vinton turned to Doc and took a menacing step toward him. "Sounds like you're a goddamn Union man, Doc." He put his hand on his gun and stared at Doc. Wilson Meyers and the men from the mill stood up behind him.

"You best watch yurself or ya might find

yurself 'n yur friends in my jail." Loud laughter
rang out behind the sheriff.

"And just what would the charges be,
Sheriff? Being loyal to the Union?" Wilson and
his men chuckled. "I don't know when that
became a crime. Seems like you'd be smart to
rethink your attitude. I know we have some
southern sympathizers here, but as far as I know
it's still a free country and there aren't any battles
being fought in Fairfax." Doc crossed his arms
over his chest and waited.

The sheriff and the gang made angry
noises and some started to move toward Doc and
Wilson. Mr. Bender was behind the bar with
Samuel and he leaned over and picked up his
shotgun that he kept under the bar. With a loud
click he closed the barrel and levelled it at the
rowdy gang.

"I think you boys better take yurselves
outside an' go yur separate ways now. It would
be a shame to have tuh clean up blood on my
tavern floor. I don't want no wars fought in my
tavern." Bender motioned with his gun, "Go on
now."

More men got up and stood with Wilson
and the mill men behind Doc. It seemed like a
standoff until the sheriff looked at Bender.
"Won't be no need to shoot anyone, Jacob.
Seems like these men'll be havin' their own
battles shortly. I just want to remind y'all to be
careful now, ya hear?" The sheriff smirked,

"Times are gonna be dangerous now that that bastard in the White House thinks he can tell the south how to run its bizness, ay boys?" Colby's men guffawed and hooted. Doc thought it was a good thing they were outnumbered by men with level heads.

"All its gonna take's a few short months for you Yankees to realize that the south is gonna set yur britches on fire. This town just might find out how powerful a few men can be." The sheriff holstered his gun. "I heard tell the only reason this war's been declared is cuz the north wants to make slaves of the southern whites an' not to free the blackies atall!" The sheriff huffed out his chest and hitched up his pants, "Come on boys. Let's do our drinkin' someplace else. Don't like the smell in here no more." The sheriff and Colby's men backed out of the tavern keeping their eyes on Doc and the mill men. The sound of horses' hooves riding out of town was a relief.

After they were gone, Wilson spoke to Doc and the men, "I don't like the sheriff's attitude. I think it's time the town council votes out the sheriff and appoints a new one and a new deputy. What do you think men?" There was a resounding *yeah* from the men. "I think I'll go on over and talk to as many of the council members as I can find and tell em about the sheriff and Colby's gang. Want to come along, Doc?" Wilson started for the tavern door.

"I have some work to do, so I'll trust you

to handle this, Wilson. You might want to take a few men along. In fact, you all ought to be real careful now. I do believe the gauntlet has been thrown."

The men with Wilson looked confused. "Whatcha say, Doc?" Wilson looked perplexed.

"I mean that a divide is now between some of us…. North versus South. Now that war's been declared, tempers are going to be high. You can't trust the sheriff or that gang. Watch your back." Doc picked up his bag and walked out with Wilson.

"You better be careful, too, Doc. You're the one who rides out alone to help folks who are ailin.' Seems like it might be a good thing to just treat folks in yur office in town til we all know how things are gonna be." Wilson patted Doc's shoulder and walked with him back into town. Over his shoulder Wilson said, "And you might keep a gun close by."

The town council lost three out of the seven members who resigned when Wilson told them about the incident in Bender's Tavern. The members who sympathized with the south refused to vote against the sheriff, but the majority voted to fire the sheriff. By the next day they had appointed the assistant sheriff as the new sheriff of Fairfax. Doc had always liked Sean Gleason. He was only twenty-five, but he was mature for his years and honest. Doc hoped he would stay and not join the army and leave the town without a sheriff. It was going to be as important to keep towns safe from danger as it was to fight for the Union. They would need a good man in the days to come.

More and more each day the flurry of activity increased in the town. People who before paid little attention to the newspaper headlines, lined up to buy the first copies of the Fairfax Courier. Editor Homer Sutton, was constantly sending his assistant, Nelson Grady, to pick up the constant flow of information that was coming in by telegraph. Nelson had even picked up week old newspapers from Cincinnati that arrived on the train. Mothers and fathers were worried that the new information would influence their sons to enlist in one of the Ohio infantry divisions that were forming.

Doc received a letter from a doctor he had gone to medical school with who was in Washington DC attending meetings with the newly appointed Surgeon General whose new job was to form medical units for each division of infantry before that group was sent to fight. There would be one doctor/surgeon, an assistant medical officer and a unit of soldiers who would help with safety, supplies, and setup. And, two wagons of medical supplies and equipment, and another wagon for transportation of wounded soldiers would be given to each group. Doc's friend urged him to sign up and he would be assigned a division in Ohio, and the rank of

Captain. He could choose his assistant or be assigned someone to serve with him.

Gussie saw Doc when he returned from the post office. His face was stern and he went into his office and closed the door with a firm click. She knocked, "Doc, can I get you anything?" Opening the door she peeked her head in. Doc was at his desk concentrating on a letter he had spread out on the desk top. Both of his hands braced his head as he stared down at the letter.

"This looks pretty serious. Is everything okay, Doc?" Gussie folded her hands and waited for Doc to look up and talk to her.

Doc finally looked up, "You're not going to go away until I tell you about this letter, are you?" He looked down and picked up the letter, "This is a letter from a friend I attended medical school with urging me to enlist in the army and take care of the wounded soldiers who are fighting for the union."

Gussie's hands dropped down to her sides and she opened her mouth without saying a word. Doc calmly folded the letter and put it back into the envelope. He placed the letter on edge against a small box at the front of his desk. The return address stared back at him.

"You gonna think 'bout that letter?" Gussie walked up to the desk, "You ain't thinkin' 'bout goin' are yuh?"

Doc looked away then back at the letter. "I

don't know, Gussie. I'm going to give this some thought and read it again. I never considered being a soldier or going to war before. The war is not supposed to last long but they will need doctors for the sick and wounded." He hesitated and ran his hands through his hair, "I just don't know."

Spring turned to summer and the news was full of talk about how many men were dying, not just from skirmishes being fought, but from diseases like mumps, measles and chicken pox. More than ever doctors were needed. Doc had received three more letters pleading with him to enlist and help the north win the war. He had spent several nights not sleeping, pacing his bedroom floor. Gussie worried and fretted and was short-tempered which was not like the normally placid woman.

Then on July 12, 1861, a major battle took place at the Battle of Bull Run. Many hundreds of soldiers were killed and wounded, shocking everyone. Then, there were bloody riots in St. Louis, Missouri and Baltimore, Maryland. Doc felt he was standing on a precipice and he was slipping and about to slide down. Homer Sutton's editorial that day talked about the difficulties there would now be for compromise with the southern states and that more were seceding from the union. Homer said in his opinion, from what he was reading in the news coming in to his newspaper office, was that many leaders now felt

234

that there was every possibility that a long and bloody war could not be avoided. There seemed to be no hope of a settlement between the states except the certainty of a devastating war.

Doc had made his decision. He told Gussie not to have any patients in the waiting room unless it was an extreme emergency and to let everyone know he would return by noon. He hooked up his buggy and rode out of town at a fast clip, not even taking the time as he usually did to admire the countryside now in bloom with green stalks of corn, their yellow silky tops waving in the hot summer breeze. Doc had a destination in mind and he wasn't stopping or slowing down.

He only slowed down as he made a wide turn into the Lelands' yard. Tom was hanging herbs along the veranda roof when he saw Doc. His first thought was that something was wrong. Doc usually was smiling when he stopped by. This day there were deep vees in his cheeks where he held his mouth tightly closed.

"Hey Doc. You on an emergency this morning?" Tom walked down the steps and caught the bridle of Doc's horse, and pulled it down. The horse side stepped and tried to pull its head back. Tom reached around and patted the horse's neck and it calmed and stood still. "Do you need Ma? She's gone to the Bradleys' and I don't know when she'll be back. They've got some baggage for transport, if ya know what I mean." Tom said referring to escaped slaves. "Seems like one of um's ailin' so she went to see what she could do and still let 'em leave tonight." Tom took a lead that was hanging on the porch rail and hooked it on the horse's bridle.

"No, Tom. It's you I came to talk to. I'll take some lemonade if you've got it. We can talk over there under the oak tree."

"Okay. I'll git us a cupla mugs and be right out. I've got the lemonade in the cellar and it's stayin' pretty cool.

Tom and Doc settled under the tree and quietly sipped the lemonade. "You hear talk about the big battle that was fought in Virginia?" Doc leaned back and looked at Tom.

"No, can't say that I have. I haven't been to town for a cupla days and I didn't have time to stop in at Bender's Tavern." Tom waited for Doc.

"The war's escalating. A lot soldiers are dying. They need doctors now more than ever." Doc looked at Tom, "I've received several letters from a friend. He's a doctor I attended medical school with and he wants me to join up as a Captain and go to war."

Tom held his mug up to his lips and froze. He was stunned! Doc was going to go to war! "Shoot Doc, what're we gonna do without you here in Fairfax? Me an' ma have gotten used to you. We need you here for all the serious things we can't help with. Do you have to go?"

"Yeah, I have to go." Doc watched Tom

and waited for him to take a sip of lemonade. "I came out here to ask you to go with me as assistant doctor. What do you think?"

Tom spit out the lemonade and choked. Doc pounded his back and waited. "I'm glad your ma isn't here. I want to talk about this before she comes home. I want to take you with me to Camp Dennison and enlist. I'm allowed to have an assistant. If you don't go with me the army will assign one. I'd rather have someone I know and can trust." Doc put his hand on Tom's arm, "And that's you, Tom."

Tom looked down on Doc's arm then up in his eyes. "You want me? I....I can't think. I never left home before. Never been without ma." Tom's eyes widen, "Will I wear a uniform?"

"Yes, we both will. It will have special markings that show we're in the new medical corps. You will be a sergeant and I'll be a captain. We'll travel in wagons filled with medicine, equipment and supplies, and with soldiers to protect us and help us set up camp." Doc set his mug down on the ground and pushed it around in the grass. "I don't know how long we'll be gone, Tom. Some say the war will be over in a few months, but since this big battle, it might be longer." Doc looked up, "I know it's a lot to put on you. What's your first thought? Want to consider going with me?"

Tom took another sip and wiped his

mouth with the back of his hand. "I dunno, Doc. I can't quite take it all in." Tom looked around, "How soon d'ya think we'd be going? I'd have to make sure ma's got wood chopped and plenty of supplies. I gotta get someone to take my place conductin', too."

"I'm going to talk to Miss Beatrice and Miss Kathryn about some things. Maybe they can assign one of their men to help out your ma and you, too. I know they're real fond of your ma. I think she'll be okay. She's a strong woman, your ma."

"Yeah, yeah. I suppose so." Tom squinted his eyes and blew out a deep breath, "How soon would we go, Doc?"

"Does that mean you'll go with me?" Doc asked.

Tom didn't answer. He just looked at Doc. Tom poured out the rest of his lemonade and stood up. "I want to think about this." Tom turned to Doc, "Can you give me til tomorrow? I'll know by then." Tom picked up his mug and took Doc's mug and walked back to the veranda. He placed the mugs on the steps and started hanging the herbs again. Doc could tell he was thinking very hard about leaving his home.

Doc got up and unhooked his horse, got in his buggy and turned to leave, "I'll see you tomorrow, Tom. I'll drive out and stop by on my way to the Bradleys'. I've got some things I'll need to see them about. Should see me about noon. Is that enough time?"

Tom stopped hanging herbs and looked at Doc, "Yup, that'll be enough time. See yuh tomorrow, Doc."

The next day when Doc stopped at the Lelands' house, Tom was sitting on the porch playing his harmonica. He stood up and waited for Doc to stop the buggy before he walked down to meet him. Doc waited for Tom to speak.

"I thought about going with you, Doc. I spoke to ma and she cried, but said I could learn a lot and it would be something I should do for the union. I agree. I want to go along and be your assistant. I'm not sure about joining up with the army. Wearing a uniform and all that….would I have to do marching and all that kind of thing, do you suppose?"

Doc looked serious and frowned, "I hadn't thought about that, Tom. I don't see why that would be necessary for us. We'll be doctors treating the wounded so I think we'll be in a different kind of unit from the soldiers." Doc pushed his hat back, leaned forward and crossed his arms on his leg, "Besides, we'll only be gone a few months the way I hear it. And, we'll be together so I guess we can put up with a little inconvenience if we have to. It's all strange to me, too, Tom."

"Yeah, it is. Maybe once we get there to sign up it won't be such a strange thing for us to do." Tom leaned back on the porch fence and looked around his home and the apple orchard, "How soon do you want to leave?"

"I talked to Miss Beatrice and Miss Kathryn yesterday. They were dumbfounded when I told them what I was going to do. I impressed on them that I wouldn't leave before my replacement arrives. I think that should be in a few days since I received a telegram that my friend will be glad to take my place here. So, I think you should be ready by next week. You might want to make arrangements with one of the men at the mill to look out for your ma. I mentioned it to Miss Beatrice and Miss Kathryn and they both said that they would visit regularly. Big John can help you find one of the men who you can trust to help her. You can pay him out of the army pay you're going to earn." Doc smiled at Tom's surprised look.

"What? I'm gonna get paid?" Tom scratched his head in wonder, "Well, I'll be. How much you think they'll be payin' me?"

"We'll know that when they sign us up." Doc fixed his hat and picked up the reins. "I'll stop by again when I can. Just be ready to go. You don't have to take much in the way of clothes since you'll get at least one uniform." Doc looked at Tom's feet. "Do you have a good pair of boots?"

Tom looked down, "These'er the only boots I own. They used to be my pa's. Ma gave 'em to me last fall when I outgrew my old ones."

Doc made a quick decision, "I'm going to buy you a new pair. You'll need a good strong pair to wear with your new uniform, especially if you have to do any marching." Doc laughed as he turned the buggy around and drove out of the yard. "Come into town tomorrow and we'll get those boots. As long as I'm taking you to enlist in the army with me, the least I can do is make sure you've got good sturdy footwear." Doc slapped the reins and chuckled.

Tom didn't say anything. Boots cost a lot of money. Tom never had new shoes before. Ma always got him shoes from the church barrels. Folks gave their old clothes and shoes to the reverend's wife. She made sure that they were always available for children who needed dresses, shirts, pants and shoes to go to school. For the last three years, Tom had been wearing his pa's old clothes. He hadn't needed the church barrel things since then. Course, some of them were getting pretty thin. But he had one good shirt left that he kept for going to church and his pa's good pants that he had only worn once for Grannie Rose's funeral. Guess he'd wear those to report with Doc to the army. His coat was a little ragged around the sleeves and neck but it would do, too. They might give him a new coat for his new uniform. Boy! Wouldn't that be sumpthin?

Tom made sure all of his chores were finished, then he washed and dressed in his good shirt, fairly good pants and pa's jacket for the day was still chilly. Ma was working making salves this morning. The stove was filled with boiling pots and the air was heavy with the smell of roots boiling. Tom liked the smell of the herbs and roots. He took a deep breath and walked up behind his ma. "Looks like a big batch this time. You plannin' on a lot of people needin' yur salves?"

Mary turned to look at Tom. She reached up and straightened his shirt collar, "No, I thought I'd make up double batches of all my medicines so that you and Doc would have a good supply to take with you." Mary's eyes teared up and she looked back at the stove and sniffed.

"Oh ma." Tom put his hand on Mary's shoulder. "I'm gonna be with Doc taking care of wounded soldiers, not firin' a gun. Besides, it's only gonna be for a few months and I'll be right back here beside you, you'll see." Tom smiled down and patted her shoulder.

"It's just that I've never been without you, son. Won't seem right havin' an empty room and only one at the table for meals. I'm so used to your help gatherin' and grindin'….I just will miss you so much," she sniffed louder and put her hankie to her nose.

Tom stood silent not knowing what else he could tell her. He felt guilty hearing her need of him. He would have to find someone who could be here and do all the chores he took care of for her. Maybe Big John could tell him about

242

someone who would help his ma.

"It's okay, Tom. I'll be okay, it will just take a little while for me, that's all." Mary looked back at Tom, "You look all dressed up. You goin' into town?"

"Yes. Doc's gonna buy me some boots. Said it was becuz I was goin' with him to enlist and he owed me some sturdy boots. He said the army would give me a uniform, too. They're gonna make Doc a captain and me a sergeant. And, I'm to be paid for it, too."

Mary turned around and looked at Tom, her eyes like saucers, "You mean you get paid for being in the army? Well, I'll be...." She crossed her arms, "Now see here, Tom. You will not be usin' that money for any drinkin' or gamblin' or anything you know the Lord would frown on. I want you to spend it on things you need like food or clothes or books. I expect to see money in your pockets when you come back to Fairfax. Why you might have some to put up in the Fairfax bank! Wouldn't yur pa be so proud of you?" Mary turned back to her bubbling pots and spoke with her back to Tom. "Don't make it any easier for me to have you gone, but it will be a nice thing for you to have a payday like workin' folk."

Tom smiled, "You don't have to worry 'bout me, ma. Doc's a good man and I'll be like his shadow. I ain't traveled or been on my own, so Doc's gonna look out for me. I cain't see Doc spendin' his money on sin. Although, I might share a beer with him from time to time. Seems like it's a part of bein' a man and I think I might like to set down and have a beer in a tavern like all the others do."

Chapter 16

Preparing for War

Mary watched Tom leave the house. He was more of a man than she had realized. Going to the army with Doc and seeing what men fighting with guns and cannons do would probably change him. She knew Tom was a good person. She hoped he was strong enough to live in the middle of war and come home as good and strong. The Lord was gonna' be weary of hearin' from her, she thought. Life was makin' a change bigger than she was ready for. She would have to be brave and strong as well.

Tom walked into Doc's waiting room and greeted the two people still waiting to be seen by Doc. He kept walking back to the kitchen where Gussie and Desdemona were preparing lunch. Gussie's daughters greeted him. "Hi, Mister Tom," they said in chorus. "Whatcha doin', comin' for lunch with us?"

"No, me and Doc are goin' to the Mercantile. I just didn't wanta wait in the front room. So I thought I'd see what smells so good back here," he smiled at the girls and leaned over Desdemona to see what she was stirring. "Mmm, smells good. Whatcha makin', Desdemona? I swear you're as good a cook as Floreen is."

Desdemona smacked Tom's arm with a

wooden spoon. "Git on back, boy, and set yursef down. They's a lot of chickin' n biscuits fur yu's well. You kin wash up over there near the back door." She smacked his arm again, "An' ah shure am as good a cook as Floreen. She taught me ever'thin' I know 'bout cookin' an' bakin' and I'm 'bout da best." She cackled and pulled bowls down for the food. The little girls giggled and got down from their chairs to wash up with Tom.

"Mr. Tom, can you hep us to wash up?"

Tom looked down at the precious faces, "Of course I can help you." Gently Tom took each little hand and scrubbed it with soap and used his hands to rinse them off. "Now stay right there so's I can dry you off. They held their arms out straight and waited. The towel hanging by the wash bowl was as big as the little girls. When Tom was done he helped the girls back onto their chairs and sat next to them.

Gussie had been watching Tom as she set the table. "You'll be a good papa someday Tom." She winked at Desdemona and Tom blushed.

Doc came in to join them and they ate together while Lottie and Lissie kept them entertained with stories of Big John and church. They had met other little children and made friends while attending church. The stories about Big John showed how much the girls liked the big kind man. Both Doc and Tom smiled when they told them that he was always bein' real nice to their ma. Gussie ducked her head and didn't say

246

anything.

As soon as lunch was finished Doc and Tom walked down to the Mercantile Store. Tom felt awkward trailing after Doc as he picked up clothes as he walked. Finally, Doc handed Tom the stack of clothes he had collected and pushed him into a dressing room.

"Try these things on, Tom. I can't have you looking like I dragged you out of a cornfield to be my assistant. I want Colonel Franklin to know you have already been working as my assistant and for you to look like it."

Tom pulled the curtain closed, "I'm gonna give you back your money for everything you buy me, Doc, just as soon as I start earning that money you told me about. And, I ain't gonna' take any charity from yuh, that's for darn shure!" Tom jerked the curtain closed, took off his boots and pants, he pulled on the new pants, then he peeked around the curtain, "Psst, Doc."

Doc walked back to the curtain, "What's the matter -- too shy to let me see how the pants fit?"

"Aww Doc! They fit good." Tom's expression was stern, "I ain't gonna come out there where the whole world can see me and laugh."

Doc grinned and held the curtain while looking at Tom, "The whole world isn't out here and why would anyone laugh at you?"

Tom pulled the curtain away from Doc, "Why, tryin' on clothes in public, that's why!

Someone could see me in the altogether!" Tom backed inside the dressing room and picked up a shirt that Doc had added to the pile for him to try on, "Whyn't you go on and do your business. I'll try on all this stuff and keep what I like. I don't need to try on everything. I don't need all of it anyways."

"You are my business right now. We don't have time to waste. Soon as we're done here we're going to the Wagon Works and talk to Wilson Meyers about a special wagon for you and me." Doc sat down on a chair near the dressing room, "There's two pants, two shirts, two sets of drawers, two long johns, four pairs of socks, gloves, a scarf and a coat. When you come out, you can try on the boots."

"Long johns!" Tom moaned. "What'll I need with them? Ain't never needed em before." Doc could hear Tom softly complaining, "Darn things'll prob'ly itch and ball up around my front. Not to mention my pants'll look all puffed up…"

"Try the coat on and then come out. It's going to be important to have a warm coat since we're looking at some cold months living in a tent or the back of a wagon. That's why you'll be glad I threw in those long johns. And, they won't itch because they're made of soft cotton. Now stop complaining and try on the coat and let me see."

A red-faced Tom came out of the dressing room wearing a new shirt, pants and the coat.

Doc looked him over and thought to himself that just wearing new clothes made Tom look older than his eighteen years. He would look just fine to introduce to Col. Franklin.

"I look okay to you, Doc?" Tom waited.

Doc smiled, "You look just fine, Tom. You might want to wear those pants and shirt next time you go to see Tessa. She'll be right impressed for sure."

Tom ducked his head and if possible, turned a brighter red, "Aww Doc." He turned and hurried back into the dressing room. Doc heard him mumbling again, "Guess it couldn't hurt to dress up to say goodbye to her."

Tom had been a regular visitor at the Bradley home since helping Tessa get well from her ordeal with Hank Colby. Everyone knew they were sweet on each other. Tessa was afraid to venture very far from the house without having someone accompany her. Tom thought if she knew Colby was no longer a threat, life would be easier for Tessa. It was a shame he couldn't tell her. Tessa had become important to Tom. He would miss their walks in the orchard and picnics together. He hoped she would feel the same when he told her he was now a sergeant in the Union Army and was going to war with Doc.

When Doc made the final decision to join the Ohio medical unit, his conscience refused to allow him to leave the town of Fairfax without a physician. It took only a few days to think of his perfect replacement. Someone who would not join the war effort and who would be a good fit for the townsfolk. The man he was thinking of wouldn't break any hearts with his scholarly looks and he wouldn't be inclined to drink beer and discuss politics at Bender's Tavern, but he would take care of all the medical needs of Fairfax. His kindness and knowledge would help him make friends in the community. Doc had also considered someone who would have an open mind for Mary Leland. He respected her too much to have a doctor replace him and ridicule Mary's unique healing ability.

Doc sent a telegram to a classmate from medical school, Dr. Hollis Harrington, asking him to take over his practice in Fairfax while he served in the army. He was surprised at the rapid response he received from Hollis. He told Doc that he would gladly take over his practice. Hollis made his decision because he knew he wasn't soldier material for the army, so this would be his way to help the union which he loved.

Dr. Harrington boarded a train from New York and arrived in Fairfax with several suitcases, boxes, and a fancy carrier for his cat, Louis. Doc was at the train station to greet Harrington and they hugged and patted each other on the back. They loaded up a wagon Doc had rented and drove to his medical office. Desdemona and Gussie were waiting at the back of the house. They both walked down to meet Dr. Harrington and help unload the wagon.

Gussie compared Harrington to Doc. Doc was tall, broad-shouldered, with dark wavy hair, bright blue eyes and chiseled facial features. Dr. Harrington had a small build, was not as tall as Gussie, with thin grayish brown hair, small light brown eyes and spectacles. His voice was soft when they were introduced, and he seemed a little shy. He smiled and held out his hand to shake with Desdemona and Gussie. She could tell by his face that he was a kind man. She knew for sure that he was kind and gentle when he carefully removed the carrier and spoke softly against the wire door, soothing his cat. "It's all right, my beautiful boy. I'll have you out of this cage in a jiffy. You can stretch out and make an examination tour of our new home."

Gussie took the carrier from the doctor's hands and peeked inside, "My girls are gonna love this cat. Won't be any time a'tall they'll be havin' it in their arms more than you, Dr. Harrington."

"Oh! You have children, Mrs. Brown? I'm not sure Louis has ever experienced children, they might be a bit much for him."

"I'm Gussie, Doctor. I have two of the sweetest and cutest little gals you ever saw! They'll be underfoot soon and you'll be able to meet them. They're twins but you won't have any trouble tellin' them apart."

Desdemona carried a large box up to the house and Dr. Harrington hurried to catch up, "Excuse me miss, I shouldn't allow you to carry that heavy box. If you'll allow me I shall take it and let you carry something much lighter."

"Doncha worry 'bout me, doctah. I been carryin' heavy things all my life. Ain't never give me aches or pains I cain't handle. Beside, this will be my only trip as I got a meal to git preparin' for y'all." Desdemona opened the kitchen door and held it for the troop of people behind her carrying in the first batch of Dr. Harrington's belongings.

Gussie led the way upstairs, "I gave you the second biggest room. I figured you'd be happy here with the light coming in and to look out on the purty back yard an' trees." She placed the cat carrier on the bed and had all the other boxes and suitcases placed along the wall. "Do y'all want me to see to yur unpackin' while you take a tour with Doc?"

Dr. Harrington looked at Doc, "Well I guess that would be all right if you have the time, Bradford?"

"I believe we have a little while before dinner. Gussie will do a great job of this. Let's take a tour, shall we?"

"Fine. I'll just take a moment to allow Louis his freedom. Gussie, can you please keep the door closed while you unpack? Louis will take a while to adjust to his new surroundings." Dr.

Harrington hesitantly looked around at everyone, "Ahhhh….I never asked if it would be permissible for me to bring Louis. He and I are such great friends I didn't think about you not approving of him." He opened the door and pulled out a large, orange and white tabby cat and held it against his chest. Louis snuggled underneath his chin and started purring. "We've been together since he was an itty bitty kitten." He looked at Doc, "He won't be any trouble, I can promise you Louis has the best manners. He will find a most comfortable spot and make it his own and stay there most of the day until he has his business to attend, then right back until we go up to bed together."

Doc and Gussie shared a smile and Gussie reached to pet Louis who immediately leaned into her hand and licked her finger. "He'll be all right I can tell. Desdemona won't mind a'tall an' like ah tole ya, my girls will give him more lovin' than he'll want, probly." Gussie took Louis from Dr. Harrington, "Now you go on now. Me and Louis has to straighten up this place afore dinner. You'll need to get out dishes for his vittles and water an' put em in the kitchen so he can eat when we do. Thata way he won't be 'fraid of bein' down there."

Hollis opened a box and took out Louis's dishes and followed Doc downstairs. When he entered the kitchen he was greeted by Desdemona's puzzled smile. "Whatcha got there,

Dr. Harrington?"

A little embarrassed, Dr. Harrington held out the dishes, "Ah ---- these are dishes for my cat, Louis. I hope you don't mind. Gussie said I should put them here in the kitchen. Perhaps you could show me exactly where would be the best spot?"

Desdemona smiled and waved her wooden spoon, "Y'all kin put em ovah there by de pantry. Ain't no problem addin' a cat tuh dis household. I kinda always've liked em. He'll enjoy hangin' 'bout in here anyways cause there's aways good food bein' prepared. If ya don mind, I kin slip im some from time tuh time."

Hollis was relieved that Louis wasn't going to be a problem. "No, I don't mind a bit. I'm so grateful that no one objects to his presence. You know there are many who dislike cats." He placed the two dishes carefully side by side, "I keep his water fresh daily. If perhaps you wouldn't mind, if I am unavailable could you make sure there is water here in his dish? I shall endeavor to feed him each evening. I assure you he won't be a bother." He smiled at Desdemona and quickly left the kitchen.

Doc showed him the house and they ended up in the examination room. Hollis looked pleased when he slowly walked around and looked at all the equipment and supplies he saw. "I think this is most satisfactory, Bradford. You have assembled an impressive medical office. I shall be quite content here. I can see why the big city didn't hold you. I'll admit, when I heard you had left Cincinnati and came out here I was very surprised. But I guess after your engagement came to an end, I imagine you wanted a change."

"Yes. My parents were none too sympathetic. I rather shocked them when I made my decision. They are still waiting for me to come home with my tail between my legs. God only knows what they'll do when they hear I have enlisted." Doc grinned at Hollis. "What about you, Hollis? You probably surprised a few people when you up and left the big city." Doc sat in one of the office chairs and motioned for Hollis to sit, too.

"I had taken a position at the New York City Hospital. My salary afforded me only a cramped, one bedroom walk-up in a rather shabby part of the city. It would have taken me years to work up to a better salary and I had only Louis and one other friend. This is a palace and the town is quite lovely from what I have seen." Hollis got up and walked to the microscope and rubbed the brass fitting, "I shall endeavor to make myself worthy of your choice. And when the time comes that you return to Fairfax, I will hope to find a practice close by where I shall remain." He patted the microscope and made a short bow to Doc.

"I can already see that I have chosen well. Gussie has a good sense about character and she approves of you. She's smart and loyal, and I would be hard-pressed to replace her. You can depend on her for advice, assistance with the patients, and, to keep this office organized, clean and fully supplied. Also, you have two patrons: Miss Beatrice Bradley and her sister, Mrs. Kathryn Granger. They own this house and office and made sure that every piece of equipment that was needed is here. If you have any questions or problems you can address them. I will introduce you to them and another interesting person that I think may fascinate you. She is a healer. Have you heard of them?"

"Umm, well yes, but not without some skepticism. Aren't they the type of people who hawk medicines to cure all ills like at a fair or circus?"

"Oh, my goodness, no. At least not in this case. Mary Leland is an amazing woman who has potions, ointments, salves and poultices that even I use. Before I came to Fairfax, she and her mother saved this town from a measles epidemic. Besides, you will enjoy her friendship and it will be welcome, I'm sure. I am taking her son, Tom, with me to enlist. He's to be my assistant. She and her mother have taught him how to make the medicines and use them. We'll drive out there tomorrow. You'll be impressed, I'm sure." Doc got up, "And now I can hear Gussie coming downstairs. We should be ready to eat if I'm not mistaken."

Doc sat at the head of the dining table and looked around. Gussie, her two daughters, Desdemona and Hollis all sat together quietly talking. The two women were giving Hollis a rundown of the patients he would be seeing. Louis had eaten in the kitchen and walked into the dining room with his tail up as if he owned the place. Doc sighed with relief. He had definitely chosen well and it gave him a sense of peace. He could now concentrate on preparing to leave and join the medical corps of Ohio. The morning's Courier sited large numbers of dead and wounded. Doc had a feeling he would be thrown into a nightmare with no time to slowly get acquainted to dealing with such high numbers of patients needing his immediate help. He hoped he was up to the challenge.

The next morning, Doc introduced Hollis to his patients. He was well received which gave Doc an additional reason to feel relieved. After lunch, he and Hollis took his horse and buggy out for a drive. Doc pointed out businesses, people and places so that Hollis could start to feel at home. As they started to leave the town behind Hollis leaned over and patted Doc's arm, "You can be secure in knowing that I already have a fondness for Fairfax and its people. I shall deport myself with care. You can be assured that I am very glad to be here and I thank you for this opportunity."

Doc laughed, "I'm very glad to hear you

say that, Hollis. Watching you this morning in the kitchen with Gussie's girls and Desdemona, I was sure you were ready to take over. Even the patients were very accepting of you." Doc nodded at the front of the buggy, "It's a beautiful town and has a lot of really nice people. Listen to Gussie for advice about the patients and people in town. As for other advice, Miss Beatrice and Miss Kathryn are another trusted source. They practically run this town even though we have a mayor. The men you can rely on are Homer Sutton of the newspaper, Wilson Meyers of the Mill and Wagon Works, and Jacob Bender, owner of the tavern. The other person I'm hoping you will like is Mary Leland, the healer I spoke of. We're stopping by her cabin on our way to the Bradley home.

Mary was on the porch hanging herbs when Doc pulled into the yard. Tom came out carrying a basket of herbs and a large roll of twine. "Hi Doc! You're just in time to help hang the herbs up to dry." Tom laughed.

"I don't mind helping. I brought a friend along for you both to meet." Doc and Hollis got down from the buggy and walked up onto the porch. "This is Mary Leland and her son, Tom."

Mary wiped her hands on her apron and shook Hollis' hand. "Glad to meet you, Dr. Harrington. We're glad to have you here while Doc and Tom are off to the war."

"I'm very glad to be here. I'm very

impressed with what I have seen so far." Hollis held out his hand to Tom, "I am pleased to meet the man who will travel with Bradford." He looked over at Mary, "I will be most happy to pay a call on your mother each week. I shall endeavor to learn about herbs and poultices and such whilst I see to any of her needs as directed by Bradford and yourself." Hollis smiled and stepped over to the basket. Taking a sprig of herbs in his hand he held it up to his nose, "And this is what type of herb, please?"

` For the next hour as they all tied the herbs into bunches and attached them to the ceiling of the porch, Mary and Tom talked about each herb, how it grows, and how it is used to heal. Hollis was very quiet and watched Mary closely. He seemed to memorize each herb she described and was careful to match Mary's style of tying the herbs together.

"Well, we've enjoyed spending time with you, but we must move on to Miss Beatrice and Miss Kathryn. I'm pleased that you will get on with Hollis, Mary. He's curious and a quick learner. It won't take you any time to make him into a fine healer like yourself." Doc chuckled as he watched Hollis' ears turn red.

"You are a scoundrel, Bradford Phillips." To Mary he said, "I will enjoy more of your kind tutelage, Mrs. Leland."

"Everyone calls me Mary, Dr. Harrington." Mary smiled and leaned against the porch post. "I'll be glad to have your company any time. Mayhap you'd like to take my walks and pick the herbs and such?"

Hollis looked at her in surprise, "Why, I think that would be most informative." He hesitated, "Mary. And, you may call me Hollis." He turned and hurried back to the buggy calling out to Tom, "Glad to meet you, Tom."

"Thank you for calling on us, Dr. Harrington, Doc. I'll be seein' ya."

Doc took Mary's hand, "I'm glad you will allow Hollis to visit and learn from you." Doc looked at Tom, "I will do my utmost to look after Tom. I'm sure he'll be doing the same for me. Please try not to worry. We will not be in battle, but we will have our hands full taking care of the fallen. I will always make sure Tom has a way to send letters home to you. Until we meet again, goodbye." Doc held Mary's hand a moment longer and gently squeezed. Then he stepped up into the buggy, waved at Tom and Mary and left the yard.

"He's a good man, Tom. You will learn a lot from him, maybe even as much as becomin' a full on doctor," she said wistfully.

"I know he's a good man, ma. I trust him to guide me. I gotta lot to learn, but I believe I'll be a good assistant for Doc."

The driveway to the Bradley home was lined with beautiful green lavender bushes, still attractive while not in bloom. Hollis was impressed with the grandeur of the home as they approached the large porch. They were greeted by a tall, thin black man who took the bridle of Doc's horse and held it while they disembarked.

"Afternoon, Doc. Miz Bea and Miz Kathryn er waitin' on yuh." A young black boy ran up and tied the horse to a large ring on a pole near the porch. "I'll take yuh to 'em. They's prepared a nice tea fur ya. Right dis way, please."

"Afternoon, Deke. Thank you for the help. How's your wife doing with her lumbago?"

"She's doin' fine, Doc. Thank you kindly for askin'." Deke led them into the house where he took their hats. "The ladies a waitin' fur yu's in the front parlor. Jus' go on in."

The two men kept walking and entered a bright and colorful room with deeply padded chairs and small settees. Beatrice and Kathryn were sitting side by side on the settee and preparing to pour tea and serve small sandwiches on delicate plates. Doc and Hollis stood in front of them and offered their hands.

"Good afternoon, Miss Beatrice and Miss Kathryn." Doc moved aside, "May I present my colleague, Dr. Hollis Harrington?" Hollis took each lady's hand and made a short bow.

"I am pleased to make your acquaintance, Miss Beatrice." Then again, "Miss Kathryn."

"We are pleased that you could join us for tea, Dr. Harrington. Now that you know the way, we hope to see a lot of you. Thank you for

bringing him to us, Dr. Phillips." Beatrice
motioned her hand to one of the padded chairs
near the table and settee, "Please won't you be
seated."

Doc pulled the other padded chair closer
to the table, "My pleasure, Miss Beatrice. Thank
you. Before we came here we stopped at Mary
Leland's cabin. Dr. Harrington will make it a
habit to stop in and check on her as well as take
advantage of her healing knowledge. I know that
Tom spoke to Big John about having one of the
men make regular visits to help her with chopping
wood and any repairs she may need."

Beatrice handed Doc a plate, "I know you
take your tea just black, what about you, Dr.
Harrington?" Kathryn handed him a plate and
held his cup and saucer while she waited.

"I take one lump of sugar, please." They sat
together eating and sipping tea for a few
moments.

"Big John has taken care of making sure that
he and some of the men will regularly visit Mary,
as will Kathryn and I. You tell Tom he will have
no worries there. Mary is our friend and as such
will be a guest at our table each Sunday and tea
several times during the week." She smiled and
Doc noticed a dimple on her right cheek. Her hair
was not as severely pulled away from her face.
Several wisps of hair curled around her cheeks.
She was a good looking woman. Doc wondered
why she had never married. He knew her sister,

Kathryn was a widow, but could there be no men in Fairfax or the surrounding area that did not see her beauty and admire her intellect?

"I will tell Tom. That information will make it considerably easier for him to leave his mother here. I thank you, Miss Beatrice." He held his cup for a refill, "Now that we have that covered, what is it that you need to talk to me about? I assume it is not confidential as we are all together here in your front room."

"Yes, well Kathryn, why don't you tell Dr. Phillips what we have planned."

Softly, Kathryn said, "We are now at war. The Bradley Mill and Wagon Works, Mercantile, Bank and rich fields of produce offer an abundance of goods to help our nation. In order to do that we will maintain vigilance that none of these are used by or destroyed in any way. We want to be your supplier of goods, medical supplies, and food while you are on the move during your time in the war. We have wagons always transporting lumber, and other mill products. It would be just as easy to furnish you with your needs by simply moving them from Fairfax to the railroad depot and having them available at the depot where you direct us to have them delivered."

Doc was dumbfounded! "I don't know what to say, Miss Kathryn and Miss Beatrice! We were going to be at the mercy of the government for our medical supplies and equipment. I hadn't even thought about food, which now I realize I cannot take for granted. I would be most grateful for any help you can give us in addition to what the government will provide."

"I am glad for that. Now all we will need is for our fastest communication so that we know which depot will be available for you to receive our shipments." Beatrice folded her hands in her lap.

"I am not sure there will be any way for us to know too far in advance of where we will be, but using the telegraph will be our best and fastest communication." Doc had no way to know, since he had never been in the army or in a war, that he was not going to be able to send information of where they would be until after the fact, and even then, telegraph lines and rail lines could be sabotaged. He was going to learn the hard way about how to survive.

"You will probably not need anything for the first several weeks, but we wanted you to know about our aid to you and Tom." Kathryn smiled and passed the sandwich tray to Doc and Hollis.

Doc wiped his face and placed his napkin and his plate on the table. "I can't thank you enough for your continued generosity." He paused and looked at Beatrice, "You will have to excuse us. I have much yet to accomplish and time is moving most rapidly." He stood up and Hollis followed him.

"I thank you, too, ladies. It is a pleasure to

be here in Fairfax and I hope to see you again."
And again, he made a slight bow.

"We hope to see you at tea and our Sunday table as well, Dr. Harrington. Please let us know if there is anything at all you need. We find it our responsibility to keep you well supplied."
Beatrice and Kathryn stood. "Let us say goodbye until Thursday morning."

Doc took Beatrice's hand, "I was hoping that we could exchange letters while I am away. It will be a source of pleasure to know about the happenings and events in Fairfax. I would consider it an honor to be able to write to you."

Beatrice's cheeks grew pink as she gazed at Doc's face. "I….I would like that as well, Dr. Phillips. I am sure you will have much to share as well."

At the door, Beatrice and Kathryn watched the doctors get in the buggy. The little black boy unclipped the bridle and as they moved away, Doc tipped his hat and smiled at Beatrice.

"Why, I think Dr. Phillips has a sweet spot for you, Beatrice." She smiled at her sister and squeezed her hand.

"Nonsense! He just needs reliable and useful information about his home from someone who will be honest and trustworthy and not some simpering gossip," she huffed.

Kathryn was enjoying her sister's obvious discomfort, "Just the same, I saw a definite twinkle in his eyes as he spoke to you." She was giggling as she walked back into the house.

Beatrice lingered at the doorway, watching Doc's buggy disappear down the road. She couldn't help feeling surprised that she felt a tingle in her tummy with the thought that she would have regular letters from Dr. Phillips.

Chapter 17

The Medical War Wagon

Doc and Tom boarded the train early in the morning and traveled to Columbus, Ohio, where Camp Jackson was established. They met with Col. Franklin who was very relieved to see Doc. Between the camp population suffering from measles, chicken pox, whooping cough, and mumps, the battles and skirmishes being fought in Virginia, the Ohio regiments' deaths and casualty numbers were increasing because there was not enough medical personnel to take care of the men.

Doc was immediately sworn in as a captain and Tom, as his medical assistant, was sworn in as a sergeant. They were taken to a large warehouse where stacks of uniforms were piled along with various equipment soldiers required. The soldier who had taken them to the warehouse when summoned by Col. Franklin, proudly told them about the importance of his job to outfit every soldier in the Ohio regiments.

After signing several papers, Tom received a dark blue coat with a chevron made of three stripes on his shoulder and shiny brass buttons that ended at the top of his legs. He was also given two white linen shirts, two pairs of navy blue pants, a thick black belt and gold buckle with a large US in the center, and wide black suspenders. His uniform cap was a typical round army hat with a small bill, but on the band was a silver MS on the cap front which signified the newly created medical corps. The calf-high boots that Doc bought him made him stand proud when he put his uniform on for the first time.

Doc received the same uniform, but with captain's bars on his shoulders made with gold thread. His navy blue hat had a brim with a band around it that crossed in the front with a medical insignia in the center. His shirt collars had small gold captain's bars on them and his belt buckle was a large metal rectangle with an eagle holding a palm leaf in one claw and arrows in the other. They stood and looked at each other after they both tried on their new uniforms and grinned. Now it was time to gather up the rest of their papers and instructions and tell the colonel they were returning home to Fairfax where they would pick up their new specially-made medical wagons.

Captain Bradford Phillips was assigned soldiers to accompany him to drive the wagons back and then remain with him as part of his unit. Privates Robbie Coglin and Edwin Birdwell were country boys and friends since childhood. They had enlisted together and requested to serve anywhere as long as they were together. Col. Franklin assigned them to Doc and they were relieved but uncertain what a medical corps would mean for them. When they asked Doc, he could only tell them they would take care of the sick and wounded. Little did they know of the enormity of death and destruction they would face within the coming months beginning with the battles of the West Virginia Campaign.

Col. Franklin, upon learning about Doc's medical wagons, had no problem allowing him and Tom to go back to Fairfax. At the beginning of the war, the doctors were furnished with what they believed was suitable equipment for service on the battlefield which proved to be quite primitive. Doc was going to have a medical unit incomparable to other units in the medical corps. The wagons being built for him and Tom would enable them to treat any illness or surgery more professionally and would contain enough supplies to last much longer than other medical wagons. Col. Franklin told Doc he would be assigned more soldiers when he returned and that he would be reporting to Cincinnati to a newly constructed camp: Camp Dennison.

The Bradley Mill and Wagon Works built large wood wagons using Conestoga wagons as a model. Built extra-long, the wagon could accommodate up to 30 wounded lying down in three rows; rows on each side and one row down the middle of the wagon. The second wagon held medical supplies, tents and blankets for personnel and patients. The third wagon was filled with cooking supplies, canned jars of fruit and vegetables as well as bags of corn, flour and sugar

269

as well as feed for the horses. All were staples designed to last more than the three months promised by Doc and Tom. If needed, Doc could send a telegram notifying Miss Beatrice to send more supplies to them by train.

Each wagon had outside attachments which held large water barrels and kettles for boiling water as well as the andiron arms to place over the fires to hold the kettles for cooking and boiled water to clean wounds and medical instruments.

The Bradley sisters also donated six large draft horses to pull each wagon for Doc and Tom. Traditionally, the wagons were built 18 feet long, 11 feet high, and 4 feet in width and could carry up to 12,000 pounds of cargo. There was no front seat. The driver stood alongside the front horses and drove them from there as he walked. That wouldn't work for their needs so a front seat had been added to accommodate a driver and passenger with a small canopy overhead to help protect them against rain and sun. The seams in the body of the wagon were stuffed with tar to protect them from leaking while crossing rivers. Also, for protection against bad weather, stretched across the wagon was a tough, white canvas cover which had been treated with oil to make it as rainproof as possible. The frame and suspension were made of wood, and the wheels were iron-rimmed for greater durability. In addition, the back end of each wagon had a platform which held toolboxes and supplies for repairs and extra feed for the horses.

Doc and Tom were hailed by a large crowd when they arrived at the Fairfax train station. Even Jacob Bender, his wife and Samuel Washington were there to greet them. Bender had temporarily closed the tavern just for this purpose. Both Bradley sisters were present and Doc and Beatrice made eye contact before he stepped down from the train. Beatrice looked concerned as she approached Doc, "I hope you don't mind. Everyone was so excited to hear you were returning and wanted to greet you. I'm glad we all came. It would have been a shame if everyone didn't see you in your uniforms." Beatrice smiled shyly, "You both look quite different now. I'm rather impressed with the Union uniforms. We are having a community picnic at our home and hope you and Tom will join us this evening."

Doc smiled down at Beatrice, "I thank you. Tom and I will be pleased to attend." He looked down and smoothed his uniform coat, "It seems rather strange to wear a uniform. I guess Tom and I will become accustomed over the next few months." Beatrice smiled and she and Kathryn moved away into the crowd.

Big John approached Doc and put out his hand, "I thank you, Doc, fur joinin' this war. I've been prayin' 'bout dis an' ahm movin' to think ah'd like to be wif you 'n young Tom."

Doc shook Big John's hand and placed his

free hand on his shoulder, "Well I think that's a fine idea Big John, but you know the Bradley home and the ladies would be lost without you after all these years."

"Ah know dat. I shure do, but you know ah would be able to hep you out and take care a lot of thangs what need doin' so's you can do yur work on the wounded men. I can do a lot of good cookin' fur ya an you know I'd be right good fur doin' dat." Big John stood firm in front of Doc and crossed his arms, "I wudna offered mysef if'n I hadn't done sum powerful thinkin' an' prayin' 'bout it. So's ahm ready to go. Ah awready got a man in the Bradley house who kin take mah place. He's a trained man, he'd be jus' fine. I awready got a time set aside this evenin' to tell Miz Beatrice 'bout mah decision, so ah hope you won't be tellin' me you ain't gotta place fur me, Doc."

Doc was quickly spinning Big John's offer in his mind and considering all the positives it would be to have someone like Big John to take care of responsibility like cooking and organizing his things. That would certainly make it easier for him, not to mention having better food to eat. He was a good man and could be trusted to handle anything he was assigned. As far as Doc knew, there was no regulation that he couldn't have personal workers for his benefit. But he would notify Col. Franklin.

"All right, Big John, I'd be very glad to have

your help and support. Make sure you advise Miss Beatrice and Miss Kathryn and they know the fellow you chose can handle your job." Doc shook Big John's hand and they parted.

Tom had seen Tessa in the crowd and pushed through the handshakes and pats on his back to get to her. "Hello, Tessa." He removed his hat, "I'm glad to see you here."

Tessa blushed pink, "I'm very glad to see you, Tom. You look very nice in your uniform. Very different from before. I don't rightly know what to say."

"Well, I feel different, that's for sure. Miss Beatrice invited me and Doc to your house for a picnic. I look forward to sitting next to you."

"Of course. I look forward to being with you, too." She looked around, "Well, I'd better go. My cousins will be looking for me. "Good bye, Tom. Please come early if you can. We can find a good place for just you and me."

Tom's heart swelled with her words. She was so pretty standing there with her blonde hair shining in the sun. Her dress was made of a thin white material dotted with tiny green leaves which was matched by a shiny green ribbon around her waist and tied in a bow at her back. The little freckles on her nose stood out because of her pink cheeks and her lips. He would sorely miss seeing her. Tom was going to talk to her about writing and exchanging letters.

The picnic was an affair that seemed to

include the whole town of Fairfax. Doc and Tom had difficulty eating the bountiful and delicious food as they had to stop frequently to talk to town folk and say their goodbyes countless times. Mary finally gave up and joined Gussie, Desdemona and Dr. Harrington. Gussie's daughters had found a teeter totter and Big John was helping them play on it because their weight wasn't wasn't sufficient to go up and down without his help.

"My girls are sure gonna miss that man," she sighed.

"You mean *you* and them girls er gonna miss dat man." Desdemona sniffed.

Dr. Hollingsworth smiled at Mary. "I'm sure we will all miss Big John. I don't know what I will do without him always available to lift and fix anything he's asked to do."

Mary watched Big John and the girls, "I know I will miss them all. I've never been without Tom. Doc comes several times a week to visit and Big John as well. My cabin's gonna feel mighty empty. She reached into her pocket, brought out a hankie and wiped her eyes. "Three months seems like forever right now."

Gussie also had a hanky and wiped her nose, "I shure wud like yur comp'ny anytime, Miz Mary. Me and Desdemona wud welcum you any time. An' Doc Hollis, yud be okay wif dat, too?" Gussie sniffed.

Dr. Harrington looked at the women with

astonishment, "Why of course! Mrs. Leland is more than welcome anytime." He lifted Mary's hand, "I would find it most interesting to visit your cabin and have you show me more of your herbs and things. Dr. Phillips has told be so much about your potions and ointments. I think you have much to enlighten me about." Mary blushed and looked down. Gussie and Desdemona exchanged knowing looks.

Mayor Brodt stood and called for attention: "People of Fairfax, we have gathered here today to say goodbye to Dr. Phil, er, Captain Phillips and his new assistant, Tom, er, Sgt. Leland. They will be leaving us for a few months – at least we are hoping it will only be for a few months, but they are going to war and we send them with our good wishes and prayers. Thanks to the Bradley Mill and Wagon Works, they will go in the best style that can be made. At this time I want to acknowledge the other families here who have sons that have recently enlisted in Ohio regiments. They, too, will go to war representing this fine state. I understand from Homer Sutton that President Lincoln said that the state of Ohio has the third largest number of soldiers in the nation." There was applause and Mayor Brodt raised his hands, "Early on Thursday morning, the town band will play various selections while Captain Phillips and his unit leave town. I would like to have as many of you as possible present to say our final goodbye, eh eh eh…." the mayor cleared his throat. Now at this time I would ask that you all bow your heads as the Rev. Hawthorn says a prayer."

Rev. Hawthorn stood up, "Thank you, Mayor Brodt, I too am proud of the men of this community. You honor us as you go forward helping to save this Union. I will pray for you and your families during this most difficult time. Now will you all please rise. Dear Lord, we send you our dear ones into this war which tries to separate our nation. We pray for your constant guidance and support for those who fight the battles, as well as, for those of us who remain behind. *"When Your people go out to battle against their enemy, by whatever way You shall send them, and they pray to the LORD toward the city which You have chosen and the house which I have built for Your name, then hear in heaven their prayer and their supplication, and maintain their cause."* Rev. Hawthorn raised his arms over the people, "May the Lord be with you in defeat as well as in victory. May He guide you and hold you in the palm of His hand. Amen."

Gradually, the people said their goodbyes to Doc and Tom. Tom was surprised by several young men who shook his hand and said that he may see them somewhere during the next months. One young man joked that he hoped he wouldn't see Tom in his medical capacity. Doc listened and felt a chill down his spine.

The next day was filled with loading supplies into the three wagons. Doc had made several lists of what he wanted packed into each one. One list was from the government detailing the surgical instruments which were furnished to each medical officer. They were contained in four cases. Doc would sign receipts for each one and be responsible for them while they were in his unit. The cases were divided into what they would be used for: one was for major operations, one for minor operations, one was a small case, and one was for using in the field. This one would be carried by Doc if he entered the field of battle.

A false bottom on each of the wagons held yards of canvas and poles for makeshift tents and covers, and boxes of candles for the lanterns. On the outside of the wagons, panniers or hoops held water barrels made of wood. Some panniers held large pots which swung back and forth on their handles. They would be used to boil water for cleaning and surgeries.

The wagons were lined up at the Bradley Wagon Work where they were being loaded and set up by Privates Coglin and Birdwell, who proudly stood guard when the mill workers went home for the night. The men had made beds in the back of one of the wagons and had a large lantern for after dark. During the day, the men ate with the mill workers in the mill canteen. The Bradleys' cook, Floreen, sent food to the men for dinner.

"Robbie, I do believe I'm gonna like this 'orderly' job we got. We go with these fine wagons and I think this grub is the best I've had since I left home. My ma was a good cook, but it's sure more plentiful here. I cain't remember when my belly was so full. And, so far the Doc seems like a real likeable sort. What do you think, Eddie?"

Eddie leaned back against the flour sack he used as a pillow and sighed, "You're right on the dollar, Robbie. My family was just poor farmers my whole life. My dad gave my sister away to a widow-farmer 'cause he give 'em a bunch of layin' hens and a big hog." When I told he and ma I was enlistin' all he wanted to know was how much the pay was 'n I'd better be sendin' it all home if I knew what wuz good fur me." Robbie frowned, "I always thought you lived a lot better'n me. Likeways yur ma and pa seemed like real nice folks ever' time I visited with ya."

"Yuh, I dearly love ma 'n pa. They were good folks and did the best they could for me and my brother, Billie. He's just a little guy, not old enough to enlist. My ma stood on the porch and cried like a baby when I left. Pa had his hankerchief out in one hand while he held on to ma with the other one. Billie refused to come out a'tall cuz he was cryin', too 'n didn't want me to go. My pa said I should put aside as much of my pay as possible to bring it on home for a stake after the war. He didn't want none of it." Eddie smiled, "Yup, that's my pa. He'd want more for me than he has." He rubbed his nose and sniffed, "Gonna miss 'em somethin' fierce."

The next day Doc and Tom arrived at the Wagon Works early. Wilson Meyers had set up time for all four men to practice driving the big draft horses since there would be two on each wagon. Privates Robbie and Edwin as well as Tom became proficient faster than Doc. He finally got the hang of when and how to apply the brake and how to use the heavy reins to direct the horses. One of the drivers of the transport wagons made them all practice putting on and taking off the harnesses and hooking them up to the wagons. It was hard work and all the men were sweating by the time they were through. Big John showed up while Doc was finishing the last buckle on the harness.

"I thought you was gonna let me do those kine of thangs fur yuh, Doc." Big John stood next to Doc and patted the horse.

"Well, Big John, there could come a time that I would be required to hook up the wagons. I don't want to be unable to do so." Doc looked proudly at the job he'd done on the harness.

"Ok, Doc. Jus' so's yuh know – ah'll be follerin' yuh 'round like a hen, hehehe."

Big John I'd like you to meet the two orderlies who are assigned to me. This is Private Robbie Coglin and Private Edwin Birdwell." As Big John stepped forward to shake hands, the two men gawked at him. "Men, this man will be along to help Sgt. Leland and myself. I'd like it if you would treat him like a fellow soldier."

Robbie was the first to put out his hand and shake Big John's, then Eddie moved forward and did the same. They didn't say anything but exchanged puzzled looks.

Doc was watching the men with concern, "Is there a problem, Privates?"

Robbie ducked his head, and Eddie looked guiltily at Doc. "Well, Sir, we didn't know you'd have a darkie servant to take to the war."

"What! This man is a freeman who has volunteered to accompany us and help make life easier! He will be as much of a soldier as anyone and deserves as much respect! Do you have a problem with that? If so, privates, let me know now and I'll have you packed out of here and replaced as soon as possible. Now what is it going to be?"

Robbie looked shocked! "No sir, Captain, sir! Me 'n Eddie jus' ain't used to havin' blackies aroun'. I ain't never seen 'em afore bein' here. We kin work 'long side of 'im no problem." He looked at Eddie for confirmation and they both nodded their heads.

Eddie looked at Big John, "I don't have a problem workin' with ya, ah, Big John. I didn't mean no disrepeck to ya. Jus' that you's a surprise, that's all."

Robbie nodded his head vigorously, "Same

fur me, Big John. I kin work side by side with ya, no problem."

Big John was grinning, "Ah'm right proud to be along wif you all. Yuh won't have no pro'lem wif me long's we all do ar work." He turned to Doc, "I don' think we'll be havin' no pro'lems a'tall, Doc. Don' yuh worrin' 'bout nothin'. Ah'll see y'all tomorrow mornin'."

Doc and Tom went to the Leland cabin, one last time. They packed up bags of herbs and eucalyptus leaves to make potions, poultices, and teas as well as ointments and salves. They included bags of herbs in order to make them in the field. Lucky for Doc, Tom would be in charge of that. Beatrice had sent a note saying that Doc could see her privately before he and Tom left on Thursday. So Doc excused himself and told Tom he would return to town and see him early Thursday morning. Tom was relieved that Doc didn't need him any longer. He wanted time to be with ma and make a trip to the Bradleys' home to see Tessa one last time alone.

Doc pulled up in front of the Bradley house and was greeted by the same young black boy, "Hiya Doc! I gotcha horse. We'll be waitin' on ya right here." He smiled and Doc could see he was missing his right front tooth. Doc reached into his pocket and pulled out a nickel and tossed it to the boy. "You need a peppermint stick for that missing tooth."

"Jus' loss it this mornin', Doc. I do believe yur right. A stick of peppamin'll make it right fine." He tossed the nickel up and down in his hand and smiled.

The front door opened before Doc reached the top of the porch. Big John welcomed him in to the house. "Right glad to see you, Doc. I mos' packed an' ready to go. Not's as easy to leave as I thought. Don't rightly like saying goodbye atall." The big man looked sad.

"I understand, Big John. If you decide you aren't able to go with us, we will certainly understand."

Big John looked at Doc with surprise, "Oh no, Doc! Ahm leavin' Thursday mornin' fur shure! I got God's work to do an' I ain't gonna let Him down." Big John led Doc to the front parlor where Beatrice was waiting.

Chapter 18

Love Before War

"Every heart hears a song, incomplete, until another heart whispers back."

"Afternoon, Miss Beatrice. Thank you for receiving me." Beatrice motioned for Doc to be seated. He wanted to sit beside her on the settee, but sat in the chair next to the settee.

"I wanted to speak to you privately. It seems that we are always surrounded by people. I hope you don't think I am being too forward by my request to see you alone."

Beatrice's cheeks were pink, "Not at all, Dr. Phillips. What can I help you with?"

Doc hesitated. He had been thinking about something since he was at Camp Jackson. "Again, I am most grateful to you for the wagons, horses and everything you have given Tom and me. I also want to thank you for allowing Big John to accompany us. I know he will be sorely missed here."

Beatrice looked sad for a moment, then sighed, "I would never stand in his way when he has a wish to help someone. I will pray that he stays safe with you and young Tom. After all, he is a black man and could possibly be in a difficult position. Not all people are totally accepting of a black man. I was raised differently than most people. My father and mother had deep respect for the black people. If you didn't know, Kathryn and I have as many blacks employed as we do white people."

"Yes, I am aware of that. I am most fortunate that he will be along with us. Our lives will be quite improved by his presence." Doc hesitated, then charged forward, "I know we have only known each other for a relatively short time. I am very glad that we will be exchanging letters while I am away," Doc struggled to say the right thing. He got up and sat down next to Beatrice on the settee. "I do not want to overwhelm you, but I would like your permission to court you upon my returning from the army." He felt sweat on his forehead and was afraid to move while he awaited her response. "Indeed I find I am pressed to ask you now as I will soon be leaving, but I hope that will not detract from my offer."

Beatrice froze. She felt lightheaded. This can't be happening! Heaven alive!

Doc took Beatrice' hand, "Miss Beatrice, did you hear me? Have I offended you?" Doc patted her hand.

"Yes, yes, I can see that I have surprised you. But are you willing to consider my request? I am afraid that I feel compelled to ask this of you now before I leave. What with the war, I am afraid that some other man of your acquaintance could approach you with the same request and I would be sorely upset that I had not taken this opportunity first." Doc still held Beatrice' hand and she felt herself adding pressure and holding it tighter.

"I am a little overwhelmed. I never thought that I would ever consider another man in my life, but I find I am quite willing to consider your request. If you will kindly give me a moment to gather myself." She smiled faintly but didn't release Doc's hand.

"Beatrice, if I may call you that," she nodded her head, "I have found my visits with you here and in town of great interest to me. You are such an intelligent woman; well-read, and capable of being in charge of several companies. I am in constant admiration of you. I was having dinner the other night with my staff and it occurred to me that I would enjoy sitting at a table with my own family. That it was time for me to consider taking a wife and planning for children. My hope is that perhaps you could possibly feel that way, too."

"Bradford, if it pleases you, I give my permission for you to proceed to a courtship upon your return to Fairfax. I, too, enjoy our talks and time together. It has been a long time since I have found a man that I enjoy being with as much as you." Beatrice put her other hand on Doc's arm, "You see, I was engaged to be married a few years ago. He was a minister and was here in

Fairfax as a tent revivalist. He died in an accident during a storm while driving his wagon. But I will always believe that he was murdered because he had preached against slavery. My fiancé was very proficient at driving and loved his horses. The storm was blamed, but Ben would not have driven his team if it would have endangered them." Beatrice looked intently into Bradford's eyes, "I thought never again that I would be offered marriage. It gives me great happiness to think that we could be together after the war. I shall write you constantly and wait faithfully until your return."

Doc leaned over and kissed Beatrice' velvet cheek. "I am most proud that I am the man whom you want be your husband." He bent over and carried her hand to his mouth where he kissed the top, then turned her hand over and kissed her palm.

Beatrice sighed and had tears in her eyes. "I do believe these next few months will be the longest I have experienced in my life."

As soon as Wilson Meyers said that he thought they were proficient at handling the harnessing of the draft horses and driving the big wagons, Doc let the men go. Tom walked over to the Bradley home and requested permission to take a walk with Tessa. Beatrice was busy but Kathryn gladly gave permission with a big smile for Tom. When she told Tessa that Tom was there to see her, she sailed down the stairs. Tom

was waiting for her and his heart swelled as she
slowed down her rapid descent and sedately
approached him, putting out her hand to take his.

Tom walked Tessa into the Bradleys' apple
orchard holding her hand up against his chest
with both of his hands. Tessa walked close
enough to put her head against his shoulder.
They were both silent, each contemplating the
important things they had to say to each other.
He had a lot to say to her before he left to go
south to join the battles that would soon take
place, and Tessa because she would be leaving
Fairfax until the end of the war. Both were afraid
of their future. They each had promises to make:
promises with their whole heart.

Tom smiled and held out his hands. Tessa
stepped forward and shyly reached out for him.
When they touched he felt a tingle go from his
fingers through his entire body. It was a thrill
he'd never experienced before. He pulled her
against him and tucked her arms under his,
holding her close. Her head reached right below
his chin. She was a perfect fit.

"I have something to tell you. Cousin
Beatrice is sending me away." Tessa looked into
Tom's eyes as they grew round with surprise.

"But why? Why don't they want you to live
with them anymore? I don't understand, Tessa."
Tom pulled her back into his arms. "I'll talk to
Ma. She'll let you stay with her, especially when
I tell her yur my girl." Tom pursed his lips in

thought.

"No, Tom. It's not what you think. They're sending me away to school and they also don't want me here in case the war comes too close to Fairfax." Tessa pulled back and looked adoringly at Tom. "I promise I will write no matter where I'm at, Tom. And when you come back home, I will come back, too," she smiled.

Tom looked grim. "Where are they sending you?" He frowned, "What happens if you meet some other fella who turns your head? What then? I'm not educated like some of those town folk. You'll find someone much better'n me. What'll I do then?"

Tessa put her arms around his middle and squeezed, "Don't be foolish, Tom. There won't be any men except some dowdy old teachers at the Litchfield Academy for Women. Besides – I will never meet anyone as kind and caring as you." Tessa leaned back and waited, her big blue eyes sparkling with affection. "Besides, I'll be so busy with all my classes I can't imagine I'll have time for too many social events."

Tom wasn't convinced. He stared at this beautiful girl and doubted he would ever see her again. "What kind of classes will be you doing?" Tom was thinking she would forever be bored with someone who had only read the Bible and Doc's medical books.

"Well, there's ancient and European history, composition, geography, Latin, art and embroidery, as well as lessons on proper deportment." The names of Tessa's classes just tripped off her tongue while Tom sank deeper into doubt about her ever wanting to be with him in a small town like Fairfax ever again.

"What the heck is proper deportment for?" This was just getting worse, thought Tom when he didn't even know what some classes were.

"Those classes are important for young ladies because they teach proper behavior and emotions for proper conduct in all aspects of life," she said as if quoting a book. "If I'm going to be a teacher I have to know these things to teach properly." Tessa looked as if it made perfect sense to her.

Tom had more doubts, again, because it just seemed like this would take her further away from someone like him. Here he was -- about to ask her to promise herself to him and now he was wondering if he should just say goodbye. His chest felt heavy. What was going to be so joyful was now so sad. Tom pulled away and turned his back on Tessa. His eyes were burning and he wasn't about to let her see him cry.

"Well, say something." Tessa looked at Tom's back with a puzzled expression on her face.

Tom took a breath and blinked away his tears before he turned back to Tessa. "Maybe we oughta just say goodbye and see what happens after the war. I don't know what's gonna happen between now and then. You should just go on away to that Academy and not worry 'bout me."

Tessa's mouth was open and her hands were on her hips, "Now wait just a minute, Tom Leland! I thought we were going to be 'promised' to each other before you left! Now you want to say goodbye!"

"Well, that's before you told me you were gonna be someone else when I return," he said angrily.

"Someone else? What in heaven's sake are you talking about?" Tessa stalked toward Tom and was almost nose to nose with him. "I happen to love you, Tom Leland. I am of an age that I could marry you. But you're leaving to go to war. *I* am going away to school so that I can be a teacher – for no other reason. I don't need to meet anyone else. I want to be with you. Now you don't want to be with me...." Tessa's eyes filled with tears and they started sliding down her cheeks. "You don't love me as I thought." Tessa put her hands over her face and sobbed into her hands.

Tom stood stock still for a moment, uncertain what Tom stood stock still for a moment, uncertain what to do. He pulled out his big hanky from his back pocket and put it into Tessa's hand forcing her to pull it away from her face. "Please don't cry, Tessa. I don't want to leave you and I do love you. Honestly I do."

Tessa kept crying and held Tom's hanky against her face. Tom pulled her into his arms and held her, fighting his own tears. "Shhhh, don't cry now. I'll never want anyone but you, Tessa. No matter what happens when you go away. You're the only girl for me. I'm just afraid you'll see that I'm just a plain ol' country boy without much to offer a pretty, smart girl like you. Those city boys dress different, talk different and live in fine houses. How can I measure up after you bein' around them for the next…..how long're you gonna be gone there?" Tom leaned back, pulled his hanky away from her face and looked at Tessa.

"I am enrolled for the next two years," she said meekly.

"Two years! Well if that don't beat all! What happens if I come home from the army in three months? What happens then? You just gonna leave that academy and come back to Fairfax? Yur Cousin Beatrice ain't gonna like that, no sirree!" Tom rubbed that back of his neck and walked away murmuring to himself in frustration.

"I will be home on holidays and during the summer months. Cousin Beatrice *promised* I can come home regularly," she pleaded. Tom stood with his back to Tessa.

"Tom. Please, Tom. Nothing will ever change the way I feel about you. Nothing."

I oughta just walk outta here right now, Tom was thinking. He turned back to Tessa, "Two years! Two Years! That's forever, Tessa. Two

291

years." He stood and looked at her.

Tessa looked at Tom then suddenly she launched herself at him. He caught her and swung her around in a circle. She put her lips on his and he stopped moving.….stopped breathing and just felt her body against his and her mouth against his mouth. The world was silent except for the pounding of his heart. It was an awakening --- a longing for something neither of them had ever experienced or knew about.

After several minutes of deep kisses, Tom pulled away and put Tessa's head under his chin and held her tightly against him. They were both breathing hard.

"What would it be like," he sighed.

"What do you mean?"

"What would it be like to wake up in the morning and see your beautiful face next to mine?"

Tom kissed Tessa's cheek. She blushed but leaned forward for another kiss on her lips. "I think it would be like waking up in heaven," she whispered and kissed Tom again.

Several minutes later, "I remember when I was little I watched my ma and pa when they didn't know I was nearby. They'd lean against each other, smilin' and ma giggling. Pa would reach up an' touch her chest. Now I know what he was touching." Tom blushed. "Pa would touch her cheek and put his arms around her then he'd kiss her. It made me feel warm an' safe----

like I was in a warm cocoon. I want that, Tessa."
Tom took her hand, "I want that kind of being
together. They loved each other an' had a real
happy life. I want that with you."

"That's what we'll have, Tom. I know we
will." Tessa patted Tom's chest. You have a big
and loving heart. Even though we will be apart,
our letters will keep us together. Promise me you
will write as often as you can. I want to know
how you are and what you are doing. I will do the
same, although my life will be very dull I am
sure." Tessa sighed, "I wish I had your picture to
keep with me. Can you have a photograph taken
in your uniform and send it to me? I promise that
I will have one taken as well and send it to you."
Tessa's tears returned and she sniffed, "Oh why
do we have to leave each other? I will miss you
so very much, Tom."

Tom pulled her back against him and kissed
her with more passion. Tessa's arms were tight
around his neck. He didn't want to ever let her go
but he knew that he couldn't keep her here much
longer. Even though they were 'promised' it
wasn't proper for him to be kissing and holding
her like this.

"I better walk you back to the house. It's
best if we say goodbye here. Tomorrow morning
we won't have a chance to be together alone."
Tom put his hand under Tessa's chin, "I love you,
Tessa. I want to marry you and be with you for
the rest of my life." He lifted her face, "I think

you are the most beautiful girl in the world. How you want me will always be a mystery." Tom smiled, "But I ain't gonna let that stop me from lovin' you an' dreamin' 'bout bein' yur husband." He chuckled, "Yur gonna have me all over you when I come home to Fairfax and see you for the first time." Tessa was breathless when he pulled away. He took her hand and led her back to the Bradley house. When they reached the back gate Tom kissed her once more. Tessa smoothed away his hair where it had fallen over his forehead. Tom took her hand and kissed her palm, "I love you, Tessa."

"And I love you, Tom," she whispered.

Tom ran his thumb over her bottom lip, "These beautiful lips are gonna be bright red from all the kisses I'm gonna' give 'em. An' when we get married you won't see the light of day for the first week if I have my way." Tom surprised himself by his boldness. He kissed her and pulled her body against his so there was no space between them from their lips to their knees. He held her bottom tightly against his front and rocked gently side to side.

Slowly, she raised her eyes and looked at Tom, her blue eyes dark with passion, "I think I will dream about this tonight." Tessa turned away and left Tom yearning for more.

Tom stood and watched as Tessa sat down on the swing he had made for her in the apple orchard. He had a feeling that overwhelmed him for the first time in his life as he watched Tessa gently swinging. He couldn't wait to claim her as his own and protect her for the rest of her life. It was a longing of first love. But Tom knew it would be his only love.

Wilson Meyers had been the Manager of the Bradley Mill and Wagon Works for eighteen years. He had been working closely with Kathryn Bradley Grant for months now and had come to realize that he was very attracted to her. Each day he was with her he found himself wanting more and wondered if it was possible to have more.

His three young sons also worked at the mill as helpers and apprentices. He had loved his wife, Maybelle, very much. They had been married almost fifteen years when he lost her. She went down to Kentucky to take care of her mother who had the 'fever.' Maybelle became ill, too, and died. After a lonely weekend Wilson decided to take the bull by the horns and speak his mind with Kathryn. He was as nervous as a young lad when he requested to talk to her

"Miss Kathryn, my three boys are getting older now. I have 'em working at the mill. I miss comin' home to a woman in my house. I don't have a big fancy house like you're used to, but the one I built is a good, warm-built house. I got a parlor and a dining room big enough to entertain guests in if yore of a mind to do that. I'm not a fancy educated man, but I'm God fearin' and clean, and a hard worker. My wife said that I'm an easy man to live with and my mama raised me up with the bible and good manners."

Wilson took a deep breath, paused and looked away as if he was remembering a script. "I find myself yearnin' to see you each day since you took up the care of the books for you and your sister. My boys hold you and your family in high respect, Miss Kathryn, and I would consider it an honor to have your permission to court you. I know you're a widow and might still be pining for your husband, but it's been a while now and I thought you being young and not attached to anyone you might want to remarry and have a family. Is there is someone else I need to speak to, I'd be obliged to do that, too." Wilson pulled his arms together and clasped his hands, waiting.

Kathryn noticed that Wilson had a sheen of perspiration on his forehead and around his mouth. He was nervous, that and his speech made him very charming, Kathryn thought. He was a big burly man over six feet tall. His eyes were a greenish color and his hair reddish brown with some gray hair at his temples. Wilson had a pleasant face and she had always thought he was a good and kind man --- but NEVER --- never had thought about marriage with him.

Wilson stood patiently waiting while Kathryn perused his face as she was obviously deep in thought. He smiled at her, just a little smile at first, then larger as he watched her eyes move over his face. When she reached his big smile, she blushed and quickly looked away.

"I….I don't know what to say," she whispered.

"Are my intentions something you might consider?"

Kathryn looked at Wilson in wonder. "I…I, ah, think I would like that, Mr. Meyers." She blushed again, but didn't look away. "I don't believe there is anyone to ask permission. My sister Beatrice has respect for your counsel and has relied upon your opinions on more than one occasion. I doubt she would be anything but pleased for you and I to court." Kathryn laughed softly. "I think she will be as surprised as I am to think you'd even consider me." She smiled at Wilson.

"I can't imagine anyone wouldn't consider me to be a fortunate man to have you on his arm, Kathryn." Wilson took Kathryn's hand in his, "Would this evening be too early for a dinner at the hotel and a walk through the park?"

"Well….I think that would be very pleasant, Wilson." After they parted, Kathryn floated through the house in search of Beatrice. What a surprise she had for her sister. Along the way she stopped at a mirror in the hallway and studied her face. Her cheeks were flushed. Her eyes were shiny mirrors. But for the first time in months she looked radiantly happy.

Chapter 19

Reporting for Duty

Thursday morning finally arrived. The sun was just starting to appear and the town of Fairfax was still in shadows. A small crowd had gathered to send them off. Beatrice, Kathryn, Homer Sutton, Wilson Meyers, Jacob and Stella Bender, Gussie, and several men from the mill all gathered together. Doc heard a whooping noise and looked around to see what it was.

Suddenly he saw Samuel Washington running with a large bag over his shoulder, "Wait up, wait up, wait up!! Ahma comin'!" Samuel ran through the crowd and the Benders looked with surprise to see him push through.

"Hey Samuel!" Jacob hollered, "What's goin' on?"

Samuel hollered over his shoulder, "Ahma goin' with Doc an' Big John, Mr. Bender. It's the best way to try an' find my Suedie. Ahm gonna help the doc an' see how close to our old plantations I kin git. Safest way to travel fur me." Samuel stopped when he got to Doc's wagon and leaned against the side, "Hope you understan' Mr. Bender. You folks have been nothin' but good tuh me. I 'preciate y'all, but it's time to try an' find my gal." He looked up at Doc, "I'd like to go 'long wif yuh. Won't be no trouble. Jist wanna help y'all an' travel south." Samuel waited.

Doc looked up and heaved a sigh. He looked at Big John and raised his eyebrows. Big John smiled and nodded his head.

"All right Samuel. You can go with us. I'll expect you to do your duty to us first. You'll have to look around on your own. Big John vouches for you. Don't make me regret my decision." Doc looked at Robbie, "Private Coglin, this is Samuel Washington, he will be your wagon partner. Private Birdwell, you will have Big John. Make the changes quickly – time's wasting away the morning."

The men clambered down and made the switch. Samuel stowed his bag behind the big seat and settled in. Private Coglin looked at him then put out his hand, "Glad to meet yuh."

Doc hollered, "Git up!" and the wagons started forward. He tipped his hat and smiled at Beatrice. Tom smiled at Tessa who had tears on her cheeks and she waved goodbye. He and Doc proudly sat high up on their wagon seat wearing their uniforms. The four men were all dressed in uniforms looking clean and sharp as they passed through town. Several people stood outside shops waving goodbye and wishing them a quick return. Bender's Tavern door was open and a group of sullen men silently watched the passing caravan. Many of Hank Colby's old gang were missing. Word was that they had all gone south to join up with the Rebels.

The caravan slowly drove north to Camp Dennison, near Cincinnati, the new army camp where Doc would receive his medical supplies: liquid bottles of chloroform, opium pills, liquid bottles of morphine, liquid bottles of ether, and boxes filled with rolls of bandages. Several boxes of cones and pads to be used with the liquid sleep medication as well as splints to apply to broken limbs.

The caravan arrived at a teeming Camp Dennison after five long days of travel. The six men easily fell into a routine with each establishing their individual jobs. A camaraderie was made fast and the evening campfire was enjoyed with Tom's harmonica and stories they shared about their lives before the army claimed them. Big John always ended each evening with a prayer for them and the unknown they were about to face.

Doc left Tom in charge of the wagons and men, and went to report in to Col. Franklin who had been told of their impressive arrival with the large wagons and draft horses. The colonel advised Doc he was the most organized and would be first to be assigned duty in the field. He told Doc to report to a supply warehouse with his wagons where he would receive the government issued supplies for reporting for field duty. Anxious to be on their way, Doc hurried back to the wagons and had them forego setting up camp for the night until after they were loaded with supplies.

Doc and Tom were given two field packs called "a surgeon's field companion," also known as a "hospital knapsack" because they were a bulky, uncomfortable boxy piece of equipment worn over the shoulders that weighed when filled, about twenty pounds. When the doctors found themselves on the battlefield trying to treat the wounded soldiers, they discovered it was difficult to move quickly and low to the ground to avoid getting shot while trying to move around the field moving from soldier to soldier.

Col. Franklin arrived and was given a tour of each of Doc's wagons. It was clear he was very impressed with all he saw. He congratulated Doc and wished him 'God's speed.' "You need to know that Camp Dennison has been fortified against a confederate invasion. Cincinnati is a major source of navy vessels because there are several shipyards along the Ohio River. Due to our location, close to the slave states, the confederates want to invade the camp and take all the supplies that are much needed. We are the major distribution point for meat, grain and cannons as well as other military supplies such as you have been issued. As you leave through the eastern gates you will see fortifications along the hillsides. We have 12,000 soldiers defending Camp Dennison. I wish I could keep you here to see to our sick and wounded, but you are better served to report to Col. Godman where he is fighting in northern Virginia."

After the final boxes were loaded and stowed away, Doc gave the order to leave the area and find a place to camp for the night within Camp Dennison. Col. Franklin assigned six more soldiers to assure they would have protection in order to reach their destination as safe as possible. Doc spoke to Robbie, Eddie, Tom, Big John and Samuel telling them they were going to embark on the beginning of their difficult journey into the war. By the expressions on the men's faces it was clear that they all realized their undertaking was about to become real. That night it was quiet around the campfire, each man deep in thought. Doc started writing notes in his journal, as well as a letter to Beatrice telling her it might be a week or so until he could write again. He had one of the new soldiers deliver his letter for mailing before he finally was able to lie down for the night. Sleep, however, was only a fitful couple of hours. By dawn Doc was awake and anxious to travel. He was not hungry but allowed Big John to force a biscuit and coffee into his hand.

Tom was already up and had eaten as well at Big John's urging. All the men were anxious to leave and quickly broke camp. Looking at the hillsides as the wagons passed by gave a chill to Doc's small group. This was their first look at soldiers who were waiting to fight. They all wondered what it would be like when the fight began for them.

After a week of travel, Doc's wagon train arrived at the camp of Col. Godman who was relieved to see the arrival of his medical unit. The soldiers had recently been involved in several skirmishes and had sustained injuries needing attention. In addition to that, several men were sick with stomach ailments and dysentery. Doc was directed to a place where he set up camp and immediately started receiving patients. Big John and Samuel got the pots of water set on large fires while privates Coglin and Birdwell set up tents with the soldiers assigned to Doc. After a while, Doc had Tom tending to the stomach and intestinal illnesses and he worked on the wounded soldiers. Long after dark, they were able to take a break for dinner and coffee. Tom thought coffee never tasted better. He and Doc talked about what they had treated and compared notes. Tomorrow they would start in and finish with the less sick and wounded soldiers.

That night, Big John prepared beds in a tent for Tom and Doc to share. They were both too tired to do more than wash their faces and necks before falling onto their cots and immediately falling asleep. During the night, instead of the sounds of crickets chirping they heard gunfire, but they did not awaken enough to be concerned. Big John said his prayers beside Samuel and they quickly retired as well. This routine continued for the next week. The medical caravan moved only fifteen miles down the road before they were again stopped by an ambush of the troops ahead.

Doc set up camp and began treating the wounded. The last group of soldiers he and Tom treated had been put back into duty except for three who had to be transported to the railroad station in a nearby town. They would be taken back to Camp Dennison where a large field hospital was established to receive the battlefield wounded.

The regiment was engaged in many skirmishes along their route deeper into the south. Doc's unit celebrated Christmas by eating one of the precious hams Beatrice had added to their supplies. Big John made three delicious apple pies that were quickly and noisily eaten amid puffs of steam from their breaths in the cold air while they sat around a bonfire. Doc surprised everyone with gifts. He gave a book of plays by Shakespeare to Tom who was speechless with gratitude but felt bad that he had nothing to share with Doc. To the two orderlies, Coglin and Birdwell, Doc gave a small bottle of brandy to share with a warning to use it sparingly. Doc gave Big John a new bible he had been given but never used (be could never admit that to Big John). And, to Samuel he gave a warm jacket that he had purchased at the Mercantile before he received his officer's coat. The men received Doc's gifts with shy gratitude and all wished they had something to share with Doc.

Later, Tom played tunes on his harmonica
and Doc took the time to write in his journal and
included a letter to Beatrice. After dark, Doc
heard a scuffling noise and heard the orderlies,
Robbie and Eddie, struggling with something they
were dragging into camp. Big John, Tom and
Samuel were with them and they finally appeared
carrying a large bath tub. They stood with big
smiles on their faces. Doc looked up with
surprise, "Well, what do you have there,
privates?"

"We gotcha somethin' Doc. Merry Christmas!
Yur gonna have the best bath you've had in a
long time. Even got somethin' to put in the water
to make you smell real nice."

Big John directed the men to drag the tub into
Doc's tent while he stoked the fires and made
sure the large tub of water was warm. When the
tub was filled and the scent was added, Doc
looked down, inhaled and breathed in the smell of
vanilla and spices, then looked at the orderlies,
"You couldn't have given me anything nicer,
men. I'm going to crawl into that tub and I'm not
getting out until I'm a prune and the water is ice
cold." Doc started to undress, "I don't know how
we'll do it, but this tub is going be a part of our
unit if I have to give up riding in my wagon and
put it on my seat." All the men chuckled as they
left the tent and tied the flap closed for privacy.
Eddie and Robbie patted each other on the back
and laughed when they heard the water splash as

Doc got into the tub. Before they walked away Doc was singing as he bathed in his new bathtub.

The New Year was filled with news of battles being fought and hundreds of casualties. Doc's unit had not yet been engaged in a large battle but they all knew it was only a matter of time. Back home, Homer Sutton published lists of casualties and posted them on the window of the Fairfax Courier. Tearful mothers patiently waited each morning for the lists with hankies clutched in their hands. As the war extended into years, the lists grew and the young men coming home were forever changed in appearance and in spirit.

Chapter 20

From Skirmishes to Battles

"The art of war is simple enough. Find out where your enemy is. Get at him as soon as you can. Strike him as hard as you can, and keep moving on."
Ulysses S. Grant

Doc's medical unit caravan approached the area where the wagons would be set up with tents to treat the wounded. It was still dark, almost dawn. The heavy snowfall would not permit the sun to shine. Tom got down from the wagon and stretched, his breath making a cloud around his face. He stomped his feet and shook his arms to warm up. Doc was shouting orders to hurry with the setup. There was so much to be done before the battle began. More orders and soon Tom was inside a large tent organizing medical supplies and instruments. Tom was shocked to see that his hands were shaking. He had no way of knowing what the next hours would be like. He was scared, he realized. Soon he would see what happened during a war – a battle that would kill and wound men. By daybreak, he heard the first roar of the cannons and the pounding of horses' hooves. Across the valley more cannon roared into action flattening trees where union soldiers were firing their guns. Tom hoped the battle wouldn't come too close to their medical unit.

It was December, 1862, and the Ohio regiment was about to fight in the Battle of Fredericksburg. Standing outside their tent and waiting for the first casualties and drinking coffee, Doc's and Tom's breaths turned to steam in the cold morning air. They would be confronted for the first time with wounded soldiers who needed to be put to sleep for surgery. Tom was quick to learn how to position the cone on the patient's face and how much chloroform to put on the pad. Doc taught both privates, Coglin and Birdwell how to use the chloroform as well just in case they were ever needed. Which, as it turned out, was a godsend for following battles and the enormous amount of casualties.

Doc performed his first surgery to amputate a badly broken arm caused by a mini ball that crushed the bone. He peeled back a dirty hanky that had been tied around the soldier's arm and grimaced when he saw the damage. Doc's hands were shaking as he applied the saw on the soldier's arm. Robbie Coglin applied the sedative and did not look at the arm being removed. Soon, Doc was so immersed in taking off the arm that he was unaware of the sounds of battle outside the tent.

When Doc finished, Tom walked in and saw the arm lying in a bucket on the ground near

Doc's feet. He stopped and stared, his stomach flaring up and his head swirling around with black spots dotting his eyes. Before he fell to the ground, Doc saw him and caught him and lowered him down where he forced Tom's head between his knees. "Take some deep breaths, Tom. This won't be our first amputation. You're going to have to get used to a lot worse than this." Doc tapped Tom's head, "I need you to help me, Tom. Can you do that, son?"

Weakly, Tom replied, "I'll be okay, Doc. Just gimme a minute."

Doc looked at Private Coglin, "Private, I need you to clean the table for the next man and dispose of this arm. Tom, there are more wounded. I need you to have Samuel bring in the next wounded men and start treating them now. Tom! Are you ready to help me?"

Tom stood up and staggered to the tent opening where he motioned for the medical unit soldiers to bring in the stretchers bearing the wounded. "Keep them coming until they're all done." He was as white as his shirt but Doc saw he was ready to take care of the patients. Big John peeked in the tent and saw that Tom was going to be alright. He looked at the bucket, then at Doc.

"I'll take care of this for you, Doc. Y'all keep workin' on the soldiers. There's a mighty big group comin' in fur yuh. Me and Samuel'll keep the fires burnin' an' the water hot." He held

309

the tent flap wide to allow a stretcher with a soldier whose face was covered by a dirty shirt sleeve that had been torn off to cover his face.

"Thank you, Big John. Bring in a kettle of hot water for Tom and me, please." Doc motioned for the stretcher bearers to place the man on the table. "When you can, I would appreciate a cup of coffee. You might bring a strong cup for Tom, too."

The arrival of Col. Godman in the medical tent was met with concerned quiet. He had been seriously wounded and needed both Doc and Tom to treat his injuries. Afterward he was transported to the hospital at Camp Dennison. The regiment was without a commanding officer and everyone was concerned how this would affect the soldiers' morale. The wounded were coming to the medical tents in alarmingly high numbers and Doc thought there must be some way for the commanders of the units fighting to end the battle.

Doc looked down and started working again. He glanced over at Tom who was working on a soldier with a wound to his shoulder. Doc smiled. Tom was tough. He'd be alright. They both might have some nightmares about that arm lying in the bucket, but for now they would take one patient at a time. There were many more amputations and serious wounds. Both Doc and Tom became fairly immune to the legs and arms thrown on the ground. Periodically, they were removed and buried. The snow fell heavily most of the day and covered the battlefield almost a foot deep in places.

The operating tent flap was tied open to allow air to circulate but it was cold, wet air. The area was surrounded by wet dense fog. The battle went on for four days and was a Confederate victory. All the medical units were overwhelmed with wounded and dying soldiers. Doc was told by a colonel who came by the tent to see how Doc's supplies were holding up that there was as many as 10,000 killed or wounded. Doc didn't have time to be shocked at this news. He did become concerned when he was told that the battle had been lost by the Union. Briefly he worried about his medical supplies being captured by the Confederates then dismissed his thoughts. No use fretting about something he could do nothing about.

The regiments moved on after the battle was over, but Doc's unit stayed to make sure all the wounded who could no longer fight were transported to the nearest train station where they would be shipped out. There was talk about a large number of Union soldiers who had been taken captive or were missing from the regiment. Doc dismissed this news because he had no time to worry about men he couldn't help. He had his hands full. His doubt about his prowess as a doctor who had never treated such horribly wounded men troubled his mind.

If this was only the beginning and he was overwhelmed, what would future battles bring? Doc was grateful for Big John and Samuel who had made a large pot of rabbit stew. Even though they had to eat standing up, he and Tom were grateful for the warm food. Their once shiny boots were covered with a mixture of muddy dirt and blood from the operating tent floor. After each surgery the orderlies took a large bucket of water and threw it on the table then took a rag and pushed the bloody water, cloth that had been used, and bits of flesh onto the ground. The next patient's body was placed on the table and the process began again.

Tom went in search of a cup of Big John's coffee. As he walked to the cook fires, he thought about the day he had just experienced which wasn't over yet and would probably last through the night and through the next day at least. This had been the first big battle for him and Doc. The medical tent had been prepared to treat wounded soldiers, but they had not been prepared to deal with the wounded and dying soldiers that flooded in by the hundreds.

Tom felt hatred like a hot branding iron pressed against his chest and burned for these soldiers, blue or gray. After this first battle, Tom now could feel the dark days of conflict and war -- the devastation of death and dying. He hoped these emotions wouldn't overwhelm him and make him feel like his skills were inadequate. What would happen if he couldn't continue to help Doc? What if he wanted to run away home?

This horrific day, Tom wondered, what must the soldiers feel like to spew cannon balls and fodder, bullets and mayhem on men across a battlefield? Men who could very well be brothers, cousins, uncles or neighbors. At the end of each battle in the bloody, moaning aftermath – would they mourn them or would their minds be as dead and mangled as the men on the war-torn field?

Doc's unit was assigned to a new officer, Brigade Commander Samuel Carroll. Their unit moved on to the Battle of Chancellorsville in Virginia. The three-month war had now become something that would last a lot longer. Doc had been asked by Commander Carroll to sign on for the duration of the war. He talked to Tom and privates Coglin and Birdwell, who decided together that they would sign up for three years. Both Big John and Samuel refused to leave and told Doc they were a part of his unit now and would stay until the "war was finally finished." Doc felt guilty because he had praised the men about how well they all worked together and because of that they made a difference for the Union. He thought perhaps it made them feel obligated to stay. But they remained firm saying it was their decision to stay in the army. They wanted to stay with Doc and see the war to the end.

The battle lasted until the first week in May.

Doc had needed to send word to Beatrice for more supplies. He sent Private Birdwell to headquarters to send a telegraph message to Fairfax for emergency supplies. Doc feared that his list was so long that Pvt. Birdwell would not be able to send it in one message. The Union Army had delivered a wagon load of supplies, but all the medicine and supplies had to be shared and there wasn't enough chloroform or ether for all the surgeries. Doc had to have soldiers hold down his patients while they held a small twig between their teeth. He had become strangely deaf to the agonized moans and groans of the soldiers while he tended to their injuries.

Beatrice and Kathryn were true to their word, within two weeks they sent a railroad car full of supplies for Doc and Tom as well as a large packet filled with letters and newspapers from Homer Sutton. When Big John opened the box car door it was like Christmas! There were barrels containing coffee, chocolate, a dozen hams hung on nails across the back wall, bushel baskets of potatoes, yams, apples, jars of honey, barrels filled with bags of sugar, flour, and salt. Several barrels were filled with rolls of torn linens for bandages, and more ointments, salves and herbs for healing potions from Mary Leland.

When Doc received notice of what the rail car contained, his eyes filled with tears and he vowed to send a special letter to Beatrice but knew there was no way he could express his gratitude for her kindness and support.

As Doc's men were sending the last group of soldiers to the railroad station, Tom saw a group of wagons coming down the road toward them. Tom thought to himself that he'd seen a lot of strange things since he and Doc had been travelling during this war, but tonight just beat it all.

It was about supper time when he saw the first wagon pulled by two very big mules driven by a scruffy-looking old man that pulled into their camp. Four women wearing fancy hats and bright colored dresses sat in two rows of seats smiling, waiving and hollering 'howdy' to everyone. Another covered wagon driven by a woman dressed in overalls like a man stopped behind them. Tom, who had never seen women so fancy, stood paralyzed as they started to climb down with no help. Their layers of petticoats flounced and whirled around them as they backed down from the wagon. He saw their ankles and lacey white, red and pink drawers flashing in the breeze.

The women stood with their backs to the wagon and waited for the old man to get down. Tom looked at their faces and saw that they all had curls of hair along their cheeks and necks that were colors he had never seen; bright red, almost pink, black as night and silver white. Somehow they didn't look natural and Tom had a desire to touch them to see if the hair was real. Just then,

Doc came out of the tent wiping his face and hands with a towel. He didn't look pleased to see the folks and Tom wondered why. A crowd of Big John's men and wounded soldiers gathered behind Tom. Many were returning smiles with the women. Others just stood like Tom and stared.

"Evenin' y'all," the old man said with a big toothy grin. "Thought you folks could use some cheerin' up after bein' on the road and all. My ladies will be glad to spend some time with ya and it won't cost ya'll that much ifn' ya'll kin throw in some food." The old man smoothed his jacket and removed his hat, waiting. He looked at Doc, "Name's Wilbur Farrow. You look like you'd be in charge, sir. Whatcha think? Yah got some time and room for a little pleasure tonight?"

Doc's face looked like he'd eaten something sour. "I am unable to welcome you here, but I cannot stop you from camping further down the road. I will not forbid these men from visiting your camp, but I will insist you conduct yourselves without causing fights or any disturbances, or I will make sure you are driven away without any food or money. Is that understood?" Doc planted his hands on his hips and looked sternly at the old man. The women tittered and whispered to each other, smiling at Doc.

"Thank you kindly, sir," the old man swept his hand across his belly and bowed. "We'll get along down the way an' set up our camp. You're all invited to stop on by. Appreciate some vittles – anything will do. We'll put the coffee on fur yah." He turned to the ladies, "Ok gals. We found us a place fur the night. Git on up in there and we'll move on down the road a piece."

The women all moaned and whined. "Awww! We ain't gonna climb back up, Wilbur. We needta walk a bit an' pull out ar legs. Besides, we ain't had a pee break in ah awful long time."

"Aw-right, Nettie. Git on behind the wagons an' you can find ah place as you walk on down the road. Hurry up, now. We got bizness to atten' to." Wilbur slapped the reins and the two mules pulled the wagon around and back onto the road. All four women waited until the second wagon pulled behind him before they started walking. Tom could hear them talking and laughing.

Tom looked at Doc and motioned to the women and wagons, "Why can't they stay here with us, Doc? They seem like friendly folks."

Doc rubbed his face and smiled at Tom. "You know what kind of women those are, Tom?"

Tom looked perplexed, "Why they're prob'ly entertainers I figure." He looked at Doc with a frown.

"Just how much do you know about what goes on between a man and a woman, young

317

Tom?"

Tom looked sheepish, "Well I know about how babies come 'bout if that's what yur askin' Doc."

"Yes, well there's a lot more to it that you're about to find out. I will tell you that I don't want to see you down there with those women. They are paid to take care of a man's needs, if you understand what I mean. The problem is that you can get a lot more than you pay for. There are diseases that those women can carry and can pass on to men who use them for having sex." Doc looked down the road with a frown on his face, "I can't order them to leave the area, but I will tell you like I'm going to tell the rest of the men, that I would prefer they resist the temptation of relieving their needs with those "ladies" no matter how tempting they look." Doc looked at Tom, "You don't want to take something back home if you're wanting to return to Tessa. There is danger in having a few moments of relief." Doc waited for Tom to answer him.

Tom looked down the road at the women walking hand in hand in their fancy dresses. "I don't find a need for that sort of relief, Doc. I thank you fur tellin' me 'bout them. I thought they were somethin' different. Ain't seen nothin' like 'em before. Now I know why they have such fancy looks," Tom looked at Doc and smiled, "They're entertainers all right, ain't they, Doc?" Tom laughed and walked back to his tent to help prepare for the night. Big John watched Tom and looked at Doc. They exchanged knowing looks. There would be lots of noise coming from down the road tonight.

Camp followers such as this lot would be difficult to avoid, but he would protect Tom and make sure he was never tempted. Over the months, it was a common occurrence to have large groups of camp followers who became a part of every regiment. Besides prostitutes, there were wives and children of some of the soldiers. They would set up camp outside the tent area of the soldiers and would help with cooking, laundry and give loving support to the men. Some women were widows with no way to support themselves. They too helped with cooking and laundry, and spent time with the men who used them for sexual comfort.

Tom had accidentally seen couples together late at night when he had a need to use the latrine. He had been shocked to see half-dressed men and women on the ground oblivious to their surroundings in the throes of passion. Tom learned to make a wide path around the area where the camp followers had their wagons and tents. He was well aware that he was being exposed to a lot more than just fighting, death and dying while being a part of the army. He and Doc talked late at night when sleep avoided them. Doc was very open and honest when he answered Tom's questions and observations. In addition to his two books, Doc had brought a box full of medical books, Shakespeare, poetry, and other books about European and US history. Both he and Doc treated the books as if they were made of gold, which was about right anyway. Without knowing it, Tom was receiving the equivalent of a college education from Doc and he was loving every discussion and passage that he read. In their sea of destruction he saw the light of learning and knowledge.

Chapter 21

Amidst Carnage and Angels

> "Forever float that standard sheet, where
> breathes the foe but falls before us!
> With freedom's soil beneath our feet, and
> freedom's banner waving o'er us."
> Banner on Union soldier's stationery

On January 1, 1863, President Lincoln using his war powers issued the Emancipation Proclamation which made it possible for former slaves to be employed by the Union Army. This proclamation ended the 1850 Fugitive Slave Act and set all slaves free as long as they were no longer within the Confederate states.

In May, Big John and Samuel Washington were sworn in as enlisted men now on the payroll of the Union Army. It was a proud moment for the men and there was much back-pounding and handshaking among Doc's medical unit. Even wounded Union soldiers joined in the celebration.

There was another major battle in urgent need of Doc's medical unit because of thousands of wounded soldiers. Doc's unit was ordered to leave the south and were soon on their way to Pennsylvania where the battle had started July 1, 1863. Doc's unit was ordered to a place aptly called Cemetery Hill which they reached in the middle of the night. The next day the sound of battle seemed to come from every direction. The roar of cannons kept any conversations to grunts and brief orders. Days went into night. Doc and Tom, and the men of his unit tried, sometimes successfully, to take turns catching an hour or two of sleep every ten to twelve hours. Doc couldn't remember when he had sat down to eat. He barely had time to relieve himself. When word came that the Union Army was losing the battle and they had to move the medical units so that they wouldn't be captured by the Confederates, Doc swore a blue streak. They had so many wounded soldiers that he couldn't fathom how to move them all. An additional unit of soldiers arrived and moved all the soldiers who were ambulatory. The ones who couldn't walk or were unconscious were moved by the wagons, crowded in like sardines. The Rappahannock River was close by and Doc yearned to swim in the clean flowing river. He vowed to do just that as soon as possible. The water would feel good, too, because the weather was very hot and Doc felt like he was smothering with the heat.

As Doc's wagons approached Gettysburg there was an overwhelming smell. It got so bad that everyone pulled bandanas over their noses and mouths to help divert the smell. Soon they could see several piles of horse carcasses that were being burned. By the end of the battle, Doc

learned that over 3,000 horses had been killed
during the battle and a continuous pile burned for
days. More devastating was the piles of dead
soldiers who needed immediate burial. Tom
looked away as they passed the area where they
were being buried. A company of soldiers, their
heads covered with bags cut with holes so that
only their eyes and lips were visible, were digging
a field of graves. In the end, over 14,000 soldiers
were wounded and needed medical attention.
More than 3,000 were dead. The people in the
nearby town were made ill by the smell of the
fires burning.

   Torrential rain was falling which filled the
roads with deep mud and ruts that made travel
difficult. The battle raged on for over three days.
Even the town buildings and homes had been
damaged from shrapnel because of the number of
cannons being fired from so many angles. At one
point, Cemetery Hill where Doc's unit camped,
was almost overrun by Confederate riflemen. A
division of Union soldiers arrived and drove them
back. The sound of rifles firing soon stopped as
the soldiers fought in hand-to-hand combat.

   On the Gettysburg battlefield it was a fairly
quiet evening….finally. The roar of the cannons,
gunfire and explosions had ceased, and even the
moans of the wounded had quieted down. The
battle was finally over. Doc and Tom were still
operating on the worst injuries. The soldiers with
less serious injuries still waited to be treated. It

would be two or three days until they could be treated. Doc and Tom were past wanting to hear who won or lost.

Tom was taking a break before returning to the operating tent. He was too tired to be hungry but knew he needed to eat for his own well-being. As he sat down on a chair in front of his tent he saw a light out on the battlefield moving around. Curious, Tom rose up from his chair and went to follow it. He had seen lights before, but was either too busy with wounded soldiers or just too darned weary to care about what moving lights on a battlefield was all about. The possibility of dangerous men briefly entered Tom's mind as there were people who stripped the dead of any valuables and they might not take kindly if challenged, but he was too curious to care. Besides, he thought, Big John and Samuel would hear him if he hollered their names and would come a'runnin to help him.

As he approached the lantern light, he saw a dark shape and soon realized it was a woman! She was walking among the bodies, periodically bending to touch a bloody face or hand, sometimes murmuring to herself. Tom wondered if she was a wife or mother searching for a lost son or husband.

As Tom approached her she turned and raised the lantern to see him better. "What are you doing out here, ma'am?" Tom slowly approached the woman. "These men are all dead. You have no business being here. If you are looking for your son or husband, you will be notified as soon as all the information is available." Tom was not pleased to see the woman smile at him.

The woman's face was gaunt and her eyes were shadowed with dark smudges of fatigue.

"I am a nurse, young man. What business do *you* have here?"

Tom was shocked! A nurse….alone out here? "Ma'am, I'm Sgt. Thomas Leland of the Ohio 4th Medical Corps. Are you from a local hospital? Where did you come from? And, how would you remove any of these men if there *was* still some life in them?"

"I'm sorry. My name is Clara Barton. I have been helping to evacuate the patients who were transported to the rail station. Sometimes I walk the battlefields just to make sure no one is overlooked…..it doesn't matter which side they fought for," she smiled but still looked sad. Tom's mouth dropped open in surprise. Clara Barton was well known as a tireless angel of mercy who had done much to clean up hospitals and make doctors pay attention to their hygiene practices with wounded soldiers and the hospitals. She had even let President Lincoln know that soldiers were going without food in hospitals because there wasn't enough help to take proper care of them. Tom knew that without Big Sam and his people that he and Doc wouldn't have been able to give their patients the care that they did.

"Yes, ma'am, I do know about you. I'm sorry I was rude just now, but I don't like to see these men picked over like trash."

"Nor do I Sergeant. Nor do I," she sighed. "I must go. There is still so much to be done at the station." She held her lantern up once again and looked at Tom, "Take good care of your patients." She turned and slowly walked away, still checking the bodies as she went. Down the way there was a road at the end of the fence line where she was slowly walking. Tom saw a small buggy with a horse attached waiting. She had walked a long way checking the bodies. Doc had said she was tireless when he told Tom about her and what she had been doing to improve care of wounded soldiers. Even generals let her do as she wanted with the hospitals and wards of patients. What an amazing lady, he thought. The soldiers called her the "Angel of the Battlefield."

When Nurse Barton arrived at Gettysburg she found wounded soldiers that had received no food or water for two days. She found that there was no food storages for patients so she immediately prepared them a kettle of cornmeal which was all that was available. Then, after this was gone she made a concoction of what meager provisions the other nurses found: crushed army biscuits called "hardtack," some wine, water, and brown sugar. Doc had told Tom that he would remember that concoction for use in the future.

Tom quickly walked back to the surgery tent. He wanted to tell Doc about meeting the nurse they had heard so much about --- that he saw her searching for soldiers who might still be alive in all the carnage!

Tom stumbled. He had stepped on a hand. Oh God! He mumbled an apology. He had to hurry now and get away from this field of bodies. The early morning light would find a group of soldiers who would separate the dead soldiers; north from south. Some would be buried with markers, others would be put into large holes together. If no one came to bury the Confederate soldiers, they would be laid together in one large hole. The only word their families would have about them would be that they died in the Battle of Gettysburg in Pennsylvania.

Tom tried to stop thinking about the dead. It was enough that he and Doc had to take care of the living soldiers' mangled bodies. Word was that they would pack up and leave in two days. Another trek through towns and fields to another battle.

He wanted Doc to take a break now. They were both exhausted and had more work to do with the wounded before they could sleep and the battle began again. He didn't look forward to sleeping either. Nightmares interrupted Tom's sleep almost every time he was able to try to get some rest. Big John prayed for him and wanted Tom to pray as well, but Tom was having difficulty believing that God was even real anymore. What he had seen during this war was a nightmare itself. If God was truly up in heaven He had given up on everyone and everything. Tom had become bitter after seeing what war did to men's bodies.

When the war started, very few doctors had performed surgery to amputate limbs. Now, it was standard practice to remove arms and legs that had been hit with minie balls fired from rifles. When a soldier was struck by a minie ball it shattered the bone. The bacteria in the grooves of the minie ball caused infection and then gangrene would set in and they would lose the soldier they fought so hard to save. Tom didn't even ask Doc when a leg or arm had to be removed. He calmly handed Doc the cutting instrument and got the chloroform or ether ready. It was nothing for him and Doc to scoop up a wounded soldier's intestines and push them back inside the body. Then Doc would tell Tom to stitch him up and walk away to the next patient. Tom had learned so much from Doc just watching him. Doc told him as good as he was getting at helping him stitch and mend the wounded, it was only a matter of time that he would be as good as Doc himself. Tom couldn't imagine being as good as Doc. True, he could handle most any kind of injury now. Even some of the doctors watched him and asked ques-tions about how to perform some of the operations and mending that he and Doc did.

Doc and Tom were promoted to Major Bradford Phillips and Lieutenant Thomas Leland by battlefield commission due to their incredible competency handling the massive amount of wounded soldiers during the battle of Gettysburg. Later, Doc laughed at Tom when he asked about a raise in pay. "We're almost three months behind in our pay now. I don't think you're going to see much of a difference."

The loss of 12,000 Confederates at Gettysburg changed the course of the war. The heavy bombardment had been deafening, and at the end of the battle Doc and all his men had a constant ringing in their ears. Later it was determined that the Gettysburg battle had the largest number of casualties of the entire war. By that time, Doc and Tom were deep in the state of Virginia struggling to keep their flagging spirits and stamina up to maintain their quality of care for the wounded.

Many of the injured soldiers were treated on the battlefield by Tom using the surgical field pack. Doc's soldiers then transferred them after surgery, as soon as they could be moved. If they were severely wounded they were taken either by wagon or train to hospitals or the soldiers forced local farmers and people in houses nearby to billet them. Many soldiers died on their way to the hospitals.

Morticians started coming to the battlefields.

Soldiers were identified and then prepared for shipment to their homes. To preserve the bodies for the long journey, they were injected with arsenic and zinc chloride. When the soldiers' bodies arrived at their destination, people who saw the bodies were dumbfounded that they were not decomposed but still intact except for their war wounds.

Because of the large numbers of wounded soldiers and the small number of surgical units and competent doctors, many soldiers lay around on the ground, sometimes for days, waiting to be treated. Their wounds, some only simple flesh wounds, became infected with gangrene which caused more amputations. Some soldiers died of fever from infection before they could be treated. Doc and Tom had to treat more and more soldiers for dysentery, typhoid fever and malaria. The marches through humid swamps in the south infected large numbers of soldiers before they ever reached the battlefield. Many died during transportation to the large hospitals where they could be housed and treated.

Working late into the night trying to save the lives of young men and old, Tom and Doc's legs felt stiff and dull like they had gone to sleep. After hours of cutting off limbs with blood flowing like small rivers over the wood planks holding each soldier, they continued working without much thought other than trying to stay awake for the next soldier. One day grew into the next during each major battle with no time for Doc to write in his journal. Except for a few entries, he gave up trying to write down his thoughts. His letters to Beatrice were very few. She still wrote weekly and sometimes he received five or six letters at a time.

My Dear Beatrice,

I have much to remember when I am finally away from this war. In the chaos I have found the people I trust with my life and the lives of others; they are true friends and the best that humankind has to offer. But I will, I am sure, have dreams and nightmares triggered by certain smells or sounds for the rest of my life.

It is of some comfort that those men who suffered from painful wounds and those who lay dying had good thoughts of home – of loved ones, often sighing and moaning their names. Of those who called for comfort it was most often "mother" or a woman's name, most likely a wife or sweetheart. For a few it was "father" they called for. I wonder, if it was I who sought a loved one's comfort – who would I call for?

Your letters have become of the utmost importance for me. I keep them close as I re-read them when I can. They are my source of comfort, dear Beatrice. Your thoughts and tales of daily life are both entertaining and comforting. I can take myself away and be with you, your sister Kathryn and the town of Fairfax.

When I return and resume my practice there it will be a new age. People will have died, moved away or be eternally changed forever due to this wasted war. I do look forward to being back there. I am going to be bold and hope that you will continue to wait for me. If there is another who takes my place and holds your heart while I am gone, I hope you will tell me. Otherwise, let me stake my claim – again -- for it now. I dream of you, my sweet. My heart yearns to feel the warmth of your returned affection.

I am being far too bold, dear Beatrice, but I find that life can change so quickly that I must grab for my happiness and throw caution to the wind.

Until we are together, my fondest wishes for your health and happiness.

Yours most truly,
Phillip

Chapter 22

The War Rages On

That it will never come again is what makes
life so sweet.
Emily Dickinson

In early May, 1864, the Battle of the
Wilderness in Virginia, was fought in an area of
dense, dry shrubs and tall grass. Doc had been
told that General Ulysses Grant, a new general,
was in command of this battle.

In the distance Tom could see dust being
stirred up and the sound of horses and heavy
equipment moving on the road ahead. Doc called
his name and Tom trotted over to him. He was
eager to prepare for the chaos that would soon
erupt. They relished this calm before the storm of
fighting and agony began.

This battle raged for three days of intense
misery. Tom and Doc would never forget, no
matter how hard they tried, that they had
transcended into a living hell from which
thousands of soldiers were injured. Many of the
more than two thousand soldiers who died during
this battle were burned to death by a raging fire
that burned through the battlefield killing them
and a herd of cattle. There was little they could
do to care for the soldiers who were badly burned

and came into their tents. Big John spent days without sleeping moving among the suffering, reading his bible and praying over the men.

The order to move on was given. The battle was weeks over. Everything that could be done for the survivors had been done. They were still burying the dead. The morticians were doing their jobs on the bodies that would be shipped home, and the last wagon left carrying the wounded to the large field hospitals that could continue their care before shipping them home.

Doc and Tom were thin from exhaustion and poor diet – there was never enough time to sleep or eat. It was now April, 1865 and Doc's unit was following the regiment, chasing the Confederates toward Farmville, Virginia. They had been told that several battles were being fought in the area where they would make camp. General Robert E. Lee was the commanding officer and his soldiers were spread out for miles trying to move toward North Carolina. Doc was warned that the Confederates were becoming desperate. They scavenged the battlefields for anything they could find: food, rifles, bullets, clothing and boots. If they thought they were going to be captured, as desperate as they were, they destroyed their own supplies before surrendering. Many of the Confederate soldiers' feet were bloody and wrapped in rags. Near starvation their bodies were emaciated. So many of their comrades had been killed or severely wounded. They were constantly being driven back by Union forces so they began to sneak away from their units and flee for their homes. Many would find that there was nothing left for them there. Large numbers of Confederates were taken prisoner near a place named Appomattox.

Doc took stock of the Virginia countryside. The sky was getting dark and it was only mid-morning. That meant they'd have rain soon and from the looks of the sky it was going to be a real downpour. There were several big trees with large branches that he would have the men chop off for firewood. They never had enough of that. Once they had that done, the men would spread the large canvas amid the tree trunks for coverage for the soldiers who would be stacked up like the firewood once the battle commenced. Hopefully, they could save a few more soldiers if they didn't have to lie in the mud with their wounds. It wouldn't be an easy time for the next few days for the surgery and wounded but they had gotten used to harsh conditions. Doc just hoped they didn't have to worry about high winds.

The rain had been ceaseless for it seemed like a full week. Water ran in small rivers everywhere – even through one of the operating tents. Big John's "crew," as Doc called them, a group of black men who joined their unit to be with Big John and Samuel, had to dig trenches inside the operating tent to block the water from flowing around Doc and Tom's feet. The crew made such a difference in setting up the tents and fire and moving the wounded that Doc kept them as a part of his medical unit and made sure they had clothes and food and a place to sleep. The men dug a trench around the outside with an opening to drain away the rainwater so it would cease to flow like a river of blood.

After another long drive, Doc's unit set up camp near a large grove of trees. Big John's crew took over and turned the entire area into the medical unit. Because the rain was still falling with no signs of stopping, Big John and Samuel knew they had to make an area to protect the wounded. The crew had taken all the canvas they could find in the wagons and placed it under the trees. A few men climbed into the trees while the men on the ground used ropes and laced the canvas together. Slowly, they men pulled the canvas pieces up into the trees and tied them around the tree trunks making a canvas roof so that wounded soldiers had a place to stay out of the rain. Several branches attached to the canvas made little hills and valleys so that the rain water wouldn't accumulate and pull down the makeshift roof. Tom watched the men working to protect the wounded soldiers and thought it was darn clever of Doc to figure out a way to help the countless bodies of men who overcrowded the area. It was difficult to walk between the bodies, but it was better to try to give these men a chance to recover from their injuries.

The number of wounded and dying was so great that there was not enough medical staff in all the units surrounding the area of the battle to properly look after them. Once treated and put aside, only the most severely injured were monitored. The rest helped each other or lay waiting for someone to come to them. Corpses piled up in mud filled trenches for days. Union soldiers were lined up on the top of the trenches and the Confederates were left in the trench to be covered over.

Tom was now able to treat almost any injury that came before him. Many times he never looked up as one patient was moved away from his table and another one was placed before him. Big John and Samuel now referred to Tom as 'Doc Tom.' He just kept giving directions for more hot water, bandages, needles and thread for stitching. Tom had even done emergency amputations without gagging or feeling like he was going to faint without Doc standing by for support. After days running into nights and again into the morning --- both Tom and Doc were able to go without sleep and stand for hours trying to treat all the wounded coming into their operating tent. Were it not for Big John, Samuel and their crew, it would have been impossible for any efficiency to take place in moving the patients around and organizing where they would be placed after treatment or surgery.

During the battle a terrified horse came running full gallop into the area covered by canvas with wounded soldiers filling the ground. It was dragging a soldier. Several men stood and captured the panicked horse and tried to settle him down. Samuel came running and while the men held the horse he removed the soldier from the stirrup that was twisted and had kept the man from falling free. Although he knew the soldier was dead, Samuel gently lowered him to the ground. He carefully removed any identification and letters from the body so that someone could notify his family of his death. Most 'Johnny Rebs' were just put in a large hole and covered up. Doc tried to keep their information so that he could send them back to families when he had time to write letters for them. Samuel didn't think that other medical units had doctors with Doc's kindness and caring. He was a special man, that Doc, he thought. Didn't matter color of skin or uniform to him, nosirree.

Doc and Tom were used to harsh conditions and were becoming immune to everything except the mosquitos and black flies that sometimes filled the air. Big John had made large fans out of pieces of canvas attached to branches. Soldiers who were able were given the task of waving the fans in the operating tent to keep the flies away from the tables where surgeries were being performed.

Tom enjoyed the early morning. He had

taken a few hours to sleep after working nonstop for nearly eighteen hours. A light breeze fluttered the leaves of the trees surrounding the medical tents, making their silvered undersides flash as they moved. Soon they would move to another place of battle, but for just a few moments --- he could take a deep breath and pretend the world was at peace. He went to get a cup of coffee before making Doc take a break.

Doc needed to get out of the operating room tent. His last patient had lost so much blood that when he removed his arm he bled to death. The tent sides were closing in; the smell had become a part of him and made his stomach roil and tighten like he was seasick. He couldn't see another stretcher with a bloody patient while he was ready to vomit on the next body put before him.

Quickly, he walked outside to see how many patients still needed immediate attention. Too many. The bodies were stretched out surrounding the tents and wagons as far the eye could see. Acres of land were covered with other medical regiments' wagons and tents. He winced when he heard the cannons still thundering but still a ways out from his encampment. There would be more dead and dying to come. Doc sighed and decided to take a short walk around the other side of the big operating tent. He wanted to clear his head and try to smell something besides blood and death.

Up ahead he saw something yellow in the

grass. Dandelions! Any other time he wouldn't have bothered with them, but he needed to see them up close. The yellow color was so vibrant. Bending down he picked a large blossom and held it to his nose. It brought back memories of his sister during the summer when she would tie them together and make a circle like a crown for her head and a necklace for him with the pungent flowers. He would laugh when his sister held one under his chin and told him it turned his skin yellow.

He knew he needed to get back, but he bent down and picked a hand full of dandelions and put them in his pocket. Slowly, he turned and once again surveyed the area. Just ahead he saw an officer holding the body of another soldier. He knew this area was for the dead. The officer was wounded and obviously needed treatment. Doc decided to approach him and make him move to the waiting area for treatment.

"Soldier!" Doc ordered. Then more gently, "You need to let him go, Captain. He's dead now, there's nothing we can do for him. I need to take care of your wounds." Doc kneeled down and pulled the captain's hands away from the dead soldier and tried to make him stand. The captain growled and sobbed, "He's my brother! Let me be! I can't leave him here alone!" He held his brother tighter and put his face against the dead man's bloody shoulder.

"He's gone now, Captain. We'll take care of

him and see that he's shipped home. It's you we need to tend to, so let my men have your brother and you come with me." Doc placed his strong arm around the captain's back and made him stand.

Doc looked up and saw Big John approaching him. "Big John, take care of…. What was your brother's name, Captain?" The captain stood at attention, saluted his brother's body, his own body weaving and swaying, "This is Corporal Jordan Lewis Hawkins, sir, my bother. I'm Captain Joshua Lewis Hawkins." Tears were running down the captain's face. Doc felt his chest tighten up in sympathy with this poor soldier.

Suddenly, the captain's legs started to bend and Doc knew he was going to faint. He caught him against his chest, "Samuel, help me out here, please!" Samuel came running and helped Doc soften the captain's fall to the ground. Together they lifted him and placed him on a stretcher. Doc pulled his stethoscope up to his ears and listened to the captain's heartbeat and breathing. "Let's get him into the tent and take a look at his wounds and see how bad they are."

Tom stood next to Captain Hawkins, holding his arm and felt his pulse. He was moaning in pain. Tom felt bad that he couldn't give the Captain any pain medication. They were short of laudanum and only used it for the most painful injuries and surgery.

"How are you doing, Captain Hawkins?" Tom held a cup of water and pulled him up so that he could take a drink. "You need to have some water. Try to take a few swallows now," Tom urged.

The Captain pushed his hand away, spilling the water all down his neck. "They're all dead, he moaned. "I led them all to a field of slaughter and death including my own brother!"

"I'm told we won that battle, Captain. The Rebs all ran away...."

"It's was too late," he groaned. "The damage was all done before then."

"Well, the war will soon be over I'm told. Union troops are moving south and we'll all be going home soon." Tom was hoping this was the truth. He was weary of war, death and dying.

"Home's all gone now. Folks are all dead, too. Now Jordan's gone. I've got nothing left! There's no place left for me to go except back to the war." The Captain tried to roll over but the cot was too confining.

"Just lie still and try to rest. Try some more water 'til we get you fixed up, then I can get you some food." Tom gently poured the water into the Captain's mouth. This time he was able to swallow.

Big John took his bible and wandered among the soldiers who lay in rows on the ground. He paused now and then and touched a shoulder or a hand of one of the men and whispered to him, quietly giving him a kind word or prayer. Tom told Doc that his friend, Big John, was a 'bible man.' Like me he learned how to read from the bible. Only for Big John it was against the law to learn to read. The aunt of the man who owned him was kind and taught Big John his letters after the master and his wife went to bed. After that he never went to bed without reading his bible.

Big John had become a preacher as well as the manager of the Bradley household when he came to work for Mr. and Mrs. Bradley. When he joined Doc and Tom and went to war, Big John brought his bible with him. He took it upon himself to read to the soldiers who Doc and Tom couldn't save and were dying. Big John read to them and gave them comfort. "They's gonna be ready to meet der Lord," he'd always say.

Chapter 23

Love Brightens the Gloom

*For nothing is less under our control than the heart –
having no power to command but we are forced to
obey.*
Heloise in a letter to Abelard

As the caravan travelled down another long
dirt road, in the surrounding trees Tom could hear
birds chirping and he turned to watch the sky
slowly change color from dark blue to pinkish
orange. They passed through a small town that
had been damaged during a battle. The only
buildings left were a small church, a bar and a
few sad looking houses. Tom saw the sullen,
angry eyes of the people who had gathered to
watch as they passed by. The only men left in
southern towns now were very young boys and
old men. All had the look of angry defeat on their
faces when the wagons passed by.

"One of our scouts says there's a big barn
not far ahead, Doc. Maybe we can camp there
and use it," Pvt. Coglin hollered. He and Pvt.
Birdwell had been discussing the use of the big
barn since they first saw it when they came over
the hill. A large barn would come in handy if the
casualties mounted up when the next battle
started. The medical train was over three miles

long and they could have the barn set up for operating on the worst cases before all the wagons were stopped and unloaded.

"Should we ask the farmer if we can use it or just take it and tell him we acquired his barn for the purposes of the war?"

"Nah, if he comes out just tell him we'll share some food with him. But you can let him know we're here for the next few weeks or so." Doc stopped his wagon and climbed down. "Big John, come on with me and we'll take a look and see how much has to be cleaned out of this barn." Doc looked at the two privates, "Why don't you two see what's around here for us to use?"

Private Birdwell was never shy when Doc's medical unit needed food, water, or anything they wanted for the wounded soldiers. He and Pvt. Coglin were known scavengers for the unit. Doc had stopped asking where they got most things they 'found.' Since Pvt. Birdwell was their cook, his resourcefulness made sure that when food ran short, something always turned up so that their group always had some sort of rations. They were good men as far as Doc was concerned. They accepted Big John, Samuel and their crew and worked very well together. That was all that counted to Doc and Tom. The war was bad enough without having to worry about his medical unit fighting amongst themselves.

Doctors in other medical units criticized Doc for tolerating "Darkies." Without Big John,

345

Samuel and the others Doc would not be one of the top units in the regiment.   Both he and Tom had received battlefield promotions because of their care and ingenuity during battle and afterward. Doc was now a Lieutenant Colonel and Tom a Lieutenant.   Tom was able to handle almost any medical emergency except amputations, which Doc knew he could do, but wouldn't without Doc standing next to him while Tom operated.

"Privates Coglin and Birdwell, when you're done looking around ---- take the crew and remove any livestock in the barn and clean away as much debris as you can." Doc was thinking as he gave orders, "And, if there's any chickens --- corral 'em up so we can get some eggs, and see if we can put 'em in something and carry them away when we leave. I have a hankering for eggs."

"Yes sir, Doc." The privates hurried away to take over the barn calling to Big John and Samuel to bring the crew.

Meanwhile, the sound of heavy pounding could be heard. Sledge hammers hitting something solid reverberated in the air. "What's dat noise, Pvt. Robbie?" Samuel was listening with his hands on his hips. "That don' sound like dem cannons bein' pulled up fer firin' – whatchu think, man?"

Privates Coglin and Birdwell exchanged looks. "Sounds like it's comin' from the railroad over that way, tuh me." He looked at Birdwell, "Whatcha think?"

"I think ah'll finish up here and go take alook." Birdwell kept walking around looking at what was left in the barn and surrounding area.

"We'll both go take a look and let y'all know." Coglin lifted up a roll of canvas and walked near the opening of the barn. Doc's soldiers and Big John's crew would have the area set up and ready to take on the wounded when they started to arrive.

Privates Coglin and Birdwell decided to take a walk and see what all the noise was about. Carefully, in case it was Confederate soldiers, they creeped through the woods until they reached a large field. Union soldiers had built a massive bonfire and were taking apart the railroad tracks that ran for miles in each direction. They separated the iron rails and put the wood on the fire. After the flames were high, they placed the rails over the wood and heated them until another group of men removed the rails and bent them so that they couldn't be reused for train tracks. The trains couldn't bring supplies and arms to the Confederates, but no more supplies could be sent to Doc from this point forward.

They had all seen so much death and destruction that it was hard to remember easy times of laughter and happiness in just being alive. The war had brought large areas of fields and towns to almost complete devastation. Black tree trunks stood in fields that had previously been lush forests and were stark reminders of what had transpired there. The men who followed after the battles were over dug huge craters and pushed bodies of confederate soldiers into them and pushed the dirt back over the holes. Tom briefly thought about the sadness of the families who would never know where their loved ones were because no one was present who could identify the dead. Forever after they would only guess as to where they had fallen and died.

Tom mentally shook himself. He couldn't worry about the losses of the southern soldiers. He had enough losses of the Union soldiers every day so that he passed by the piles of bodies and tried not to find the sight appalling. Tom tried not to think about how easy it was to disregard death and dying and was sometimes afraid his heart would harden for his own soldiers that he treated. Even Doc had talked about how he barely thought about what he was doing as he took care of body after body, not looking to see if they died after he was done with them or not. It was a cold thought that they had learned so much and come so far but had lost so much feeling in their hearts.

A small group of black men and women slowly came out of the woods and stood watching as the wagons stopped to set up camp. They were emaciated and wore torn, dirty clothes. Tom saw them and motioned for them to approach.

"Hello. You look like you could use a meal. We'll have a pot of stew and some coffee soon's we get set up here. You're welcome to join us." Tom held out his arm and waved them over to the wagons.

The old man of the group spoke, "We've come a long way, mistah, an' we'd 'preciate a meal from yuh. We ain't lookin' fur no trouble. Wouldn't mind pickin' firewood or any othah chores to hep yuh. We ain't askin' fur nothin' wid out doin' sum hep." The others with him nodded their heads. There were three women standing behind the two men. They looked scared.

Big John and Samuel were taking off the harnesses of their horses. Big John looked over and saw Tom with the people and nodded to Samuel to look. He leaned his arms on the horse and turned to look at what Big John was watching. Suddenly, he dropped his arms and wiped his face. Then he took off running toward the people with Tom. When he reached them he stopped in front of one of the women. They just stood looking at each other.

Finally, Samuel reached out and tenderly touched the cheek of the woman. He whispered, "It's really you, Suedie?" Samuel's voice cracked, "I cain't be dreamin' but I cain't b'lieve this is you standin' right here."

Tears were running down the face of the young black woman. She gulped a sob and smiled, "Ah cain't b'lieve you kin rekanize me all dirty an' worn out."

"Aww Suedie my gal, I cud rekanize yuh anywhere." Samuel pulled Suedie into his arms and held her while he, too, had tears on his cheeks. "I wanna hold yuh forever an' ever." He pulled back and cupped her cheeks with both hands, "Ah came wif dese folks hopin' somehow ah'd see you somewhere. Closer we git to North Carolina where I thought you might be, ah determined I'd leave them an' go on by m'self." Samuel laughed and sniffed, "Now you saved me a *long* trip."

Suedie leaned her head on Samuel's chest. "I dreamed 'bout seein' you someday. Truth tuh tell – I was 'fraid you'd gone an' found anothah gal. So much time's past y'all cud be a daddy to a whole passel of chilren." She rubbed her face on his shirt and neck. Suedie felt so worn and dirty but she just couldn't let go of Samuel.

Big John approached them, "Welcome y'all," he smiled, "Right glad to see you." He turned to Suedie, "And, you're a right gift from heaven." He pointed at Samuel, "An' this here young fellow been lookin' out fuh you since we left home four years ago. Now lookee what we got ahead ah us. This boy's not about to let you git away, so ahm a thinkin' we gonna be havin' a jump de broom." Big John laughed and hit Samuel on the back practically knocking him over. Samuel just kept looking at Suedie. They stood staring at each other.

The other folks with Suedie were smiling, too. The man who first spoke said, "Well ain't it jus' God's work on this day? We found y'all an' the youngins found each othah!"

Tom walked up to Samuel, "What's a 'jump the broom' mean?"

Before Samuel could tell him, Big John spoke, "Well ah'll tell yuh. Since de time all my people bin slaves, they's no sucha thing as a weddin'. So when a young couple wants to be like a man an' wife we got us a special time we call "Jumpin' the Broom." We git us all together, take up a broom. Some likes to make it purty with some flowers but it don't hafta be. Then we have a table full of food, dress as fine as we all kin, an' have us a real time." Big John looked at Samuel and Suedie still holding on to each other, "You's gonna have both – ahm a preacher wid a bible an' we gonna find us a broom so y'all gonna have a knot so tight you ain't nevah gonna git free, hee hee hee." Big John laughed and laughed with joy for Samuel.

Doc came out of the barn, saw the gathering and walked over. "What's going on Big John?" He smiled at the people and put out his hand to shake the men's hands, "I'm Lt. Col. Phillips, but most folks just call me Doc."

"Pleased to meet you, Doc. Ahm Zeke, this here's Daniel, Bessie, Sally, and Suedie." Zeke pulled out a dirty hanky and wiped his face.

Doc exclaimed, "Suedaleen! Well, saints be praised!" He moved over to Samuel and slapped him on the back. "You found her, Samuel! My God, what luck is this?"

Samuel was grinning from ear to ear and tears were still running down his cheeks. "Don't this jus' beat all? Suedie and these folks here jus' walked outta the woods an' here she is!"

"I'm certainly glad to make your acquaintance, Suedaleen. You are all welcome to join us." Doc smiled at the other people.

Zeke looked at Doc, "We bin travelin' a long ways, hidin' an' aways tryin' tuh find food. Ain't been a time we cud sleep well an' we ain't found many meals. But we knew we had to keep headin' to de north cuz sooner er later we was gonna find some yankees who might hep us. An' glory be – we done found you an' Suedaleen found her fella."

Doc turned to Samuel, "Looks like this is your lucky day, Samuel. I couldn't be happier for you." He took Suedie's hand, "It's a miracle that you happened along and found us. We needed something like this to remind us that there is still happiness in this world."

Tom spoke up, "We're gonna have a celebration for Samuel and Suedie."

"Is that right?" Doc looked at Samuel. "Are we going to have a wedding, Samuel?"

"Well, Doc, we're gonna have us two celebrations: one with Big John an' one 'jumpin' the broom.'

Doc's face beamed, "Well that's just wonderful. How soon is this to take place, and what's this about jumping the broom? We might be short of time what with a war on and all."

Big John spoke up, "Soon's that barn is ready, we'll git it done. We got us some time till dark so if we all hurry up, we kin make fast work of de cleanin'.'"

Softly Suedie whispered to Samuel, "Ah jus' cain't get wed without ah git mahsef clean. Kin you figure outta way fur that, please?"

Samuel smiled down at her and touched her nose with his finger, "We got us a bath tub and ahm gonna fill it up with hot water so's you all kin have a bath. We even got us some good smellin' soap. Cain't do much 'bout yur clothes, but ah'll see what I kin muster up." Samuel turned to the others, "Y'all kin make use of the bath tub. We'll set it up in the back of the barn an' use some canvas sheeting to make it private." He still held Suedie's hand as he led them to the barn, "Hurry up y'all. We've got us some celebratin' to do!"

Zeke's group helped Big John's crew and they made short work of organizing the barn into several areas for treating patients and operating. The canvas sheeting made the perfect bathing area as they attached the canvas to the ceiling, then draped it over a horse stall. It was the perfect size for the tub and even had a bench to place clothing and large pieces of material which served as towels for drying bodies and hair. Samuel pounded in a nail and hung part of a mirror they had found and used for shaving.

Big John had made sure all the large pots were filled with water while the barn cleaning had taken place. The people formed a bucket brigade and quickly filled the bath tub. Suedie was first to use it. Samuel had walked back to where the camp followers were setting up their area and found one of the wives who sold him a dress for Suedie. It was too large and a little threadbare, but Suedie was thrilled to have something clean to wear.

Big John placed Suedie and Samuel in front of him underneath the branches of an old oak tree. They held hands and looked at one another as he united them in marriage. Doc, Tom, Privates Coglin and Birdwell as well as the soldiers with Doc's unit stood and watched. Some of the camp followers gathered behind them, many holding covered plates of food to share after the ceremony.

"Samuel and Suedaleen, the good Lord has brought you together to be part of each other's lives from now 'til you pass from dis earth. Da bible ask that you pledge yoreself for better or worse, whether you be sick, healthy, or poor that you love each other no matter what happens in dis life." Big John placed his hand over theirs and looked up at the sky, "Dear God these young folk stand b'fore yuh this day an' make der vow to each other an' to you. If it please yuh, Lord, we'd like to have yur blessin' on them as they is joined as husband an' wife. Amen." Everyone applauded while Samuel kissed Suedie and hugged her.

Big John held up his hands and waited as the crowd got quiet. "Now it's a custom for us folks to do a ceremony called 'jumpin' de broom.' After dat, deys well-fixed as married." He picked up a broom on the ground behind him and placed it in front of Suedie and Samuel who faced the crowd. They held hands and jumped over the broom and everyone laughed and applauded again.

Doc walked in front of the crowd and waited until he had everyone's attention, "We don't have but this evening to celebrate with Samuel and Suedie, but we have a big pot of stew we'd like to share with you. You'll need to bring your own bowls and spoons, but you won't leave hungry." Everyone laughed and came forward to congratulate Samuel and Suedie. The women camp followers who had brought plates put them out on the tables that had been set up and soon there was music from a banjo, guitar and harmonica. As the evening wore on, people danced with or without partners.

Big John and Doc took Samuel aside and told him that a special place had been made inside the barn in one of the stalls back near where they

355

had set up the bath tub. It wasn't much of a honeymoon night, but it was all that they had to offer the couple. Samuel was grateful when Doc gave them a beautiful quilt that he had brought from his home in Fairfax, as well as a fluffy pillow as a wedding present. Tom gave them a pouch of sweet lavender to make their 'room' smell better, and Privates Coglin and Birdwell gave them a bouquet of flowers they picked and put in a large mason jar.

Soon the music and the crowd was gone and the camp was quiet. Tomorrow could bring a new battle with endless casualties but for now they enjoyed the night. Big John, Doc and Tom sat around the fire drinking coffee and enjoyed the peace and quiet together. Tom wrote a letter to Tessa telling her about Samuel's wedding. He told her he hoped that soon they would be having their own wedding ceremony.

Chapter 24

The End is Near

"Here, in the dread tribunal of last resort, valor contended against valor. Here brave men struggled and died for the right as God gave them to see the right."
Adlai E. Stevenson I, Vice President

By dawn the thunder of horses' hooves and the wheels of cannons being pulled into place reverberated across the fields. Black clouds of smoke still rose into the sky from the burning railroad ties. Col. Templeton, from General Grant's staff, stopped to have coffee and tell Doc that they expected the numbers of casualties to be large, but that the Confederates were definitely on the run and they hoped to 'finish them off' in the next few weeks.

That news didn't make Doc feel any better or relieved. He and 'Doc' Tom, as Suedie called him would have their hands full trying to help as many wounded as possible. Tom would be forced, again, to take a medical field pack onto the battlefield and treat the wounded where they fell. Big John would accompany him, bible in hand, to help both the casualties and Tom. Doc prayed that they wouldn't be casualties themselves as the Confederates weren't particular who they shot if they were wearing blue.

As he gazed out at his encampment, Doc marveled at his good fortune that Big John and Samuel had joined him when he left Fairfax. Suedie and her 'gals' were another gift from God. They were already helping with the cooking as well as laundry and the boiling water pots that were so important for Doc and Tom. Big John was tireless and demanding but it kept everyone on their best mettle to help Doc and Tom and the hundreds of wounded soldiers. The new men, Zeke and Daniel, were busy helping Privates Coglin and Birdwell unload the rest of the medical supplies and carrying them into the barn.

No other unit could match Doc's people for dedication and tireless work to help the wounded. Some doctors were jealous of Doc's reputation and tried to disclaim his ability to save more men than their units were able to do. When Doc heard this he angrily said that it was ridiculous to compete with something as sacred as their duty as doctors. Still, General Grant had told Colonel Templeton that "he wished he had a hundred more doctors like Lt. Col. Phillips. He had more success saving amputees than any other surgeon in all his regiments." Tom was learning fast and becoming extremely competent under Doc's guidance. He was no longer afraid to handle patients on his own using his own judgement as to what was needed.

The morning mist was rapidly deteriorating into a deluge of rain. Doc was seriously disappointed that the rain had not ended for the year. It was impossible to find room for all the wounded soldiers, many of whom would lie on the battlefield injured while the rain encased them in mud before they could be brought in for treatment. Even then, the canvas covering the men erected in the trees couldn't serve as a roof for as many as would need it. The wounded would be placed under wagons and anything else they could put together.

As the day and the battle progressed, more and more lines of Confederate prisoners were marched past the medical encampment. The women camp followers booed and hissed as they limped past. A sorrier group of men had never been seen; covered with mud and blood, many without shoes and all wearing ragged uniforms. Even Big John's crew, who had reason to dislike the men, looked sorry for their desperate appearance.

Colonel Templeton sent word to Doc that several battles were being fought simultaneously and to expect more casualties than he first anticipated. Doc just kept his head down and worked on one soldier after another.

On April 6, 1864, massive numbers of Confederates were either taken prisoner or were no longer able to fight due to hunger, disease and injuries. Three days later, General Robert E. Lee finally surrendered to General Ulysses Grant at a place called Appomattox Court House.

While Doc and Tom were still operating, a disturbance was heard outside of the operating tent. They could hear voices growing louder, then suddenly a loud cheer!

"Suedie – can you see what that's all about?" He motioned with his head toward the tent flap to the outside.

"Sure, Doc. Ah'll see and hurry back." Suedie peeked outside and saw Big John and Samuel with big smiles on their faces. She ran to Samuel and he caught her and swung her around as he laughed and cried with joy.

"It's over Suedie! It's all over!" He kissed her with a loud smack. "We kin all go back to Ohio now! The south done lost the war an' General Lee signed papers giving up!"

Suedie started crying, "I was so afraid that we'd have to run away and keep running 'til we was safe! Now we don hafta run no more. None ah us has to be 'fraid no more!" She pushed at Samuel, "I gotta tell Doc and Tom. Let me down so I kin tell them the news!"

Suedie ran back into the tent. Doc and Tom could hear the celebration outside the barn where they were still working to save as many wounded soldiers as they could. Suedie hollered, "It's over, Doc! The south gave up and war's over!"

Doc hesitated and looked over at Tom, "Well, what do you know?" He put his head back down and kept working.

The rain had ceased, but mud was everywhere and covered anything they put down to walk on to get from the barn to the wounded outside. Doc ordered his entire unit to stay clear of the camp followers who were drinking and firing weapons into the air, hooting and hollering that the Union had been saved. All the medical units had days left to take care of the wounded and see them transported to hospitals or homes.

The last week of April, Doc and Tom were supervising the cleanup and packing of their unit when the farmer whose barn they had been using ran into camp screaming for help. Doc and Tom stopped him and were told his wife had been in labor and was dying because the baby wouldn't come and the woman helping her said there was nothing she could do for her. Crying and sobbing the man begged, "Please, sir. I'm begging you to help my wife. It's our third child and she ain't never had a problem like this before. I can't lose her after all thats happened."

Doc grabbed his medical bag and some supplies and stuffed them into Tom's arms, "You take these and I'll get the other things we'll need." Doc smiled at Tom, "You're about to bring a baby into the world, Doc Tom."

"I'm glad you're here, Doc. I can't birth no babies. Don't know the first thing about it."

Tom's cheeks were blazing pink. He'd help Doc, but he didn't want to pull a baby out of a woman and hear her in pain.

As they neared the farmer's house they could hear a woman's screams. The man grabbed Doc's arm and pulled him, "Hurry up, man. Can't you hear her? I been listening to this for almost two days."

The woman who had been helping the farmer's wife was wringing her hands outside the bedroom door when they entered the house. Two little girls sat huddled together on the hearth, their eyes wide with fear. Doc paused and knelt down in front of them, "Your mother's going to be fine. I'm here to help her bring your new baby out so you can see them. Don't you worry now," he said.

The woman in the bed was wet with perspiration and moaning. She looked exhausted and Tom thought her stomach was much larger than it should be. He had seen a couple of pregnant ladies before when they had visited with his ma before the birth of their babies and their size looked nothing like this woman's.

"You're about to learn something new and exciting today, Tom," Doc said as he rolled up his shirt sleeves and began laying out tools. He looked up at the farmer who was standing next to his wife's head and holding her hand. "What's your names?"

I'm Floyd Nelson and this here's my wife, Ginnie." He looked at her then Doc. "Can you help her doctor?" His face was almost as pale as his wife's.

"I'm going to do my damndest, Floyd. I need you to put on a larger pot of water to boil. You stay out with the little ones until I tell you to come back in. Understand?" Doc was pulling down the sheets as the man left. Tom turned to leave, "Where do you think you're going?" He growled.

"I'll wait out there with Floyd and you can call me when you need anything."

"The hell you will. You're going to help these babies to be born." Doc pulled up the woman's nightgown and she groaned. "Ginnie, I'm Dr. Phillips. I'm going to help you give birth to these babies. I think you're about to have twins and they're fighting to see who's going to be first."

Ginnie groaned again and tried to sit up. "I don't think I can help you anymore, doctor. I'm about worn out." She fell back onto the pillows.

"I know you're tired, Ginnie, but you have no choice. Doc Tom here is going to help you and between the three of us we're going to get these babies out if I have to open you up to do it."

She screeched and grabbed the covers as the pain overtook her. Doc looked between her legs and motioned for Tom to look, too.

Bright red now, Tom forced himself to look at what Doc was showing him. "Do you see that she is partially open down here? That dark blob you see is one of the baby's heads. Let's see if we can bring it out." Doc opened the carbolic acid and poured some into his hands and rubbed them together. He had Tom do the same thing. "Ready?"

"I guess as much as I'll ever be," he gulped.

"Try not to push when you have your next pain, Ginnie. I'm going to try and get this baby out."

"What makes you think there's two babies, Doc?"

"Her distended abdomen. She's way too big. When I palpitated her abdomen it was solid." Doc worked on the woman and gave directions for Tom. Together, they pulled the first baby out who wasn't breathing.

Quickly, Doc worked on the baby and soon a high-pitched wail filled the room. The door was flung open and Floyd came flying in, his face alight with joy. "What is it, Doc? A boy?"

"Tom, wrap this baby up and give him to his dad." Doc smiled at Floyd, "It's a boy, Floyd. Congratulations. Now keep him warm while I bring the other one out."

Floyd was astounded! "The other one! You mean there's two?"

"That's what I mean." Doc was working on Ginnie. Tom wrapped the baby with a flannel blanket and handed him to Floyd. "Go on now and introduce your son to his sisters. We'll see you in a little while."

Tom had lost his embarrassment and was completely enthralled with the birthing process. "How come that other woman couldn't help get these babies out?"

"Because they needed to be turned. Sometimes they try to come out the wrong way. That one was crowded and just needed a little turning, the next one might need turning completely around. I'm about to check." Doc proceeded to examine Ginnie again. Her face was contorted with pain and she was breathing very hard. "Almost done, Ginnie. I'm going to have to turn this baby. It's going to be a little painful for a minute. Bear with me and it'll soon be over." Doc put both hands inside Ginnie's body and Tom could see him pushing and pulling the baby. "Do you see what I'm doing, Tom?"

"Yes, I do, Doc. How do you know when to do that?"

"Babies should come out head first. When the back end presents itself it's called breech birth. Usually I would need to operate to get the baby safely out of the mother's body. But this little one is a lot smaller than the other one and was already turning to come out." Doc gently pulled and the baby popped out! He

365

severed the umbilical cord, tied it off and checked the baby over. "There! Welcome to the world, little one!" Doc smiled and handed it to Tom as the baby started squealing and crying.

"This one's a little boy, too." Tom wrapped the baby up and walked to the head of the bed. "Both babies are boys, ma'am. This one's a little smaller, but he's a loud one."

Ginnie smiled, "Thank you, doctor. I'm so glad you came to help me. I'm afraid they both would have died without you." She closed her eyes and relaxed for the first time.

Tom gave Floyd the second baby and the two little sisters excitedly stood on their tiptoes to see his face. They were oohing and aahing over the babies as Tom returned to help Doc. Tom realized they were not done with the birthing process and Doc talked him through what needed to be done and what to watch for when the babies are born.

The woman who had been helping before Doc and Tom arrived finished cleaning up the room, including Ginnie. Floyd Nelson was a grateful man. He tried to pay Doc and Tom, but they declined any money. Doc told Floyd that it was an honor to bring the baby boys into the world that had been so filled with death and devastation. They were done with the war and soon to return to their homes in Ohio. It was a splendid way to end the war!

When Doc and Tom returned to their encampment, Big John asked about the farmer's wife and was happy to hear about Tom helping to bring twin boys into the world. He told Doc that Colonel Templeton was going to talk to the Confederate prisoners and had invited Doc to come and listen. Doc was surprised but decided to take Tom and go to the area where the prisoners were being held. When they arrived, they saw that there was a large group of prisoners separated from the others. They stood at attention facing a Union flag and the colonel was talking to them with a bible in his hand. As they listened they were astounded to understand that the Confederate soldiers were being given an Oath of Allegiance! Another Union officer standing next to Doc explained that if the Confederates volunteered to take the oath, they could be released to go home as free men. The oath made them promise *to "faithfully support, protect and defend the Constitution of the United States, and the union of States thereunder."* The oath had to be given and sworn to if they wanted a presidential pardon.

Doc was sad to hear what the prisoners who had refused to take the oath were saying to the ones who had taken the oath. Several soldiers, fists raised, tried to accost the oath takers. Colonel Templeton kept the men apart and told them they were free to go but without horses, supplies or weapons of any kind. They were told to be careful on the road and if they were stopped, they were to tell Union soldiers that they had taken the Oath of Allegiance. The men stayed in a group as they left the area talking among themselves.

Several prisoners hollered that the traitors best not go home as they would be tarred and feathered, and their homes burned to the ground. One soldier addressed the prisoners, "We ain't got nothin' left back home. No crops, families starving, houses already burned down – what difference does it make if I swore not to fight anymore? Ahm sick of this war! At least I ain't gonna be in some prison camp where I'm gonna die! An' if'n I am gonna die, I wanna be south in Dixie!" With that he gave a loud rebel yell. He rejoined the other men and with their heads hanging in shame, hunger and exhaustion, they began to walk down the muddy road toward what was left of their beloved south.

Later that night, Tom wrote his final letter to Tessa. He had so much to tell her:

Dear Tessa,

I apologize for this piece of paper that I am writing on. Because we no longer receive shipments from Miss Bradley, we've almost run out of paper. What we have is in short supply and we have to share it. You will see that the other side of this scrap of paper is a list of supplies that we needed but never got. It was in the operating tent and that's why it has some blood drops and is a little dirt-scuffed around the edges. But I feel the need to write to you as you will see. I have the best news yet! The war is over! General Lee surrendered to General Grant and the fighting and dying is done. When we heard the news Doc and I were still operating on the wounded soldiers so we didn't have a chance to celebrate. And then we had to go and help a woman give birth to twin boys! I am still in a state having seen a birthing and helped to bring the babies into the world. I have seen a lamb born, and once a horse, but it is a real wonder to see a baby come out of a woman's body and breathe and cry and want to be fed! Doc and I both agree that it was a real good end for us after so many years of war operating on soldiers who suffered and died no matter what we did to help them. I am coming home to you Tess. I hope you will be there to greet me. I hope you are enjoying being the teacher in Colton Springs. We should arrive home sometime 'bout the end of May. Hope that means you will be done teaching for the year. We have much to talk about and lots to plan. I think of you every night and dream of our last kiss. I will stop writing now as I am running out of room to tell you my thoughts. I remain your devoted Tom.

Tom folded the wrinkled odd-shaped letter and sealed it with a dot of Doc's sealing wax. He gave it to one of the unit's soldiers and told him to see that it was mailed. He hoped his letter made it to Colton Springs before he and Doc arrived in Fairfax.

A week later Doc and Tom were still treating the wounded. Colonel Templeton stopped at their camp to give them the official notice of war's end. He had papers he wanted Doc to have that gave information of what the Ohio regiment had accomplished during the war. The regiment had lost a total of 8 officers and 95 enlisted men. Three officers and 155 enlisted men died from disease. Doc and Tom suffered through 24 skirmishes and five major battles before the war ended. Each battle had a name to separate the horror from each one. Doc's regiment had a total of 950 soldiers who had volunteered to serve and represent the state of Ohio. From the beginning of the war until the end they marched a total of 2,500 miles.

Surgeon General Barnes, a new position made by President Lincoln, was in charge of all medical regiments. He issued orders that all medical units were to be disbanded after the last wounded soldier was dispatched. Doc was ordered to either sell or dispose of any supplies that were left after that.

This information was not well received by Doc. He had made good use of these materials and had no intention of destroying or selling any of it. It could still be used for good purpose. So he patiently listened to Colonel Templeton and waited for him to leave, then issued his own orders:

- He would return to Fairfax, Ohio with both wagons that had been built and outfitted by the Bradley Wagon Works and all they contained.
- Any of Big John's crew was welcome to travel to Fairfax with him and Tom.
- Privates Coglin and Birdwell could leave for their homes by way of train as soon as possible or they were welcome to travel with Doc.
- They would leave for Fairfax in two days.

Chapter 25

The Journey Home

If my people who are called by my name will humble themselves, and pray and seek my face, and turn away from their wicked ways, then I will hear from heaven and forgive their sins and heal their land.
2 Chronicles 7:14

The sound of the rifle firing from the nearby trees was as startling as a crack of thunder. Big John stopped his wagon and searched the tree line on his left where he thought it had come from. Only Samuel had the good sense to order everyone to take cover. Private Birdwell jumped down behind his wagon and searched the trees with his gun ready to fire.

"Get down y'all! Take cover under the wagons!" Private Coglin hollered at Doc, "Doc! Stop and take cover!"

Doc's wagon just kept moving. He was alone because Tom was riding with Samuel. It wasn't like Doc to ignore danger. Then Daniel, one of Big John's crew who had been sleeping in the back of Doc's wagon started hollering, "Doc's been shot! Help us!"

Samuel ran to Doc's wagon and stopped his horses. Two more shots were fired, this time from Privates Birdwell and Coglin. Samuel stayed holding Doc's horses. Tom handed his reins to Zeke, jumped down and ran to help Doc. Private Coglin returned fire into the trees. Suddenly, a Rebel yell rang out and slowly a body fell from a tall tree and onto the ground. Tom was so angry he hollered, "Make sure he's dead!" He ran to Doc's wagon and pulled Doc up onto the wagon seat and held him. Samuel and one of the other men was trying to hold the skittish horses still.

Privates Coglin and Birdwell went looking for other shooters. "I think he was alone, Tom! And he's a dead Reb now," Private Coglin hollered, then used his foot to turn the man over.

"Yup! Got him in the heart yuh did," Private Coglin looked at the men standing nearby. "Whoever got 'im – either Eddie or me did a good job." All the men looked grim, no one smiled as they watched Doc being supported by Tom.

Quickly, Tom and Big John pulled Doc down onto the ground. Suedie grabbed Doc's medical bag and opened it for Tom but he wasn't looking at anything but Doc who was bleeding profusely from his chest. Tears were streaming down his cheeks as he clutched Doc to his chest. "You stupid bastard! The war's over!" he sobbed. Tom screamed to heaven, "The war is over! You shot a doctor you stupid bastard!" Tom hung his head. He looked at his bloody hand; turned it, watching the pink and red of

Doc's blood dripping on the ground. What was the sense of this? Was God punishing all humans because of their folly – was God even up there? These doubts had begun to plague Tom. He had always believed in God without exception until the war. But now this just made no sense!

Suedie put her hand on Tom's arm, "Doc's hurt real bad, Doc Tom. He needs your hep now." She pulled his arm down and pushed Tom back. She called to one of the girls, "Bessie -- gotta get Doc's shirt off now. I need ta have yuh get the wagon ready fur us ta hep Doc." Big John's crew were gathering around Doc, "Back away now an get dem wagons settled in an the camp fires up an burnin'." She pulled on Tom so he would look at her, "Doc needs you ta save him, Doc Tom."

Big John pulled at Tom, too. "Gonna lay Doc in de back of his wagon now, Tom." Big John motioned for the men in his crew to come and help him move Doc. "Look lively men, careful now, y'all, Doc's hurtin bad here. Gotta move fast." Big John pulled Tom up to face him. "Looky hear, Tom. Doc needs you. It's up to ya to save him. You's de on'y one here who can do dat. Time's awastin' now. Buck up an' save Doc." Big John gave Tom another shake and Tom wiped his arm across his face and took a deep breath.

"I'm okay now, Big John. Bring Doc's bag and make a camp here. Get the kettles boilin' with plenty of hot water." As he walked to the back of the wagon he hollered over his shoulder, "I'm glad one of you men shot that stupid Johnnie Reb dead!"

"Y'all heard Doc Tom! Get a move on now." That put everyone into motion. Quickly, Big John and Samuel pulled the wagons around and started directing the rest of the folks to make camp and set the fires. Tom felt sick -- he had a soldier's cold heart; full of stress from too many battles, too many dying and wounded. He had to save Doc or his own life was over.

"All right, Suedie. I think the bullet's still in here. Can you see if we have any more chloroform or ether? Doc's unconscious, but I don't want him to wake up in pain while I'm working on em." Tom swabbed the bloody wound so he could see the hole where the long probe would be inserted to remove the bullet. Then he poured carbolic acid on the wound to sterilize the area. Sweat was running down his face. Gently, Suedie wiped his brow and cheeks without being asked.

Tom heard Suedie talking softly, "Doc Tom, ahm here fur ya. Jus' tell me whatcha need from me an ah'll do it." Suedie laid out tools: long-handled forcepts, a needle for stitching, scissors, scalpels, more carbolic acid, and then proceeded to cut bandages in long strips.

While Big John stayed near Tom, Samuel took over and organized the wagons and set up camp. The fires were burning and heated water for Tom to use. Bessie, Sally, and Daniel made coffee and biscuits while Zeke went hunting with Robbie and Eddie. They had told everyone that they were to be called 'Robbie' and 'Eddie' since the war was over and they weren't soldiers anymore. They would hunt for game to make stew for everyone to eat.

Tom squared his shoulders and hunched over Doc as Suedie finished cutting away his uniform shirt and undershirt. Tom recognized that the wound was near Doc's lung. Hopefully there was no damage there. He looked at Doc's unconscious face and lips which were slack and open. Suedie laid out his tools and Tom opened the area around the wound. He blanked out Doc's face and operated on him as if he was just another wounded soldier. Confidently, as he had done for the past three years, Tom worked to remove the minie ball, stop the bleeding, and sew up the damage done by its entry into Doc's body.

Tom worked on Doc for over an hour. Suedie never left his side and was quick to know what Tom needed as he operated on Doc's chest. Private Coglin administered the ether so Doc slept peacefully as he worked. The minie ball had gone deep, tearing skin and muscle as it travelled. A rib was broken but hadn't punctured Doc's lung, and the ball had stopped before it reached Doc's heart – that was a relief, Tom thought. But -- it had caused a lot of damage. Tom remembered Doc's teaching him to work a layer at a time when working on wounded soldiers. But this was Doc. One slip, or an artery that he couldn't stop from bleeding could end Doc's life. So Tom stood motionless except for his hands and put Doc back together a stitch at a time.

After Tom took the last stitch and closed the gaping wound, he sat next to Doc, staring at his pale face. His breathing was shallow. He had regained consciousness only briefly, urging Tom to look in his leather case for important papers for Tom to read. Tom was concerned about the amount of blood Doc had lost. If he developed a fever and fluid filled his lungs, he would be a goner. The use of his ma's poultices and powders had to help him. Tom prayed it would be enough. Big John was outside the wagon and Tom could hear him quietly saying a prayer. The camp was filled with whispers and a very somber mood.

Suedie had left Tom after the surgery and cleaned all the instruments. She returned to the wagon, lifted the canvas flap and pulled herself up into the back of the wagon. "It's time for ya to eat now, Doc Tom. Doc ain't gonna like it if'n yu gonna fail yursef an' not take care now." She waited for Tom to look at her. In a more stern voice, "Look here, Doc Tom. Don't make me call on Big John an' Samuel to haul yu outta here, cause ahm a right ready to do jus' that."

Tom looked at Suedie, "I'm all right, Suedie. I can't leave im. Not until he comes awake. I just can't." His eyes were full of tears as he looked back down at Doc.

Softy Suedie answered, "I know how you love this man, Doc Tom. We all do. He 'bout de bes' man we know. But we care 'bout y'all as well. An' if we don' take care ah yu, Doc's gonna be mad's ah hornet when he wakes up." She smiled at Tom and pulled on his arm. "Now yu git on up an' outta here right now. Big John's got a good pot a soup an' a hunk ah dos good biscuits waitin' on yuh."

Slowly Tom got up to leave. He placed his hand on Doc's chest and felt his heart beating. He wiped his eyes and sniffed, "If God doesn't save Doc, I'll never forgive him. An' ain't nothin' that's ever gonna get me in a church as long's I live."

Big John had heard Tom's vow and waited until he was seated eating his dinner before he sat across from him holding his bible. Tom looked up and saw the bible and frowned. "Ah heard ya words in anger 'bout being' mad at God, Tom. Ah unnerstan' yuh bein' grieved but yuh gotta know dat de Lord works mysterious. We nevah know who's gotta go on ahead tuh heaven. May be dat Doc's needed up der. Ain't ar place tuh decide. You's suffered a big time an' had tuh change up into a strong man right quick these years. Doc's trained yu up to a doc yursef now. The Lord's been wif you bof an' held yu up thru mean times an' strife. Don' give up on im

378

now, boy. He's gonna be wif Doc an' if he decides to leave im here wif us, den we gonna lift up ar voices an' sing his praise. If'n he takes Doc, den we gonna let im go an' unnerstan' dat he's up wid de angels watchin' ore us poor folk, an' we'll praise Him for dat, too." Big John opened his bible and began to read: *The Lord is my shepherd, I shall not want…… "*

As he heard the words of the psalm, Tom tried to let go of his anger and concentrate on Doc. His ma would agree with Big John and would want him to think only of healing and not wasting his energy on being mad at God. But so much had happened to him and Doc. They had experienced things that the people back in Fairfax would never understand. He had a right to be angry! Doc was someone who should be untouchable! He was good to his core and helped so many! War shoulda never touched someone as perfect as Doc. He was a better man than was ever born!

Tom sat next to Doc, staring at his pale face. His breathing was shallow. He had regained consciousness only briefly, urging Tom to look in his leather case for important papers for Tom to read. Tom was concerned with the amount of blood Doc had lost. If he developed a fever and fluid filled his lungs, he would be a goner. Only the use of his ma's poultices and powders could help him. Tom prayed it would be enough. Big John was outside the wagon and Tom could hear him quietly saying a prayer. The camp was filled with whispers and a somber mood.

To please Doc, Tom opened his leather case. A packet of letters from Miss Beatrice were held together by a red ribbon. An envelope with Tom's name on it was next to the letters. Carefully Tom opened it and read what Doc had written. It was Doc's will naming Tom to receive Doc's estate if anything happened to him. Doc had paid for Tom to take the medical examination for doctor at the Columbus Hospital. Because of Tom's experience during the war he qualified to take an examination which would make him a full doctor if he passed. The fact that Doc had already paid for the certificate made it clear to Tom that Doc had confidence he would have no difficulty in passing the exam. Tom was overwhelmed with love for this man. Doc was his friend, his mentor and a father figure.

It was a week before Doc was well enough to resume the journey to Fairfax. Big John hung a bed from the roof in Doc's wagon so that he wouldn't feel each rut in the road as they traveled. The bed gently swayed back and forth and kept Doc as comfortable as possible. Tom was still worried about Doc because he had developed a fever three days after surgery and the incision was an angry red. He used every potion he could think of to fight the infection that was trying to take over Doc's wound but he had few herbs left. It was more important than ever that they get him to Fairfax where there was more medicine available.

When the weather was nice, Tom opened the back flap and allowed the sunshine and breezes to fill the wagon. Doc was weak but he was able to eat and drink small amounts of broth and bread. But there were times when his fever took over and he was unconscious, murmuring orders and asking to see Beatrice.

It seemed to take forever to reach Fairfax, but they finally arrived in town early one evening the end of May. Only a few people saw the wagon caravan arrive. One of them, Homer Sutton, grabbed his notebook and pencil and raced out calling to Big John to stop. After learning of Doc's illness, he urged Tom to pull around to his former medical office while he ran ahead and had Dr. Harrington ready to take Doc into the office.

Soon, Doc was in a bed in his old home and Gussie was fussing and fluttering over Doc. He smiled wanly at her and greeted his friend, Hollis who was standing by his side. "Sorry to be so much trouble, Hollis. Had a little run in with a Johnny Reb. He must have thought I was someone important, else I can't imagine why he shot at me." Doc smiled and closed his eyes.

Hollis questioned Tom about what had transpired and together they removed Doc's bandages and inspected Doc's wound. Together they worked on Doc; replacing the bandage after a fresh poultice had been applied and making Doc drink a tea to reduce his fever. Tom hadn't been able to make Doc a tea since he had run out of herbs for that purpose and was unable to replace them.

By the next afternoon, Doc had improved. Miss Beatrice had been notified the night before about Doc and had arrived within an hour. She sat in a chair next to Doc's pillow all night helping Tom and Hollis swab Doc's face and chest with cool water. When Doc awoke and saw her, she leaned over and kissed him on his lips in front of Hollis, Tom and Gussie. He told everyone he would be well very soon.

EPILOGUE

July 1865 -- Home and Healing

"I shall look at the world through tears.
Perhaps I shall see things that, dry-eyed,
I could not see."
Nicholas Wolterstorff

Beatrice looked out over the meadow and fields where the people of Fairfax were celebrating on the same place where she first met Rev. Ben Pattison. This gathering wasn't for a tent revival – it was to celebrate the birth of a nation and the end of a war. Ben would be so pleased she thought. His handsome face would beam with pleasure to know that freedom of the slaves had prevailed. But at what cost, she lamented.

Several young men were in a group chatting together. It was obvious they had served the Union as they still wore the proof: one leaned heavily on a crutch, another was missing an arm, while another young man's head was bandaged covering one of his eyes. Yes, they had paid a high price for their support of this nation to save the union and stop slavery. Beatrice silently said a prayer for all who returned and needed to heal, and for all who were left behind never to return.

It seemed that everything had changed. A nation and its people so divided and filled with such hatred for four long years! Could they come back together, united again in faith of democracy? What would the future be like for the wounded people of the southern states; their homes burned, economy destroyed?

Just then she spied another injured man. This one made her heart beat faster. His arm was in a sling he held against his chest with his other hand. A little bent over as he walked, he slowly made his way to her. Gussie's little girls danced around him laughing as he walked toward Beatrice. Dr. Bradford Phillips -- Doc, shared their laughter and looked up at Beatrice, his smile growing larger. He was thinner than before he left for the war. Three months that turned into what felt like a lifetime of four years. Bradford was still healing from the outside as well as the inside with Beatrice's determination and care. They were to be married next month and would live here on the Bradley estate. He would, again, be Fairfax's doctor. Dr. Harrington had obtained a practice in Bellington, a town near Columbus. He had been a competent and good doctor while Dr. Phillips had been gone. She would miss his quiet manner and gentle humor.

Beatrice smiled as Bradford placed his arm around her. Together they watched the people of Fairfax laughing and celebrating. Her sister, Kathryn, appeared on the arm of a very solicitous

Wilson Meyers. She was pregnant with her first child. Their wedding had been a small affair unlike her first wedding – but just as happy nonetheless. Wilson's home was under construction with new rooms being added and the living area expanded for his increasing family.

Tom and Tessa strolled into view. He was a handsome man, not a boy now. There was nothing left of the boy who went to war with Doc. A self-confidant doctor came home. He had saved Bradford's life and Beatrice forever owed him a debt of gratitude. She was helping him set up his new medical practice in Colton Springs where Kathryn had lived briefly before the death of her first husband. As soon as Tom returned from taking his medical boards in Cincinnati he and Tessa would be married. She was already a teacher there. Beatrice saw lines around Tom's eyes when he smiled down at Tessa. When they arrived in town with Bradford's unconscious, fever ridden body, she had seen shadows in his eyes. The same shadows she saw in Bradford's eyes. Hopefully time and love would banish their shadows.

His mother, Mary, was seated near the garden with Dr. Hollis Harrington. They had become close friends while Tom was away. She had talked to Tom about Dr. Harrington, telling him they had affection for each other. Tom had been surprised, but told his mother that he liked the man and wouldn't keep her from being with him.

385

Doc heard the news and told Mary he thought she could do a lot worse than being courted by Hollis. Beatrice had been very pleased when Hollis asked her advice about courting Mary. She deserved happiness especially now that her Tom would be marrying his sweetheart, Tessa, and leaving Fairfax to live in another town. Mary planned to give her cabin to Samuel and Suedie. It would be the perfect place to raise their family. Suedie was already carrying their first child.

Bradford gently squeezed Beatrice's shoulder. She gazed up at him and they smiled at each other. He nodded his head toward the meadow. Beatrice looked out and saw Big John, Gussie, Suedie and Samuel happily playing a game with horseshoes with some of the men and their wives from the mill. Black and white together as if it was a natural thing to see. Big John had told Beatrice that when Samuel brought Suedie home to Fairfax she told him that they didn't have to go any further --- this was 'the Promised Land" for her.

"Ah…..it's so good to be up walking again and not a hopeless lump in bed," Doc sighed.

Beatrice felt Bradford lean into her. "You are getting tired. It's time for you to rest." She turned him around and led him to a large white wicker chair on the veranda and helped him sit down. He held her hand as they continued to watch the people.

"I would say don't fuss, but I love that you

do," he smiled and kissed her hand.

Willie Colby with his sister, mother and Luther waved at Beatrice and Doc. They were part of the community now. Their farm was plowed and the field that had been vacant and ignored for years was fully planted with corn. Men from the Bradley fields had done the work and would share the profits with Mrs. Colby. Willie and Luther still worked at Bender's Tavern. Jacob Bender made sure they both attended school when they weren't working. They had been his only help when most of the young men left for war.

Beatrice looked out over the meadow where Ben's tents once stood. She could feel his presence. She imagined he stood proudly, his dark hair shining in the sun watching over his people. Tears trickled down her cheeks as she looked at Bradford.

Big John saw Beatrice and Doc and walked up to the veranda, holding Gussie's hand. They would be married and 'jump the broom' next week now that Doc could attend their celebration. "Good to see you up and out on such a beautiful day, Doc," he said with a big toothy smile. "God's smilin' down on us this day. I kin feel his love, yessuree!"

Doc held Beatrice's hand against his cheek as he spoke, "It's so good to feel the warmth of the sun on my chest. It seems like I've been cold for so long." He looked up at her, "Life will be good again for all of us now. We have so much to live for."

Beatrice wiped her cheeks with one hand while her other hand held Bradford's. Looking over the meadow she replied, "Yes, my love." She closed her eyes and saw Ben in her memory. He smiled at her one last time as he walked through the meadow into the sun.

Fly now with the angels. If heaven awaits, may they watch over you and be the first with open arms to greet you. Author unknown

THE END

"*The past is dead; let it bury its dead, its hopes and its aspirations; before you lies the future--a future full of golden promise.*"
Jefferson Davis

About the Author

Juliann Dorell grew up always having stories in her head. When her mother was in hospice care, they talked about her stories and her mother urged her to write them and get them published. After her mother's death – that is what she did to fulfill her promise to the wonderful woman who always supported and loved her.

Juliann lives in southern California and Minnesota where she enjoys writing, reading, fishing and crafts. Her husband, children, grandchildren and two wonderful dogs complete her family.

54134508R00226

Made in the USA
San Bernardino, CA
08 October 2017